# A "Business" Arrangement . . .

Jeremiah took her shawl and flung it onto a chair back. "Wine?" he asked. "A business arrangement should not be conducted without wine." He poured two glasses and handed her one. Lifting his in a salute, he said, "To a successful arrangement."

Paulette merely touched the cool liquid to her lips. "I am willing to pay you well for obtaining . . ."

Before she could finish the sentence, Jeremiah took the glass from her hand, set it carelessly on the table beside his and swept her into the cradle of his arms. "I know your part of the arrangement," he said, "and I think you also know the price."

**Books by Parley J. Cooper**

Dark Desires
The Devil Child
Golden Fever
Marianne's Kingdom
Moonblood
My Lady Evil
Reverend Mama
San Francisco
The Shuddering Fair One

Published by POCKET BOOKS

Another *Original* publication of POCKET BOOKS

**POCKET BOOKS, a Simon & Schuster division of
GULF & WESTERN CORPORATION
1230 Avenue of the Americas, New York, N.Y. 10020**

ISBN: 0-671-81476-1

First Pocket Books printing March, 1981

10 9 8 7 6 5 4 3 2 1

POCKET and colophon are trademarks of Simon & Schuster.

Printed in the U.S.A.

# Golden Fever

### PARLEY J. COOPER

PUBLISHED BY POCKET BOOKS NEW YORK

*Dedicated to my mother,*
*Dorothy McKinney Wade,*
*and my uncle and aunt,*
*George William and Dorothy Freytag*

# Part I

---

# THE
# JOURNEY

# Chapter One

PAULETTE FAVIÈRE arrived late at the supper table.

Ordinarily she would have been chastised, at least with a glance from Clabe or Vienna, but today was an exception. She slipped into her chair beside the younger Bella, eyes averted, and helped herself to a small portion of food.

"The heart of the South must survive the daggers of the Abolitionists," Clabe was saying. "They are our real and present danger." With a troubled sigh, he leaned back in his chair at the head of the long, elegantly set table.

Walter and Rebecca Whitely, unexpected afternoon guests who had been convinced to linger for the evening meal, hastened to agree with Clabe's statement although their sympathies lay with the movement he was maligning. They were comparative newcomers to Louisiana and wanted no difficulties with their neighbors over politics, especially not the most powerful plantation owner in the vicinity.

Walter Whitely understood his lack of enthusiasm for the topic of politics would go unnoticed. Their host had been preoccupied all afternoon. "Amen," he murmured after a mouthful of possum. It was unclear if he was punctuating Clabe's remark or the deliciousness of the meal.

Clabe stretched his long legs under the table. He

was a handsome man, the image of his father, with a large frame, chiseled features and unruly blond hair, now going white at the temples. Today, the furrows of his brow and the sadness behind his blue eyes drained away the aura that contributed so much to his good looks. He was troubled and his troubles were multiple.

The issues he had forced himself to discuss with Walter Whitely—the debatable principles of slavery and the complexities of the growing problems between the North and the South—were only secondary in his mind, a shield behind which to hide a more pressing anxiety.

His family was being pulled apart.

First, his son Dester had abandoned Plantation Bend after a heated argument over the slavery question. Wild and stubborn and eager to declare his independence, Dester had eventually written—not to him—from the western village of San Francisco. He had referred to the West as "the land of the free." *Free soil, free speech, free labor and free men!* How unoriginal of him to have used the slogan of that new Northern party of *locofocos*. He had related stories of separating golden grains from the stream beds of the Sierra Nevada, of one day being richer than his father by his own deftness and not through slaveholding.

Clabe, having read Paulette's letter with her consent, had then crumpled it in his hand in anger. "The young fool thinks like a Northern mudsill!" he had bellowed.

He remembered Paulette bending to reclaim the letter from the hearth where he had flung it. She had smoothed out the creases, folded it and returned it to the pocket of her gown like some cherished possession. "Our Dester," she had murmured, "is the product of this year of our Lord 1848." Then she had fled the room in tears.

Now Paulette was leaving them.

Clabe glanced down the lengthy table at his wife, Vienna.

Dester's desertion had aged his mother, brought fine, hardening lines around the corners of her mouth that Clabe had not noticed previously. He wondered if she blamed him, and he felt a twinge of guilt tug at his heart. What else could he have done? denied his convictions? agreed with their son for the sake of keeping peace? No, Vienna would not have expected that of him. She was as strong willed in her beliefs as he was in his. She understood him—she loved him—and she would have to love him deeply to have survived with him through his bad years of gambling and drunkenness. He realized with a sudden jolt that he had thought of Vienna as invincible and ageless. The early, rocky years of their marriage and the difficult burgeoning years of Plantation Bend had touched her without visible effect, but now, sitting opposite him, eyes downcast, her youth and zest appeared to have abandoned her.

Vienna glanced up, met his gaze briefly, then turned to speak to Rebecca Whitely.

Clabe continued to stare at her questioningly. If she didn't blame him for Dester's forsaking them, was she considering his inability to convince Paulette to remain? No, he again reasoned, she wouldn't blame him for that, either. He had no firm control over Paulette. He had loved her like his own daughter since his mother had brought her from the burning plantation of her parents, but he had no authority to forbid her to go chasing Dester. He could not even deny her finances because she was wealthy in her own right since the sale of the Favière plantation. He had pleaded, even begged, but she had proved as stubborn as his son whom she loved; once her mind had been made up, she would not alter her decision.

Clabe turned his attention to Paulette, his gaze taking in her dark, French beauty, the black hair piled high with ringlets cascading down the right side of her face to her pale shoulder, and it was difficult to remember her as the quiet, frightened child first sheltered in his home. Even then, in those early years, he and Vienna had talked of the bond between Dester and Paulette. The fact that they had fallen in love had surprised neither of them. They waited for the day they would marry, the day they would take over Plantation Bend from them as they had taken it over from his parents. Clabe cast his eyes down at his untouched meal and was thankful Walter Whitely had not pursued the topic of politics.

Paulette looked lovingly around the supper table at her adopted family. Her heart felt near to bursting with love and regret, the two emotions mingling and prodding her close to tears. She knew Clabe and Vienna were also struggling with their emotions.

Bella had long since ceased to struggle; quiet tears were streaking her cheeks. She sat staring at her plate, while across the table Rebecca and Walter Whitely devoured their possum with ravenous appetites. Bella understood why her father had insisted the couple remain for the evening meal, but she considered it unfair of him. No number of guests would lessen the pain of this last supper with Paulette. If Clabe felt a need to hide his emotions behind conversation with strangers, so typically male, then let him—but he need not have restrained her mother and herself with inflicted company. She trembled as Paulette reached out beneath the secrecy of the table and gave her hand an encouraging pat. She turned a tear-streaked face toward her adopted sister and felt herself begin to choke with sobs. She loved Paulette more than her real sister, Katrina—she always had—and now she wanted, needed to confess this to her, not to prevent her from going, but because it might speed her return to Plantation Bend. Whether she came back with Dester did not matter—Bella had never been close to her brother—but she could not imagine a long separation from Paulette. The separation tomorrow morning would be like tearing away a part of her own being.

"Isn't the possum to your liking, Bella?" Clabe asked.

Bella felt the color flood her face. She knew he was demanding that she control her emotions. She was nearly seventeen, and a lady avoided emotional displays in front of guests. "I've . . . I've no appetite," she murmured. Excusing herself, she fled the dining room.

The slamming of the door echoed in the silence that followed.

Rebecca Whitely lay her fork aside and turned her pinched face to Vienna. An expression meant to convey sympathy flickered behind her small eyes. "Poor child," she said. "It isn't easy being the last in the nest. First your Katrina marrying and moving to New Orleans, then Dester, and now . . ." She tossed a disapproving glance in Paulette's direction. "Oh, well," she concluded, "it is, I suppose, a sign of the times that a young woman can travel alone." Outrageous, her tone conveyed. "But don't you worry about your Bella. She'll soon settle on a beau and then . . ." She ended with a knowing smile.

"We've never worried about Bella," Vienna said quietly.

"Nor should you be," their guest agreed. "She's a good head on her shoulders, that one." Again, a disapproving glance in Paulette's direction.

Vienna met Rebecca Whitely's gaze and held it. "All our children have good heads on their shoulders," she said in the same quiet tone. "They were raised with independent spirits." She turned her dark eyes on Paulette and smiled faintly. "All *four* of them," she said.

Rebecca Whitely took the opportunity of Vienna's transference of attention to dab her mouth daintily with the linen napkin. She knew she was being too forward, but she found the desire to express herself almost obsessive. "California," she murmured distastefully, "is one of the primary reasons for all this trouble between the states. It's an outpost, barbaric. I certainly don't think of it as a proper place for a genteel Southern lady."

Vienna opened her mouth to speak, but Paulette spoke first. "Gentility," she said, "true gentility, has been known to survive under the most devastating conditions. I believe when my grandparents came to Louisiana it was also known as barbaric."

"That it was." Walter Whitely stammered. He was embarrassed by his wife's familiarity. Even if they had been close friends instead of mere acquaintances, one did not presume to criticize a Granville, even their adopted daughter. If she chose to travel like a scarlet woman, to follow her lover-adopted-brother— wasn't that almost incestuous?—on a journey not yet taken by a member of the weaker sex, then it was no affair of theirs. Still, he felt sorry for their host and hostess. Surely they were aware of the dangers that awaited the young, dark beauty sitting across from him. If she had been his daughter, even his adopted daughter, he would have locked her in her room until this insanity left her. *Southerners,* he thought with uneasiness. *He'd never come to understand them.* He nudged his wife with his knee to silence her. "Delicious meal," he said, touching his overfilled stomach. "Your Mati must be the best cook in Louisiana."

"Easily," Clabe said.

"You wouldn't consider selling her?"

"We don't sell or trade slaves at Plantation Bend," Clabe answered flatly. He rose, grateful that the meal was at an end, and invited Walter Whitely into the study for cognac and a cigar. There, away from the women, they could discuss politics and he could continue to avoid thoughts of Paulette's departure.

Bella slipped into Paulette's room and perched on the foot of the bed. She had put on her nightdress and plaited her hair into braids that fell over her small breasts. Her eyes were red from crying, but she was determined to put on a brave front for Paulette. "I see you escaped the Whitelys," she said. "Poor Mama is still stuck with them."

Paulette turned away from her vanity mirror. "You

wanted to talk to me without Mama, didn't you, Bella?" she said with understanding.

Bella nodded. "I want to apologize for crying at supper. I . . . I don't want you to think . . . to think I don't want you to go after Dester, not if that's what you want." She lowered her eyes in confusion. "I don't and yet I do," she explained.

Paulette said simply, "I understand," and turned back to her reflection.

Bella left the bed, came up behind Paulette, and began brushing her dark hair. "I've always loved you more than Katrina or Dester," she said. "Losing them wasn't the same."

"You didn't lose them—and you're not losing me," Paulette told her. "Katrina's in New Orleans and visits regularly, and Dester . . . perhaps I'll be able to bring him home to Plantation Bend."

The hairbrush stopped in mid-stroke as Bella's hand was stilled by a sudden thought. "And if Dester won't come home?" she asked. "If he can't reconcile his differences with Papa? What will you do then, Paulette? Will you stay in San Francisco?"

Paulette stared at Bella's image in her mirror and knew she was again on the verge of tears. She reached around and took the hairbrush from Bella's hand and pulled the younger woman onto the bench beside her. "I've never lied to you, Bella," she said, "nor to Papa and Mama. The truth is I'll stay if I must. I love your brother. I don't think there could ever be another man for me. Do you understand that?"

Bella nodded uncertainly. It sounded so romantic, like something out of the novels her father forbade her to read. But Paulette and Dester? She turned the names over in her mind, trying to equate the two people she loved with the fiery romances of literature. *Dester and Paulette. Romeo and Juliet.* Dester was no Romeo. He was her brother and she loved him, but she could not imagine him as a romantic hero. He was, she supposed, handsome, with his blond hair and chiseled features and dark eyes, but she also saw him as ill-tempered, easy to anger, and often childish, traits never applied to the heros of her novels. "I heard Mama and Papa talking," she told Paulette. "Mama said you and Dester had been in love since you were small children." It was a statement, but her eyes transformed it into a question.

Paulette's lips moved away from her even, white teeth in a broad smile. Her eyes took on a distant, thoughtful expression. "Yes, that's true," she said scarcely above a whisper. When had she actually realized it? how long ago? Perhaps it had been that day on the riverbank when Dester had taken her for the first time. No—before—she had fallen in love with him in a forgotten faraway moment of their childhoods. She tried to recapture that moment now in her mind, but she could not. Every time she thought of Dester, she experienced a sensation of timelessness, of possession, of a relationship foreordained by unknown forces. "Yes," she repeated, "I've loved him as long as I can remember."

"Then I'm glad you're going after him," Bella said firmly. She leaned forward and brushed her lips against Paulette's cheek. "I also think you're extremely brave," she said. "They say no other woman has made the trip across the Isthmus."

Paulette laughed at Bella's reference to bravery. She had never thought of herself as brave. There was a twinge of fear plucking at her heart whenever she considered the journey. But she decided against confessing that fear to Bella. "It isn't as if I'll be traveling alone," she said. "I'll have Aaron and Pearl's daughter Mati with me." She was referring to the two slaves Clabe had insisted accompany her; she had agreed only after he had permitted her to give them their freedom once they reached San Francisco. That, she thought, should please Dester.

"Mati is a twit," Bella said critically, "and Aaron is a stubborn mulatto who'll be a maroon if you don't watch him. You're braver still for agreeing to take them with you."

Outside, the sound of carriage wheels crunched along the gravel driveway. The entryway door closed and presently there were footsteps on the stairs.

"It's Mama come to say good-bye," Bella said. "She'll want to speak with you alone." She leaned forward again and kissed Paulette. "Do come home to us, dear Paulette," she pleaded, and rising, left the room just as Vienna was about to knock.

Vienna, without glancing at Paulette, crossed to the windows to draw the heavy draperies. She stood for a moment, looking out, her back to the room. The darkness had not yet settled. A mist was hanging along the creek bank. The sky over the gulf was a deep crimson. How often she had stood at this window in the past; it was her room then—and Clabe's—that was before his mother had died and they had moved into the master bedroom down the hall. Dester and Katrina and Paulette had been small, Bella not yet born. It seemed so long ago, and yet only yesterday. Their lives had been secure; they had been a family. Now only Bella would be left. What had it all been for? the planning? and working? and dreams for their children's futures? She steadied herself and pushed the thoughts from her mind. The music from the slaves' quarters could be heard through the walls of the house. The people were celebrating the departure and eventual freedom of Aaron and Mati. A few short years ago freedom would have frightened most of their people. It was another symbol of the changing times. Drawing the draperies, she sighed and turned to Paulette. She felt almost incapable of uttering a word. Her heart was heavy; she felt weary to the point of collapse. She went to where Paulette sat and nestled Paulette's head on her lap. Vienna's wrinkled hands stroked her adopted daughter's soft, shimmering dark hair as she cradled her head. "I somehow fear this is our final farewell," she said quietly.

Paulette made to pull away. "But I . . ."

"No, don't promise me you'll return by any given time," Vienna interrupted. "I don't want to spend the remainder of my days watching the road and expecting every carriage that passes to be bringing you back to us. Even you don't know what lies ahead for you. I know my son and he won't easily be convinced to return." She stepped back and held Paulette's head firmly between her hands, their eyes locking. "But tell him we love him, his father and I, and want him home. This plantation will be his one day. Then he can run it as he chooses, with freed labor. After you're married, you'll be the rightful mistress of Plantation Bend. That and your own inheritance will make you one of the most powerful women in Louisiana. Even a man as stubborn as Dester couldn't deny you that right. If he does . . ."

Turning, Vienna moved to the chaise longue and sat down. "When he was younger, there was a streak of the devil in Dester's father," she said. She smiled at Paulette's shocked expression. "It's no secret," she told the younger woman. "They still tell tales of his escapades in the casinos in New Orleans. But he changed when our first child was born." Her smile faded and her expression became serious, troubled. "Dester, I fear, has inherited some of his father's deviltry. I only hope he sheds it as easily." She brushed a stubborn strand of gray hair away from her face and tucked it beneath a comb. "Some men need to be tamed," she said. "Dester may be such a man."

*Tamed,* Paulette thought. *Dester's wildness was part of his appeal.* She loved him as he was; she did not want him changed—except, perhaps, in small ways. Nor did she truthfully feel he would change for her. In all relationships there was one who loved more. If change was to be made, it would be on her part.

"I only hope after you're married that Dester will also prove to have inherited his father's thoughtfulness and loving spirit," Vienna went on.

Despite her effort to conceal it, a ring of doubt had crept into Vienna's voice.

That doubt troubled Paulette through the long night and even the next morning, when she bade her tearful farewells and the carriage drove her away from Plantation Bend.

Paulette, snuggled deep into the plush goosedown mattress, awoke and suffered momentary disorientation. She sat upright, staring at the muslin-draped canopy of the bed and the strange furniture, her heart beating rapidly, thinking she had been caught in the netherworld of a nightmare. Then familiarity came rushing back to her. She sighed, smiled, and lay back against the pillows. She was in New Orleans, at Katrina's, where, as a houseguest, she had displaced their daughter from her room because of inadequate sleeping accommodations. The muslin canopy was pink with white doll-like figures at play. The same printed muslin draped the windows, a bright light now behind them. The furniture looked handmade and had been scaled down to a child's size. A small vanity table against the opposite wall had its top laden with cloth dolls, the sort the slaves at the plantation made for their children; more dolls filled the seat of the only chair. Katrina had always been good with a needle, Paulette recalled. It was a good thing, too, since she had married a bank clerk who could not afford to keep her in the fashion to which she had been accustomed. Clabe and Vienna had not approved the marriage, but they had said little to deter their oldest daughter. Perhaps they had seen the futility of discouraging the marriage, just as they had seen the futility of discouraging Paulette from following Dester.

Paulette rose, went to the window, and drew back the muslin draperies. The malodorous New Orleans air stung her nostrils as she pushed open the shutters and stepped onto the narrow balcony. The humidity brought instant moisture to her skin. Below, in the

courtyard, the topiary trees, enameled dark green by
the dampness, rose out of a thin layer of morning
mist. Beyond the stone wall she could hear the street
peddlers hawking their wares in singsong voices, the
wheels of their rickety carts clattering over the cobblestones. Old Jacob, Katrina's only male slave, came
out from the house below and crossed the courtyard,
the mist swirling about his legs. He went through the
gate and returned with a bucket of fish. He was singing to himself in a language unfamiliar to his listener.
When he glanced up and saw Paulette, he fell silent.
He nodded curtly and disappeared inside the house.
Paulette drew back from the railing. Something in
Old Jacob's eyes had made her feel apprehensive.
The apprehension was not new to her; she had felt it
in the past few months from the slaves at Plantation
Bend . . . a restlessness, or, as Dester had warned,
rebellion being born.

There was a gentle rapping on the door, and Mati
entered without waiting to be invited. She scarcely
glanced at her mistress, at the open French doors.
"Mornin'," she said. She crossed to the closet where
Paulette's gowns had been hung the night before and
began checking to see if the wrinkles had vanished.
"What'll you be wantin' to wear today?" she asked.
"Somethin' special, I reckon, since you'll be goin' to
the bank to see Master Sinclair." She fingered the
emerald-green silk, her choice for the occasion.

"The beige with the brown blouse," Paulette told
her. "Visiting Katrina's husband at the bank doesn't
call for a party gown."

"Yes, ma'am." Mati had never been a lady's slave,
but as a house worker, she had watched the ladies'
slaves with envy and had sworn to herself she could
do better. The suggestion of the emerald-green silk
had been meant to prove her worth, but, from her
mistress's tone, she had failed. She would have sulked,
maybe even have defended her choice of gowns, but
she remembered her mother's warning. In San Francisco, she and Aaron would be freed. They would be

married and live as free as any white folks in the new
territory. She took down the beige gown and searched
the trunks for a brown blouse. She was aware of her
mistress pacing the floor behind her. *Maybe she's as
afraid of this new land as me and Aaron,* she thought,
and she wished she could allow herself to be bold
enough to ask. But few of the slaves at Plantation
Bend dared claim familiarity with Mistress Paulette.
Even to the young slaves like Mati, who could not
remember the day when she was a stranger to the
family, Paulette was always treated differently. The
rumors of her family, of the devil Favière, who was
her father, were still whispered about in the slaves'
quarters. Then there was the difference between
Paulette and the Granvilles, they being blond and
fair, and her with her black raven's hair and dark
complexion. Mati stole a glance at her mistress and
thought that it was true—she was almost as dark-
complected as Aaron, a mulatto. A question that could
never be asked formed in Mati's mind, but she
quickly pushed it away. What did anything matter except that she be a "good girl," as her mama had
warned her. In San Francisco, she and Aaron would
say good-bye to Paulette Favière—and to slavery.

Paulette stopped pacing as the door opened a second time and Katrina entered. Katrina was already
dressed for an outing, even to her hat and gloves. "I
trust you slept well," she said. She crossed to the bed,
where Mati had laid out the beige gown, and fingered
the material. "I'm sorry Tom and I couldn't do better
for you," she said, "but on his salary . . ."

"It was fine," Paulette assured her. She disliked it
when Katrina apologized for her lack of affluence.
"In fact, the decor made me feel younger. The room
is charming."

Katrina picked up the gown from the bed and held
it against her, turning to catch her reflection in the
child's mirror. "I miss gowns like this," she murmured.
Sighing, she returned the gown to the bed. The grandfather clock in the downstairs entryway was striking

the hour. "You must hurry," she told Paulette. "Tom
hates it when I'm late." She crossed to the tiny vanity
table and bent over to inspect her appearance, twist-
ing the blonde curls until they lay against her cheekbones.

Paulette motioned for Mati to help her with her
petticoats. She forgot about Katrina until after Mati
had pulled the beige gown over her head and was
lacing it. Then she saw Katrina leaning against the
vanity table watching her with a curious expression.
Again she felt apprehension—as strong as with Old
Jacob; the expression in Katrina's eyes was not unlike
the old slave's. Restlessness? Rebellion? Why, and
against what? "Is something troubling you, Katrina?"
she asked.

"Troubling me? No, nothing, my dear." Katrina
pushed away from the vanity table and crossed to the
door. "I'll have Jacob bring around the carriage," she
said. She smiled back at Paulette, but the smile was
belied by the expression that remained behind her
blue eyes.

Mati, instinctively trained to be aware of the ways
and moods of white people, accurately read the expression, but she said nothing. She understood her
mistress had not interpreted Katrina's expression, and
she felt a momentary surge of sympathy. She shrugged
it away. They would be gone from this house tomorrow—and that suited her fine—one step closer to
freedom.

Paulette and Katrina rode quietly inside the carriage.
Paulette, an infrequent visitor to New Orleans,
pretended interest in the sights. The heat was oppres-
sive. The sun seemed to burn directly through the
carriage roof, and her body was baking inside the
oven of her gown. She leaned forward, hoping for a
slight breeze through the carriage window, but there
was none. The stench added greatly to her discomfort.
She glanced at Katrina, but Katrina's gaze was averted
to the opposite window. She was nervously twining

her fingers. How, Paulette wondered, could Katrina have preferred New Orleans to Plantation Bend? Her marriage to a poor man, she understood—wouldn't she have loved Dester even if he had been poor?— but Katrina's Tom had been offered a position on the plantation and the two had chosen New Orleans in preference. What magnetism did city life hold for them? Paulette glanced again through the carriage window, as if seeking an answer to that question. The buildings were made of stucco or brick, roofed with slate or tiles, in the Spanish style, built around patios or courtyards. Logs had been pegged into the ground for sidewalks. Black convicts, burdened by iron collars and heavy chains around their ankles, were cleaning the ditches on either side of the street. They wore handkerchiefs or scarfs over their nostrils and mouths. It was from the ditches that the stench came, from garbage and unnameable refuse they were shoveling into vats.

Paulette searched her handbag and brought her nosegay to her nostrils, practicing taking short breaths of air that did not draw the stench deep into her lungs. At that moment she missed the country, Plantation Bend, more than she would for days to come.

When Old Jacob handed Katrina down from the carriage, she slipped out of her silent mood and became a model of charm and chattiness upon entering the bank. With Paulette trailing behind, she moved from cage to cage, greeting the tellers as if all were her dearest friends.

"For appearance's sake," she whispered to Paulette as they approached the door of her husband's office. "Tom is very popular at the bank. He expects to be promoted soon—as well he should be." Her gaze became momentarily distant. "Tom is a financial genius" she went on after the moment of reflection had passed. "If he only had luck—or, to be more precise, capital—he would make us more money than Papa ever imagined."

Paulette refrained from mentioning Katrina's dowry,

a sizable sum, that Tom had poorly invested and depleted within their first six months of marriage.

"But Tom is stuck at the bank," Katrina said with obvious resentment. Shrugging her shoulders daintily, she forced a smile to her lips. "But we shall endure. It's only a matter of time." She flung Tom's door open and both women swept into his office unannounced.

Tom was not alone. His small eyes darted from the face of his client to the intruding women with unveiled annoyance. His expression turned to apology for his client. Rising, he said sternly, "Katrina, how many times have I requested you to . . ."

Katrina, laughing, dismissed his irritation with a Southern-lady's gesture of the hands. To Paulette, she said lightly, "I do believe we're in error. Come, my dear." She took Paulette's arm. "We'll wait outside until these gentlemen have concluded their business."

Paulette allowed herself to be guided back toward the open door.

"But our business is concluded."

The chair creaked beneath the weight of Tom's client as he rose quickly to his feet. He had been sitting in profile to the two women. Now, turning, Paulette felt Katrina's grasp tighten around her arm and she glanced at the stranger. He was strikingly handsome, tall, with skin sun-colored to a leathery tan that enhanced the extreme darkness of his eyes. He wore the clothes of an Easterner, tailored and trimly cut to flatter his lithe form. His high boots had been freshly polished, but the New Orleans street mud had already claimed the lower portions. His lips, Paulette thought, were the most perfectly shaped she had ever seen on a man, almost feminine, and accentuated by the cleft of his chin. He was thirty, no more, but he had the aura of an older, worldly gentleman. There was also visible humor sparkling in his pale eyes— humor and obvious interest as he stared at Paulette.

He bent slightly from the waist. "Jeremiah Walker," he said when Tom neglected to make the introductions. The gesture of bowing seemed to amuse him. He smiled, revealing even, white teeth.

Tom came from behind his desk. "My wife, Katrina," he said. "And Paulette Favière."

Jeremiah took Paulette's hand. "At your service, ladies."

Paulette felt a shudder at his touch. Despite his fancy dress and manners, she felt there was something of the savage animal in him.

"Mr. Walker will also be debarking on the *Falcon* tomorrow," Tom announced.

The amusement faded from Jeremiah's face. He stared at Paulette intently. "A lady such as yourself crossing the Isthmus?" he asked increduously. "Forgive me, Miss Favière, but have you been advised of the dangers?"

"Repeatedly," Paulette answered coolly.

"And you're traveling alone?"

"With two servants."

Jeremiah looked at Tom, as if for verification.

Tom shrugged his shoulders to express his disapproval and helplessness. "She can't be swayed," he said.

Katrina, still staring at the handsome stranger, could hold her tongue no longer. "Perhaps Mr. Walker could speak to Paulette," she suggested. "He seems to be a man who understands the dangers of a lady traveling alone."

Paulette, irritated at Katrina's suggestion of drawing a stranger into her private affairs, extracted her hand from Jeremiah's and crossed to the chair he had vacated. "A stranger could not succeed where my family failed," she said firmly. "I must reach California quickly, and if crossing the Isthmus is the quickest route, then cross the Isthmus I shall." Something about Jeremiah Walker both attracted and repelled her; she could still feel the current surging through her hand at his touch, and when she sat down she realized her legs felt weak and were trembling. She folded her hands in her lap. "And now, Tom, if we could get our business concluded?"

Tom, his face flushing with color at having Paulette dismiss his client in such an abrupt manner, looked at Katrina in confusion. Katrina, still the social butterfly, came to his rescue by inviting Jeremiah Walker to join them that evening for supper.

"Unless, of course, you have friends in New Orleans with whom you've committed yourself for your last evening," she continued.

Jeremiah, not taking his gaze from Paulette's profile, said, "I have no friends in New Orleans. It would be a pleasure to sup with two such beautiful ladies." He took his hat from the hat tree. "Until tonight, then." He gave another quick, mocking bow, then left them.

Katrina slipped into the chair beside Paulette. "Why were you rude to him?" she asked. "He's so handsome, and he could be a great service to you during your journey."

"I'm not accustomed to eliciting the services of strangers," Paulette answered, even more irritated that Katrina had invited the man for supper.

Katrina drew in a deep, weary breath. "Mr. Walker seems to be a gentleman," she said defensively. "I suspect you're wrong if you think he would expect favors for his services."

*And I suspect you of being naïve,* Paulette thought, but did not say. To Tom, who had settled back behind his massive desk, she said, "Now, what must I sign? You know I understand nothing of finances."

"That is something you must remedy," Tom told her as he searched through a stack of files and extracted one. "The sale of the Favière Plantation made you a very wealthy young lady. Without someone to properly instruct you . . ."

"I'll leave that to Dester after we're married," Paulette interrupted, glad for thoughts of Dester to push away thoughts of the stranger she had just met. "Papa suggested I carry five thousand dollars on my person and arrange for you to transfer other sums, should I be longer in San Francisco than anticipated."

"Yes, yes," Tom mumbled. He placed metal-rimmed glasses on the tip of his nose and examined her file. "Very wealthy, indeed," he murmured, and exchanged glances with Katrina. "It astounds me that a man about to marry a woman as wealthy as you would be in California sifting sand for gold."

"Then you apparently don't know your brother-in-law," Paulette said stiffly. "Dester doesn't want Papa's money—or mine." How often had they had that battle? Dester's anger flared every time she mentioned the money she had made from the sale of her parents' plantation. It was almost as if he resented her wealth. "Dester will make his own fortune," she concluded.

Tom pushed papers across the desk toward her. "If you'll sign these," he said, "it will give me the authority to transfer future sums."

While Paulette signed, Katrina began to chat with Tom about what she would have the cook prepare for Mr. Walker's visit that evening. "Tell me about him," she insisted.

Paulette listened with half-interest.

"There's not too much I can tell you," Tom told his wife. "He's from New York, apparently a man of some means, since he's leaving a goodly sum with this bank."

"Then why is he going to the gold country?" Katrina inquired.

"To open a business, I believe," Tom answered. "Not all people going to San Francisco are adventurers and fortune hunters." He glanced warily at Paulette, but she seemed to take no offense. "He has a business acumen; I can tell you that. He questioned every detail of the bank's policies and argued . . ."

"But is he married?" Katrina demanded.

"Married? My dear, I didn't pry into his private life," Tom told her. He pulled Paulette's signed papers back to him from across the desk. "And I forbid you to pry, also," he said. "What Mr. Walker wants us to know, he'll offer voluntarily at supper." He stuffed the papers into Paulette's file and pushed it shut. "Now, ladies, if you'll excuse me, I have a bank to manage."

"Will your wife be joining you in San Francisco, Mr. Walker?" Katrina, smiling at their guest, avoided glancing in her husband's direction. Let him be angry with her. She was also angry. Her supper party had been a complete disaster; Paulette, feigning a head-ache, had refused to join them, and then Mati, forced to help in the kitchen, had made a sham of good serving. The least she could do was satisfy her curiosity about Jeremiah Walker.

Jeremiah wiped the corners of his moustache with his napkin and then laid it aside. He had been quiet during supper, speaking only when spoken to. "I'm unmarried, Mrs. Sinclair," he answered flatly. A noise outside the dining room door drew his attention, but his interest quickly turned to disappointment when Mati appeared with strong chicory and coffee.

"A handsome man like you unmarried," Katrina went on. "It must be the times we live in. It's inconceivable some lucky woman hasn't landed you."

"You make Mr. Walker sound like a fish," Tom said abruptly. "Excuse my wife, Mr. Walker. Her curiosity is insatiable." Had the expanse of the table not separated them, Tom would have made Katrina feel the toe of his boot.

"I have curiosities of my own," Jeremiah admitted.

Katrina leaned forward with anticipation.

"About Miss Favière," Jeremiah explained.

"Oh," Katrina murmured and leaned back in her chair. "I regret Paulette was indisposed and couldn't join us for supper. The excitement of the trip, I suppose."

"Possibly," Jeremiah murmured. "Is Miss Favière your sister?"

"Not my blood sister," Katrina told him. "Her parents had the plantation next to our Plantation Bend. There was never a man more evil than her father.

The French Devil, they called him. Just the mention of him and the slaves started to quake. His older daughter was even worse. She was given to . . ."

"Katrina, I'm certain Mr. Walker has no interest in this plantation gossip," Tom said sternly.

"Oh, but I do," Jeremiah assured his host. "Go on, Mrs. Sinclair."

Katrina needed no further encouragement. "Her mother was mad, driven that way by her husband, so the rumor goes. After her husband died of a heart attack, she never left the plantation house, never let Paulette out of her sight. They say she was afraid her husband's daughter by a former marriage would kill the child to prevent sharing the inheritance." Pausing, Katrina drew in a deep breath. "Ironically, it was the mother, in her madness, who almost killed Paulette. She set the plantation to the torch. It was Papa who saved Paulette. He carried her out of the burning house and he and grandmother brought her back to Plantation Bend. She was raised as one of our family."

"Then the mother and half-sister perished in the fire?" Jeremiah prompted.

"The mother perished," Katrina told him. "But the fate of Claudine Favière is another story. During the fire our people discovered a shed of tortured and mutilated slaves, some of them ours, slaves we had thought were maroons. The woman was more of a devil than her father."

"Claudine Favière," Jeremiah said, musing. "Yes, I knew the name was familiar. In the North, they cite her name as an example of how Southerners treat their slaves."

"Outrageous!" Tom cried. "The Southerners would have hanged her or worse if she had not escaped back to France!"

"Even there she was badly received," Katrina added. "Her infamy reached even that country ahead of her. We heard she was shunned by shopkeepers and neighbors and eventually died by her own hand.

Papa went to great expense to have her death verified before Paulette could claim her inheritance."

Mati, serving Tom's coffee, began to tremble, the cup in her hand rattling in its saucer. Her grandmother had been a victim of Claudine Favière; the stories still haunted her and awakened her anger. Sometimes at night she remembered the scars and burns on her grandmother's face and arms and she would awaken in a cold sweat, crying out against the injustice. Always, in these dreams, Claudine Favière's image resembled Paulette.

"What is the matter with you?" Katrina demanded.

Mati poured Tom's coffee and quickly left the dining room.

"Paulette's girl," Katrina said to Jeremiah as an explanation. "She spoils them, always has."

Jeremiah ignored the remark. "Miss Favière must be greatly affected by her past," he murmured, more to himself than his host and hostess.

"Not that you'd notice," Katrina answered, "although once I heard her ask Mama if madness was hereditary."

Tom studied Jeremiah Walker over the rim of his coffee cup. Had he not known Jeremiah to be wealthy, he would have thought him a fortune hunter, with Paulette as his mark. Well, regardless, he would get nowhere with Paulette; her heart and mind belonged solely to Dester Granville. Her money would also belong to that scoundrel after she reached San Francisco. He sighed wistfully, as he always did when he considered the wealth of others, and returned his cup to its saucer. Katrina was still prattling about the past, Paulette's and her own. He had heard the stories so often it was as if their past belonged to him; it was definitely preferable to his own, the son of a poor seaman.

Jeremiah was beginning to show boredom. The conversation had all but eliminated Paulette and now focused on his hostess. He saw there was nothing else to learn from Katrina about the woman who had so interested him. He ran a long, slender finger around the rim of the coffee cup and fixed his gaze on the steaming, foul-tasting brew.

When supper was finished, Jeremiah declined cognac giving the excuse of having to pack for tomorrow's departure. Both his host and hostess followed him to the door, the latter still chattering about life on Plantation Bend and her girlhood.

Tom brushed his wife aside. "Have a pleasant journey."

"And do look after our Paulette," Katrina added without conviction. "We would rest easier knowing she had the protection of a strong gentleman."

Jeremiah, assuring them he would be at Paulette's service, escaped from the couple into the humid night air. In the courtyard he paused, lighted his pipe, and stared up at the second-story windows. For an instant, he thought he detected movement behind one of the shutters, and he felt that Paulette was watching him. He gave a mock, sweeping bow from the waist, thinking how comical he must appear, a black-draped figure in the moonlight bowing to a woman who might or might not be observing him from above.

Laughing at his own sense of the romantic, he swept the folds of his cape back over his shoulders and strode out onto the cobblestones of the busy street.

# Chapter Two

PAULETTE WAVED good-bye to Katrina and Tom from
the railing of the *Falcon* and made her way through
the throngs of passengers to the stairs leading below
deck. Descending, her nostrils were assaulted by acrid
and stale smells. The timber of the handrail was worn
and sticky. The unpleasant scent of tar and rope clung
to the air and permeated her clothing.

The passageway was filled by passengers and crewmen. They were laughing, joking, excited over the
ship's sailing. Silence fell as Paulette left the stairway;
all eyes turned in her direction, some with curiosity,
others with obvious lust. She knew from the passengers' manifest that aside from Mati and an older
woman named Maude Mason, she was the only female
on board. Men, Tom had told her, were superstitous
about women on board a vessel. Masculine nonsense,
she had answered him. Now, moving down the passageway with the men stepping aside to clear the way
for her, she felt like an intruder into their male world.
Damn them, she thought, and their superstitions. She
tilted her chin defiantly and glanced neither to the left
nor right, her gaze fixed on the closed door of her salon.

Whispering reached her from behind as she passed.
". . . piece of skirt . . . don't mind being shipwrecked
with that one." She fought to control her trembling.

Their laughter cut through her like a knife and she felt the color rush to her cheeks. *Animals!*

Then a hand touched her arm; she felt the prickle of rough skin against her flesh and she froze, expecting to have to scream and fight off an attacker. Still clinging to her attitude of defiance, she turned to confront the man who had touched her.

Jeremiah Walker smiled down at her. "Miss Favière." He said her name with that air of mockery that so annoyed her.

The other passengers and crewmen had become silent, listening, perhaps wondering if this gentleman, so much more elegantly dressed than they, would meet with success in his approach.

"Mr. Walker," she said with a hint of mockery to match his own. "I had forgotten we were to be fellow passengers."

The smile left his dark eyes. "I had not," he said. He glanced at the passageway, crowded with men. "And a good thing, too," he added quietly. "May I see you to your room?" He positioned his arm and she laid her hand gently across his elbow, hating herself for the security she felt because of his presence, and they moved to the door of her salon like a couple on their way to supper.

Someone behind them snickered, but a quick glance from Jeremiah silenced all of the onlookers. Despite his elegant manner of dress, his size made him a man to be reckoned with.

Paulette opened the door and was relieved to see Mati busy unpacking her trunks. She turned to Jeremiah.

Before she could speak, he said, "A small cognac would be appreciated." The mockery had crept back into his voice, the smile to his eyes.

"But I haven't . . ."

Before she could complete her protest, he produced a flask from his breast pocket. "I'll supply my own," he said and moved past her into the salon. When he turned back to her, he saw the anger in her eyes and explained, "It will be to your advantage if I remain for a short time. You wouldn't want them to think of you as a woman unescorted."

Paulette was about to close the door when Aaron appeared. "I have Aaron for protection, should the need arise again," she told Jeremiah.

"Not if you prize his life," Jeremiah answered. "A nig . . . a slave on ship can easily be thrown overboard with a knife in his back, should some scoundrels want to get to his mistress."

Mati, busy smoothing the creases from one of Paulette's gowns, became stilled, fear for Aaron creeping into her eyes.

"And a white man wouldn't?" Paulette asked.

"Not without an investigation and some consequence, enough to make the scoundrels think twice." Jeremiah moved to the counter and flipped open the built-in bar. He took out a glass and poured himself a generous cognac. Glancing around the large salon, he moved to the table and took one of the two chairs, seating himself without waiting to be invited.

Paulette motioned for Mati and Aaron to continue with their chores. She took the chair opposite Jeremiah. "Then," she said, "if entertaining you in my rooms is going to ensure my safety, I am obliged . . . for the short time you suggested." She folded her hands properly in her lap and watched him sip his cognac.

He stared at her for some moments over the rim of his glass without speaking. Then he said, "Tell me, Miss Favière, were you really ill during last night's supper at your relatives' home? Or was the illness manufactured to avoid my company?"

Paulette was taken aback, but only momentarily. "You're very forward, Mr. Walker. You will be pleased to learn that I am the same. I was not ill. I have never been ill a day in my life. I did not feel like tolerating Katrina's chattering, or Tom's pompousness, *or* your company."

She thought she detected a flicker of hurt in his

dark eyes, but could not be certain. She had meant it to be there; she wanted, for some unexplainable reason, to hurt him, to wipe that mockery from his expression.

Jeremiah raised his glass to her in the form of a salute and then drained the contents. "I must be cautious when I question you," he said. "Honesty in a woman is something I am not accustomed to." He set his glass aside and rose. "I believe I've remained long enough . . . for the purpose given," he said. "Good day, Miss Favière. This will be the most pleasant leg of our journey. I hope you enjoy it."

Paulette rose to see him to the door. "I believe we'll meet at the captain's dinner table tonight."

Jeremiah smiled at her again. "Forgive me," he said, "but it's your first voyage and I would not advise you to count too much on being capable of sitting at anyone's dinner table." He bowed slightly and moved into the crowded passageway.

Paulette leaned against the closed door. "What did he mean by that statement?" she asked of Mati and Aaron.

"Seasickness," Aaron answered.

"Oh, that," she said. Outside, she heard the crewman yelling and casting off the lines. "I'm not the sort to give in to anything so foolish."

Paulette felt as if she were about to die. Had it not been for Jeremiah's watchful eyes—and her defiance—she would have excused herself from the captain's table and sought the seclusion of her salon. As it was, she had to feign interest in the conversation, and, worse, in the food placed before her by the steward. She tried to force her attention to the conversation.

Reverend Shirr, an old man with gray hair and badly wrinkled skin, had been holding the topic of conversation for what seemed to be an eternity. "I'll be savin' souls for the Lord in that heathen section of the country."

Jeremiah, not attempting to conceal his boredom

with the subject, leaned across the table and faced the reverend. "Of course," he said, "that heathen section of the country existed before the discovery of gold. Why have you waited so long, Reverend, to save those lost souls?"

Reverend Shirr, ignoring the implication, said with enthusiasm, "The Lord moves in mysterious ways. Perhaps the discovery of gold in California was another of His divine moves to draw the heathens together for salvation."

"The men who do the Lord's work seem to move in even more mysterious ways," Jeremiah persisted. "Wasn't that gold-mining equipment I saw you store beneath your berth?"

The reverend's mouth remained open, his ill-fitting teeth appearing ready to cascade onto the table, and the color drained from his wrinkled face. All eyes were turned toward him. "Well, I . . . I see no wrong in . . . I'll do my share of gold-diggin' . . . but only between savin' souls," he murmured. "The Lord's work, of course, comes first."

"Of course," Jeremiah said pointedly. He smiled at Paulette, but she quickly averted her gaze.

Mrs. Mason, attempting to alleviate the silence that fell about the table, began chattering about her son in San Francisco. "Sent me the passage, he did," she told them. "He lives in a place called Nigger Hill, if you can imagine that. Such names they've given these camps! Dutch Flat, Chinese Camp, Hangtown, French Corral. My Jamie says they'll all turn into big cities, and that a person with foresight can make a fortune by anticipating the needs of the miners."

"And what will you be doing, Mrs. Mason?" Paulette asked.

"Me? Oh, any number of things," the older woman answered cautiously. "I'm a worker, always have been. That's where my Jamie gets his ambition. His father was a lazy loafer. He thought it was a disgrace to have calluses on his hands." She glanced briefly at

Jeremiah's hands, resting on the table, and made an obvious comparison to those of the husband she mentioned. "Never had a dollar in his pocket earned through honest labor. But Jamie's different. If anyone will make a fortune in the gold country, it'll be Jamie." She punctuated her belief in the statement with a jerking nod of her head and then went back to eating.

Paulette stiffened as the ship began to roll. Her stomach heaved and for the horror of a moment she thought she would be ill at the captain's table. She knew she had paled and dared not look at Jeremiah for fear he would be smiling at her in that sardonic way of his.

"Just a bit of bad weather," Mrs. Mason whispered into Paulette's ear. "Nothing to be afraid of."

"I'm . . . not afraid," Paulette assured her.

Mrs. Mason patted her hand, anyway.

Paulette reached for her wineglass, hand trembling. Glancing up, she met Jeremiah's gaze. He was not smiling, but instead was looking at her with concern. Oddly, his concern irritated her as much as his mocking smile. Rising, she excused herself and hurried from the captain's quarters.

The air in the passageway was cooler and she felt relief at the absence of the smells of the food. Not wanting to face the confines of her salon, she pulled her shawl around her shoulders and climbed the stairs to the deck.

Despite the restlessness of the sea, it was a clear, starlit night. A gentle breeze was blowing, rustling the silk of her skirt. She could hear the water splashing back from the bow. Drifting up from below deck was the occasional laughter of passengers in the mess hall. The sails were gray, ghost-like in the moonlight. Paulette moved to the railing and stood staring out across the dark water. The fresh sea air and the wind, with its beads of moisture, began to drive away her sickness. She blamed her stubbornness for having

forced her to attend the captain's meal and allowing
Jeremiah to witness her weakened condition. Damn
him and his mocking smiles; damn that look of concern, also. She puzzled at why she disliked him so; she
had seen mockery in other men—even Dester—and
it had not offended her. Perhaps it was his self-
assurance, his poise, his habit of always being impec-
cably attired. Katrina had told her he was a gambler;
that meant he was masquerading as a gentleman. But
she had disliked him even before she had learned this.
He was handsome—that she would give him, with his
dark eyes and tall frame. He commanded respect from
men and, she supposed, admiration from women other
than herself. She wondered vaguely if she had not
been in love with Dester if Jeremiah would also have
been an object of her admiration.

But she was in love with Dester.

She pushed thoughts of Jeremiah Walker from her
mind and thought ahead to when she would be reunited with Dester. She closed her eyes and his image
appeared stamped on the insides of her eyelids: blond,
blue-eyed, chiseled features like his father's and a softness about him inherited from his mother. There
was no softness in the way he held her, made love to
her; it seemed an eternity since they had been together.

The wind had torn her hair away from its combs.
As a strand whipped across her face and into her eyes,
she was brought away from her memories and back to
reality. Without understanding the origin, she felt shivers of fear plaiting along her spine. Turning, she
peered into the darkness, but she distinguished nothing
in the shadows to frighten her. A sudden gust of wind
snapped and filled the sails, and as if taking a cue, the
moon was hidden behind a high-moving cloud. She
gathered up her skirts and was about to return below
to the safety of her cabin when a movement to her
right caused her to halt. Someone was lurking in the
deeper shadows cast by the bridge.

*Jeremiah,* she thought, *come to gloat over her sea-sickness.*

He must have been disappointed to find her leaning against the railing like a dreamer rather than over the side losing her supper. She smiled, deciding to pass by him without acknowledging him. If he spoke, she would ignore him.

But she did not reach the door of the stairs before a man—not Jeremiah—stepped out from the shadows. Even in the dim light she could make out his scruffy dress and unkept beard. He wore the knit cap of a seaman, but his coat was checked, torn at the sleeve, the cast-off garment of some gentleman. Her breath caught in her throat and the plaiting along her spine turned to visible trembling. She hastened to move on, but the hand inside the torn sleeve shot out and clutched at her arm.

"You're lookin' like you're awantin' company," he said in a rasping voice.

"No!" she managed to say. "Release me!"

"Release you, I will, my pretty," he snapped, then laughed.

Paulette attempted to pull her arm free, but he only increased the pressure of his grip. "Don't be a fool," she said. "They'll hang you if you touch me!"

He pulled her to him roughly. "Only if you live to tell about it."

She opened her mouth to scream, but before sound could be forced out, a hand clamped over her mouth from behind. Two of them—they had seen her climbing to the deck and had followed her, watching from the shadows as she had unsuspectingly stood dreaming of Dester.

Dester—the thought of him gave her strength. She was going to be raped and murdered; she would be lost to Dester and he to her. She managed to force her jaws apart beneath the pressure of the hand clamped over her mouth. Her teeth sank into hard, foul-tasting flesh. She tasted blood and heard a groan of pain. Then a fist struck her back and winded her; explosions of light erupted before her eyes and she thought she would faint. Still, she clung to consciousness and continued to struggle. She kicked out at the man in the checked coat, but her own skirt and petticoats prevented the blow to his groin from delivering any serious damage. In return for her effort, he struck her across the face. A hand was forced beneath the bodice of her gown and the silk was brutally torn away. The man behind pinioned her arms with one of his without releasing the clamp across her mouth. The man in the checked coat lowered his head to her breasts. The coarse wool of his cap scratched her throat, and the smell stung her nostrils. But those sensations were quickly lost to the pain of his teeth on her flesh. Hands groped and tore at her skirt; she felt the material tearing, felt her petticoats being lifted, torn. Visions passed before her of Clabe and Vienna, of Dester and Bella, of Plantation Bend; she remembered the warnings—a lady of quality traveling alone, unheard of; you'll be raped, killed, dishonored at the very least—and she had scoffed at them. Tears stung her eyes and further blurred her vision. With the hand clamped over her mouth, she could not even plead for mercy, or for them to kill her before they took her.

"Christ, Almighty!" the man in the checked coat whispered to his companion. "I've never felt no skin like this. Soft as a baby's bottom side." His fingers greedily kneaded her thigh, his fingernails digging into her flesh as they sought to remove the final, awkward barrier of fabric keeping him from the even softer flesh he would violate.

She tried again to bite the hand clamped over her mouth, but more pressure was applied and her teeth cut into her own inner lips. She was bent backward, a knee in the middle of her back pushing her loins forward. She felt the tearing of her undergarments, felt the rough fingers searching for entry, and she prayed to God she would faint.

Then she felt herself being jerked, flung away. She
fell, had been cast aside as if she were no more than a
rag doll. There was shouting, curses. She struck the
deck and rolled onto her back. Staring up, she saw
the shadows struggling in the darkness, outlined by the
moon, now unhidden by clouds. There was the sound
of other footsteps on the stairs, lanterns glowing, cutting through the darkness. The man in the checked
coat was lifted, seemed to float for an instant, and
then was thrown screaming over the railing. The sea
claimed him soundlessly.

Mrs. Mason appeared at Paulette's side. "Darling,
darling," she murmured. She removed her shawl and
draped it over the young woman's naked breasts. "The
beasts!" she screamed. "The brutal savages!" She
pulled Paulette to her bosom and held her protectively.

The deck was now well lighted by lanterns. Paulette, clutching at Mrs. Mason, saw Jeremiah lifting
another man above his head. Growling like an angry
giant, he spun the screaming man around and then
flung him as he had the first. Instead of going over the
railing, the man struck the base of the mast. There
was a crunching sound as his back snapped, and he
slumped lifelessly to the deck.

Jeremiah, pushing away the crewmen who approached him, strode to where Mrs. Mason held
Paulette. He stood, the glow of the lanterns lighting
his face, and stared down at Paulette.

Paulette pushed herself closer to Mrs. Mason, her
eyes locked to Jeremiah's. There was no longer mockery in his gaze, nor concern. What she saw reflected
there was fury—fury so intense that it terrified her.

He bent and scooped her up into his arm and
started toward the stairwell. She could feel the power
of his body through his fancy coat, could feel the studs
of his shirt poking against her flesh through Mrs. Mason's shawl. She felt protected, safe. Then the terror
of her experience struck her. The scream that had been

denied her through her ordeal finally broke in her throat. She slumped against Jeremiah's chest in a faint.

Paulette rose slowly through levels of unconsciousness. At first she had difficulty adjusting herself to her surroundings; there was the gentle rolling motion of her bed, the sound of wind and splashing water, and whispering. She listened, eyes closed.

". . . warned her, they did, all of them," Mati was saying. "Beggin' your pardon, Mrs. Mason, but sea travel ain't something for a lady—especially Miss Paulette."

"Nonsense," the older woman countered. "You're scared for your own skin, not your mistress's. She's young and strong. California's the place for her. She's got a drive. You can see it in her eyes."

"Her drive's for Mr. Dester," Mati said knowingly.

"Whatever it's for, it's there," Mrs. Mason said.

"It's like a fever she's got for him," Mati murmured. "And them raised like brother and sister."

"Don't gossip, child!" Her voice softened. "I'm sorry. I've no call to speak to you in that manner. Even if I wasn't a Northern woman, you're not my slave."

"I won't be anyone's slave after we reach San Francisco," Mati informed her proudly. "That's the only reason I came instead of runnin' away. Aaron and me, we're goin' to be freed—that is," she said with a dwindling voice, "if we live to cross the Isthmus."

"We'll live, we'll live," Mrs. Mason repeated with assurance.

"I'm not so sure as you. I've listened to people, and they say of the few women—two to be exact—who've attempted the crossin', one died of cholera and the other drowned."

"Strictly gossip," Mrs. Mason said, but with fading conviction, "probably started by men to scare us. Look, I think your mistress is coming to."

Paulette felt a cold cloth pressed against her temples. She opened her eyes and stared up into the older woman's kind and wrinkled face. Then her experience on deck came flooding back over her and anguish caused her to whimper in fear.

"There, there," Mrs. Mason soothed. "It's over and done with, and those savages got their just rewards." She patted the pillows under Paulette's head and fussed at making her comfortable. "A good thing Mr. Walker was concerned about you and followed you from the captain's table. If he hadn't, God only knows what those evil ones would have done to you."

"He's waitin' in the other room," Mati said from behind Mrs. Mason, "waitin' to make sure you're all right. Shall I tell him he can come in now?"

"No! I don't want to see him!" Paulette cried. She clutched at Mrs. Mason's hands, holding them tightly, as if drawing from their strength.

"He deserves to be thanked properly," the older woman told her. "He did save your life, child."

Paulette remembered the sight of him as he flung her attackers around as though they were weightless bundles. She also recalled the fury in his eyes, fury that had not been quenched by the two men's deaths.

Mati shrugged her shoulders; she'd never understand white women. "I'll send him away," she said, "even thinkin' it's not the thing to do."

Paulette lifted herself on the bed. She was about to shout at Mati, but Mrs. Mason urged her back against the soft pillows.

"She may be a slave," she said, "but she's right. Wait a few moments and then decide if you'll send him away or thank him, as a lady should."

Mati, hand on the doorknob, hesitated, waiting for instructions. Paulette nodded her acquiescence.

"But I won't see him like this," she said, "not in my dressing gown. Mati."

Mati went to the wardrobe and began sorting through the array of gowns.

When Paulette was properly dressed, Mati and Mrs. Mason left her. There was a gentle rapping on the door and Jeremiah stepped in. Paulette had dimmed the lanterns, not wanting him to see the bruises on her cheeks and forehead; she somehow felt he would take satisfaction in seeing her injuries, and she did not wish to give him any satisfaction.

"I believe your drink is cognac, Mr. Walker," she said, and she motioned him to a chair where she had had Mati pour out a small glass of the strong liquor on the side table.

He took the chair, leaning forward to see her better in the poor lighting. "Are you in pain?" he asked.

"None to speak of," she answered. She folded her hands tightly in her lap. "I must thank you for saving me from a fate far worse than pain." Her words were curt, clipped.

He remained silent for several moments. Then, leaning back, he picked up his cognac and drained the glass. "I promised your adopted sister to look after you," he said as coldly as she had thanked him. "I considered it my obligation."

"Obligation?" Why did he anger her so easily? "I'll be no man's obligation."

"Not even the man whom you're traveling to San Francisco to meet?" he asked bluntly.

She rose, moved to the porthole, and stood staring out at the moonlight shimmering across the restless water. "Not even to him," she answered. She heard his chair creak as he shifted his position, but he did not rise, as she expected. She turned to face him; he sat in the shadows cast by the dim light of the lantern and she could not make out his expression. "Again, I thank you," she said. "Now, if you'll excuse me, I'm very tired and want to retire."

He rose without speaking and moved to the door. Hesitating, he turned. "Don't go on deck alone again," he told her. "Don't go anywhere on the ship alone. Those men were only two of many who would not hesitate to take what they want from a defenseless lady."

"Thank you for the warning," she said. "I'll see that Mati or Aaron is always with me."

He opened the door, but again he hesitated. "You could always change your mind and return to New Orleans before crossing the Isthmus," he said. "It's not going to be an easy journey."

"I didn't expect it to be. Good night, Mr. Walker."

He gave her a short, stiff bow. "Good night, Miss Favière." The light from the outer room caught the mockery in his eyes before he closed the door.

# Chapter Three

"Good Lord, Miss Paulette!" Mati cried. "Are they expectin' us to travel in those?" She pointed from the porthole to the canoes being rowed across the shallow water from the shoreline.

Paulette glanced through the porthole at the approaching canoes. Her heart quickened, but she hid this from the slave. She turned back into her cabin. Their luggage had been packed and was waiting for Aaron to carry it topside. "Quickly," she said, "I can't wear a gown like this in a canoe." She indicated the green velvet dress."

"But we didn't bring no simple gowns," Mati protested.

Paulette thought for a moment, then said, "Then I shall have to wear one of yours, Mati. We're about the same size."

Mati looked horror-stricken. Her simple dresses, stitched up by her mother, were rolled into bundles, some of them with the color worn away, some torn and sewed so many times the tiny stitches seemed like part of a design. Then the thought of her mistress in one of her dresses amused her. She forgot about the dangerous-looking canoes and went searching through the luggage for her most tattered serving dress.

When Paulette emerged on deck, the weather had taken a turn for the worse. The sunny skies of morning had given way to a gray overcast. A light mist was settling on the crowd waiting to disembark. Men were jostling, cursing one another. Those who saw her fell silent. The story of what had happened to her attackers had spread quickly among the passengers. Since that night some of the men would not even glance in her direction; she did not know if it was from fear of Jeremiah or if they considered her a symbol of ill fortune.

Mrs. Mason was already on deck, jostling and pushing her way through the crowd of men. When she saw Paulette emerge, she pushed her way back from the railing through the crowd, her black bonnet disappearing and then reappearing among the sea of masculine shoulders. She glanced at Paulette's dress and nodded her approval. "They've prepared a chair on ropes—Mr. Walker and the captain—to lower us to the canoes," she said. "Don't be afraid. They tested it by sending one of the heftiest crewmen over the side in it. Except for submerging his legs in the water, he made it without mishap." She took Paulette's arm and led her forward into the crowd. "It's lucky that with us being women," she whispered, "we have Mr. Walker on our side."

Paulette halted. "What are you saying, Mrs. Mason? What has Mr. Walker done for us now?"

"Why, he's seen that we're among the first to disembark," the older woman said. "Canoes are the sole means of conveyance across the Isthmus, and even though they've all been pressed into service, it'll take several days to take everyone from the *Falcon*. That's why some of the men are fighting mad. They say Mr. Walker cheated them, being a professional gambler."

Paulette still refused to be urged forward until she fully understood what had transpired.

"The order of our disembarkment was determined by gambling," Mrs. Mason explained. "Jeremiah Walker took the liberty of gambling for us ladies. Now, hurry before there's a brawl on board and it's everybody for themselves."

Paulette allowed herself to be urged forward to the railing. The chair from the galley, ropes tied to its arms and back, was being hoisted back on board. It looked frail despite the burden Mrs. Mason had told her it had survived in its test.

Jeremiah was standing at the railing. Despite the journey ahead of him, he wore his customary suave clothing and looked more like a man on his way to the theater than on a canoe ride. He smiled at her and touched the brim of his hat in greeting.

She nodded curtly. She had not seen him since the night he had saved her, although he had been constantly on her mind. She had even dreamed of him, confusing him in her dreams with Dester, something that disturbed her greatly. When he stepped up beside her now, she avoided looking up at him.

"It's not as delicate as it looks," he said of the chair.

*Neither am I,* she wanted to add, but she held her tongue. "I understand I owe you another debt," she said.

"And what might that be?"

"Getting us to be among the first to disembark."

"Ah, Mrs. Mason told you," he said. "And I swore her to secrecy." He laughed and slapped the older woman playfully on the back.

"Do you always win at gambling, Mr. Walker?" Paulette asked.

"Not always," he answered, "just when it's of major importance." Turning, he joined the crewmen in lowering the chair to the deck. He parted the ropes for easier seating. "Which of you ladies will have the honor first?"

Paulette glanced over the side of the *Falcon,* realizing for the first time how far down the water seemed. Fear toyed with her, but she quickly pushed it away. "With your permission," she said to Mrs. Mason, and slipped into the chair. "Hoist away," she said.

With a signal from the captain, the crewmen hoisted the chair up and it was pushed out over the railing. Paulette caught her breath when she was suspended

above the water. She would have closed her eyes had
not Jeremiah and Mrs. Mason been watching and
would have taken it for fear. The chair began to swing
in the wind during its descent. The mist was growing
thicker, beading on her eyelashes and creating a blurring of her vision. She could see the canoe below, see
the crewman reaching up to receive the chair. Her
heart was fluttering against her rib cage. Should the
rope break or the chair suddenly decide to splinter,
she could swim, but not with the weight of Mati's
dress pulling her down. She told herself not to anticipate disaster. To lessen her fear, she turned her attention to watching the men who were climbing down
ropes to the other canoes. Those canoes already moving away from the *Falcon* appeared too heavily loaded
and were sitting low in the water.

She felt the crewman grab the legs of her chair and
heaved a sigh of relief. From above came a cheer
from Mrs. Mason. She glanced up and waved.

"All right, ma'am," the crewman told her. "Move
forward in the middle of the canoe and take a seat."

Easier said than done, she decided. By the time she
was seated, her head covered with her shawl against
the mist, the chair had already been returned above.
Presently, Mrs. Mason appeared over the railing. She
was laughing and shouting instructions about the lowering of the chair.

"Something to tell my grandchildren," she said
when she was seated beside Paulette, "that is, if my
Jamie ever takes a wife."

"I'm sure he will," Paulette told her absently.

"Not that many women in San Francisco, I'm told,"
the older woman said with concern. Then her expression changed and she laughed. "Bad for Jamie, but
good for me. Who knows, I might even find myself a
husband. I've been without one for too long."

There were seven passengers in the canoe when it
moved away from the *Falcon:* Paulette and Mrs. Mason; Jeremiah and Reverend Shirr; Mati, concerned
because Aaron was in the canoe behind theirs; and two

crewmen. When the canoe had left the main body of water, it moved with greater ease, but even then the weather made every moment miserable. Jeremiah and Reverend Shirr rigged a canvas beneath which the three women eventually huddled, but the wind blew the mist in from the sides, so they still became wet and cold. Mati made matters worse by continually lifting the flaps of the canvas to see if Aaron's canoe remained in sight.

"Can't swim, my Aaron," she explained and bit her lower lip with worry.

"Hush," Paulette told her. "If the canoe overturns, someone will save him."

"Save a nigger slave," Mati murmured. "Not likely." She huddled with her head hunched down into her shoulders and closed her eyes.

The mist turned to rain and the rain grew steadily heavier until it was impossible to see the canoes ahead or behind. The wind continually tore the canvas covering away until finally Jeremiah was unable to retrieve it and it was claimed by the murky water. He removed his coat and put it over Paulette's shoulders, but it was quickly soaked through and was nothing more than a burden. The three women huddled together; even the brave Mrs. Mason gave way to her fear of death by drowning and whimpered that she would never see her Jamie again. Mati cried out Aaron's name, and Paulette tried to take comfort in thoughts of Dester. Reverend Shirr shouted a prayer, but it was not one to still their fears, and Jeremiah demanded he be silent.

It was difficult to estimate how long they had been traveling by canoe, nor could time be told by nature. The sky was darkening steadily, but Paulette was uncertain as to whether it was from the storm or the end of day. She heaved a sigh of relief when the crewmen turned the canoe toward shore. The waves were now lapping over the sides of the canoe and filling the keel. Jeremiah and Reverend Shirr put themselves to scooping out the water so that the canoe wouldn't suddenly sink.

Mati started wailing, unable to see Aaron's canoe and thinking they might pass by without turning ashore. She tried to stand, and Mrs. Mason was forced to slap her to keep her from overturning them.

It was not Mati who caused the accident, but Reverend Shirr. As he stood up from scooping water, he lost his balance and pitched to one side. His upper body struck the side of the canoe. He went head first into the churning water and disappeared beneath the surface. The canoe rolled despite the men's efforts. The women, in a flurry of wet shirts and screams, tumbled against one another and fought to cling to their seats.

Paulette was the last to hit the water. In the instant before, she saw Jeremiah, his dark hair flattened against his forehead, his eyes blazing with the same fury she had seen the night he had saved her on the *Falcon*. He was attempting to reach her, but both knew it was hopeless. Then she understood the intensity of his fury. It was born out of frustration. On the *Falcon* he had thought he had come to her rescue too late; now he could not reach her and might lose her to the dark water.

The water closed around her face. She tasted its foulness and flayed her arms to bring herself to the surface. Her wet skirt and petticoat clung to her legs and drew her down farther into the murky depths. She touched something solid and knew by the feel that it was Mrs. Mason's coarse woolen skirt. She grabbed at the older woman's arms, kicked with all her strength, and brought the two of them above water.

Jeremiah was there almost instantly to relieve her of the burden of the unconscious Mrs. Mason. "Hang onto my coat!" he shouted above the wind. When she had clutched at his collar, he started for shore with the two of them, Mrs. Mason's chin cupped in the crook of his left arm.

Mati and Reverend Shirr were already pulling
themselves onto the muddy bank. One of the crewmen stood knee-deep in water, stretching out his hand
to assist Jeremiah with his charges. The other crewman was nowhere in sight. The canoe was bobbing
upside down away from shore. When it drifted into
the path of the canoe that had been behind them,
Paulette heard Aaron's tortured scream; so, too, had
Mati.

Mati pulled herself from her knees. Cupping her
hands about her mouth, she screamed Aaron's name
in return to let him know she had been saved.

Jeremiah half-dragged, half-carried Paulette onto the
embankment. When she felt ground beneath her, she
pulled away from him, her independence returning.
Through the veil of rain she saw Aaron's canoe, saw
him stand and suddenly dive into the water. It wasn't
until Mati screamed again that she remembered the
slave telling them that Aaron had never learned to
swim. In his panic, he had dived into the water to
reach Mati.

"Oh, my God!" Paulette cried. "He can't swim!"

Jeremiah followed the direction of her pointing finger. Shedding his coat, he plunged back into the water, powerful strokes taking him quickly to where
Aaron was floundering.

Paulette restrained Mati from following Jeremiah.
"He'll save Aaron," she assured the slave. "You'll
only hinder him." She left Mati and went to Mrs.
Mason. The older woman was pulling herself up from
the mud, sputtering and spitting out the dregs of water. She leaned into Paulette's arms, accepting her assistance in rising to her feet.

"Thank the Lord," she murmured, "for saving me
to see my Jamie again."

"Yes, thank the Lord!" Reverend Shirr shouted beside them. "He has taken one of the crewmen whose
time it was, but He has spared us." Dropping to his
knees in the mud, he clamped his hands together in

front of his face and began to pray in a loud, singsong voice.

Paulette led Mrs. Mason away from him to the protection of the base of a tree. Had it not been for the wind, they would have been shielded from the rain by the heavy foilage. At least they were out of the mud. From there they watched Jeremiah help Aaron to shore and into Mati's waiting arms.

Jeremiah, completely ignoring Reverend Shirr on his knees, walked past him and joined Paulette and Mrs. Mason. He sat beside Paulette, his chest heaving from the ordeal. "We've lost the canoe," he told her. "When the rain stops we'll have to start out on foot. For now I'll try to find a place where we can get out of the rain and build a fire."

The three women huddled together for warmth. The tree gave them little protection and they trembled with the cold. Mati, so happy Aaron had been saved by Jeremiah, was too thankful to complain. Mrs. Mason clung to Paulette's hands.

The men struck out in different directions seeking shelter. It was Aaron who returned and told them he had found an overhang against the cliffs where they would at least be protected from the rain. Cupping his hands to his mouth, he gave a call to signal the others.

Mati gathered dried leaves and twigs from among the cliff's crevices to start a fire while Aaron and the crewman collected bark and branches. Within minutes a fire was blazing within a circle of stones.

Paulette drew back into the shadows away from the fire and attempted to wring the water from her skirt and petticoats. The fabric was so splattered with mud that it felt rough and grimy; she had never felt so dirty, so uncomfortable, or so unattractive. But I'm alive, she thought. She could have been lost instead of the crewman; perhaps she would have been if it had not been for Jeremiah. Another debt she owed him. She returned to the fire and huddled beside Mrs. Mason.

The older woman sat staring into the flames. She lifted her head suddenly and sought Jeremiah. "We'll never make it on foot, will we, Mr. Walker? There's swamp and quicksand and any number of unspeakable dangers out there." She glanced past the men toward the darkness that surrounded them, as if expecting something to plunge into the light and devour them.

Mati pulled closer to Aaron and clung to him, her eyes wide.

Paulette placed her arm around Mrs. Mason and held her. She also felt fear, fear of the darkness in this strange land, and fear for their situation, but she would not give in to that fear because of Jeremiah. If he thought she was afraid, he might mock her.

"We'll make Chartres," Jeremiah said with conviction.

"Aye," Reverend Shirr agreed, "God willing. But even then the *California,* out of New York, may have sailed without us."

"Where is your faith?" Jeremiah asked him. He laughed, but his laughter rang hollow. Moving around the fire, he crouched beside Paulette and Mrs. Mason. "If you can, get some sleep," he told them. "We're going to need our energy tomorrow." He touched Paulette's shoulder, but she pulled away from him. As much as she wanted to have him near her, to feel the protection of him, she would never submit. He moved away from the fire and lay curled up, his head resting on a rock, his arms folded, and his legs drawn up. Within moments he was asleep.

"How can he sleep?" Paulette murmured.

"Because he knows he must," Mrs. Mason answered absently. "You must sleep also, child."

"And you."

"I require little sleep," the older woman said. She straightened her legs and made a headrest of her lap for Paulette. "Dream of pleasant things," she said. "Dream of your fiancé in San Francisco. Perhaps when you arrive there, he will have made his fortune.

The hardships you suffered on this journey to be reunited will then be of little consequence." She stroked
Paulette's wet hair with her wrinkled fingers. She
leaned closer to Paulette's ear. "Mr. Walker is quite
taken by you. Why do you treat him so coldly?"

Paulette pretended to sleep so she would not have
to answer. Eyes closed, still trembling despite the fire,
she listened to the rain beating down beyond the
overhang of the cliff. It seemed to have lessened;
hopefully, it would have stopped by morning.

She awoke to shouts.

Sitting up, she saw that Mrs. Mason, Mati, and
Reverend Shirr had also been awakened by the same
disturbance. Jeremiah, Aaron, and the crewman were
not in sight. The rain had stopped, the sun was out,
and steam was rising from the ground and foliage.
The shouts came again, but they were incoherent,
excited.

"I'll go," Reverend Shirr said, and he hurried away
from them.

Paulette rose. Her dress had dried, or rather Mati's
dress, but the mud was caked around the hem and
bodice. She brushed at it, but without success. Fortunately, most of her clothing had been in Aaron's canoe; that would obviously reach Panama well ahead of
her. She pushed back her hair and wished she had a
mirror. Then the idea of primping in the wilds of the
Isthmus suddenly struck her as amusing and she
laughed aloud.

Mrs. Mason and Mati looked at her as if she
had taken leave of her senses. Her laughter ended
abruptly as she remembered the money she had been
carrying on her person. As Vienna had instructed her,
she had tied a small pouch around her waist and kept
the money there. She hoisted her skirts and heaved
a sigh of relief. The pouch was still there, the money
inside, wet but unharmed.

Jeremiah came through the foliage unexpectedly.

Paulette uttered a cry of alarm and dropped her

skirts. She saw the mockery in his eyes and felt her anger growing. Then she realized that he looked no better than she; his stylish clothes had been as badly treated as hers. There was dried mud on his forehead and caked in his hair and his shirt had been badly torn and hung open, revealing one side of his strong, powerful chest.

He motioned for them to come with him. Forgetting Paulette, excitement showed in his expression. "Canoes," he said. "They were headed for the *Falcon* and we managed to coax one of them ashore. The owner will take us to the port of Panama—for a price," he added, "double our original passage."

Mrs. Mason broke into delighted cheering. "And we'll get there well ahead of the *California*. And here I thought I'd never live to see San Francisco and my Jamie."

She grabbed Paulette's hand and the three of them hurried after Jeremiah.


"The *California*'s three weeks late, and each day there are new arrivals," Mrs. Mason said, "all of them headed for the gold fields."

Paulette, setting her tea cup aside, rose and moved to the closed shutters. The room was stiflingly hot, and yet Mati had neglected to open the windows. The slave was becoming lax and forgetful; she would have to speak to her. She opened the shutters and stared out across the square to where a crowd had gathered around a fountain.

"What's worse," Mrs. Mason continued from behind her, "is that they're all expecting to gain passage on the *California*. It's impossible, of course. They're now talking of using the lottery system to determine who goes and who stays behind."

Paulette, alarmed, spun around. "They can't do that! We booked passage well in advance."

"Little do they care," Mrs. Mason scoffed. "You haven't been out there, confining yourself to your rooms as you do. You don't understand what it's like,

what this gold fever's done to everyone. If there isn't
a lottery, I wouldn't be surprised if men started killing
one another just to lessen the number of travelers
competing for passage. Only last night in my hotel
there was a knife fight in the hallway outside my
door—two men fighting over passage one had won in
a card game."

It was true that Paulette had not left her rooms except to visit the dining room in the three weeks since
their arrival in Panama. The first few days she had
kept to her bed due to exhaustion, not even venturing
out for supper; then she had not felt well and had
developed a slight fever. The fever had frightened
her because the cry of cholera had gone up among
those who had crossed the Isthmus. It was rumored
that several had died of that dreaded disease. Panic
had struck. People with the slightest malady that
might be thought to be cholera were being turned into
the streets from hotels and private homes where they
rented rooms; some, Mati had told her, were even
driven from the city and forced to live on a restricted
section of the beach in makeshift tents, the authorities leaving food for them in a designated spot each
afternoon. "Like animals," the slave had said.

Mrs. Mason rose and moved to the window beside
Paulette. "Look at the square," she said quietly.
"Each day it becomes more filled. Each night there
are more sleeping on the cobblestones. I can't imagine what will happen if the *California* arrives much
later. As it is now, our odds for boarding her are not
good."

"But surely . . ."

"There's nothing sure about men driven to reach
the gold," Mrs. Mason said. "Don't think we'll be
given special treatment because we're women; indeed,
it may prove to be our disadvantage. Mr. Walker
says that the rooms will be packed beyond capacity
even if they go to the lottery system. As far as I know,
there are only five women traveling to San Francisco.

The steamship company isn't going to favor five in a room that could hold ten."

"Then we'll pay double," Paulette suggested.

"That we must do, anyway," the older woman informed her. "The steamship line's representative announced an increase of all fares effective immediately."

Paulette leaned her forehead against the window-frame. In the square beneath her window, a child was playing with a mangy dog. Two men were setting up a table, spreading out cards and inviting passersby to join them in a game of poker. Several men stopped to watch, but none agreed to join the game until finally a familiar figure emerged from under the arches of the hotel and took one of the chairs.

"Jeremiah," Paulette murmured. Despite herself, she felt her pulse quicken.

Mrs. Mason leaned out to follow Paulette's gaze. "Hmm," she mumbled. "Jeremiah's changed since our arrival in Panama, and I think you've something to do with it. He drinks heavily and spends most of his afternoons and evenings gambling."

"That's his profession," Paulette said stiffly.

Mrs. Mason ignored the remark and the tone with which it had been delivered. "He asks about you daily —calls on me for that purpose only. He also told me he tried to call on you several times, but was turned away."

Paulette, afraid Jeremiah would glance up and catch her watching him, straightened and moved back to her chair. "More tea?"

"No, thank you, dear. It's much too warm for tea. They have a wonderful drink here made with coconut and rum. You must try it." The older woman also resumed her chair. "About Jeremiah Walker," she said after she was settled. "I think it most unkind of you to treat him as you have. After all, my dear, he did save our lives, yours twice. He's quite fond of you and would be a great asset to you until you reach San Francisco."

"I'm grateful for what he's done already," Paulette said, "but I would prefer to avoid him."

"For heaven's sake, why?"

"I can't explain," Paulette admitted. She sipped her tea and found it bitter and lukewarm. She did not want to offend Mrs. Mason, but she decided that if the older woman persisted in speaking of Jeremiah, she would be forced to tell her to abandon the topic in the future.

Mrs. Mason apparently read her thoughts, for she said, "Then I shall say only one more thing on the matter. Should there be a lottery, should you not be one of the fortunate ones to win, there is probably no one better qualified in Panama to get you aboard the *California* than Jeremiah Walker."

"And how would he succeed in doing that?"

"With what is occupying him at this very moment," Mrs. Mason answered. "A drunken man will gamble anything, even his passage to San Francisco, and, my dear, as you said, Jeremiah is a professional gambler. Should he be playing for a lottery ticket on your behalf, I think he would win even if he was forced to tamper with his usual honest method of gambling." She leaned forward across the tea table. "He may be a gambler, but he's an honest one, a good one also. I've watched him. My husband was a gambler, not of the quality of Jeremiah Walker, but he taught me cards. I can tell when a man's cheating, and Jeremiah doesn't cheat."

"I'm pleased to learn of his honesty," Paulette said flatly. "I'm also pleased you think he'd cheat for me, but since it might not prove necessary . . ." She turned from Mrs. Mason as the door opened and Mati slipped into the room. "Mati, where have you been? And where is Aaron? I told you I wanted him to move the bed away from the window. All night long I'm kept awake by noise from the square."

Mati, eyes lowered, moved to the tea table and began removing the china. "Aaron . . . he'll be along soon," she said quietly.

"It was Mrs. Mason who saw the tears in Mati's eyes. "Here, dear, what's troubling you? Have some of these hoodlums been bothering you?"

Mati glanced quickly at Paulette. Her lower lip was trembling, the tears flowing faster. Suddenly, with a moan, she dropped at Paulette's feet, clutching her mistress around the knees.

Paulette, never having seen anything but rebellion in the slave, was taken aback. She took Mati's shoulders in her hands and held her back so she might see into her face. "What is it?" she demanded. "It's not Aaron? He's not run away?" She remembered hearing Mati and Aaron talking when they thought she had slept, the young slave telling Mati he thought they'd never reach San Francisco and never be free.

"No . . . not run away," Mati wept.

"What, then?"

"Aaron . . . he's got the fever . . . the cholera," Mati cried.

"Oh, dear Lord!" Mrs. Mason moaned, and she rose to her feet, as if about to flee the room.

Paulette also rose, pulling Mati to her feet. "How do you know it's cholera? Have you called in a doctor?"

"No!" Mati answered. "A doctor would send him off to die in some pit! There ain't no niggers livin' on the beach, only white folks. No one knows where they'd send us to. Please, please! Don't let them take Aaron away!"

"But the cholera . . ." Mrs. Mason mumbled as she saw the expression in Paulette's face.

"We don't know that it's cholera," Paulette said firmly. "Mati, stop that crying at once!"

Mati fought to control her emotions. Wiping her eyes on the corner of her apron, she shuffled away from the two white women and dropped helplessly onto a chair by the open windows. "Aaron says for me to stay 'way from him," she murmured. "He's afraid for me. But I can't stay 'way. I can't let him die. Please, Miss Paulette, please help him."

"Where is Aaron now?"

"In one of the stables," Mati told her, "hidin' in the hay loft."

To Mrs. Mason, Paulette said, "Is there a doctor we can trust—one who won't go to the authorities unless we're certain nothing can be done for Aaron?"

"There's a doctor in my hotel who's on his way to the goldfields. Then there's Reverend Shirr."

"Reverend Shirr?" she asked with surprise.

"He was a doctor before he became a reverend, or, as he put it, before he found the Lord," Mrs. Mason informed her. "He's not, I'd say, the sort of doctor I'd turn to unless it was an extreme emergency."

"This is an emergency," Paulette said. "Please find him, Mrs. Mason, and bring him to the hotel stables." Turning, she motioned for Mati to follow her.

The three women left the rooms together, Mrs. Mason hurrying down the outside steps into the square, Paulette and Mati skirting the lobby and exiting in the rear courtyard. There were two guests, women with books open in their laps, reclining beneath the bougainvillaea trellis; their books were apparently too interesting to waste attention on a lady and her slave passing through the courtyard.

The stables were ill kept, the odor of horses and horse dung clinging to the humid air. A small boy was shoveling hay from the loft. He went wide-eyed to see Paulette entering the stable.

Mati caught her breath in a gasp. "Aaron," she whispered. "He's hidden under the hay." Her eyes were glued to the prongs of the pitchfork.

Paulette remained calm. "Come down, please," she told the boy.

He scampered down the ladder, but he hung back when she motioned him forward.

"Are you afraid of me?" she asked with a smile.

The boy nodded that he was; he apparently didn't trust any of the strangers who were pouring into his hometown.

"My slave girl has misbehaved badly," Paulette explained. "I've brought her to the stable to punish her so I won't disturb the other guests."

Mati, with a nudge from her mistress, began to moan fearfully.

Again, the boy nodded his understanding.

Paulette bent so her eyes would be on the boy's level. "If you'll guard the stables until I've finished, I'll reward you," she told him. "Don't let anyone in except a woman in a black dress and a man with a dirty gray beard. Do you understand?"

The boy's head bobbed affirmatively. He fled the stable and slammed the doors behind him.

Paulette reached the loft with difficulty, her skirts making the ascent of the ladder almost impossible. "Aaron? Where are you? It's Miss Paulette."

A mound of hay moved and a black arm protruded, pushing away the covering.

Paulette caught her breath, but said nothing. Aaron's face and naked chest were covered with perspiration, glistening, the fragments of hay sticking to his skin like a second covering. His eyes were glazed, the heavy lids scarcely capable of remaining open. He attempted to rise, but she forced him back with instructions not to move until the doctor arrived.

"No doctor, Miss Paulette," he said scarcely above a whisper. "Doctor will have me taken 'way. Don't want t' die in some pit . . . don't want t' be covered over with dirt and no Christian marker tellin' . . . where I am."

"Don't worry about that," Paulette assured him. "We can trust this doctor." She only hoped her statement was true; she hadn't seen Reverend Shirr since they had crossed the Isthmus, and they had never been particularly friendly. "Mati, get some water and cloths," she instructed. "Then wait at the door for Reverend Shirr and Mrs. Mason. Hurry!"

Paulette tore away the bottom of her petticoat and began wiping the perspiration and bits of hay from the slave's forehead and cheeks. She remembered Vienna taking care of a sick slave—in fact, Aaron's father—and the memory filled her with homesickness. If she had not insisted on making this journey, she reminded herself. Aaron wouldn't be here now suffering with what she prayed was not cholera. She had promised them freedom, but instead Aaron might find freedom of a different sort.

Mati returned with cloths and a pitcher of water. Close behind her was Reverend Shirr, his long canvas coat dragging across the hay as he crawled to them. He looked even older since the crossing of the Isthmus, his beard now almost entirely white.

"I came because Maude Mason chided me into it," he explained, making it clear he had no wish to be in the presence of a possible cholera victim. "But even then I expect to be paid handsomely for my services."

"So much for the Lord rewardin' you in Heaven," Mati said angrily.

Paulette silenced her with a glance. "You'll be paid," she assured the old man, "handsomely, if you save him."

The reverend bent over Aaron. "Saved some in the epidemic in New Orleans," he murmured. "Lost more than I saved, but I saved some."

Mati began to cry softly again.

"Don't sniffle," the reverend snapped. "If you must make sounds, make sounds of prayer. Now, fetch me blankets and hot broth and pick me a dozen of those sour limes growing alongside the hotel. I'll need hot water and plenty of salt and a bottle of bourbon." He glanced up at Paulette. "After that I don't want to see either of you here until tomorrow morning. By then he'll either be dead or his fever will be broken."

Paulette sent the stable boy for the limes. She dared not go to the kitchen herself for fear of arousing suspicion, so Mati was given the task of getting the broth and hot water. She went into the hotel and ordered a bottle of whiskey to be sent to her rooms. When everything the reverend had ordered was collected, Mati was sent back to the stable.

Mrs. Mason knocked on Paulette's door shortly before sunset. "How is your slave?" she asked.

Paulette told her they would not know until morning.

"Well, I've one bit of good news for you," the older woman told her. "The *California* has been spotted. She should arrive tomorrow. A committee is forming to begin the lottery."

The crowd was noisy and excited. The local authorities, expecting the worst, had guards placed around the square. Locals, remaining in doorways and windows, watched with interest as the lottery proceeded.

Paulette clung to the fringes of the crowd, and Mrs. Mason, among the first chosen, stood at her side whispering encouragement as each lot was drawn. There was shouting and cursing in French, German, English, and languages Paulette could not identify. She stood on tiptoes when she heard Jeremiah Walker's name called and saw him pushing through the crowd to claim his lottery ticket.

"He's lucky," Mrs. Mason murmured, "a gambler with luck." She mumbled something about what else could one ask for, but Paulette ceased listening to her.

With the calling of each name, her hopes dwindled. To have come through so much to have been stopped in Panama—it weighed heavily on her and she struggled to keep back her tears.

"You'll be next," Mrs. Mason predicted.

But the next name was one Paulette could not even pronounce, a burly man with flame red hair and beard who shoved the complainers roughly aside as he strode up to the makeshift podium. He waved his ticket, a symbol of victory, and leaped back into the crowd to push his way to the nearest *cantina*.

Paulette was not aware of Jeremiah standing at her side until he touched her elbow.

"Good evening, Miss Favière." He bowed slightly.

She nodded and could not refrain from a dry "Congratulations."

"Only luck," he said.

"So Mrs. Mason mentioned."

"I've called at your hotel repeatedly," he told her.

"I haven't felt like seeing guests."

Jeremiah touched the brim of his hat. "Should you feel in the spirit for receiving me after the lottery, you'll find me at Casa la Labia." He moved away into the crowd without waiting for her to reply.

"Oh, Paulette!" Mrs. Mason cried in exasperation. "It would have cost you nothing to have been pleasant to him. If your name is not called soon, you will need him if you are to gain passage on the *California*."

"Perhaps I, too, will have luck," Paulette answered.

"And perhaps you won't," Mrs. Mason reminded her. "Dear, dear, you are a stubborn . . ." She let the sentence trail off. "I only pray you don't regret your treatment of him."

An hour later, Paulette was indeed regretting just that. The last winner for passage on the *California* had been drawn, and she was not it. She returned to her rooms, Mrs. Mason trailing quietly behind. Inside she paced, discouraged and beaten. The hats Mati had been sorting through were strewn about the floor. She kicked one in her fury; blue ribbons flying, it sailed across the room and disappeared beneath a chair.

"Maybe," she said hopefully, "I can purchase one of the winner's tickets for twice its value."

"Not likely," Mrs. Mason told her. "They all have the gold fever. I doubt they'll sell their chance at their fortunes in California."

"Then why do you think Jeremiah can help me? If a man won't relinquish his ticket for twice its value, why would he wager it at cards?"

"I've never understood that in men," the older woman admitted, "but I know most would do just that."

Paulette collapsed onto a chair and leaning back, covering her eyes with her hands. "I must be on the *California*," she said, more to herself than Mrs. Mason. "I must!"

"Other than stowing away, I can think of only one way of achieving that, and you know what it is," Mrs. Mason murmured.

"Then that's exactly what I'll do," Paulette said firmly. She rose and went for her shawl. "Casa la Labia, wasn't it?" She flung the shawl around her shoulders and stopped for a brief examination of her appearance in her mirror.

"The price may be higher than you'd now wish to pay," Mrs. Mason said knowingly. "You've been rude to him, you've refused him when he's called, and you've even treated him with worse disdain than you would your slaves. I know Jeremiah Walker's kind of man. He'll make you pay for that. But if reaching San Francisco is that important . . ."

"Reaching San Francisco is of the utmost importance," Paulette interrupted.

The older woman rose, gathering up her handbag and shawl. "Then I'll walk you to Casa la Labia," she said. "No lady as beautiful as you should be out alone on a night like tonight. There will be those who are celebrating their good fortune in the lottery and those out to release their hostilities for losing. Both good and bad fortunes have strange effects on men."

Paulette knew immediately that Jeremiah had been expecting her. Waiting as he was under the darkened arches, he had even anticipated the approximate time she would come to him. As she approached the door, he stepped from the shadows and spoke her name very softly.

"We needn't go through the lobby," he said. "We can use the outer staircase."

Paulette glanced over her shoulder and saw Mrs. Mason moving away along the crowded street. She turned back to Jeremiah; the light from the window fell across his face and she could tell by the expression in his dark eyes that he had been drinking. The look of mockery was gone, but his expression was equally as intense. Despite the warmth of the night air, she felt a chill and pulled her shawl protectively around herself. Stepping forward, he lay a hand on her arm; she felt the warmth of his touch through the sleeve of her gown, smelled the odor of liquor on his breath . . . sensed his desire for her. She instinctively made to pull away from his touch, but she restrained herself.

"I've lost in the lottery," she said quietly.

"Yes, I know," he answered. Taking her arm more firmly, he led her toward the outside staircase. As they ascended, he asked, "Are you afraid of me?"

Paulette did not answer.

"Or are you afraid of yourself?" he asked, being persistent.

"A gentleman would not question me," she managed to say. "You pledged your services. I need your assistance in gaining passage on the *California*. I have come to discuss a business arrangement." She was attempting to keep her voice calm, even cool, but she detected its trembling, and she knew she had not fooled him.

They had reached the second-floor terrace. The air was heavy with the fragrances of unfamiliar flowers. Jeremiah released her arm. Stepping away from her, he leaned against one of the arches, his back to her, and stood silently staring down into the courtyard.

The sudden change in him alarmed her. Her desperation to gain passage on the steamship had brought her to him, but now she feared she had offended him and he would refuse his assistance. She puzzled at her reaction to this man—perhaps it was herself she feared; he stirred something inside her, something she had not been able to explain or accept. It was for this reason that she had always treated him coolly, sometimes even with hostility. He had known why she had come—knew what she would ask—but he apparently expected her to be more submissive, more pleading. She bit her lower lip in frustration.

"How," he asked, "do you expect me to help you gain passage? Do you expect me to surrender my lottery ticket?"

"No. Mrs. Mason suggested you might gain an extra passage from one of the winners through cards."

"I thought you found gambling and gamblers repulsive," he said pointedly. He turned to her then, his eyes boring into hers. "Is that why you have rejected me? Because I'm a gambler and not your typical Southern gentleman? Because I don't wear outdated styles of clothes and speak with a twang?"

"I . . . I don't . . ."

"Don't trouble yourself so with searching for the answers to my questions," he said. "As you said, you came to discuss a business arrangement." The mockery had returned to his eyes; he bowed stiffly and made a sweeping motion with his hand to indicate the open doors of his room.

Paulette moved reluctantly past the sheer curtains. The room was brightly lighted, but, unlike her accommodations, Jeremiah's consisted of a single room with a large bed with carved headboard in one corner. A davenport and two chairs were arranged in the opposite corner as a sitting area. Here, two glasses were set waiting beside a silver bucket containing chilled wine.

Jeremiah took her shawl and flung it onto a chair back. "Wine?" he asked. "A business arrangement should not be conducted without wine." Without waiting for her reply, he poured two glasses and handed her one. Lifting his in a salute, he said, "To a successful arrangement."

Paulette merely touched the cool liquid to her lips. "I am willing to pay you well for obtaining . . ."

Before she could finish the sentence, Jeremiah took the glass from her hand, set it carelessly on the table beside his, and swept her into the cradle of his arms. "I know your part of the arrangement," he said, "and I think you also know the price."

"No, please!" she protested. "Jeremiah, please!" But she made only a weak effort at freeing herself. When his lips sought hers, she felt herself becoming submissive and did not struggle against his lingering kiss. *For my passage on the* California, she told herself, but she knew it was more. She clung to his neck, returning his passion. The image of Dester flashed through her mind, but she quickly pushed it aside.

When Jeremiah broke the kiss, he buried his face in her neck and repeated her name several times, as if unable to believe she had responded to him as she had. "I've wanted you since the first moment I saw you," he murmured.

She said nothing.

Taking her hand, he led her to the bed.

He swept her up into his arms and lay her on the bed as gently as if she were some precious, fragile object. But it was his only display of gentleness.

Trembling, she watched as he undressed—his coat, cravat, shirt, and stockings. Hooking his thumbs into the waistband of his trousers, he rolled them down off his hips and pulled them free. He stood there for a moment, staring down at her, his nakedness exposing him for her admiration. Then he extinguished the lamp. Moonlight flooded the room. Jeremiah's hands explored her body while his lips pressed against hers with greater and greater demands.

Despite herself, Paulette found herself responding. She clung to him, her fingernails digging into his back as he penetrated her.

"This," he whispered, "will seal our business arrangement." And then he began to make love to her with a savageness she had not imagined.

When she awoke she was alone in Jeremiah's room. His clothes were missing from the chair where she had watched him throw them. She sat up, her body aching, and dressed as quickly as possible without assistance. Guiltily, she glanced through the open doors along the upper terrace to make certain she would not be seen leaving his room by anyone who could later whisper about her sin. It must have been late; even the noise from the square had quieted down. She slipped out into the night and hurried down the staircase. She had reached the bottom steps when she heard laughter from inside. A window was open and four men sat

around a round table; one of the men, although his
back was to her, was Jeremiah. He was spreading his
cards slowly, but she could not distinguish the hand he
had drawn—not, she knew, that she would understand
a good from a bad hand of poker. The man who had
been laughing was obviously drunk; there was no
laughter in his eyes. She stepped closer to the window
and realized he was the burly, red-haired man who
had won at today's lottery. On the table before the
men was a pile of money; on top of the money was a
lottery ticket. Her heart skipped a beat and she
pressed her hands to her chest.

Afraid she would somehow jinx Jeremiah's game—
even though it was more important to her than to him
—she moved away from the window and walked
quickly toward her hotel.

Mrs. Mason and Mati were waiting for her; the
slave was asleep on the floor by the window and Mrs.
Mason was on the sofa. The older woman opened her
eyes and rubbed them with her fingers. Stretching, she
rose and came to take Paulette's arms. "Well?" she
asked. When Paulette hesitated, she persisted: "Will
he get you passage? Tell me. I've waited all night."

Paulette glanced toward the window above Mati's
head. The first sign of daylight was edging over the
horizon. "He's gambling for my passage now," she
said. She nodded toward the sleeping Mati. "And
Aaron? Has there been any word?"

"Aye," Mrs. Mason said happily, glancing at Mati.
"The poor thing wouldn't sleep until the reverend sent
word that the fever was breaking."

"Thank God," Paulette murmured. She sank into a
chair and covered her face with her hands. She
wanted to cry, not only because Aaron would live, but
because of guilt for having submitted to Jeremiah, no
matter what the circumstances, had begun to seep
through her exhaustion.

"There, there, dear," Mrs. Mason soothed. "May I
fix you a cup of tea?"

Tea seemed of little comfort, but Paulette agreed so

the older woman would be kept busy and question her less. Besides, she reasoned, she would not be able to sleep until she heard from Jeremiah. If he lost at poker and was not the gambler Mrs. Mason thought him to be, she would have submitted to him without succeeding in reaching her goal; then her guilt would be intensified. She forced the tears away from her eyes. When she and Dester were eventually reunited, the episode of this night would remain a secret. What would he think of her if he learned what she had done to reach him?

"Oh, look!" Mrs. Mason cried. She stood at the open window with tea cups in hand.

Mati stirred and pulled herself up drowsily from the floor.

Paulette rose and hurried to the window.

Entering the harbor, white sails turned golden by the rising sun, came the *California.*

"She's a beauty," Mrs. Mason murmured.

"Yes, she is," Paulette agreed. "But if I'm not on her . . ."

"You will be," the older woman said cheerfully. "Have faith in Jeremiah—and in your fate." She pointed down into the square. "What did I tell you? Look, there."

Jeremiah, still in the shadows of the buildings, was crossing the square, distinguishable by his stride.

Paulette pulled back from the window, not wanting to be seen. "You go down," she requested of Mrs. Mason. "Tell him I'm sleeping."

"But surely you should . . ."

"Please. I can't see him now."

"Oh, very well, my dear." Mrs. Mason set down the tea cups, took her shawl from the sofa, and slipped out of the room.

Paulette turned to Mati. "I'm happy Aaron's fever has broken," she told the slave. When Mati did nothing but nod, Paulette dismissed her and then paced back and forth across the room, waiting impatiently for Mrs. Mason's return.

When the older woman slipped back into the room, she held the lottery ticket above her head triumphantly. "I told you he could do it!" she cried. "That man is a genius at cards!"

"Or a cheat," Paulette mumbled. Nevertheless, she took the ticket and kissed it. "San Francisco!" she cried. "Dester!" She spun around in a happy dance of victory.

Mrs. Mason was watching her without expression. Finally, when Paulette quieted down, she said, "Jeremiah looked troubled. He didn't even protest when I told him he couldn't see you. He merely gave me the ticket and walked away."

"Don't concern yourself with Jeremiah now," Paulette told her. "Be happy with me! I have my passage!"

"Yes, dear, I'm very happy. But, then, I didn't doubt you'd get what you wanted."

The following morning Paulette had Mati and Aaron pack her belongings and deliver them to the dock. When they returned, she called them together and told them since they wouldn't be proceeding to San Francisco, she would give them their freedom in Panama. She also gave them enough money to return to New Orleans if they so chose. She took Mati and Aaron to the proper authorities, had the papers drawn up, and had her signature witnessed and sealed. When she handed them the papers, Aaron dropped to one knee and kissed her hand; Mati merely smiled, fighting back tears.

"Will you return to New Orleans?" Paulette asked. "There are people at Plantation Bend who love you. You could work there for wages now."

Aaron, head lowered, reached for Mati's hand and held it. "No, ma'am," he said. "We'll miss those we loves, but Mati and me are goin' North—maybe to Boston or New York."

"Boston? New York? Whatever would you want to go there for?"

" 'Cause things are easier for us there," Mati said when Aaron didn't answer. " 'Cause Aaron says there's goin' to be trouble in this land."

Paulette's happy mood faded; she remembered the arguments between Dester and Clabe, remembered the expression she had seen on the faces of Katrina's slaves, the hostility and unrest of blacks working in the fields, the rumors and speculations. "I see," she said quietly, drawing herself back to the two standing before her. "Wherever you go, I wish you the best," she said. She stepped forward and kissed Mati's cheek. She felt Mati's impulse to draw back, but she pretended not to notice.

"Mati and me, we wish you happiness with Mr. Dester, too," Aaron said. He pulled Mati against him. His arm around her shoulders, they walked away.

When the *California* finally departed Panama, the steamship was crammed well beyond capacity. Paulette and Mrs. Mason, the only female passengers, shared their room with crates and ship stores; they were scarcely left any space to walk around their bunks. They ate in their room and went on deck only during the early morning hours, when the men who slept there were still sleeping.

Jeremiah Walker, although they were certain he was on board, made no approach to call on them.

On the fourth day out, when they were on deck for air and Paulette made mention of this, Mrs. Mason looked gloomily out to sea and said, "There are rumors Jeremiah killed a man . . . for a lottery ticket."

# Chapter Four

WHEN THE *California* sailed through the Golden Gate strait, every passenger was on deck. Men cooped up under the worst conditions for the duration of the journey put their anger and discomfort aside; those who had become enemies forgot their hostilities. There was much laughter and cheering—and much impatience for the last few minutes of the trip.

"I'm headin' straight up the Sacramento River!" one man shouted. "The gold's awaitin'!" And the shout of *"The gold's awaitin'!"* went up throughout the passengers.

Paulette and Mrs. Mason were allowed to be at the captain's station during arrival. The excitement of the other passengers touched them, but they each had an excitement of their own—Paulette one step closer to Dester, and Mrs. Mason closer to her son, Jamie.

The old woman hugged Paulette. "We're here, dear! We made it, and many were the times I doubted I'd see this lovely sight!"

*Lovely sight* echoed in Paulette's head as the steamship drew nearer to their point of disembarkation. San Francisco looked more like a battleground than a village. Tents and lean-tos were pitched on the sandhills. Cargo was strewn about the docks and muddy streets. Several ships lay at anchor in the harbor and looked like abandoned ghostships. The water itself was

murky, tinted, she was later to learn, from the mining
along the Sacramento River.

Surprised and disappointed by what she saw,
Paulette lowered her gaze. Standing on the deck below
was Jeremiah. He was staring up at her. Dressed in his
usual finery, he looked out of place among the other
men. He touched the brim of his hat and nodded before pushing his way to the railing. She wondered how
he had faired on the journey, and how many men had
shared his cabin. And remembering Mrs. Mason telling her of the rumor, she wondered if he had indeed
killed a man to obtain her lottery ticket. He glanced
back at her from the railing; there was no smile, no
hint of mockery in his dark eyes. In attitude, he was a
changed man.

When the captain dropped anchor, it was announced that independents of the steamship company
were charging $1.50 to put passengers ashore. Paulette
and Mrs. Mason were among the first to be lowered
into open launches. On shore, it cost another $2.50
each to have their luggage carted over the planked
streets to the Union Hotel. Mrs. Mason objected to the
high cost, but she was so glad to finally have her feet
on solid ground that she complained little.

She did catch her breath angrily when she heard
the desk clerk tell Paulette, "The best room in the
house is seven dollars a day. That, of course, includes
board."

"Fine," Paulette said. "I'll take a room." She
reached into her handbag and drew out Dester's letter.
"Is Dester Granville still registered in room 202?"

Pressed because of the line forming behind Paulette,
the clerk impatiently checked the register. "No one registered by that name, ma'am." He read her disappointment and added, "Men come to San Francisco
from the gold fields and take rooms for a couple of
days, a week at the most. Then they head back up the
Sacramento. You can leave a message in case he comes
in again."

Mrs. Mason begrudgingly paid the high price of the

room. "I'll reach my Jamie without a dollar in my pocket," she complained.

Because of a shortage of help, the two women were forced to carry some of their own luggage up the four flights of steps. Their rooms, beside one another, turned out to be no larger than six by five feet.

"The best in the house," Mrs. Mason sneered. "You must have had closets bigger than this at Plantation Bend. When I first married Mr. Mason, my sewing room was twice this size. Oh, well, oh, well, at least we're here, and I'm leaving soon for Nigger Hill." She closed the door of her room and Paulette was left standing in the hallway staring into the tiny cubicle she must occupy for God knew how long.

Heartsick, she went inside. Homesickness again swept over her; she missed Vienna and Clabe, and she missed Mati. Never in her life had she unpacked her own luggage; never had she had to see to her own wants and needs; never had she felt so lonely or so vulnerable. She sank onto the lumpy mattress and cried until there were no tears left. She rose and began to unpack, wondering how Mati had been so apt at something so tedious. Most of her gowns had to be hung against the walls, the hangers hooked over the molding; the gowns were wrinkled and crushed, and she doubted that the Union Hotel employed anyone who could see to them. First thing tomorrow she would have to employ a servant.

She fell back onto the bed, closed her eyes, and slept.

The noise of a brawl outside her room awakened her. Men were shouting, crashing into doors. She sat up, shaking with fear, trying to orient herself. When the pandemonium ended, there was a knock on her door.

"Paulette, dear, it's Mrs. Mason."

The older woman had changed into one of the nicest gowns Paulette had seen her wear: emerald-green with lacework around the throat and cuffs.

"I thought we'd go down to supper together," she said.

Paulette nodded; she had no desire to face a dining room full of men on her own. When she asked about the disturbance, Mrs. Mason told her two men had been fighting over "a woman of questionable character" who occupied the room at the end of the hallway.

"You've already met people?" Paulette asked with amazement.

"Naturally, dear. I've been asking everyone if they've heard of my Jamie. How else would I get news of him? And you must ask people about your Dester if you're to find him."

"Yes, I suppose I must," Paulette murmured, "or it's possible that I'll spend weeks in this dreadful hotel."

"Dreadful and expensive," Mrs. Mason said. "I'm wondering if the hotel rent is comparable to other expenses. If so, I don't know how my Jamie has survived. He's always been tight with a dollar."

The meal served in the hotel dining room was tasteless. Paulette, despite her hunger, pushed her plate aside. While Mrs. Mason ate, she watched the crowd. Most were men, a few accompanied by brightly dressed women. No table was private; if there was space for a plate, a man sat down without invitation, some even squatting on their haunches if there was no empty chair. Food was eaten quickly, supper being something merely to get through for other adventures. A small stage held a piano: the piano player was oblivious to the customers; the customers were oblivious to his tunes. Boys in red-and-white-striped shirts and long aprons moved around the room collecting dirty dishes; some boys were scarcely old enough or large enough to handle the burdens they collected. Everyone talked at once, making conversation impossible without shouting. Pipe smoke clung to the air in a heavy haze. The most amazing aspect was the mixture of men; men who were well dressed, obviously gentlemen, sat elbow to elbow with men of lower stations. Conversations were in many languages, and appearances varied greatly, denoting the different nationalities.

When Mrs. Mason finished her meal, she dabbed her mouth daintily. She would have tarried at the table had not Paulette urged her from the dining room. Then, saying she was exhausted and needed sleep for tomorrow's journey up the Sacramento River, she excused herself and returned to her room.

Paulette requested paper and pen from the desk clerk and wrote a message to Dester in the event he should return to the hotel. She then wrote a short letter to Tom and Katrina, informing Tom to send her another sum of money. What she had carried with her was dwindling rapidly, the three unexpected weeks of delay in Chartres having forced her to dig deep into her finances. Dester, when she found him, would surely have money, but exactly when she would find him remained a disturbing mystery. *Ask people,* Mrs. Mason had instructed her. But whom would she ask? And if she approached one of the men, what if he took her for one of the prostitutes who seemed to frequent the hotel? Disturbed, she was about to return to her room when she saw Jeremiah enter the hotel lobby.

But it was on the woman clinging to Jeremiah's arm that Paulette's attention focused. She was tall, slender, with hair tinted a reddish shade by use of a tinting comb. She wore a blue gown of good quality, but designed to accentuate her too-large breasts and tiny waist. The shawl draped loosely over her pale shoulders had golden threads woven in with the white lace. When she walked there was a glimpse of awkward boots showing beneath the hem of her gown, giving her the appearance of a traveler whose entire wardrobe had not yet arrived. She moved with grace, her lips slightly parted in the hint of a smile. The necklace she wore was simple, made with gold nuggets spaced out on a thick chain; her earrings were also gold nuggets.

Not understanding why, Paulette felt a tug of jealousy . . . and of curiosity. Jeremiah was a man of many surprises. In Panama, she had never seen him with a woman. Now, in San Francisco for less than a day, and he had acquired the company of a lady who attracted the attention of every other man in the hotel lobby.

Gathering her skirts, she started for the stairway.

But Jeremiah had spotted her. Calling her name, he came forward, leaving the woman he escorted unattended. Instead of bowing, as she was accustomed to his doing, he merely nodded. "I see you are alone," he said. "You apparently have not located your fiancé."

She searched his face for an expression of mockery, but she saw none. "No, I have not," she answered. She cast her eyes down, not wishing him to see the extent of her upset. "I wrote, but he apparently did not receive my letter."

"And your hotel room?" Jeremiah asked to change the topic from Dester.

Paulette started to answer, but she was stopped by the woman who had been accompanying Jeremiah. She came up behind him, her skirts rustling, every male eye in the lobby on her. She stopped beside Jeremiah, her high-piled hair scarcely reaching to his shoulder. She smiled at Paulette. "Men," she said teasingly. "Only a man could look at this hovel and ask how your room was." She turned to look up at Jeremiah. "Why didn't you tell me about your lady friend? There's room for her at my house."

"No, I think . . ."

"How kind of you," Paulette interrupted. "I would be most grateful to escape this hotel."

The smile that had been missing from Jeremiah's face now spread from his eyes to his lips. The expression of mockery also returned. "Miss Favière, allow me to introduce Theodora Hodge. Dora, this is Paulette Favière, a fellow traveler on the *California.*"

Both women nodded.

"We're having supper in the hotel dining room for lack of a better place," Dora said. "If you'll have your luggage ready, I'll have my man come for it when I return home. I don't live far from here. The street has no name as of yet, but it's being referred to as Maiden Lane."

Jeremiah laughed unexplainably. "Until we meet next," he said to Paulette. Lifting his arm for Dora, the couple turned and proceeded into the dining room.

Paulette went immediately to the desk and changed her message to Dester. Then she climbed the stairs, knocked on Mrs. Mason's door, and told her of her good fortune of finding residence in a private home. "Through your friend Jeremiah Walker," she told the older woman.

"He's a guardian angel, that one," Mrs. Mason murmured. She stepped forward and hugged Paulette affectionately. "This is good-bye then," she said. "I'm off to join Jamie at Nigger Hill first thing tomorrow."

Both women shed tears; since meeting on the *Falcon,* they had become closer than they realized until it came time for parting.

"We'll meet again," Paulette assured her.

Mrs. Mason shook her head doubtfully. "Traveling as we did and sharing so many hardships brought us together," she said quietly. "But we've arrived now. We belong to different classes and our lives are separating."

"Class distinction doesn't seem to exist here," Paulette told her. "It's one of the better things I can say of San Francisco." She kissed Mrs. Mason's wrinkled cheek. "Until we meet again." She left Mrs. Mason and hurried to her own room to prepare her luggage for Dora Hodge's man.

The house was small, two stories, made of brick and stucco and lumber, giving the appearance that not enough of any one material existed, so the three had to be combined. The sidewalks, as throughout most of the village, were of planks. Because of an earlier rainfall, the narrow street was a river of mud. Planks had been laid across at intervals for those brave enough to test their strength at crossing from one side to the other.

Dora's man was Chinese. He hoisted Paulette's luggage and almost ran across the planks, depositing the bags in front of the house and returning for her trunk. She held her breath as the plank swayed beneath him; she had visions of the Chinese man and her trunk disappearing beneath the mud and being lost forever. But, again, he reached the other side with ease, returned, and extended his hand to her, speaking encouragement in his native tongue.

"Yes, yes, all right," she told him. She moved carefully onto the plank, sliding one foot cautiously in front of the other. She could feel the plank swaying beneath their weight.

The door of the house opened and Dora stood in the threshold. "You'll get accustomed to it!" she shouted. "Just close your eyes and walk. We haven't lost anyone to the mud yet on Maiden Lane. They haven't been so lucky on Battery Street—found three bodies the last time the mud dried."

Paulette shuddered at the thought and quickened her step. She heaved a sigh of relief and smiled when she reached the safety of the narrow porch.

"Welcome," Dora greeted her. She stepped back and showed Paulette into a small entryway. Lamps were ablaze, but their glow was deadened by the dark red, flocked wall covering. "It's simple, but it's home," Dora said, "and much nicer than the Union Hotel."

"Much," Paulette agreed. "I'm deeply grateful." She followed Dora into a sitting room decorated with heavy wine-red draperies and with matching upholstery on the chairs and sofa. A life-size marble statue of a woman stared down from a pedestal in one corner. A table in front of the window held an enormous arrangement of wildflowers. Another table was cluttered with bottles of liquor.

Dora slipped onto the sofa and stretched one pale arm across the back. "Your room is on the second floor next to mine. The walls are comparatively thick, so we'll not disturb one another. I'm seldom home in the early evening. Chang does the cooking. It's not much better than what you had at the Union Hotel, but he does find luxuries for us. Eggs are one dollar apiece, and fresh vegetables are as sought after as gold. Occasionally, one of my friends brings me venison." She stopped talking suddenly and stared directly into Paulette's eyes. "How well do you know Jeremiah?"

Taken aback, Paulette did not answer immediately. It crossed her mind that Jeremiah may have told Dora about Panama; then she decided he had not, or the woman would not have asked so pointed a question. "Mr. Walker was most helpful during our trip," she answered. "In fact, he saved my life when our canoe overturned."

"Hmm," Dora mumbled. "He's very taken with you. But, then, I'm certain you're aware of that."

Paulette's back stiffened; apparently she had been invited as a guest in order to be questioned about her relationship with Jeremiah.

"We knew one another in New York," Dora said. "Jeremiah owned a club there, but he was having difficulties with the authorities. One night he disappeared and I didn't hear from him until he wrote saying he was on his way to San Francisco. He had apparently kept track of me." She smiled, pleased with what she had related. "He's quite a man, *our* Jeremiah."

"*Your* Jeremiah," Paulette said expressively. "I've come to San Francisco to marry my fiancé. I doubt that I shall see Jeremiah again."

"Neither of us shall . . . for a time," Dora told her. "Jeremiah left for the gold fields."

Paulette couldn't repress a laugh. "I can't imagine Jeremiah mining for gold," she explained.

Dora also smiled at the thought. "It won't be mining he'll be doing," she said. "Jeremiah needs more capital to build the sort of gambling casino he wants in San Francisco. He's gone to the mining camps to relieve the miners of some of their gold—through gambling, of course. It's the only occupation he knows."

The noise at night on Maiden Lane proved scarcely less than that at the Union Hotel. Paulette spent sleepless hours listening to the brawls or the traffic of boot heels crossing the wooden planks. There was much laughter and drunken shouting. Even the interior of the house was noisy; Dora apparently entertained into the late evening. Music drifted up from the sitting room, and footsteps went up and down the stairs. By morning, Paulette wondered if all San Francisco was on an around-the-clock schedule; the village did not seem to sleep.

When she rose, she felt more tired than when she had retired. Dora's door remained closed, the sound of heavy breathing coming through the cracks beneath. Chang, bobbing his head in a smiling and happy greeting, welcomed Paulette to the kitchen. She did not know how to ask him for what she wanted, so she settled for whatever he prepared for her—strong tea, a bowl of rice, and a tasteless scone. He also offered her a cognac, indicating it was his employer's habit to begin her day with a small glass of it. She waved the drink away. The small room where she ate was bright and sunny; the window commanded a view of the fields beyond and the incline of the hills —a view that would soon be blocked, judging from the foundation now being constructed across the street. Indeed, as she listened she became aware of a chorus of hammering and sawing. San Francisco was busily being transformed from a village to a town, even, perhaps by the number of ships setting sail for the gold fields, to a city.

Chang was busy cleaning the sitting room when she finished eating. She washed her own dishes, dried them, and put them away in the cupboards. Upstairs, the heavy breathing still came from behind Dora's door. Paulette took her cape from the trunk, went downstairs, and let herself out into the morning.

A workman across the street waved at her. *Friendly, these San Franciscans.* She nodded a greeting and moved off along the plank sidewalk toward the Union Hotel, hoping Dester would have returned and found her message.

As she approached the hotel entrance, Mrs. Mason was emerging, struggling with her own luggage. "You look dreadful," the older woman said.

"It was impossible to sleep," Paulette explained. "The noise in this city is unbelievable. Are you on your way to the docks?"

"Aye. I'm going upriver on a launch, then crossing by coach to Nigger Hill." Mrs. Mason set her luggage on the edge of the planks, out of the way of the pedestrians, and looked around hopefully for a young boy she might coax into assisting her. "You're lucky you didn't spend the night at the hotel," she said. "You would have had even less sleep. The active young woman at the end of the hallway managed to catch her draperies on fire. After the fire brigade extinguished the flames, she entertained them until dawn. A sinful place, this is."

"It seems everyone entertains late," Paulette murmured.

But Mrs. Mason was not listening; she had spotted a young boy and was bartering with him over the price of carrying her luggage to the docks. "All right," she finally concluded, "but it's robbery."

The two women said good-bye a second time, and Paulette stood on the sidewalk and watched until the older woman had disappeared into the crowd.

The hotel clerk told her her message had not been claimed.

Discouraged, she returned to the street.

She did not feel like returning immediately to Dora's and decided to walk. She passed the streets under heavy construction and climbed the hill. From above, the view was breathtaking: the blue of the bay, the circle of green hills beyond. There were many more ships in the harbor than she remembered seeing the day before. Two launches were moving away from the docks; one of them was probably Mrs. Mason's. She regretted losing the older woman's companionship; in the short time of their acquaintance, they had become close. Sighing, Paulette stretched out on the grass, her head resting on her hands, her eyes scanning the horizon. Oddly, she began to feel more at peace than she had since leaving Plantation Bend. There was no doubt Dester would eventually return to San Francisco; she need only survive until he did. Then, if she couldn't convince him to return to Louisiana, they would build a home here—perhaps on this very hill. It was a lovely spot, commanding a breathtaking view. Still, she didn't understand the people she had met since her arrival—she understood even less the gold fever that seemed to motivate everyone—but the land itself was magnificent. She felt she somehow understood more of what she had heard Clabe and Vienna discussing about their parents forging their home out of the wilderness that was Louisiana.

Voices caused her to push away from the grass and sit up. A man, three women, and four children were crossing the knoll toward her. All were dressed in black and resembled a funeral party. They did not see her until she sat up, and then they halted, talking among themselves.

The man, about forty, with graying sideburns and bushy eyebrows, stepped away from the group and approached Paulette. He tipped his hat and made a feeble attempt at a smile. There was something severe about his expression. "We do not wish to intrude," he said, "but we had set our minds to eating on the hill. May we share your spot?"

Paulette nodded.

The man's voice was deep, polite, but not particularly friendly. His request had been more of a demand. He motioned to the women and children and they came forward. The women solemnly bowed their heads. They were of various ages, ranging from a few years older than the man to Paulette's age. All were pale-complected and wore no makeup. Their black dresses were all similarly stitched, designed to cover the body and not flatter it.

"It is a beautiful spot," Paulette said in an effort to make conversation.

One of the women, the youngest, glanced up and smiled, but the man grumbled and she went back to assisting with the unpacking of the food baskets. The man made no effort to assist, but watched carefully, as if they were performing a ritual that needed his supervision. After a meager spread had been placed on the cloth, he removed eight black books from a canvas bag and had one of the children lay them before each plate. Until all this was done, he had not glanced again in Paulette's direction. Turning to her, his dark eyes stern and cold, he said, "I would invite you to join us, but you would undoubtedly not approve of our religious readings." His tone was not only meant to insult her, but to dismiss her.

Her anger was instantaneous. She stood up, brushing the dust from her skirt. "Your religious readings have apparently not covered the sin of rudeness," she said stiffly.

The women, still busy with the placement of food, stopped their activities. One of the smaller children, a girl, snickered and was quickly silenced by the older woman.

Color burned on the man's face. A twitch of a muscle lifted his bushy brows in an arch above his cold eyes. For an instant, Paulette thought he meant to strike her. Instead, his expression softened. "Forgive me," he said. "I thought you to be one of the women from *that* street. I was indeed guilty of rudeness and assumption." Turning to his party, he said, "I wronged this lady. We must pray for forgiveness."

"And invite her to join us, Mr. Slater," the youngest of the women said.

"Indeed. Would you share our simple repast?"

Unable to refuse without seeming rude herself, Paulette accepted.

The meal was indeed simple: bread and berries gathered from the hillside, a strong cheese, and milk for the children. The man introduced himself as Donald Slater, from Wisconsin; the women were Alice, Dorothy and Miriam; the children were not introduced. Before, during, and after the meal, each took turns reading aloud from their books. The passages Paulette listened to were unfamiliar, but then she had never been an avid reader of the Bible. When the books were closed for the final time and returned to their canvas bag, the children, with a cry of cheer at being released, ran to play on the hillside. Mr. Slater strolled away while the women gathered up their belongings. Miriam, the youngest, kept glancing at Paulette; she appeared eager to speak but was holding back because of the other women.

At last, their packing done, the two older women moved away to sit with the man and watch the children. Miriam moved up beside Paulette and spread her skirts out on the grass, her legs curled up beneath her. She was not beautiful, but her face held a promise of beauty at an older age. Her eyes were blue, but dulled by the severity of her dress. Her breasts were full and they lifted the coarse woolen material of her bodice as she drew in her breath. She stared silently down at the busy harbor, but her interest was obviously with Paulette. "Do you understand why he insulted you?" she asked quietly.

Paulette admitted she did not.

Miriam smiled for the first time, a smile that took away her dull expression and revealed even, white teeth. A wisp of hair had come from under the edge of her bonnet; it was auburn and flamed in the sunlight. "He thought you to be a woman of easy virtue," she explained. "Your gown, I suppose." She caught her breath when Paulette stiffened. "It's a beautiful gown," she said hurriedly. "But Mr. Slater thinks a woman who does not wear black is laughing at respectability and decency."

Paulette relaxed. "And what was this about a street? *That* street, he called it."

"There's a street where the men got together and built houses for the women they had brought to San Francisco," Miriam answered. "I don't know the street. I'm not even allowed to mention it. If he heard me, he'd beat me."

"Beat you? For mentioning a street?" Paulette was shocked. "Is Mr. Slater your brother? Is he that stern with you?"

Miriam laughed, then covered her mouth with her hand to stifle the laughter lest the others should hear. "Donald Slater is my husband," she whispered.

"Your? . . . I thought Alice or possibly Dorothy, but you . . . I never imagined."

"They are," Miriam told her. "We're all his wives. Didn't you understand from the readings? We're Mormons."

Paulette said nothing. She knew little of the Mormons, only the plantation gossip she had heard from travelers along the Mississippi who had stopped and chatted with the slaves.

Miriam lifted her knees and rested her chin against them. "I was married to Mr. Slater's brother Jake," she said quietly. "When Jake died during the crossing, it was the law of our church that forced Mr. Slater to marry me. It hasn't been easy on him. He already had Alice and Dorothy and the four children to care for. If it had not been for the other Mormon families who have come here for the gold fields, we would never have made it."

"Are there many Mormons in San Francisco?" Paulette asked, trying to recall if she had seen many dressed similarly to Mr. Slater and his wives.

"Yes, many," Miriam told her. "But several families are planning to leave for Utah as soon as the snows melt in the Sierra Nevadas. Mr. Slater intends to move on to Utah. He calls San Francisco the devil's ground."

"You don't want to go, do you, Miriam?"

Miriam said she did not. "But, of course, I must," she concluded. "I must do as my husband wishes."

Even though you don't love that husband, Paulette wanted to say, but she held her tongue.

"Miriam." Mr. Slater had turned and had been watching them. When he called his youngest wife's name, Miriam scrambled to her feet.

"We live on the opposite side of the hill," she said quickly. "Should you want to visit, I'm sure Mr. Slater would allow it." There was a pleading expression in her eyes as she turned and ran to join Mr. Slater and his other two wives.

Paulette watched the black-clad group disappear over the crest of the hill, with Miriam glancing back when she thought the others were not watching. After they had gone, Paulette remained, but her sense of peace had left her. Miriam's loneliness had touched her and had reawakened her own feeling of aloneness.

Fog was rolling in through the Golden Gate strait, reaching toward the ships anchored in the harbor. Within moments, only the masts remained unhidden. The sun was gone and the air grew chilled. The flurry of building below the hill ceased and a heavy quiet settled over the knoll. Shivering, Paulette rose and made her way back down into the village.

Chang was helping Paulette unpack her trunks.

Because of the fog, darkness had fallen early. With the darkness came the noises of the night before: men fighting, laughing drunkenly as they passed on the sidewalk planks.

"It's like a party every night," Paulette said to Chang, forgetting he did not speak or understand English.

He nodded for no reason. Then, bowing when the door knocker struck, he left her, backing from the room and leaving the door ajar.

Presently a man's voice came booming up the stairwell. "Dora! It's Hammond. I've brought you eggs and a bottle of wine off the steamship *Mechanic*."

Paulette heard Dora's door open. Although she had heard Dora moving around inside her room for the past hour, she had not ventured out. There was the rustling of silk skirt and an excited cry as Dora rushed down the stairs to greet her visitor.

Paulette pushed her door closed and continued with her unpacking. Some of her gowns had suffered from the constant dampness and were beyond repair. She examined the damage with a sinking heart. Vienna had made many of the gowns for her; discarding them was like cutting herself further away from Plantation Bend. If Dester didn't come soon . . .

It was late when she retired. Dora was still entertaining below, and the street noises continued, but from exhaustion and depression Paulette fell into a deep sleep almost immediately. Her dreams were troubled; in them, she wore a black dress similar to Miriam's and Mr. Slater's other wives. Dester came for her and did not recognize her. He, too, had changed, his blond beard gone gray, his eyes aged in pockets of weather-worn wrinkles. Then there was Jeremiah Walker, watching them, mocking them with his dark eyes.

At first she thought it to be the dream that brought her so abruptly out of her sleep. She lay, heart pounding, staring into the darkness of her room and waiting for the effect of the dream to leave her. But it had not been the dream that had awakened her. A shadow loomed at the foot of her bed—a man standing very still and staring down at her. Her heartbeat quickened, pounding so noisily in her own ears that she thought for certain it could be heard outside her body. When the man moved, it was with the agility and silence of a cat, only his knee brushing the side of the mattress. Paulette caught her breath in terror. Then it occurred to her that the man might be Dester; he had come for her and been told at the hotel that she was living with Theodora on Maiden Lane. Chang had let him in, had showed him to her room—but Chang would have knocked, would have awakened her.

Her eyes, piercing the darkness, distinguished enough of the man's features to realize he was a stranger. Perhaps he was the man who had been visiting Dora—Hammond—and he had entered the wrong room. She forced herself to speak with as much control as she could muster. "You're in the wrong room, Mr. Hammond. Dora's room is next door."

"It isn't Dora's room I want," he answered in a near whisper.

Paulette pulled herself up against the headboard and clutched the linen around her throat. "Please leave at once!" She had intended to shout the command, but her voice was scarcely audible.

The man now stood directly above her. She could tell by the buttons of his coat that he was a seaman. He smelled of tar and rope, familiar to her from her passage on the *California,* and of liquor. Visions of her experience the night Jeremiah had rescued her came flashing back. Again, she could feel the rough hands tearing at her clothes, searching the softness of her flesh. Gooseflesh rose on her arms.

"I'll be gentle," came the near whisper.

"No! Please leave, or I'll scream!"

"Scream, then. Who's to hear you? Dora's passed out from wine." His hands came up, pale in the darkness, and stretched toward her. "Why are you rejecting me? You're one of them. You live here on Maiden Lane."

Paulette pulled back and slipped to her feet, putting the width of the bed between them. Mr. Slater's statement of *that* street flashed through her mind. *A street where the houses were built for the prostitutes.* Reaching to her vanity, her hand closed over her hairbrush. "Get out!" she shouted in a fury. She flung the brush, but it missed its mark and shattered the glass covering a picture on the wall behind him.

The man laughed. "I like my women to have tempers," he said.

Paulette's hand searched in the darkness for her next weapon. Her fingers closed over a small bottle, too small, she determined, to do much damage, but perhaps enough to allow her to get around him and to the door. "Dora! Dora!"

The man, advancing around the bed, hesitated when she called Dora's name, but only momentarily. "Saints in heaven aren't going to wake up Dora," he said. "Now, come to Hammond. Hammond will pay you well." He began advancing again, slowly. "I leave for the gold fields tomorrow. I understand there are no women there, none worth having. You and Dora will be worth remembering on those hard, cold nights."

Paulette drew back her hand that held the bottle, but she waited, not wanting to miss again. When he was nearer, she would aim for his face. She knew she must not allow him to seize her as the men on the *Falcon* had done. If he got hold of her, she was lost.

The man was laughing softly, wickedly, perhaps thinking her terror was a masquerade for his benefit; she had read in one of Katrina's forbidden novels of women who play-acted in such a manner for their lovers.

Again she screamed Dora's name, but there was no response.

Then, just as she was about to fling the bottle, she saw movement behind the man's shoulder. The hall door had opened, and a small figure was silhouetted against the dim light. Dora? But what could Dora do against such a brute?

"Now let's stop the pretending," the man said. He lunged forward.

But before he could move close enough for her to fling the bottle, there was a crashing sound. A large vase shattered over his head. He crumpled to the floor with a thud and lay still.

Paulette did not move until the lamp was turned on.

"Chang!" she cried. "Thank God!" She stepped over the seaman's body and would have embraced the Chinese man had he not stepped quickly away.

"You go now," he said. "No place here for you. You go."

"Chang, you speak English!" Paulette cried. "Then why? . . ."

"Better not know I understand," Chang stammered. "Bad woman, Miss Dora. Bad men come here. You go."

"Go? But where?"

"Anywhere away from Maiden Lane," Chang answered. "Go back to hotel. I bring clothes later. Go before man wake up, before Miss Dora find out what I've done." Turning, Chang hurried out of the room and closed the door behind him.

Paulette immediately began gathering up what things she could carry.

# Chapter Five

THE PLANK sidewalks ended and a narrow trail of hard-packed dirt continued, as if the houses had sprung up faster along the street than the sidewalk builders could keep up with. Then the houses stopped as abruptly as the sidewalks and a dirt path snaked its way around the side of the hill. The house Paulette sought was no more than a shack, with heavy, dark fabric tacked across the windows and cracks in the door that were big enough to slip one's fingers through. The roof was made of an assortment of materials, shingles and tiles, and even sides of crates with the shippers' names spelled out across them.

It was early morning—too early to come calling even under extreme conditions—but there was smoke drifting up from the chimney and the pleasant odors of food cooking.

Paulette hesitated, her hand raised to knock. The hotel had not had room for her since the arrival of three more vessels, all rooming houses were filled, and the hotel manager, despite his sympathetic attitude, had told her he could not allow her to spend another night in the lobby. She had found herself with nowhere to turn except to the only other people she had met since her arrival. Biting her lower lip, she rapped her gloved knuckles gently against the barren boards.

There was movement inside, the running feet of

children, and then one of Mr. Slater's wives slipped the door open a crack and peered out, the children peeking around from behind her black skirt.

Alice, or Dorothy? Paulette wondered. The only one of the Mormon's wives she remembered distinctly was Miriam. It was more difficult to distinguish between the two women now because the one who had opened the door wore no bonnet; she had not seen them without bonnets on the hill. This one—Alice, she decided—had small black eyes like flecks of coal. Her hair was neither gray nor blonde, but an odd colorless shade in between. Her mouth was a mere slit in her face; the wrinkles around her eyes and mouth hinted at a pleasureless life and a hopeless future. She stared at Paulette with a baffled expression.

"Is . . . is Mr. Slater at home?" Paulette asked.

"Nay," was the woman's only reply.

Then from behind her: "Who is it, Alice?"

Alice looked as if she was about to close the door in the caller's face, so Paulette, recognizing Miriam's voice, called out. "Miriam, it's Paulette Favière. We met on the hill."

Miriam pulled the door open wide. Her expression was no less baffled than Alice's. Still, she was more friendly. She motioned for Paulette to enter and closed the door behind her to block out the morning chill. "Mr. Slater's gone hunting," she explained, moving back to the small metal stove. "If he doesn't catch a pheasant or quail, we'll have no meal this day."

"If we have no meal, it's the Lord's will," Alice mumbled. She directed the children to a corner of the shack where they huddled quietly on a pallet, their eyes fixed with interest on their visitor.

Paulette took a stool beside the stove and held her hands there to warm them. Her heart sank as she took in the interior of the shack: two small rooms furnished with a table, some stools, a long bench, and wooden shelves that held dishes and pans. The pallet in the corner was obviously the children's bed. As she turned toward the doorway of the second room, Dorothy Slater emerged.

She was a stout woman, with dark hair pulled back away from a stern face and braided in a bun at the back of her head. Her face was full, her eyes puffy. The black collar of her dress fit tightly around a wrinkled throat. She was apparently the oldest of the three wives, and Paulette wondered if she were the first. Or did they marry more than one wife at a time? She pushed the thought from her mind. She had come to plead for space to stay until a room was available— she had no call to question or criticize. There was, however, no sense in pleading for space. The shack was already overcrowded, a hovel no better than the slaves' quarters at Plantation Bend. God help me, she thought, that I've come to this. She bit her lower lip and feared she would cry. In front of these stern women, women accustomed to hardships, such an act would be unforgivable. What would they think of her? Worse than Mr. Slater had thought of her on their first meeting.

"Will you be stating the call for your visit?" Dorothy asked directly. She came into the room, skirting the stove, and moving to the counter beneath the shelves of dishes. Without turning, she said, "We don't have visitors—not unless they're of our own kind." There was no hint of welcome in her voice, only questions unasked, suspicion.

"I . . . I've had some misfortune," Paulette managed to say. "I . . ."

"Ah, misfortune," the older woman murmured. "I've known much of that. So have we all. It seems sometimes we collect misfortunes."

"A test of the Lord," Alice inserted.

"A test of us," Dorothy corrected.

Miriam looked stricken. She apparently was allowed little to say when the other two women chose to converse. A visitor to their shack was a break in their monotony, but the other two women were about to

drive the visitor away. Dorothy's manner was openly
hostile, Alice's little better.

Paulette, fighting the impulse to leave, saw Miriam's
expression and decided to brave out the visit a few
moments longer. "May I trouble you for a cup of tea?"
she asked Miriam.

Miriam's face turned pale.

"We don't drink tea," Dorothy snapped. "It's forbidden. Tea is a sin against the body."

"Aye," Alice agreed, "and a sin against the Lord.
We do not abuse our bodies, His temples." She turned
away to silence the children, adding, "Nor do we
adore them so fancifully."

Miriam sprang to her feet, overturning the stool she
had perched on. "She does not understand our ways!"
she shouted. "With treatment like this, is it any wonder we are limited to friendships with only our own?"

Dorothy's brows came together in anger. "We need
no more women here," she said sharply, "be they
more wives or outside friends. There's a recklessness
in you, Miriam Slater. It's your recklessness that al-
lows you to so easily accept strangers." She shook a
long index finger in a gesture of warning. "Jake
Slater may have been lax with your training, but you'll
find that Donald is not."

Miriam flung her hair back from her face. "How
could he possibly be lax with two harpies for wives?"
she cried. "I am ashamed of both of you. You read
The Book, and yet you can neither one love yourselves little own your neighbors."

She stormed across the room and flung open the
door. To Paulette she said, "If you'd care to visit with
me, I'll walk you back to the village."

Paulette rose. Without glancing at either Dorothy or
Alice, she marched through the doorway behind Miriam.

"Mr. Slater will lash you!" she heard Dorothy shout
as the door slammed.

They walked quickly away from the house, letting

the momentum of the hill quicken their steps until they reached its base. Paulette stopped, breathless.

"Miriam, I'm sorry," she said. "I had no wish to get you into trouble."

Miriam threw back her head and laughed. "There'll be no trouble," she said confidently. "Neither of them will complain to Mr. Slater. He knows they're both jealous of me and would beat them for the sin of jealousy." Without her bonnet, the sun glistened off her auburn hair. Her eyes sparkled with excitement. "The only way they can hurt me is by mentioning Jake," she said, her smile fading. "They know I didn't want to come to his brother as a wife. Mr. Slater knows also. Even if it is our law that a brother must marry his brother's widow . . ." She stopped suddenly and turned on the path. "But you said you had some misfortune."

"Yes, but it seems so minute in comparison with yours. I find myself without a place to stay. *That* street Mr. Slater mentioned turned out to be Maiden Lane, the place I moved to from my hotel—unsuspectingly, of course." Paulette told her what had happened with the seaman. "Now the hotels are filled, and so are the rooming houses. I was hoping Mr. Slater would have friends who might help, or who would have an extra room. I didn't realize the conditions under which . . ." She refrained from finishing the sentence.

"We lived in a fine house in Wisconsin," Miriam said sadly, "Jake and me. He built it himself. He was a fine carpenter. But when his brother suggested the gold fields, Jake became possessed. He talked of what we could build for ourselves and what we could tithe to the church. He had had other dreams. Before we married he wanted to spread the religion in foreign lands. But no dream touched him like the dream of finding gold."

"It seems most everyone in San Francisco has been similarly touched," Paulette murmured.

"Jake died of the fever," Miriam continued quietly,

"without ever reaching the West. His dream was buried with him on some mountaintop in the Sierra Nevadas." She continued walking, head bowed. "Mr. Slater married me the next morning after we buried Jake and took me into his house."

"It must be very difficult on you," Paulette said, "not only losing your husband, but being married to a man with two other wives. Oh, I'm sorry. I didn't mean to insult . . ."

"It's no insult to me," Miriam told her. "I joined the faith only because of Jake. If Mr. Slater heard me say that, he would truly beat me. But it's true. And Mr. Slater hasn't touched me as a man touches his wife—not yet . . . not because he doesn't fancy me, either, but because of them." She nodded back toward the house. "It's been easy to avoid him. But we're leaving soon. I heard Mr. Slater talking to Dorothy last night. Tomorrow he plans to leave for the gold fields. Then if the Lord doesn't help him find his fortune, we'll go on to Utah." The young woman kicked the toe of her shoe against the ground and sent up a spray of dust. "I won't be able to avoid my duties much longer. Despite those two, I know he'll take me soon, if only because our law has made me his wife."

"But surely you could protest," Paulette suggested. "You could go to the authorities and explain and . . ."

"And then what would I do?" Miriam asked hopelessly. "I am a mere woman in a strange land. How would I earn my keep? No." She shook her head despairingly. "I should end up on Maiden Lane. It's no better a fate than suffering Mr. Slater's ardor." She stopped and turned on the path. "You are a lady of quality," she said, "and you are forced to come begging of a man like Mr. Slater. No, my situation is indeed hopeless. Oh, but forgive me. I ramble on about myself and you came about your own misfortune. Unfortunately, I do not know what to tell you to do. Other than the hotel and the rooming houses, there are only the tents. You must have seen them on the sandhills."

Paulette nodded. "Yes, I remember. They looked like a battle camp. But I have no idea how to . . ."

"If you have the money, you must hire a man to pitch a tent for you," Miriam said. "And then, should you have even more money, you must hire him to stand guard for you at night."

"How do you hire any man in San Francisco," Paulette murmured, "when all they think of is getting to the gold fields?"

"There are some," Miriam told her. "Perhaps you can find one of the Chinese men. They are less greedy and, I think, less susceptible to the gold fever—or, so Mr. Slater says after calling them heathens."

A thought struck Paulette. "Yes, you are perhaps right," she said.

Miriam halted. "I cannot go beyond where the planks begin without Mr. Slater," she said. "I'll go back now. Thank you for visiting. I grow so anxious to talk to women my own age, women different from Dorothy and Alice. My greatest fear is that I'll become like them."

"I don't think you possibly could," Paulette said. She took Miriam's hands and squeezed them gently.

"God go with you!" Miriam shouted as she ran back toward the shack.

And with you, too, Paulette whispered silently.

She walked back quickly to Maiden Lane. She knocked, knowing Dora would still be sleeping.

A startled Chang answered the door. "You stay away," he warned. "Bad place for you. Bad women, bad men. You not like them. They hurt you."

"I know, Chang, I know," she quieted him. "I've come for another purpose. How much does Miss Dora pay you to look after her and her house?"

Chang cocked his head to one side and studied her carefully. "Not much," he concluded.

"Then I'll pay you one and a half times that amount if you come with me," she said.

Chang jumped into the air and clicked his heels

soundlessly together. "Me pack," he said. "Me pack now."

The tent was impossible.

Despite Chang's attempts, he could not keep the cold outside the coarse fabric. At night a fire was kept burning in the small pot-bellied stove. Paulette, in the bed Chang made for her, lay wrapped in quilts so heavy that turning was a major struggle. Boards from shipping cartons were collected, bought, and stolen to cover the hard-packed dirt of the floor; beneath these Chang had packed pine needles gathered from the nearby forest. Using Paulette's trunks, he created a division of the tent and slept huddled out of her sight between the trunks and the tent wall, coming out only to feed wood to the fire.

He never complained of the hardship here, or of the loss of his comfortable room on Maiden Lane. In fact, he seldom spoke at all unless spoken to.

Paulette wrote letters addressed to Dester and had them delivered by those bound for the various mining camps. Still, at the end of two weeks there was no word from him. She began to panic. Perhaps he was dead; she had heard stories of the battles between the miners over disputed claims, of the cruelties of the camps, of hardships that made her tent living seem like a luxury. She pined for Plantation Bend, for Clabe and Vienna and Katrina, for the softness of her goosedown mattress and the spoiling attention of the slaves.

But she also watched people, she listened, and she learned. San Francisco was growing rapidly every day. Steamships from all countries anchored in the harbor, many standing abandoned, crew and passengers disembarking before the anchors had settled and heading for the gold fields. Cargo, if unloaded at all, was strewn about the docks or stacked along the plank sidewalks and left to the mercy of the elements. For those with ingenuity and finances and a place for storage, all goods that were not edible or used for mining could be purchased for half their original cost on the East Coast.

The village of tents was growing daily. Although Paulette had had Chang pitch her tent on the crest of the hill, the spreading growth below would soon reach her. Even at her distance she could hear the nightly fights and drunken singing of the men. She had nightmares of being attacked again, and she purchased a small pistol, which she kept under her pillow. The fact that she was a lady of quality—as Miriam had called her—made little difference. Social background, position, and wealth meant nothing in this new land. People were valued for what they really were and for their ability to survive. All classes had been thrown into the melting pot of the village and survival had become a great leveler.

Chang informed Paulette that she had been named "the lady on the hill." Being the only woman living in a tent—even though hers was removed from the others—had created for her a sort of fame. It was said that a woman of her beauty could have the grandest house on Maiden Lane if she made her wishes known. When she heard this, she told Chang he would have to be more cautious at night and guard the tent more carefully while she slept. She would assume the responsibilities of obtaining their food, and he could sleep during the day. The villagers apparently considered her a bit demented, and she feared stories would encourage some of the men to approach her.

At the end of a month without word from Dester, she decided to begin construction of a small house. She went to the authorities and purchased the land on which she had had her tent pitched. Determined to remain in San Francisco until she had word of Dester one way or the other, she reasoned that the house could always be sold should he return and be convinced to travel back to Louisiana.

Chang found two of his countrymen and a Mexican youth to work for her and the construction began.

Bricks were a dollar apiece, so the youth suggested adobe. Realizing her finances were dwindling and that she had not received a draft from Tom's New Orleans bank, she agreed. Horses were borrowed and used to drag lumber up the hill. Men from below watched with interest as the new house began to take shape; then, when the frame had been completed, a few men, bored with waiting to return to the gold fields, came and offered their assistance. Chang advised Paulette to accept their generous offers.

"Not like Maiden Lane," he assured her. "Men don't expect payment. They know you not bad woman."

Paulette designed the house herself, making it as much like a small replica of Plantation Bend as possible.

"There," she said when it was near completion. "Should Dester come down the Sacramento in a launch, he'll see the house and know immediately where I'm living." But the house did not please her. It was small, only three rooms, and the sight of it as she walked up the hill only made her miss Plantation Bend more. *If we stay,* she told herself, *I'll keep adding to it. I'll make it the grandest house in San Francisco.*

Each day she made the trek down the hill to the hotel. Each day the clerk shook his head sadly when she asked if a letter had been received. She wrote again to Tom, to Clabe and Vienna, and sent out further letters to Dester at the various mining camps.

On a day when she was particularly discouraged, she climbed back up the hill from the hotel and found Miriam waiting on the porch.

"I thought Mr. Slater had taken you to the camps," she said. "Otherwise, I would have visited you again." She invited Miriam in, glad to see a familiar face, and had put the kettle on to boil for tea before remembering it was forbidden by the Mormon religion.

Miriam sat solemnly at the kitchen table. She had removed her black bonnet and was fingering the ribbon nervously. Finally, she said, "I want to leave the Mormon Church, Paulette. I don't want to go with Mr. Slater." She set her bonnet on the table and ran her hands through her long auburn hair. Moisture was forming at the corners of her hazel eyes.

Paulette slipped into the chair beside her. "Have you told Mr. Slater this?" she asked. "Have you asked him to let you go?"

"No, I haven't told him," Miriam wept. "It would do no good. He wouldn't let me go. He couldn't without losing face with our people. It's against our laws. Once married, we're married through eternity."

"Eternity," Paulette repeated. She took Miriam's hands and held them. "But surely under the eyes of God you and Mr. Slater are not truly married. You said yourself he had not . . . not taken you."

"And he still hasn't," Miriam assured her. "But I can't hold him at bay for long. Neither can Dorothy nor Alice. Even they understand their jealousy can't keep him out of my bed much longer. Oh, if only Jake hadn't died . . . if only we had not come West . . . if I had not accepted his faith . . ." She lay her head forward on the tabletop and burst into tears.

Chang, happily entering with a basket of food he had bought at the shops, surveyed the scene quickly and slipped out unnoticed.

Paulette ran her hands gently over Miriam's hair and stared thoughtfully through the kitchen window. It was a beautiful day, the sky and bay a deep, rich blue, the hills beyond an emerald-green. There were birds chirping in the yard and children laughing as they played on the hillside. *Neither of us should be unhappy,* she thought. *Yet, here we are, two women with different miseries over which we have no control.*

Miriam finally ceased crying. She straightened up, dabbing at her tears with the sleeve of her dress. "Forgive me," she murmured. "Tears are sinful."

"You sound like Mr. Slater now," Paulette told her, "or Alice, or Dorothy. Tears are healthy. Holding them in is the sin."

Miriam looked as if she would begin crying again.

"When is Mr. Slater planning to leave?" Paulette asked, hoping to cut off the fresh flow.

"Tomorrow morning," Miriam answered in a broken voice. "I should be there now helping to pack. They'll be furious with me—even more furious if they learn where I've gone." She pushed back her chair and would have risen if Paulette had not restrained her with a hand on her arm.

"When I asked before why you did not leave Mr. Slater, you told me you had nowhere to go," Paulette reminded her. "You were afraid you'd end up with the women on Maiden Lane."

"It's true," Miriam said in a half-whisper. "How else could I make my way?"

"We'll talk of that later," Paulette said. "In the meantime . . ." She rose and moved to the hearth, where the kettle was boiling. "My house is small, but you're welcome to remain here until we can find another solution."

"Oh, but . . . Mr. Slater!" Miriam cried. "He'd come for me! He find me and then his wrath . . ."

"I'm not afraid of Mr. Slater's wrath," Paulette said, although the shivers that ran the length of her spine when she visualized being confronted by the man belied her statement. "And you mustn't be afraid, either. As things are, your life is no better than the slaves we had at . . ." She broke off speaking when she heard Chang shouting in his native tongue to someone who had ridden up outside.

Miriam's eyes widened with fear. "Mr. Slater!" she cried. "He's found me already!"

Paulette stilled her trembling and went to the side window to glance out. Seeing the stranger dismounting beyond the gate, she breathed a sigh of relief. "It's not Mr. Slater," she told Miriam.

Chang, seeing Paulette at the window, came running up and pressed his face close to the pane. "Man with message for you waiting at hotel!" he shouted. His usually passive face matched her excitement. He

understood she had been waiting for news of Dester,
understood her depression because the news had not
come. "Hurry!" he cried. "Maybe message from your
man!"

"Wait for me here," Paulette instructed Miriam.

She ran from the house without even grabbing up
her shawl.

Paulette knocked on the door of the room the clerk
had told her was the man's with the message. When
he didn't answer immediately, she feared she had
missed him. She was about to go downstairs again to
question the clerk when she heard movement inside;
the bed creaked and footsteps crossed the room.

The door opened and she found herself staring at
Jeremiah Walker.

"You!" she murmured. "But I thought . . ."

Jeremiah smiled down at her. "That I had a message for you," he finished for her. "I do." He stepped
back for her to enter. He looked exhausted, dark circles beneath his eyes, his hair uncombed and needing
to be trimmed. His usually neat clothes were in need
of pressing; his boots, standing beside the bed, were
encrusted with mud. At the foot of the bed stood a
trunk. As she came into the room, Jeremiah flipped
open the top lid and withdrew a letter. "From your
fiancé," he said.

Paulette snatched the letter from his hand, ignoring
the mockery in his eyes that always so annoyed her.
The handwriting was Dester's, sprawling and slanted,
written as he always wrote, in great haste. Without
even thanking Jeremiah, she tore open the envelope.

*My darling Paulette,*
*The man who brings you this letter told me*
*you were in San Francisco and of your hazards*
*in reaching there. I received this news with sur-*
*prise—and mixed emotions—not having any*
*knowledge of your intention to join me. Walker*
*tells me you wrote, but mail, my darling, is not*

*reliable in this section of the country. I am in a
camp named Hangtown. That alone should tell
you something of the damnable place and should
help you understand why I command you not to
join me here. I shall rest easier knowing you have
the comforts of San Francisco, and I shall join
you when it is permitted. Luck has not been on
my side, neither in striking a rich claim, nor with
the bearer of this letter. Still, I feel that our separation shall now be a short one.*

*Until we are together, I remain,*

*Dester*

Paulette read the letter twice more. It did not
sound like Dester; gone was the enthusiasm of his past
letters, and it told her nothing of his health. He had not
even mentioned his family, nor had he said he loved
her. He had received news of her being in San Francisco with *mixed emotions*.

It was with mixed emotions that she now stood in
Jeremiah Walker's hotel room, the letter trembling
in her hand.

Forcing herself to gain control, she folded the letter carefully and returned it to its envelope. Jeremiah
was standing at the foot of the bed watching her.

"The letter was written in a rush," he said, perhaps
reading the confusion in her face.

"How . . . how did he seem?" she asked.

"Not knowing the gentleman previously, I couldn't
answer," he said. "And you? How have you fared? I
understand you moved from Dora's." The smile had
crept back into his eyes, the mockery.

"I have my own house," she told him stiffly.

"Then you won't return to New Orleans?"

"Not alone—not unless Dester returns with me."

He shrugged. "I also have another message for you,
Mrs. Mason told me to give you her best regards."

"Is she well?"

"As well as a woman can be living at Nigger Hill,"

he said. "It's rougher than you could imagine at the mining camps. But, then, Mrs. Mason is accustomed to hardships. She's happy because she's with her son —a strange young man, not the sort she described, with a stammer to his speech and a particularly awkward gait."

Paulette moved hesitantly toward the door. "Thank you for bringing the letter," she said.

"Ah, but you want to know more," he said, stopping her exit.

"Yes," she said, "whatever you can tell me." Let him mock her with his eyes; she didn't care. She was starved for news of Dester.

"Then have dinner with me?" Jeremiah said. "I'll even consent to spending the entire meal telling you about your fiancé."

Reluctantly, she agreed.

"Despite the stories you might have heard, nuggets aren't scattered around the ground for the taking," Jeremiah said. "Mining is a backbreaking labor and the rewards are too often few."

"Dester said he had not had luck," Paulette said when he fell silent.

"No, and neither have many of the other miners at Hangtown," he told her. "Some of the miners are lucky to pull out five dollars a day, and that for eleven hours of effort. They're a discouraged, rowdy lot."

"But you managed to relieve them of their discouragement by taking their gold in card games," Paulette murmured.

Jeremiah laughed. "That I did," he admitted. "I did well enough to raise the additional money for my casino. Construction begins within the week. It'll be called The Barbary Coast."

"And it will no doubt employ women like Dora."

Jeremiah's brow furrowed. "Women like Dora have their place in the scheme of things," he said. "I would have thought you would have learned that quickly."

"I learned only how to survive," she said.

"And that, my dear Miss Favière, is what Dora learned." He pushed back his plate and, without asking permission, lit a cigar.

She decided not to anger him by pursuing the subject of Dora or his gambling. She wanted to hear of Dester. "And Dester?" she urged. "How did you happen to find him?"

"By asking at every camp," he confessed. "It wasn't until I reached Hangtown that one of the men said he knew the name Granville. Your Dester came to the gaming table the next evening, said he'd heard I'd been asking for him, and asked if I had been sent by his father. I told him no, I hadn't been sent, but was performing an errand of mercy for a love-stricken young lady." He winked at her, but she averted her gaze. "I must admit part of my search on your part was also to satisfy my own curiosity. I had to meet the man you'd travel so far to be reunited with."

"You sound as though you were disappointed," she said with a hint of anger.

"I was not impressed," he said bluntly. "I presume your fiancé has hidden qualities, qualities another man might not recognize."

"You are being rude," she murmured, and again she wished she had not consented to the dinner. She wanted news of Dester, but not to hear him criticized, especially by a gambler like Jeremiah Walker. "Is he well?"

"He complained of no maladies to me," Jeremiah answered, "although there was one I found most obvious and, because of you, distressing."

Paulette sat forward, her dinner forgotten.

"Gold fever," Jeremiah said. "If I've ever seen a man under its possession, it's your fiancé. It's distressing also because of his background and social position at home in Louisiana."

Paulette stiffened. "He wants something of his own," she said defensively.

"Wouldn't he have inherited more than he could possibly find in California?"

"It wouldn't have been the same," she said quietly.

"But isn't that why you came to San Francisco? To convince him to return?"

She stared blankly past his shoulder and said nothing.

"I don't mean to be rude," Jeremiah continued. "I don't mean to insult or discourage you, but, Miss Favière, I see nothing but difficulties ahead for you. I don't think your fiancé is the man you remember him to be. Men change—especially here in California, where the driving force is to strike it rich in the gold fields. Dester Granville may have been the refined Southern gentleman when he lived on that grand plantation you grew up on, but at Hangtown he was merely another grubby, gold-crazed miner."

Paulette sprang to her feet, white-faced, trembling. Had not heads turned in the dining room, she would have screamed her outrage; instead, she folded her napkin calmly and dropped it beside her plate. "I'll say good night now, Mr. Walker. My apologies for expecting more of you than petty attacks on Dester."

Before she could move away from the table, Jeremiah grabbed her hand and pulled her back into her chair. "Don't be a little fool," he snapped. "The attack isn't petty. I couldn't give a damn about your Dester. But I do . . ."—he paused, still clutching her arm—". . . I do care about you. I have from the beginning, and you've known it. That night in Panama . . ."

"Please don't remind me of that night," she pleaded. "It's something I choose to forget."

"Well, it's something I haven't been able to forget," he told her. "There's never been another woman in my life who has affected me as you have. I'm as possessed by you as those bastards in the camps are possessed by their dreams of gold. I've cursed you for it; I've cursed myself. But the truth remains that I . . ."

"Please! Stop this! I forbid it!" she cried. She pulled to release her arm, but he only increased the pressure of his grasp. "Is that why you criticize Dester and try to make me think he's become less than the man he was? Because you hope to take his place with me?" Her voice had risen in her fury until all the diners had ceased eating their meals and were listening. "Then you are a fool, Mr. Walker! Stay with your own kind of women—stay with Dora and the other whores on Maiden Lane!"

The rage she had witnessed in Jeremiah the night on the *Falcon* when he had saved her flooded across his face again now. Fear mingled with her fury. She pulled again to release her arm and he let her go.

"You've a lot to learn from the women of Maiden Lane," he said with control. "In and out of a man's bed, they're all your superiors."

Paulette fled the dining room.

Chang, waiting for her outside the hotel, recognized her fury and kept several paces behind as she hurried toward home.

# Chapter Six

PAULETTE'S FURY had cooled by the time she had reached the top of the hill. It was not, however, destined to be cooled for long.

On the porch, pounding on her door and shouting Miriam's name, was Mr. Slater. Black-clad Dorothy and Alice stood at the gate, silent, smiling, encouraging their husband with unspoken words. Neither saw Paulette and Chang approaching.

"Miriam! Come out, you woman of Satan! Come out, or I'll tear this door down!" Mr. Slater yelled.

Paulette passed by Dorothy and Alice without speaking. With Chang at her side, she stepped onto the porch. "I hardly think you'll be tearing my door down tonight, Mr. Slater," she said.

The man turned on her, his face contorted with anger. "Whore of Babylon!" he shouted. His fists were clenched, the muscles in his neck expanded by his fury. "My wife is in there! Send her out to me!"

"Never!"

"I knew when I first saw you the sort of woman you were," Mr. Slater hissed. "No decent, self-respecting woman would travel alone. You've influenced her," he accused. "You've driven her to leave me! By God, you'll send her out, or I'll knock down the door and drag her out! The woman is my wife!"

"You have two other wives," Paulette told him calmly. "Miriam does not wish to be the third."

"Wish to be?" he yelled, his fury building even more. "She has no choice in the matter! Our laws . . ."

"I know nothing of your laws," Paulette interrupted. "But I'm certain there are laws of the land that are in contradiction to yours. Tomorrow I'm taking Miriam to the proper authorities. The marriage will be annuled."

From the gate behind her, Paulette heard both Dorothy and Alice gasp. Alice then cried out to the powers of heaven to strike down this woman who defied her husband.

"I would suggest you leave, Mr. Slater," Paulette said. "My house is now a sanctuary for Miriam. She won't leave and she won't be dragged out by you."

Mr. Slater, trembling in his rage, drew back his fist, but it froze in midair when Chang, leaping in front of Paulette, drew a dagger from his clothing and crouched, ready for the attack.

"Heathen!" the Mormon shouted. He lunged forward, but Chang was too quick for him. The blade flashed, and Mr. Slater cried out and leaped back, clutching his upper arm.

"You go now," Chang said, the tone of his voice no different than if he had been telling Paulette that dinner was ready. He remained crouched, the dagger waiting.

Miriam, white-faced, her cheeks streaked with tears, appeared in the lighted window. Paulette waved her back.

Dorothy and Alice had come halfway into the yard, then had stopped, both crying with fear. "Come away!" Dorothy cried. "Leave her."

"She's my wife!" the man bellowed.

"She was your brother's wife," Paulette told him. "It was your brother she loved, not you. She has a right to her freedom."

"She's one of us. She must abide by our laws." Determined, Mr. Slater removed his coat and wrapped it around his left arm, intending to use it as protection against Chang's dagger. The white sleeve of his shirt was streaked with blood.

Paulette felt her hopes sinking. She had thought Mr. Slater would have left after once having vented his anger. She had not expected him to fight, to face Chang's dagger—and death. She stepped closer to Chang's back. "Good God," she whispered. "We can't kill him."

Chang, confused by her sudden change, rose from his crouching position. "What wish me to do?" he asked.

It was Dorothy who prevented Mr. Slater's next attack on Chang. She rushed onto the porch and placed herself between Chang and her husband, her back to the man with the dagger. "Leave her," she pleaded. "She was never really one of us. The Book meant nothing to her, only Jake."

"But the laws . . ."

"The laws were meant to protect her, not you!" the woman cried. "It isn't the laws that are driving you. It's lust! She isn't worth dying for! Leave her!"

Roughly, Mr. Slater pushed her aside. "I can't leave her!" he shouted. He advanced slowly toward Chang.

The small man readied himself for the attack.

The two men began circling one another slowly on the narrow porch.

Paulette, her back pressed against the house, cried out for them to stop, but it was now beyond her control. Chang had the right to protect himself. He had the dagger, an advantage, but he was also small. Mr. Slater was a strong man. Should he wrest the dagger from Chang, he would be capable of breaking the Chinese man's neck.

Just when the two men were ready to lunge at one another, there was the sound of horse hooves approaching out of the darkness.

Jeremiah leaped from his stallion before it had come to a full stop at the gate. Pistol drawn, he pushed past the two black-clad women and stepped onto the porch.

Mr. Slater backed off. He would have faced the small Chinese man with a dagger, but not, even in his fury, would he go against a giant like Jeremiah Walker, even if the man hadn't had a pistol pointed at his chest. Without speaking, he stepped off the side of the porch and his wives ran to him, taking his arms and urging him toward the gate.

No one spoke until Mr. Slater stopped outside the gate. He pulled himself erect, shedding the grasps of his wives. "All right," he said, "I'll leave without her. But she'll come crawling back." He flung his coat across his shoulders. Turning, he walked away, the three of them disappearing into the darkness before the echo of their footsteps had faded.

Paulette slumped against Jeremiah's chest, her earlier anger at him forgotten. "I seem to be constantly in your debt," she murmured. "Thank you."

But when his arms went around her, she pulled away. "Come in," she invited. "I have no cognac, but I can fix you a cup of tea."

Miriam, huddled in a corner of the room, came running forward. Paulette held her, soothed her, and then had Chang lead her away to bed. While the water boiled, she explained the situation to Jeremiah as best she could.

He sat at the kitchen table, listening, trying to conceal the smile that he knew so irritated her. When she had finished, he told her he had come to apologize. "My manners were uncalled for," he said. "And your accusation was true. I did want you for myself, not just to have you, but . . ."—he glanced away, fixing his gaze on the glowing coals of the fireplace—". . .but as my wife. However, I realize nothing could come of my desire as long as you are in love with Dester Granville. Not," he added, "that I've altered my impression of your fiancé."

Paulette said nothing.

For a reason she could not explain to herself, she

no longer felt resentment toward Jeremiah. His honesty had ended her resentment. She could not blame him for that night in Panama, no more than she must blame herself.

They sat at the kitchen table talking until near midnight, Jeremiah telling her of his plans for his casino and of the growth he expected of San Francisco. "It may seem improbable, but the ramshackle mining camps in the foothills of the Sierra Nevadas will be instrumental in establishing San Francisco as an important city. We are the lucky ones to be in on its beginning. Let the others suffer from their gold fever. The real fortunes are to be made here, starting now."

Paulette sipped her tea and stared thoughtfully at Jeremiah. "This was a part of you I never recognized," she admitted. "But it's difficult to imagine the realization of your dream—not when you look at San Francisco as it is today. It's one vast garbage heap, with spoiled food and the intestines of slaughtered animals tossed into the streets. Debris litters the wharf and the bay is already being polluted. The streets are quagmires after a rain, with the mud sometimes four feet deep."

"It's growing too quickly," Jeremiah told her. "But the conditions here are no different from other cities at their beginnings. Surely you heard your parents talk of New Orleans before it became modern."

Paulette said she had, remembering those quiet nights around the study fireplace with Clabe relating stories of the New Orleans flood, when men and beasts were lost in the mire of the street trenches. "But New Orleans was not a city of transients," she said.

"True. But the gold fever will wane. The mines will peter out. Many will leave—they already are—but many more will remain. Tent cities like Happy Valley will disappear. Those with insight who invest now in San Francisco will be the city's leaders of the future." He stared at her intently. "But it isn't your wish to remain, is it?" he asked. "You still believe you'll talk Granville into returning to Louisiana?"

"It's home," Paulette said simply. "I'd rather be there than here. I don't choose to live with the filth and the fear of going out alone, not even if I believe, as you do, that San Francisco will become an important city."

"You miss your fiancé's family?"

"They're my family also. Yes, I miss them desperately," she confessed, and the feeling of homesickness swept over her.

"I dare say your ancestors felt the same when they came to Louisiana," Jeremiah told her.

They fell silent for a moment. The wind was blowing, howling around the corners of the house. Occasionally when it was quiet, Paulette heard Miriam still moving around in the bedroom. Chang was asleep on a mat in the corner near the fireplace; it amazed her that the little man could sleep with so little covering. When the fire went out, the house always became cold, but he never complained. She made a mental note to throw an extra quilt over him before she retired.

Suddenly, Jeremiah, pulling himself erect in his chair, reached across the table and covered her hand with his. "If things do not go as you expect with Granville . . ."

Paulette pulled her hand from beneath his. "Don't, please," she murmured, anticipating his question.

But he continued, ". . . is there hope for me? For us?" His expression was intense, his dark eyes boring into hers. "I am a persistent man. When I know what I want . . ."

Paulette rose. Why had he spoken these things? And just when she had begun to feel comfortable with him! Her uneasiness with him returned, and with the uneasiness came her anger. A woman other than herself would consider him to be the most handsome of men and would welcome his advances—a woman not in love, as she was in love with Dester. "I think you'd best say good night," she told him.

Obediently, he rose. "Until tomorrow, then," he said.

"I don't think we should see one another again," Paulette told him. She saw that the words stung him, and she added, "I both hated and liked you tonight. I hated you when you attacked Dester. I was grateful when you drove Mr. Slater away, and I liked you when I listened to you talking of your dreams of San Francisco. I also believed you when you said you are a persistent man, but I could not abide persistence when there is no hope. I would never be comfortable around you again."

Jeremiah's face paled. There was hurt and anger reflected in his dark eyes. He struggled for a moment with his emotions. Then the smile that so irritated her spread around his lips, and the old mockery filled his eyes. He bowed slightly, snatched his topcoat from the chair back, and departed without a farewell.

Paulette watched from the window as he mounted his stallion and rode away down the hill. Despite her words, she felt she had not seen the last of him.

The noise began at sunup: hammering, sawing, men shouting.

Paulette leaped from bed, and pulling her robe around her shoulders to ward off the morning chill, she went to the window. The hill—her hill—was alive with activity. Dozens of men and horses were trampling the grass and wildflowers that grew just beyond her fence. Flat-bedded carriages stood filled with lumber and bricks and barrels of building supplies, the horses wet from their efforts of pulling the loads up the incline.

She bit her lower lip in frustration. It had been her intention to buy the land surrounding her house when Tom sent the bank draft from New Orleans. Someone had beaten her to it. An important part of her view of the bay would be blocked by the new house. "Damn!" she cried. She dressed quickly, woke up Miriam, and went into the kitchen to find Chang had also been awakened by the din of noise and had the kettle put on to boil.

The little man pointed through the window. "Much lumber," he said. "Big house. We have rich neighbors." He smiled, thinking she would be pleased.

She passed through the kitchen doorway and moved to the fence, motioning one of the men to her.

He was gruff looking, with an unkempt beard and bird-like eyes. There was a scar on his cheek that ran, red and ugly, from beneath his left eye to his jawline. When he rested his hands on the pickets of the fence, she noticed another scar on the back of his right hand. She prayed he was not to be her new neighbor, a ruffian who had made his fortune in the gold fields and was now building a house for one of the women from Maiden Lane.

"Is it a house you're building?" she asked, although the answer was obvious.

"Aye," he said in an accent she could not place, "and a big one it's to be." He glanced up at the sky, the position of the sun. "A shame, too, but it'll block your afternoon sun, being built so close."

"Then why don't you build it farther back?" she demanded.

" 'Cause this is exactly where we were instructed to build it," the man answered flatly.

"But it'll also block my view of the bay," Paulette protested.

The man shrugged his massive shoulders. "I'm only a builder," he said.

"Then tell me the name of the owner," Paulette said, "and I'll go to him."

The man scratched his beard. Turning, he yelled at one of his companions, "Taylor, who's paying for this?"

"Jeremiah Walker!" the man shouted back.

Paulette watched the frame of the house go up; then the walls took shape. It was an enormous structure for San Francisco, three stories, with a cupola and fireplaces in every room. A carver, an Italian who worked for wages between trips to and from the gold fields, was employed to etch the trim with grotesque faces and animals. Windows were brought by ship, as was furniture and fabric for draperies; carpets were purchased from travelers seeking to sell their belongings for grubstakes or return passages east.

"Mr. Walker must be very rich," Chang remarked.

Miriam, helping with the shucking of the peas for the evening stew, said, "It'll be the grandest house in San Francisco—and him not even a married man."

"Maybe will be," Chang told her.

The two had become extremely close since Miriam had come to live with them; they shopped together, hunted the nearby woods for berries and rabbits, and kept Paulette's life generally organized. Miriam was giving Chang English lessons; Chang, in return, taught her a spattering of Chinese—and cooking, something that Miriam had never been forced to learn because of Dorothy and Alice. Her culinary ability was quickly surpassing her teacher's. When it could be purchased, she made a dish of venison or bear that was better than anything Paulette had tasted from the kitchen at Plantation Bend.

Paulette, sitting at the kitchen table writing letters, glanced up at the two and thought how lonely she would be without them. They were her friends, her family, and she could not imagine being without them —although, since she had not yet heard from Tom, she might have to dismiss Chang. Her finances were now desperate; she had enough money for another month if she were frugal—a damnable situation, she thought, since she was worth far more than the extravagant Jeremiah. Dester had written to her only twice in the past two months; both letters had been brief, telling her of his closeness to striking a rich claim, his intuitive belief that his fortune would be made soon in the gold fields—and then he would return to San Francisco, and to her. He missed her, he wrote. But missing her had not driven him to take a launch downriver to visit her. In both letters he forbade her to come to him, reiterating in the second letter the hardships of the camps, the crassness and animalistic behavior of the miners, and the difficulties wrought by the elements. She was beginning to doubt his feelings toward her; she would spend hours pondering, remembering.

And over it all was the infernal noise of the building next door.

"He hasn't brought a woman to see the house," Miriam was telling Chang. "He comes alone. I've seen him standing under the trees, looking. Sometimes I think he's looking here instead of at his own house. A strange man."

Chang glanced only briefly at Paulette. "Yes, a strange man," he murmured, then went back to cleaning potatoes. "But he very rich man."

Paulette knew Chang was being critical; Miriam did not recognize the builder of the house as the man who had saved her from Mr. Slater, but Chang remembered. Paulette wondered if he had truly been asleep beside the fireplace that night, or if he had only been pretending, listening, knowing that she could be the woman to move into the grand house that now blocked their afternoon sun.

"The workmen say he's a tyrant," Miriam went on, "but I think they meant a perfectionist. If they build something that isn't to his liking, he makes them tear it out and rebuild it. They say he wants the house to be the grandest in San Francisco. A man would only build a house like that for a woman he loved completely."

Paulette's pen scratched across the paper. She crossed out the mistake. "Enough of Mr. Walker and his house," she said. "Isn't it enough that he's taken away our afternoon sun and the best part of our view? We needn't romanticize him and his intentions." Still, should she have admitted it to herself, she wanted to hear more of Jeremiah. She, too, had seen him standing beneath the trees; she, too, believed he stared at her simple house and not at the

grand structure beside it. What did he expect? To see
her briefly pass by a window? For the grand house to
influence her decision not to see him? For her to
abandon her feelings for Dester and accept his proposal? She folded the sheet of paper; writing letters
was impossible with Chang and Miriam chattering.

She took her shawl, and leaving Chang and Miriam
to their preparations for supper, she stepped out into
the narrow yard. The seeds she had purchased from
an eastern family had begun to sprout in a row along
the picket fence. Chang had also built a trellis near
the porch and she had planted a moonflower vine to
remind her of the one at Plantation Bend; Clabe's
mother Zelma had planted that one and it had been
in complete possession of the front veranda. Hers, she
feared, would not survive the climate here.

She left the yard and wandered to the side of the
hill overlooking the bay. The harbor was now filled
with vessels, most abandoned, flying the colors of
every nation; some, she had heard, still had the cargo
in the hold, the crew having deserted immediately
upon arrival for the gold fields. One ship had caught
fire, burned, and sunk near the wharf, the mast protruding with its shredded sails.

Paulette sat on a boulder and stared thoughtfully
across the harbor at the green cliffs beyond. Dester
was out there, past the hills. They had been separated
for longer than she cared to consider. She had had no
news from home; she felt cut off, deserted, so close to
Dester, and yet so far away. Melancholy was claiming
her reason, uncertainty.

The hammering from inside Jeremiah's house cut
into her thoughts. She clamped her hands over her
ears and was thankful tomorrow was Sunday; the
workmen didn't come on Sundays—she would have a
day of peace and quiet. But then there was that committee of women who had approached her; they
wanted her to go with them to protest the conditions
in Happy Valley. The odor of uncleanliness and the
stench of slaughtered animals were being carried

across the village by the winds from the bay. She had reluctantly agreed and now regretted it. Although her house was on the hill above the sandhills of Happy Valley, the direction of the winds had spared her. Even had she not been spared, her house had only originally been meant as a temporary dwelling until Dester had returned from the gold fields.

Closing her eyes, she turned her face up to the sun and felt its warmth on her face. How I've changed, she thought. In Louisiana, a lady would never have allowed her face to be tanned by the sun. It had been a sign of low breeding.

"Miss Paulette! Miss Paulette!"

She turned to see Chang running toward her from the house.

"Letters!" he cried, then waved two envelopes. "One of Mr. Walker's men brought them from hotel."

Paulette greedily accepted the envelopes. One was from Dester, the other from Vienna. She opened Dester's first.

*My darling Paulette,*
*At last I've struck a richer vein than on my previous attempts. Since Wednesday last I've taken well over one hundred dollars a day from the stream. I know there's more there waiting for me, a vein so rich it'll take months to mine it. Conditions here are worsening with the influx of more gold seekers from the east. A wagon train arrived last week, more than half its original party lost in the cruel winter of the Sierras. It is now necessary to guard a claim night and day from claim-jumpers. If they're caught, they are, of course, hanged. I've hired a black man to stand guard for me at night—that is, until he earns enough to strike out on his own. He's from Savannah, the home of my grandparents, and is what our ancestors would call a maroon. The fellow tells me there is now an entire underground of whites who assist slaves in escaping*

*from their bondage. How, I wonder, does my
father take to that?*

*I regret our prolonged separation. I dream of
you nightly, long for you, and pray for my success so I may join you soon. Your last letter telling me of the growth of San Francisco was
fascinating. Why should that village be growing
with such rapidity when the gold being sought is
here in the foothills? Still, I am grateful that you
are there and that I do not have to worry over
your safety while I am mining. Do not despair—
we shall be together soon.*

*Love,*
*Dester*

At least this time he had put *Love* before his name,
she thought, then chided herself for the criticism.

She sat for several moments contemplating Dester's
letter before opening the letter from Vienna.

Instantly, her eyes skipping the customany greeting, she felt her heartbeat quicken.

*. . . Clabe has been bedridden with his old mal-
ady.*

Malaria, Paulette remembered.

*The doctors say he will pull through once
again with proper care. The overseer now has
complete control of the operation of Plantation
Bend. Fortunately for us, he is a trustworthy
soul, a freed man, you'll recall, but we are still
in desperate need of our son. I prayed before
opening your last letter that there would be news
of your return with Dester, but, alas, I guess this
is not to be for sometime yet.*

*Mr. and Mrs. Whitely dropped by—you know
how I dread their visits—and Mr. Whitely argued with Clabe. The supporters of the North-*

*erners are becoming more outspoken. Clabe
ordered him out of the house, which is good for
me, but it eliminates yet another of his male
companions. Now only Mr. McKinney visits; he
sits in Clabe's sickroom for hours and diplomat-
ically skirts the topics that would upset Clabe.*

*Now, my child, I must broach something that
is painful to all of us, but which affects you most
of all. I scarcely know how to begin—at the beginning, Clabe tells me from his bed . . . and so
I shall. Katrina returned to us with our grand-
daughter. Such was her state of distress that it
was a full three hours before we could quiet her
enough to learn that Tom had been arrested. It
seems he was making use of the bank customers'
finances to further his own means and the in-
vestments he had made proved pure folly. Your
account, since he had been given power of at-
torney, was totally depleted. Clabe went instantly to New Orleans to check into the matter.
I think it was this blow and the dishonor Tom
brought to the family that awakened his malaria.
But all this aside, Paulette, the inheritance you
received from the Favières has been squandered
and the bank is fighting making restitution, especially to anyone connected with the guilty em-
ployee. Indeed, they have even instigated an
investigation into our affairs, trying to prove that
we profited from Tom's crime. Of course this is
not true, and Clabe would be furious at me
should he learn that I fear for our beloved plantation: I have never been one to understand the
workings of business or business minds. It is all
too baffling! But I do fully understand Katrina's
shame—she swears she will never leave the
house again—and your loss. You must understand that you are not penniless, only temporarily financially distressed [Clabe's words], for we
look on you as our daughter and have ensured
that you will receive an equal share in all we*

*own. As for the draft I understand you requested
from Tom, we are sending it with this letter.
Should you require more before you can convince Dester to return and accept his responsibilities here, you need only ask. Perhaps when
you tell him of his father's condition and of this
new disgrace his family must face, your purpose
will be easier achieved. Should, however, he
continue to refuse to return, we would be most
happy for your return alone.*

The letter continued with news of the happenings
at Plantation Bend: Bella's new beau, the preparations for harvest, the surprising number of maroon
slaves.

Paulette finished the letter as if in a daze, then
folded it carefully around the draft and put it with
Dester's letter into the pocket of her gown. She went
over and over the news, as if unable to comprehend
what she had read. So, she concluded, except for the
draft in her pocket, she was penniless. She felt no par-
ticular loss, perhaps because of the last few months of
frugal living in San Francisco. She felt no surprise at
Tom's crime, only pity for Katrina. Her main distress
was for Clabe and Vienna.

It was nearing sunset when Chang, worried that
Paulette had sat so long on the cliff, came out to
question her about the news in the letters and to
coax her inside. She did not hear the crunch of his
feet on the newly spread gravel, did not turn, and did
not alter her position. Her shoulders were hunched,
her hands clasped before her in what he thought was
the Christian manner of praying. Her shawl had
slipped to the ground, but it was obvious she did not
feel the chill of the crisp bay wind.

Bending, Chang touched her shoulder. "Come inside," he said quietly. "Fire is warm and supper almost ready."

Startled, she stared up at him, her eyes slightly
dazed.

"Oh, Chang," she murmured, and she seemed to shake herself from her thoughts. She gave him her hand and he helped her to her feet. Her legs were cramped, almost numb, and she was forced to stand for a moment before moving. She stared out over the bay at the abandoned ships and was struck with the thought that she was as abandoned as they were. Then she chided herself and knew that she must not linger in self-pity. She had been taught to be strong— by Clabe and Vienna, by her own family's past, of which the slaves had whispered, and by her ordeal in reaching this strange land.

Arm in arm, she walked back to the house with Chang. At the door, she stopped before entering. "Chang, I'll be leaving for a time. I trust you to look after Miss Miriam and the house."

"I do as you wish," the little man assured her. "But where do you go that we cannot go with you?"

"To the gold fields," she answered.

Chang's eyes widened, but he said nothing.

Paulette went inside, but not before catching sight of the man and stallion standing in the shadows of the nearby trees.

# Part II

---

# THE
# MINES

# Chapter Seven

THE TWELVE-TON cutter *Marcia* was readying to depart.

Paulette stood on the docks with Chang and a tearful Miriam.

"No tears, please, Miriam," Paulette said.

Miriam made a valiant attempt to stop the flow. "But the stories we've heard!" she sputtered. "And you being a fragile lady of quality!"

Paulette winced, as she always did when Miriam used that phrase. "I shall be fine," she assured the young woman. "You must not worry about me, but about yourselves." She turned to Chang. "You've hidden the money I've given you?"

Chang nodded.

"And you have the paper on the house in case anything should happen to me?"

Again he nodded. Should anything happen to Paulette, he understood that her house would belong to both him and Miriam. "But you will come back to us soon?" It was both a question and a statement.

"Soon, yes," she assured him. Depending, she thought . . .

The cutter's whistle sounded and those who had lingered on the docks began to board. The only passage Paulette had succeeded in obtaining was that of a deck traveler; she would be crammed in among thirty fellow passengers, all male, and she was forced to provide her own food. Chang and Miriam had packed a basket for her: a whole chicken, biscuits, and, as she was later to discover, two prized boiled eggs and a flask of cognac.

"Stay well," she called from the gangplank.

She stood at the railing and watched her friends grow minute as the cutter pulled away.

As a deck passenger, there was no shade to protect her from the intensely strong sun. Huddled on a crate, she opened her parasol, but the sun seemed to pierce directly through the fabric. Her one piece of luggage and her bedroll were stacked beside her. She had brought a book to read and opened it in her lap, but she could not concentrate on the words. The men crammed in around her were chattering in English, French, German, and other languages she could not identify. There were also a youth someone referred to as a Malay boy and two Indian guides. The Indians, perched on the railing like human birds, sat with their eyes closed, sleeping, oblivious to their precarious perches and the chattering crowd around them.

A man stepped through the crowd and stopped in front of Paulette. *"Bonjour, mademoiselle."* He removed his high felt hat and bowed in a manner that reminded her of Jeremiah. "You are French, no?"

"My father was French," she told him, understanding that he had placed her as a countrywoman because of her dark hair, eyes, and coloring. "But I do not speak the language." She did, of course; Vienna had insisted on French tutors. But Paulette had never mastered the language and refused to admit she spoke it at all.

"A shame," the Frenchman said. "Ah, but a woman of your beauty need not speak at all." He requested permission to sit with her, and she nodded her approval. His name was Jean-Paul Colbert. He had sailed into San Francisco that morning and immediately boarded the *Marcia* for the gold fields. He was young, perhaps her own age, with a full crop of black hair; his eyes were a forceful and penetrating brown; his complexion was swarthy. He had the habit of sitting with one shoulder cocked lower than the other, and when he moved he sometimes gave the impression of being in pain. He seemed pleasant enough, but for some reason she could not comprehend, Paulette felt she should be wary of him. He was not, she told herself, what he seemed.

Still, she had hours to while away, and Jean-Paul Colbert appeared to be better company than the other men crowded on the deck. He flattered her between topics of conversation—perhaps the reason for her quiet mistrust, since she had grown unaccustomed to flattery—and he talked of New Orleans, where he had stopped on his journey. At lunchtime, she shared her basket with him. He ate sparingly and without appetite. When it was obvious he had grown tired of talk and she was glancing longingly at the book still opened in her lap, he remained beside her, reluctant to take his leave.

Suddenly, staring directly into her face, he said, "Your name, Favière—it's familiar to me."

"Is it?" she asked. "I'm certain that in your country there are many who carry the family name." She took the handkerchief from her cuff and touched at the perspiration beading her forehead. "Although none would be related to me."

"Then your father had no other children?"

Paulette did not answer for a moment, then said, "He had two others, a son and a daughter, both older than I. Both are now dead, or so I've been told. My half-brother was killed in a duel in New Orleans. My half-sister returned to Paris and died there. My father is also dead—and my mother. I was raised by a neighboring family." As always when she talked of the Favières, she felt herself becoming upset. The mention of her father, or especially her half-sister, reawakened stories she had lived with since childhood, stories overheard from the slaves, from Katrina when she was being cruel, once even from a woman who had sat

behind her in church. Paulette would never forget the
woman whispering, "Is that the devil Favière's daughter? I've told my son the devil hides his evil in pretty
packages. Stay away from beautiful women because
their souls are dark."

"Favière, Favière," Jean-Paul repeated. "Claudine
Favière—that's it! Was she by any chance your half-
sister?"

"No," Paulette lied.

Jean-Paul laughed. "A colorful creature for a relative if she had been," he told her. "I remember my
mother telling me of . . ."

"Monsieur Colbert," Paulette interrupted, "I regret
that I am extremely tired. If we could continue this
conversation later . . ."

Jean-Paul rose and bowed slightly. "Pardon me for
tiring you," he said without offense. "Should you need
me or feel the want of my company again, I shall be
within hearing distance." Smiling, his even, white
teeth flashing in the afternoon sun, he moved away
from her.

She closed her eyes, but she still felt him watching
her. Perhaps she should have listened to his stories of
her half-sister, Claudine; sending him away had made
him suspicious, had confirmed her relationship. Would
her half-sister's infamy never die and be buried with
her? Eyes closed, she realized just how tired she was;
she had slept little the night before, packing and giving
Chang instructions. Then, before closing her eyes a
few hours before dawn, she had written to Vienna,
telling her she was to leave for the gold fields to try
and convince Dester to return to Louisiana.

The *Marcia* was moving slowly, crewmen at the
bow testing the depth of the river. Despite their efforts, there was a suddenly shuddering of timbers as
the cutter struck a sandbar. Paulette was thrown from
her crate, startled, and a man beside her tumbled over
her and struck his head on the deck. There was confused shouting and cursing. The captain appeared,

screaming orders, and hurried forward to estimate
the damages.

Jean-Paul was instantly kneeling beside Paulette.
"Are you injured, *mademoiselle?*"

She told him she was not, but she pointed to the
unconscious man beside her, whose head had been
split open and was bleeding. Together they turned
the man over and placed his head in her lap. She took
a napkin from her basket, moistened it with cognac,
and dabbed at the man's wound.

"A waste of good cognac," another man murmured.
"A bucket of water in his face would work the same."

Paulette gave the man such an angry look that he
shrugged and walked away. The man in her lap began
to moan; he opened his eyes and stared up into her
face. When he regained his senses, a twinkle came
into his eyes. "If this is heaven, it ain't half bad," he
said.

Gently, she pushed him away. Rising, she went to
the railing to join the crowd of men there who were
staring over the side. The bow of the *Marcia* was se-
curely grounded in the sand. Orders were being passed
back from the captain, at the bow.

"It seems we are all going to be put to work," Jean-
Paul told her. "The captain has ordered every man to
shore to handle the ropes. We are apparently going to
tow this beast off the sandbar."

It took over an hour for the *Marcia* to be freed.
Only Paulette and the captain remained on board.
When the men climbed back on deck they were mud-
spattered, tired, and angry . . . except for Jean-Paul—
he seemed to have actually enjoyed the exercise. His
coat was ripped and his shirt was covered with grime;
perspiration cascaded from his forehead, but there
was a smile on his face and his eyes danced like one
intoxicated. He looked down at his appearance and
laughed. "The sun will quickly dry the mud," he said,
"and the drinks the captain promised us will cure a
parched throat. Oh, but, *mademoiselle,*" he murmured,
his expression becoming serious, "I do not know if

drinking is wise, you being the only woman on board
with so many men. Men can become less than gentlemen with too much liquor."

"I needn't think we should worry," Paulette told
him. "With so many men on board, I doubt the captain carries that great a supply of liquor."

The heavy night fog was as grueling as the intense
sun had been during the day. With nothing to shield
the passengers, they were exposed to the cold and
dampness, which penetrated to the bone.

Paulette found a wedge of space and curled up in
her bedroll. She was grateful Jean-Paul was huddled
near her; she need not fear a repetition of her experience on the *Falcon* with him to protect her. Of course,
he was no Jeremiah Walker, slighter in build and not
nearly so fierce, but, despite her odd mistrust of him,
she felt secure knowing he was there watching over
her.

She slept fitfully, waking many times due to the
cold. She dreamed dreams of frozen places, a country
covered with ice and snow—something she knew only
from her earlier lessons. Dester was there standing
knee-deep in water that was frozen around him, and
he kept beating at the ice, trying to break through its
surface. *"There's gold down there,"* he kept repeating
to her. *"I'll find my fortune down there, down there,
down there."* She shuddered, awakened, and lay trembling.

When she slept again, Vienna appeared, ghostly,
her voice strange and distant. *"He's dead, my Clabe!"*
she cried. *"My son deserted us, one daughter in disgrace, another roaming a strange land."*

Then Vienna became Mrs. Mason. *"You're a stubborn one, you are, my dear. Jeremiah's good to you,
he loves you, and you treat him like the dirt beneath
your feet. You'll regret your treatment of him one
day."*

She awakened again and was determined to remain
awake to avoid her dreams. She pulled the bedroll

from around her face and peered out across the deck. The fog was so thick and heavy that she could see scarcely a few feet. She saw the bundle that was Jean-Paul; he was curled in an embryo position, knees up near his chin. Several men slept standing up, leaning against the railings or crates; some had altogether abandoned the idea of sleep and stood wrapped in their quilts talking quietly. The water lapped against the sides of the cutter; a crewman at the bow continued to shout the water's depth.

The chilled dampness was biting against Paulette's face. She again made a cocoon of her bedroll and before long was asleep again, this time without dreams.

The *Marcia* docked at Stockton and all on board disembarked. There the passengers joined another group on their way to the mines, with the Indian guides taking the lead. Six pack mules accompanied them, carrying provisions for the storekeepers in remote areas along with the party's provisions. Paulette was offered a mule to ride, but she declined; she did not want the others to consider her weak or to give her special treatment because she was a woman.

Her clothing, however, proved a detriment, her long skirt collecting the mud along the trails until the weight of the fabric pulled at her waist and made walking more difficult. The sun was again intense, the heat stifling. It wasn't long after they left Stockton that she regretted having declined a mule.

Only Jean-Paul gave her any special attention. He held back from the main party and walked slowly at her side, encouraging her when her pace slackened and they began to fall behind. "Lose them and some future party will find our bones out here," he told her.

"I doubt they should leave us here," she murmured, but she was not convinced by her own words.

Every member of the party seemed to have armed himself—pistols, Bowie knives, and some even carried shotguns in addition to the pistols and knives dangling from their belts. The jovial conversation on the *Marcia* had come to an end as soon as the cutter had discharged them. The men were as intense as the sun, something gleaming in their eyes that Paulette could not pretend to understand. *The gold fever,* she thought, and turned to ask Jean Paul if that was what she saw. But it was there in Jean-Paul's eyes also—that strange glazed expression, the firm set of his jaw, the tension of his neck muscles. She had the impression he wanted to leave her and catch up with the others, and she felt a moment of panic.

The trail, scarcely visible except for the grass those ahead had trampled down, was bordered on both sides by high trees and thick scrub. Wild berry bushes reached out their thorny tendrils to clutch and tear at her clothing. In the distance she could hear the rush of water over stones; this sound drew louder, and finally, when those ahead had stopped and she and Jean-Paul caught up with them, there was a waterfall, the white-capped water thundering into a large pool etched out of the mountain's stone.

The Indian guides made a sign that the party would rest. Men who had been striding forward with haste suddenly dropped breathlessly and without protest. The guides, tireless, saw to the mules.

Paulette moved through the resting men and seated herself at the edge of the waterfall's pool. The spray, fine and cooling, covered her face and revived her. Over the thundering sound, she heard two men near her talking.

". . . becomes more difficult from here on," one was telling his companion. "No shade from the trees and the temperature'll go up to one hundred twenty degrees. Some places the sand's ankle-deep. Then if it rains . . ."

She turned, not wanting to hear more, and stared into the clear, cold water.

Jean-Paul brought her a tin plate of beans and a chunk of bread. "There's nothing to drink," he said, "except the water from the pool behind you." He was thinking of the cognac that remained in her basket, but she made no offer of it, having forgotten that it existed.

She only wanted to close her eyes and sleep, but she knew the rest stop would not be long enough to allow that luxury. She ate in silence, scarcely tasting the food.

"The men are talking about you," Jean-Paul suddenly said. "They're questioning why you are with the party, why a lady such as yourself would want to reach the mines. I did not know what to tell them."

"Then tell them nothing," she said, then was immediately sorry for her rudeness. Better, she decided, if she let the men know. "I'm to meet my fiancé at Hangtown."

Jean-Paul stared at her intently. "He let you make this journey alone, without coming for you himself?"

"He doesn't know I'm coming," she answered.

"Oh, I see," he said, the tone of his voice making it clear he did not.

A murmur went up from the party and Paulette looked up to see a bedraggled group of men approaching along the path they had just used. There were no more than a dozen of them, haggard and emaciated, with heavy beards and badly worn clothing. There was a covered wagon, scarcely clearing the overhanging branches of the trees; on its seat sat a woman, a faded cotton bonnet concealing her face, the reins drooping uselessly in her red and swollen hands.

The men began to rise and go forward, greeting and questioning.

"We're what's left of a large party," Paulette heard one of the men explain, "from Indiana."

Paulette moved up to the wagon and offered the woman her hand in climbing down. The woman stared at her suspiciously, at the fine gown with its mud-spattered hem, at the silk hat slightly askew on the raven-black hair, and refusing the offer of assistance, she climbed down on her own.

"Come," Paulette told her. "We have food."

The woman allowed her hand to be taken; she

made no objection at being led away from the circle of men. Paulette brought her beans and bread and a remnant of the chicken left in her basket. The woman ate with appetite, scarcely chewing the food before swallowing. She was frail, small of frame, with lifeless hair the color of cornsilk and eyes that were sunken into her head. Her cheekbones were high and protruding, Indian in appearance; these combined with her sunken eyes made her resemble a frightened bird. Because of the trail dust that had settled in her pores, it was impossible to determine her age; she could have been anywhere from eighteen to forty. When the beans and chicken were gone, she wiped her plate with the bread and chewed it quickly. Then, leaning over the edge of the pool, she caught water in her cupped hands and drank thirstily.

"Imogene Lochner," she said so quietly that Paulette had to ask her to repeat the name before she heard it. "We're overlanders." She nodded toward the men. "Thirty-four of us when we started; thirteen now, countin' me. I told my husband not to make the journey, told him to be satisfied with what we got, but he wouldn't listen. That's him there, doing all the talkin'."

Paulette followed her gaze and saw the man: tall, sinewy, with a great mane of gray hair.

"The closer we got to California, the more abandoned debris we came 'cross: broken equipment, furniture, then burial mounds and skeletons. My son Jessie's buried out there; so is my sister Mary. Jessie was killed by Indians and Mary by the elements. God didn't mean for us to cross the land. God punished Zach and me for leaving our farm, for not being content with what we had. He took our Jessie, him only ten, and Mary not much older." Once she had started talking, the woman seemed incapable of stopping. She talked faster, her voice growing louder. "And for what? For gold? I'd give all the gold in the world to have my Jessie back, and my Mary. Men are fools. Fools!" Standing suddenly, she screamed at her husband, "You're the biggest fool of all, Zach Lochner!

Satan tempted you with riches and you clutched at his bait!"

Paulette, startled by the woman's outburst, remained sitting, stunned and confused. She wanted to rise, to hold the woman and comfort her, but fear held her back.

"You seen children with their scalps taken?" the woman shouted at the men watching her. "You seen your neighbors with their throats parched and their lips cracked and their eyes not able to blink 'cause there ain't enough moisture in their bodies?" She turned and glared down at Paulette, a fury burning from her sunken eyes. "You seen a baby born to a mother who knows she ain't strong enough to nurse it? And no milk? Cows and goats dead or stolen by the redskins?" Cuddling her arms, she rocked back and forth. "Holdin' a newborn and knowin' you're goin' to bury it 'fore sundown. That's what I've seen, and more. And for what? 'Cause my man wants gold! Fools, men are!" she screamed. "Satan's fools!"

Zach Lochner came forward quickly. He drew his arms around his wife and pulled her against him, her head snuggling against his chest as she broke into wails and tears. "Ain't been right since Jessie died," the man said over his wife's head. "But she'll be well again. Only woman out of six who came through, only one, my Imogene." He picked his wife up in his arms, carried her to the wagon, and lifted her inside.

Paulette realized her cheeks were streaked with tears. She wiped them away on the dusty sleeve of her gown. Rising, she went to the wagon just as Zach was climbing down. "Is there anything I can do?" she asked.

The man looked at her with the same suspicion as his wife, at her fine, though soiled, clothes, and his eyes turned dark. "I think maybe seein' you is what started her off again," he said. "Maybe it's best if you stay 'way from her 'til she's herself again." He moved away to join the other men.

Inside the wagon, Imogene Lochner continued to wail in her madness.

The party trudged on toward the gold fields.

Leaving the woods for the more open land, the temperature rose rapidly.

Paulette's throat was parched, and her eyes ached in their sockets. Jean-Paul remained at her side, but it was unclear as to whom supported whom. They were beyond speaking and trudged along in silence.

Imogene Lochner remained hidden inside her wagon and was seen only on occasion when she stuck her head through the opening and called, "Jessie? Where are you, Jessie? Mary, you and Jessie, get home, you hear?" Her husband, marching along beside the wagon, kept his head down and said nothing.

That night the party had moved away from the river and there was no water to be found. Those who had been resourceful enough to collect water in bottles shared it with their companions, but there was only enough to wet the lips and tease the throat. There was no firewood, therefore no cooking, and the meal consisted of cold tidbits. Paulette altered one of her gowns by the silvery light of the moon, letting out the waist for comfort, cutting the hem so it hung above the ankles of her boots, and stitching up the center of the skirt so that it resembled men's trousers, or, more exactly, the ballooned pants she had seen in books of Arabian tales. Her silk hat she flung into the bushes.

She spread her bedroll beneath the Lochner wagon. Exhaustion weighed heavily upon her and tortured her body. She longed for sleep, yet the howling of wolves filled her with terror and made sleep impossible. Imogene Lochner, her husband having deserted her for the peace of distance, carried on a conversation with herself, her dead sister, and son, then finally cried herself into a stupor. The mules, as terrified by the wolves as Paulette, whinnied and whined and stomped their hooves into the thudding sand. An owl hooted, then flew overhead with wings flapping, and

a night hawk screeched in frustration at having mis-
calculated its attack and lost a meal. The night fog
rolled in, silencing everything within its eerie blanket
of whiteness, including the snoring of the men. Everyone except Paulette; she felt numb, physically and
mentally, and lay staring at the underside of the
wagon until the whiteness of the fog grew thinner,
brighter, and she knew the sun was near rising.

The second day there was not the slightest drop of
water. Some of the men, panicking, licked the sweat
off the mules' bodies; they even fought for this privi-
lege. The Indian guides seemed unaffected—and un-
concerned.

"The heathen bastards," Jean-Paul murmured.
"Couldn't they take us to water?"

By noon the rush of water could be heard in the
distance. Even those most exhausted hastened their
steps. When they reached the creek, men jumped into
the cold water, clothes and all, and only Jean-Paul's
restraint stopped Paulette from joining them. He
scooped water into his hands and held them for her
to drink; she drank deeply, the cold liquid burning
her parched throat.

"Oh, dear God," she moaned, "I can't go through
this again. "Is there anything we can fill with water?
Anything? I can survive without food, but without
water . . ."

Imogene Lochner stepped up beside her, bent over,
and dunked a jug into the creek. "Jessie needs a
drink," she murmured, "and Mary, poor dear, says
she'll not make it farther without water." The woman
carried the jug back to the wagon and disappeared
inside.

"Dear God," Jean Paul murmured. "This is all madness. For a few handfuls of gold, we're all driving
ourselves insane." Not having drunk until Paulette's
thirst had been quenched, he dropped to his stomach
and submerged his face beneath the surface of the
water.

The mules, unattended, waded into the stream and

instantly the water was muddied. The men did not seem to object; they continued to splash and cavort, filling their stomachs until the pain of satiation drove them onto the creek bank.

Jean-Paul helped Paulette back from the bank to escape collision with the men crawling from the water. "I'll bet they don't think of turning back for those left behind," he said.

"Left behind?" She was astounded. "I didn't know there were any left behind."

"At least four," he told her. "We're now assured of water and wood for fires, but they'll forget them—those unfortunate four. Such is the Christianity of men."

"Then we must . . ."

"No!" he said firmly. "We are not our brother's keeper. If you want to reach your fiancé, you will continue with the others."

"But surely we would not lose our way now," she protested.

He glared at her, anger in his eyes. "Would you know the way to Nigger Hill from here? No, and neither would I."

Zach Lochner stopped on his way to the wagon to check on his wife. He stared down at Paulette, his suspicions of the past vanishing; she was sunburned, her clothes only hinting at earlier riches. "Should you be awantin' to ride in the wagon, you're welcome," he said. "She's mad, my Imogene, but she's harmless." He moved on without waiting for her answer.

"Ride in the wagon," Jean-Paul demanded. "You'll not make it otherwise, and I can't . . . I can't support you any farther." He was so weak he could scarcely speak above a whisper. "I've done my job. I've found you . . . I've earned . . ." He closed his eyes in a deep sleep, from which Paulette could not awaken him to question his statements.

The wagon was cooler because of the covering, but at times the heat seemed preferable to Imogene Lochner's ravings. The woman was quite mad; one moment she would be conversing with her dead son and sister, and the next she would be bemoaning their deaths.

"Mary bloated before we could get her underground," she wept. "Her tiny stomach looked as if she'd been carryin' child for eight months. They covered her with cotton one of the women had brung along for dresses and shoveled the dirt on top. The weight of the dirt pulled the cotton from her face and her eyes were starin' up at me, askin' me questions I couldn't answer."

"Please, Mrs. Lochner," Paulette pleaded, "turn your thoughts elsewhere."

"You think I don't want to?" the woman screamed. Then, in a moment of control, she burst into tears and buried her face in her apron. "All for gold!" she wailed. "The gold of Satan! For this I've given my son and sister!"

The trail moved upward, and the ascent was rugged. The one road was sand-covered and pitched at a forty-five-degree angle. Paulette, fearing the wagon would overturn, coaxed Imogene Lochner outside and they walked alongside.

The wondrous sight of the diggings finally came into view. Miners, as thick as ants, worked their claims along the river.

"A bustling colony," Jean-Paul said at Paulette's elbow. Men with picks and shovels tore at the earth of the riverbanks; few had interest enough to glance up at the newcomers. "And welcome to Nigger Hill," Jean-Paul murmured bitterly.

Paulette moved from miner to miner, asking for Mrs. Mason and her son, Jamie, but no one had heard the young man's name. "Probably moved on," one of the miners told her. "They come and go here. Never bother to ask a man's name 'cause I know I'll not likely see him again."

"Why is it called Nigger Hill?" Jean-Paul inquired.

" 'Cause a nigger found the first vein," was his answer, "a damned nigger from the South who'd no right to be here, let alone find somethin' that he didn't deserve."

"And what happened to that man?" Jean-Paul queried.

"Was hanged, I've heard," the miner told him.

Again, Jean-Paul murmured, "So much for Christianity." He turned to Paulette. "Are you sure you want to go on to Hangtown? I wouldn't venture it will be any better than here."

"I must," she told him. "My fiancé's there, and I've already come this far."

"Me, I'm turning back," he told her. "There are other ways to make one's fortune. I'm not an animal that can burrow in the ground and forsake humanitarianism. Look at them—they're like an army of moles." He kissed her hand, then her cheek. "We'll meet again," he assured her. "It's destined."

She stood on the riverbank and watched him go— the handsome Frenchman who had protected and looked after her, but whom she had never been capable of bringing herself to trust. His odd statements and questions during the journey flooded over her, and she had the compulsion to call him back and question his purpose, but at that moment Imogene Lochner tugged at her arm and implored her to help her find the lost Jessie and Mary.

There was no available cabin for them to spend the night. Paulette again slept in the wagon with Imogene, waking up during the night and discovering the woman gone. She rose, pulling a quilt around her, and went in search of Zach. She found him sleeping on the creek bank and told him his wife was missing.

"Searchin' for Jessie and Mary, I suppose," he said sleepily.

It took prodding to fully awaken him.

"Only harm can come to her," she convinced him. "We must find her."

Zach Lochner awakened his friends from the original overland party, and with torches alight, they began their search for his missing wife.

It was dawn before they found her.

It appeared that she had stumbled off an embankment and struck her head on the stones along the water's edge. Her skull had been opened and she lay in a pool of blood, eyes wide and staring. Zach stared down at her for a very long while; there was no compassion or sadness in his expression, no sense of loss. Simply, he said, "I hope the madness drained from her 'fore she went to meet Jessie and her sister."

The following morning half the party that had arrived at Nigger Hill moved on toward Hangtown.

Paulette had bought the Lochner wagon. Never having reined horses in her life, she was forced to hire the Malay youth to drive for her.

"I don't want no pay," he told her, "only the wagon and team when you've no longer any need of them."

She readily agreed to his demand.

# Chapter Eight

FROM THE hill above, Hangtown appeared very little different from Nigger Hill. It was late afternoon and the sun would set within half an hour; still, the miners worked diligently along the creek bank.

"Like a colony of ants," one of the men observed.

Paulette climbed down from the wagon and surveyed the winding creek and its busy miners. Her distance was too great to pick Dester out from the others, but the knowledge that he was there, one of them, unsuspecting she was among the new arrivals, excited her. She thought of her appearance for the first time in days and climbed back into the wagon and searched her belongings for a mirror. The reflection that stared back at her shocked her. The sun had turned her skin to a dark cocoa coloring; had she still been in the South, she would have been taken for a mulatto. She pushed back her black hair and tried to make some order of it. Then, sending her driver to the creek for a pitcher of water to wash herself, she stripped away her altered and tattered gown and waited in her slips. The men in the party had already gone below, eager to learn from the miners of their luck or misfortunes at the diggings. She knew word of her arrival would spread quickly and half-expected Dester to suddenly appear and throw back the wagon's flap.

Washed and changed, but still feeling grimy and unclean, she emerged from the wagon. The sun was peeking over the distant hills, golden, about to disappear for the night. The warmth of the day was quickly dwindling and there was a chill in the air. She reached back into the wagon for her shawl. Below, the miners continued to assault the creek bank, taking advantage of the last of the light. Fires had been lit at irregular distances along the water's edge; smoke, turned golden by the setting sun, drifted lazily into the sky. The smell of cooking filled her nostrils.

"Me take wagon and team now?" the Malay youth inquired.

"Not quite yet," she told him. "Don't be impatient." But she herself was impatient. Dester was down there somewhere along the creek.

She gathered up her skirts and made her way down the narrow pathway, aware that the miners had stopped their digging and were watching her descent. The shacks were on the opposite side of the creek and she was forced to cross a rickety bridge of planks and tree stumps. It reminded her of her first crossing of Maiden Lane; so, too, did the looks of lust reflected on the miners' faces. *Well, they'll have to adjust,* she thought, *and so will I. I'm here and there'll be no sending me away, even though Dester might choose to do so, because I can't be expected to make my way alone back to Stockton.*

The first miner she approached was leaning heavily on his shovel, staring up at her on the edge of the bridge. He was spattered with mud, the color of his beard scarcely distinguishable beneath the layers of dirt and grime. He smiled and revealed uneven, chipped teeth.

"Do you know Mr. Dester Granville?" she inquired, forcing a smile.

"Aye," he answered. "I know a Granville. Speaks with an accent and uses fancy words?"

"That must be him," she reasoned aloud. "Could you direct me to him?"

Two other miners stepped up to listen. One, a small man with slitted eyes and a scar across his cheek, kept his eyes lowered, a smile playing about his lips. The other was a black man, tall, his hair cropped close to his skull; shirtless, his body rippled with hard muscles.

It was the black man who answered her, his voice telling her he was from the South. "Mr. Granville works downriver," he said. "He don't come back 'til after the sun's set. Comes and goes in the dark." He pointed to a shack on a slight incline. "That's his place, if you wants to wait for him."

*His place* was built of logs and crate sidings, with a minute, paneless window covered in sacking. The roof was sagging and appeared ready to collapse. A metal chimney protruded from a side wall; that, too, leaned precariously. There was no porch, only a tree stump wedged into the ground as a step. The door was made of small saplings, stripped and bound together with cord.

"Wouldn't mind findin' that waitin' in my shack," one of the miners whispered.

The black man stepped forward and offered Paulette his hand to assist her off the bridge. "I'll see you to Mr. Granville's place," he told her and eyed the whispering miners with a look of defiance. "My name's Elisha, ma'am. I consider myself fortunate to call Mr. Granville my friend."

It was good, she thought, to find Dester practicing his free thinking by making a friend of this man. "Tell me about him, Elisha. Is he well? Has he had any luck since last I've heard from him?"

"No luck to speak of," Elisha answered. "As for his health, ma'am, I can't answer. We don't speak of our health, or our aches and pains. Mr. Granville's teachin' me my letters." Elisha's eyes narrowed, and his grasp of her hand tightened as he led her up the incline. "In Georgia that would've made him a criminal—teachin' a nigger."

"Yes, in Louisiana, too," Paulette murmured. But

that had never stopped Dester; he had organized a
school for the slave children without his parents'
knowledge, so most of the younger blacks at Plantation Bend both read and wrote. To Elisha, she said,
"Then you're from Georgia?"

"Yes, ma'am."

"Mr. Granville's great-grandparents were from Savannah," she said, "and so were his grandparents.
They settled outside New Orleans and carved a plantation out of the wilderness."

"He told me," Elisha said. "Told me also 'bout the
fight with his father." His eyes narrowed again. "I told
him he was fightin' a battle that should be left to my
own people and that sent him off, sure did. He lec-
tured me 'til we was both too tired to mine 'til noon
next day."

Yes, Dester loved to lecture, she thought, especially on the subject of slavery and the injustices of
the white men.

Elisha helped her onto the step and pushed the
door open. "I'll be nearby," he said darkly, " 'til Mr.
Granville gets back. I wouldn't go out, ma'am, if I
was you—not 'til he's explained how things are here
at Hangtown. All I'll say is that it ain't no place for
a lady."

"Then there are no other women here?" she asked.

"Only one, ma'am, and she's stronger than most
men. Could break a man's jaw with one punch, so
she's not much bothered." Nodding his farewell, Elisha
moved away.

Paulette stood at the shack's door and hesitated
entering. The smell from inside had rushed out to assault her nostrils. Shuddering, she went inside, left the
door ajar, and pulled the sacking away from the small
window. She lit the lamp and inhaled the odor of the
oil, preferable to the smell of damp bedclothes and
quilts. The shack's interior was large enough only for
a pallet in one corner, a pot-bellied stove, a single
chair, and a small table. Muddied clothes were strewn
about the floor. Books were stacked beside the pallet,

and the corner of her last letter protruded from one of the books; it was the letter in which she had pleaded with Dester to return to San Francisco.

There was kindling and wood stacked in a crate beside the stove. She had never started a fire in her life, but she had watched the slaves do it often enough. The pitch flared in her hand; she flung it into the stove and began adding pieces one at a time until a sufficient blaze was going to toss on the larger blocks. Satisfied, she closed the metal door and instantly the shack was filled with smoke.

"The damper, ma'am!" Elisha shouted from the door. "Open the damper!"

Embarrassed, she reached for the damper and turned it. The smoke ceased pouring from the lid of the stove. "Thank you, Elisha," she said.

Elisha moved away from the shack again. Paulette went to the door and saw him sitting on the knoll near the shack, waiting, as he had promised, until Dester returned. She felt secure with his being there. The sun had set and only streaks of red remained in the sky. Fires now blazed all along the creek bank. She could hear laughter and music and smell the men's food cooking. Peaceful, she thought, and probably not nearly so dangerous as Elisha thinks—or Dester, who had written to her of the miners' deviltry.

She stepped back and closed the door against the cold. There was a small shaving mirror hanging from a nail. The glass was distorted and she could not see to examine her appearance. She collected the scattered clothes and piled them in one corner. She dusted the table and drew the quilts up on the unmade pallet. Then she sat down in the chair, stared at the shack's interior, and fought to keep from breaking into tears. The slaves at Plantation Bend had lived better. She found her understanding of Dester slipping away. It had been grand thinking of him fighting for a cause, for his own financial independence, but she could not comprehend his living under these conditions. If she proved incapable of convincing him to return to

Louisiana—or even San Francisco—she had determined to stay with him. But could she live like this, worse than a slave?

Her exhaustion from the day's trip weighed heavily upon her. When the minutes passed and Dester had not returned, she stretched out on the pallet and turned her face into the damp, smelly pillow. Outside, the music from the campfires was joined by the neighing of horses and the barking of a dog. Two men were shouting at one another, their words angry but unclear. She slept without meaning to and did not hear Dester stomping the mud from his boots on the stump outside the door.

When first she looked up at him, she thought him a stranger. A scream caught in her throat; then, seeing his eyes, pale and loving, her scream turned to a cry of joy. She clung to him, kissing and receiving his kisses, whimpering his name over and over again.

She would have continued to clutch at his neck, to kiss him, if he had not suddenly forced her back on the pallet and stepped away from her. She stared at him questioningly.

His hair had been bleached even blonder by the sun so that it shone almost colorless in the light of the lamp. His beard, too, was bleached, pale against his tanned skin. His eyes were bluer than she remembered, burning now with mixed emotions. The clothing he wore was similar to what she had seen on the other miners, odd for him, who had always dressed so elegantly—the coarse overalls and heavy woolen shirt, both spattered with mud. His trousers legs were tucked into his boots, the boots laced tightly and covered with mud.

"You shouldn't have come here," he said darkly.

She had expected the rebuke, but not so soon.

"I wrote you of the conditions here. It won't be safe to leave you during the day when I go to work my claim. You should have waited in San Francisco."

"I couldn't wait any longer," she told him. She pushed herself up from the pallet, moved to him, and buried her face against the coarse front of his overalls. "Besides, I have news from home, news I didn't want to put in a letter."

"Don't tell me of home," he said, "not now." He lay his face against the top of her head. Holding her tightly, he lifted her so that their faces met. "Let me bathe," he said, "and then I can welcome you properly." He kissed her, set her down on her feet, and left the shack with a towel thrown over his shoulder.

Paulette watched him from the window. It was difficult to follow his shadow as he descended to the creek. She heard men speaking to him. She heard: ". . . prettiest woman I've laid eyes on in months." And she heard his warning reply that he'd kill any man who tried to touch her.

The flickering light of a fire caught him as he peeled off his clothes; his chest and back and arms were as deeply tanned as his face, his legs and slim buttocks pale, where the sun had not touched him. He waded into the icy water and dunked himself. When he emerged someone was waiting for him on the creek bank. Paulette caught her breath when she heard a woman say, "I hear your woman's here, Granville. Damned silly thing for a man to do, bringing a lady to a place like Hangtown."

"I didn't bring her," Dester answered with an edge of anger. "She came on her own."

"Then it was damned silly of her," the woman said, not turning away from his nakedness. "You remember the last time a woman came to Hangtown? Amy Saunders? With her man, too, she was. And ugly as sin. It got her man killed, and her . . . she'd been better off if they'd killed her along with him."

Dester was toweling himself dry, as unembarrassed by his nakedness as the woman. "Paulette's not like her," he said. "Amy Saunders may have been with her man, but she was no more than a whore."

"Can't blame the woman, her bein' ugly and not accustomed to men chasin' her like she was a great beauty." The woman stepped back closer to the fire and Paulette saw her bulk silhouetted against the flames. She was enormous in size, almost as tall as Dester, her shoulders broader. "I hear your woman is a beauty. That true?"

"It's true," Dester answered as he pulled on his trousers. "And she's a lady. Any man I catch even sniffing around her will have me to deal with." He slung the towel over his shoulder and picked up his shirt and boots.

"May be like Amy Saunders," the woman said. "Five of the bastards jumped her husband while the others . . . goddamned evil bastards!" She followed Dester up the incline toward the shack. "Well, let me meet your woman," she said. "Bein' the only other female at Hangtown, we might as well be acquainted."

Paulette stepped away from the window, not wanting Dester to see that she had been watching, and listening.

The woman who followed him into the shack was a shock to Paulette. Not only was she larger in stature than Dester, but she had a great, large head, the hair cropped as short as a man's. Her arms, protruding from the rolled-up sleeves of a shirt, were thick and hard. Her breasts were heavy, sagging, obviously without the restriction of undergarments. "Well, like they say, she's a beauty," she said in her deep, masculine voice. "Hello, my dear. Charity's my name." She extended her hand, which completely engulfed Paulette's. "I'd say welcome to Hangtown, but as I've told Granville, you shouldn't be here. It's no place for a woman."

Dester smiled at Paulette, but he said nothing.

"But you're a woman," Paulette objected.

Charity threw back her massive head in laughter. "I'm a woman, dear, but I've been raised by and have lived with nothin' but men all my life. My father never wanted girl children, and he had three—Faith, Hope, and Charity. He raised us all like boys, bless his wicked, departed soul. There's no man in this camp who can take me in an honest fight, and very few who aren't afraid to consider challengin' me dishonestly.

I've a good Irish temper and everyone knows it. I
don't expect to be treated different 'cause I'm a
woman. I work my own claim and ask no favors. I
don't give 'em, either, unless I've a mind to." She
winked one of her heavily hooded eyes.

Charity stepped back, almost through the door because of the smallness of the shack, and, placing a
long, callused finger thoughtfully against her chin, then
examined Paulette carefully. "Well, there's no way
we're goin' to make you look ugly, dear, but we've got
to do somethin' about your clothes. It'll be hard
enough with the miners seein' you sashayin' 'round,
but them silks and frills would prove your undoin'."
She turned to Dester. "I'll find her somethin' that'll
show her off less," she said, " 'til you've had time to
talk some sense in her head. Nice meetin' you, dear."
Without waiting for Paulette to reply, she turned and
maneuvered her bulk through the doorway and was
gone.

Laughing, Dester came to Paulette and drew her in
to his arms. "You've met our famous Charity," he
said.

Paulette felt the heat of his chest against her cheek.
The familiar scent of him, well remembered on long
nights when she had lay awake with longing, filled her
nostrils and awakened her desire. She pressed against
him, clutching at his back, and turning her face up to
meet his lips.

But he did not kiss her. His pale eyes were now expressing anger. "You'll leave with the next party on its
way to Stockton," he said. "Charity's right. The men
here have been without women for a long while. The
hunt for gold keeps them busy during the day, but at
night . . ."

"But you'll be with me at night," she protested.

"I can't be with you every moment." He moved to
the stove and stroked the coals angrily. "Their fever
for riches will be forgotten when they see a woman
like you, even if Charity manages to hide your body

in rags. We had another woman here, Amy Saunders. She came with her husband . . ."

"I heard," Paulette told him. "Your voices carried from the creek bank. You also said Amy Saunders was a whore."

He turned, unaccustomed to hearing her use such words. For a brief moment, she thought the anger was going to leave his pale blue eyes. But when he spoke, it was with determination. "Even though I've been obsessed by no woman other than you since we were young, I found myself looking at Amy Saunders. I found myself wanting her."

Paulette said nothing. She had not thought of Dester with other women, wanting other women. Then the memory of Jeremiah and the night in Panama flooded over her and she turned away, her cheeks coloring.

Dester rose from in front of the stove and slammed the metal door. "Tomorrow I'll ask around about those planning to leave," he said. "There are always those who become discouraged quickly and leave the camps. Fools, most of them, without any grit and unwilling to suffer the hardships. If I find a party that's suitable, you'll be on your way to Stockton."

"When you hear the news from home," she began, but he took her hand, silencing her, and led her to the pallet.

"Not yet," he murmured. "We've time enough for that."

He helped her with the buttons of her gown, then picked the shimmering heap from the floor around her ankles when it fell and tossed it onto the chair back. He watched as she removed her undergarments. Then, thinking of Charity's warning, he stepped quickly to the lamp and turned out the flame. He shed his trousers and crawled onto the pallet beside her. The moonlight was filtering through the cracks in the door; he could see the paleness of her body, the dark crescents of her breasts, and he thought before pulling her to him that tomorrow he must cover the door and make a shutter for the single window to protect her from spying eyes.

"Dester, I love you," she murmured. "I can't be separated from you again. I can't! There's so much . . ."

He pressed his mouth to hers, silencing her. His hands roamed freely over her body, savoring, teasing —her and himself—until he thought he would scream with desire for her. He took her quickly, more brutally than he intended. Then they lay cuddled in each other's arms listening to the music from the campfires and the wind howling around the shack.

She told him of Vienna's letter, of his father's illness, and Katrina's shame over Tom's imprisonment. "They need you now, Dester, unlike they've needed you in the past."

He lay silently for several moments and she thought he had fallen asleep beside her. Then he said, "That's why you came? To convince me to return to Plantation Bend?"

"But you must," she said, believing it. "You must forget your differences with your father. He may be dying, or already dead, God forbid. What will happen to the plantation if you don't return? What will happen to your mother and Katrina and Bella?"

"Katrina will shed her shame. Both she and Bella will be taken care of when they find the right men," he said quietly. "My sisters and I have never been close; you know that. From the time we were children, I only had time for you. Remember then how it was —when they first brought you from the Favière plantation to live with us? It was always you and me, Paulette." He raised himself suddenly to his elbows and stared down at her in the moonlight. "You're away from the plantation now. I have no reason to return."

She was both shocked and angry. "But what about Vienna and Clabe?"

"And the plantation itself? You forgot to include Plantation Bend." He fell back against the pillows. "I don't give a damn about the plantation," he said. "I loathe what it stands for, slavery. My father and I will never bury those differences. I came to the gold fields in the hope of making my own fortune and fighting the very things he believes in so strongly."

"But there are other ways of fighting," she said. "I was talking to a black man named Elisha when I arrived today. He told me you were teaching him his letters. You used to organize the teaching of the slaves at Plantation Bend, remember? That's a way of fighting, by helping to educate the slaves."

"It's not enough. More can be done with money. Almost everything can be accomplished with money, good or evil."

"But you'll one day be the master of Plantation Bend," she protested. "Then you can fight." She shuddered to think of Clabe's reaction to that statement, the use of his money to fight the causes he so cherished. Father and son, she thought hopelessly, there would be no peace between them even after death. "Your mother needs . . ."

"My mother is a strong woman," he interrupted, "perhaps stronger than both my father and myself. Should the need arise, she could run Plantation Bend by herself." He heard Paulette's intake of breath and added, "Why not? My grandmother Zelma did. It was she who amassed the Granville fortune. No, Paulette, you'll not get me back to Plantation Bend. I'll either make my fortune here in the gold fields—or I'll die here."

"Don't talk like that!"

"But it's true," he assured her. "So, you see, my love, your journey out here was a waste." He turned and kissed her forehead. "In those aspects, anyway."

She knew he wanted her again. But, trembling, she restrained him. "I also came to be with you," she said, "to marry you and bear your children."

"There will be time for marriage and children," he murmured, pushing away her hands and lowering himself onto her. "Let's make the most of the few days we'll have together."

*You'll never get me to leave you again,* she silently vowed. *If you refuse to accept your responsibility to your family—if you insist on staying here, dying here —then I'll stay here and die with you.* She brushed her lips against the mat of blond hair on his chest and dug her fingernails into the hard flesh of his back. She gave herself to him, not fighting his new brutality, understanding that he was as starved for her as she was for him.

When he moved off her, spent and exhausted, she cradled his head in the crook of her arm, caressing him long after he slept, and his heavy breathing drowned out the howling of the wind.

# Chapter Nine

"MEN," CHARITY said with venom. "I've been raised 'round them, raised like one of 'em, and I still don't understand 'em. I can out-fight, out-work, and out-drink any man I've met." She rammed her shovel deep into the earth of the creek bank and hoisted the dirt into the sluice box. "Your Dester, now, he's a real gentleman, but he's still got that masculine quirk of all men." She motioned to Paulette. "All right, dear, the water now."

Paulette dunked her pail into the creek and emptied it into the sluice box. The dirt and small stones were washed out the opposite end.

"Men think a woman's place is in the kitchen or bedroom," Charity went on. "I can understand Dester wantin' you to go back to San Francisco. Hangtown's no place for the likes of you. But him not lettin' you work his claim with him while you're here, that's beyond me—unless maybe he's jealous."

Paulette straightened, her back aching from constant bending and lifting pails of water. "Jealous of what?"

"Jealous 'cause maybe he don't want you there when he strikes it rich—*if* he strikes it rich," the older woman said. "You said he'd left his family 'cause he wanted to make it on his own, didn't want to touch what was his father's. Maybe he feels that your bein' here if he hits a rich vein would mean that it wasn't all his, that you'd share in it." She shook her massive head of close-cropped hair. "Like I said, men are among the strangest of God's creatures. Me, I don't mind your helpin' me. More water there, dearie."

Paulette emptied another bucket into the sluice box. She had offered to assist Charity because remaining locked in the shack had been more than she could bear. In the four days she had been in Hangtown, only Charity, Elisha, and Dester had spoken to her. The other men, she reasoned, kept their distance because of Dester's threats. Still, she was aware of them watching her, lusting for her. She never felt as though she were alone, even when undressing at night—always she had the sensation of eyes upon her.

Charity began shaking the sluice box from side to side, forcing out the remaining water. "The men," she said, "are talkin'. They're sayin' Dester don't look after you properly, like leavin' Elisha to stand guard when I take you back to the shack. They say a nigger shouldn't be allowed that close to a white woman."

"Elisha's as much a gentleman as Dester," Paulette said.

"I know that," the big woman said. "What you've got to understand is what the men are really sayin', and that is: Are you looked after well enough to keep them from tryin' somethin'?" She bent and ran her palms carefully along the bottom of the sluice box. "But you're bein' properly looked after," she said. "Elisha and me, we're seein' to that when your man's not 'round. Damn." She straightened. "Nothin'," she said. "It looks like it's goin' to be another dry day. Not a speck of color there."

Paulette sighed quietly. This was the fourth spot they'd tried that morning, Charity hoisting the sluice box on her shoulders and Paulette carrying the shovel and pails.

"We'll try down a bit farther," Charity said. "Have to watch it, though. We don't want to wander into that bastard Crimmon's claim. He's a mean one. He killed one miner for takin' a single shovel of earth from inside his boundary." She lifted the sluice box as though it were weightless and waited until Paulette had gathered the shovel and pails. "Come along, dear. We're wastin' light."

Paulette trudged along behind. "How far down-creek is Dester's claim?"

" 'Bout a mile farther," Charity told her. "But he's forbidden me to take you there, and don't even think of goin' on your own. Strange man, your Dester. Most men would want you with them. Ah, well . . ." She moved about thirty yards, set up the sluice box again, and began to dig into the bank.

Paulette was miserable under the intense heat of the sun. She was grateful when Charity told her to go up on the bank and "sit for a spell." She stretched out in the shade of some scrub, resting on her elbows. Charity had made clothes for her of the same coarse fabric used in the men's overalls; it was uncomfortable when it rubbed against her skin, but she admitted the absence of skirts and slips was a relief. The only difference between her clothes and the men's was that Charity had boiled the fabric in roots to dye it a deep brown coloring. The trousers legs were wide and almost looked like a skirt when she was standing. Bella would like these, she thought; then, thinking of Bella reminded her of home and she felt the depression settling over her again.

Daily she had spoken to Dester about returning, but he remained stubbornly untalkative, repeating what he had told her the night of her arrival. She knew he was questioning the other miners about whether any were returning to San Francisco and she knew he was still determined for her to leave. She felt it was more than his fear for her safety, but she could not pinpoint his reasons.

If it had not been for Charity and Elisha, Paulette would have gone mad at the camp. Dester left her before sunup and returned after sundown. The time they spent together was always inside the cabin; he never allowed her to sit at the campfires and listen to the men singing or watch them playing cards. When a man even came near the shack, Dester would tense up and not relax until he had passed. "They're crude savages," he would tell her. "Don't smile or talk to any of them." And so she was lonely, would have been lonelier if she had not taken to teaching Elisha his letters and helping Charity with her claim. Still, she did not want to return to San Francisco, did not want to abandon Dester. They had been parted too long, and she had gone through too much to be reunited with him to leave him again.

Since there was no minister, marriage was out of the question. She found herself watching all newcomers to the mines, hoping one would be Reverend Shirr; she knew he was roaming the countryside, preaching and searching for gold. Also, he would undoubtedly have news of Mrs. Mason and her son. But none of the newcomers resembled the reverend.

She was so lost in thought that she failed to hear the warning.

It was Charity, screaming at her, that brought her back to the present and the reality of the rattling. The older woman was standing below the bank, the visibility of her bulk hidden behind the dirt, the eyes in her massive head wide with alarm. "Don't move, dearie!" she shouted. "Don't move a muscle!"

But Paulette moved her eyes and she saw the rattlesnake out of the corners, saw it coiled, its fangs white in the sunlight, its ringed tail shimmering, rattling. She wanted to scream, to fling herself away from the creature, but fear held her. Perspiration beaded her brow and dripped into her eyes; her heart beat against her rib cage and echoed in her ears.

Charity had disappeared from view. She reappeared and raised a rifle to her shoulder. "Good girl," she said quietly. "Don't move now. Don't make the little bastard strike you." Her finger squeezed gently on the trigger. There was an explosion, and the rattlesnake, just lunging its head forward, was blown backward with the blast.

Paulette found her voice. Her scream echoed through the hills and along the creek bank. She scrambled to her feet and put distance between herself and the dead snake. She literally fell over the embankment into Charity's arms.

"Now, now," Charity said, "it's over and done with and you ain't been bitten." She pushed Paulette to her feet. "We're losin' light," she said for the twentieth time that day. "Grab the shovel and pails. We'll move on a piece. Can't go back to camp without findin' somethin'. Those bastards will laugh at me. Can't have a man laughin' at me."

Paulette, shovel and pails in her hands, moved along behind her, but this time so closely that if Charity had stopped, she would have collided with her.

It was the middle of the afternoon before Charity stepped back from the sluice box and clapped her hands together. "We've done it, dearie!" she announced. "Come! Look here!"

Paulette stepped up to the sluice box and saw the gold glistening along its bottom.

"That, my dear, is what this is all about," Charity said. "There's at least fifty dollars there, maybe more. Pray to God we've hit a vein that'll prove worthwhile."

Paulette looked at her and saw the same expression she had seen on so many of the men's faces. Gold fever, she thought. She dreaded seeing that expression on Dester's face.

Charity instructed Paulette in the use of a gold pan. "Pannin'," the big woman said, "is the oldest method used by the miners. Here, take the pan. I'll show you how."

Paulette took the shallow, slope-sided pan. They were knee-deep in water, their clothes tied around their thighs by cords; the water was freezing cold, but Charity did not seem to notice. Her excitement had grown since finding the shiny gold deposits in the bottom of her sluice box. Paulette was fighting to keep her teeth from chattering.

"Shovel in gravel and mud from the creek bed," Charity continued. She scooped a mixture into the pan and Paulette bent with its weight. "Now, bend down and let the water run over the pan," Charity instructed. "No, don't go that deep." She took the pan back and showed Paulette how to work off the excess stones and plant material. "Gently," she said and turned the pan with precision until all but a fine, dark pyrite remained. "The gold's heavier. It'll stay in the bottom, if you catch the right semi-rotatin' motion. Here, you try it. I'll get back to the sluice box."

Paulette took the pan and attempted to do as Charity had instructed. She worked the pan in a to-and-fro motion until finally nothing remained on its bottom except a few flecks she instinctively knew were gold. She started to call out to Charity, but she decided against it. Since finding gold in the sluice box, Charity had somehow changed. She had wanted Paulette away from the box, had wanted no assistance—as if she alone should pick out the small nuggets. Paulette removed the gold flecks with the tips of her fingers and transferred them into a small bottle. So little, she thought, for so much work. The process of working one pan had taken almost half an hour.

When, on the second pan, she found a nugget of considerable size, she stopped, held it up to the light, and stared at it, wondering why she, unlike the others, felt no elation. She considered carefully and decided no change had come over her; her eyes had not dilated, as Charity's had done, and her expression had not altered. Perhaps, she decided, she was immune to gold fever. She put the nugget with the gold flecks and continued to rotate the pan more out of a sense of duty than to find more gold. Her hands had turned red and felt numb; her bare feet and the lower parts of her legs were numb also. It was mid-afternoon and two hours of daylight remained.

Charity was completely ignoring her, caught up in working her sluice box. The big woman worked like a demon, shoveling gravel and mud into the box and washing away the excess with pails of water. Despite the cold, there was sweat on her brow.

Paulette tried another pan, sloughing off the first debris.

Both women were so intent that they did not see the man approaching along the creek bank. He stopped, watching them, and squatted with his rifle across his knees. Behind him, his mule, reins loose, stood chomping on the high blades of grass. There was an expression in the man's eyes that no one would take for anything but lust. He had been in the mining camps for the past seven months and, except for one trip to Stockton, where he had visited the professionals, he had not seen a woman. The flashes of Paulette's slim, pale legs excited him and removed all thoughts of gold from his mind. He stared at her and considered the risks in taking what he wanted; then he turned his attention to Charity. The only men in camp who had approached her had been beaten out of any sense of desire. Of course, he could shoot the big bitch, but then he'd have to kill the girl, too—after he'd finished with her. Justice at Hangtown was swift. If caught, he'd be hanged before sundown—that is, if Granville didn't get to him first.

He was still considering the possibilities when Paulette glanced up and saw him. She read the expression on his face instantly and the gold pan fell from her hands and was carried away by the current. Splashing toward Charity, she called the big woman's name.

Charity was alerted by the panic in Paulette's voice. Even before turning, she had reached for her rifle and had it to her shoulder. When she spun around she held the man in her rifle's sights. "It's you, then, is it, Crimmon?" she said, her voice deep and threatening. "What're you doin' here on my claim?"

Crimmon stood and casually stretched his legs. "Just passing, Charity," he answered. "Just passing. No need for your going and shooting me for that, is there?"

"It's somethin' you'd most likely do if someone sneaked up on you when you were minin'," Charity said. She lowered the rifle from her shoulder but kept it pointing and ready. She turned to Paulette, huddled at her side. "He say somethin' to you?"

Paulette told her he had not. Afraid Charity was going to shoot the man, she reconsidered what she had seen on his face . . . thought perhaps her fear had made her see what had not been there. Crimmon was ugly enough to have scared her without his look of lust. He was tall, gaunt, with bushy, black hair and eyebrows that arched above beady eyes. He had a red birthmark on the right side of his face that reached from his cheekbone to his chin—a mark the slaves at Plantation Bend would call "The Devil's Sign." There was a slight hump on his back and he stood at a bend to compensate for it. Now, smiling at Charity, he showed teeth that were chipped, uneven, and stained by tobacco.

"Uglier than the mule behind him," Charity murmured for only Paulette to hear, "and twice as mean. If you ever see him in camp, stay far away from him." Louder, she said, "All right, Crimmon, move on! You've gawked long enough. This lady's got a man, as you well know. Neither he nor I take kindly to her bein' scared witless by the likes of you."

Laughing, Crimmon took up the mule's reins and gave them a brutal tug. The beast neighed in pain and protest. "I'm going!" Crimmon shouted. "Had any luck, Charity?"

"Only fool's gold," the big woman answered and gave Paulette a warning glance not to contradict her. "He might not risk his life for a romp with you," she murmured, "but he'd cut both our throats if he thought we'd found more than a thousand dollars in gold."

They watched Crimmon leave, Charity with her rifle still positioned near her shoulder for firing.

"What an evil-looking man," Paulette said, relaxing as the bushes were separating him from them.

"He is the way he looks," Charity told her.

"Would he have really murdered us for a thousand dollars in gold?"

"Probably less," Charity answered and snorted her dislike. Then her eyes lighted up. "But we've more than that, dearie." She opened the leather pouch attached to her waist and emptied out a handful of nuggets. "At least two thousand dollars' worth here," she said proudly. "That's the biggest amount taken in one day at Hangtown in the past two months." Moving to a dry section of the creek bank, Charity settled her bulk on a boulder, her rifle leaning against her leg. "I think maybe I'd best ask Elisha to come in with me," she said, more to herself than to Paulette. "He's doin' poorly, and I need a man 'round if this strike proves as rich as it appears. Crimmon could have killed us then, taken what we had, and filed his own claim and nobody would be the wiser. It's hard to work alone sometimes, man or woman." She looked at Paulette thoughtfully, her heavily hooded eyes narrowing to mere slits. "You ever fire a pistol or a rifle?"

Paulette told her she had not. "Would you really have shot Crimmon if he hadn't moved on when you told him to?" she asked incredulously.

"I would have if he'd made a move toward his rifle, or toward you," the big woman assured her. "I think Crimmon was involved in what happened to Amy Saunders and her husband, but there wasn't any proof. If there had been, he'd have hanged with the rest." She sighed wearily and rubbed her red, callused hands together for warmth. "This ain't the city or no plantation," she said. "The men here ain't civilized. You can't treat 'em like they was. It's the gold, I guess. It does somethin' to a man's senses. You've seen the look in their eyes."

Paulette refrained from saying she had also seen that look in Charity's face when she had found the gold in her sluice box.

"I'm goin' to teach you how to use firearms," Charity announced, "that is, if you're willin'. Dester Gran-

ville wouldn't approve, so you'll have to keep it from
him. Still, there's no harm in a woman, even a lady
like yourself, knowin' how to protect herself. Who
knows how long you'll be here in Hangtown?"

Paulette's head shot up; her greatest fear for the
past days had been that Dester would come to her
and tell her she was to leave with a party deserting
the mines.

Charity was smiling; she understood. "When the
news of our find today gets spread 'round," she said,
"there won't be any parties leavin'. You'll have more
time to convince that man of yours to return home."
She pushed her bulk off the boulder. "All right," she
said, "let's get busy. We're losin' light."

Paulette could not understand Dester's reaction to
the news of Charity's success.

He had returned to the shack well after sunset, the
leather pouch tied to his belt almost empty. He was
exhausted, irritable, and silent. Taking his towel, he
had gone to the creek to bathe and had been gone a
particularly long while. When he returned she could
smell liquor on his breath.

"They tell me you and Charity brought in over
three thousand dollars in gold today," he said accus-
ingly. She was sitting in the single chair and he stood
over her, almost menacingly.

She regretted not having told him the news herself
before he had gone to bathe, but she had been hoping he would return in a better frame of mind. "We
were lucky," she told him. "Charity thinks it'll be a
rich strike."

Dester pushed his sun-bleached hair away from his
eyes with an impatient gesture. His expression was
unfathomable. "You and Charity . . . you wouldn't
have invented this good fortune because you knew a
party was leaving tomorrow?"

The accusation angered her. "I'm not accustomed
to lying," she answered, "even to get what I want."

He ignored the venom in her voice. "Women have been known to do worse."

"So have men!" She was exhausted, Charity having pushed until the last moments of light before quitting the sluice box. Then they had trekked back to the camp in the darkness, stumbling and tripping, and fearing each black clump of scrub was hiding Crimmon, who would leap out and attack her. "So have men!" she repeated. She tossed the shirt she had been sewing onto the floor beside the chair.

Dester glared at her. He had often seen her angry when they had been children—she had a fierce temper—but she had never unleashed her anger at him. He felt he had a right to question her—Charity's luck seemed too convenient. No party would leave Hangtown now, not for days, until every miner had tried his luck at equaling Charity's daily take. There would be more fights, more arguments; those running low on their grubstakes would turn to stealing, even claim-jumping. Every man would have to sleep with his pistol beside his head. He'd have to mine with one eye on the sluice box and another on the creek bank. He moved to the open door and stood with one arm resting on the frame, staring out at the campfires. There was more music tonight, more laughter—all because Charity and Paulette had come back into camp with a pouch full of gold.

What Dester would not admit to himself was that he was jealous. It should have been his strike and not that cow of a woman's. He wanted Paulette away from Hangtown not merely because of the danger, but because striking it rich with her present would somehow take away from his sense of personal achievement. He had always been secondary, even at Plantation Bend. The wealth had not been his, but his father's; when his father died, it would be inherited wealth—no sense of accomplishment there. And Paulette—she had been wealthy because of her circumstances. He would never admit to her the nagging satisfaction he had felt when she had told him of Tom's thievery. He wanted her to rely on him—he wanted to be master, he who detested slavery. Sending her back to San Francisco against her will would have inflated his sense of control over her. He loved her, but at the same time he realized he hated her also, hated her for the same reasons he loved her—her independent spirit and beauty and devotion to him. Her love made more demands on him than he thought himself capable of meeting. Perhaps, he thought darkly as he stared out at the glowing campfires, he was truly what his father had called him: *the spoiled, weak son of a wealthy plantation family.* Damn, he'd never forgive him for that—it was that more than their differences over the question of slavery that had driven him away. Paulette did not see that in him, that weakness he had always hidden from her. She felt his rebellion was strength; she thought his ideals were noble. She would never understand that his obsession with finding gold was yet another weakness, a means of proving himself through luck and not effort.

"Why do you want to send me away so desperately?" she asked from behind him.

"For your protection," he answered without turning.

She left the chair, moved up behind him, and ran her arms around his naked waist. "But Charity looks after me during the day . . . and Elisha, too," she told him. "I'm with you at night—and I'm safe." A vision of Crimmon passed through her mind, but she quickly put it aside.

"Amy Saunders had a husband," he said. "It didn't help her." He turned then, folding his arms around her. "No sense in arguing," he murmured. "There won't be a party leaving Hangtown until the yield of Charity's find peters out. You're here until then." He kissed her forehead gently. "But then you leave with the first party."

Not without you, she thought, but she said nothing.

"Perhaps you'd best not go out with Charity tomorrow," he said.

Paulette pulled back and stared up into his pale blue eyes. "But why? She needs me now. Unless Elisha joins her, she has no one."

"There will be those after her claim," he explained. "Two women on a claim that yields three thousand a day—no, you'd best stay with Elisha."

He sounded so adamant that she refrained from refusing. He left every morning before sunrise, and she would do as she thought best after he had gone. Besides, Elisha wouldn't be a fool; when Charity asked him to join her for a stake in her claim, he surely wouldn't refuse. His own claim yielded scarcely enough to pay his daily expenses.

Dester closed the door and bolted it. He went to the wall pegs, took down his pistol, checked it, and placed it under the pillow of their pallet. As he undressed, he said, "God willing, Charity's luck will spread down-creek. I'm due for luck. My money's almost gone."

That, then, is what's worrying him, Paulette thought. Money. "I've what's left of the draft Vienna sent me," she told him. "I left some with Chang and Miriam, as I told you, but the balance is in my handbag. You're welcome to it."

He continued to watch her closely as she let down her long black hair and twisted it into a braid for sleeping. He was silent, brooding, she thought, about taking money from her. But when she crawled into the pallet beside him, he said, "I'll repay you . . . after I've been as lucky as Charity."

She murmured her agreement and turned into his arms.

Late, when he was satiated, he slept soundly while she lay staring at the patterns of moonlight playing across the ceiling. There was something different about Dester, she thought, something strange. That had developed since he had left Plantation Bend. She tried to pinpoint that difference, but it continued to elude her. It gave her a sense of uneasiness.

Finally, too exhausted to puzzle further, she snuggled against his side and went to sleep.

Charity and Elisha remained by the campfire long after the others had retired. Charity was filled with the need to celebate her day's luck. The pouch with gold still hung from her waist. Elisha sat quietly, without glancing away fom the flames, chewing on the stem of an unlighted pipe. He had been very untalkative tonight; unusual, Charity thought. He was generally excited about practicing the lessons Granville had taught him.

Charity had already asked him about quitting his own claim and joining her. He had given her no definite answer.

"What about it?" she asked.

Elisha glanced up at her. "About what?" he asked.

"A question with a question," she murmured. "Granville didn't teach you that."

"Hasn't taught me at all since his woman arrived," Elisha told her.

"Is that what's botherin' you? That why you're so quiet?"

He shook his head, "No. But it's to do with Granville. I've been watchin' him, listenin' to what he says —maybe for the first time. I've been listenin' to Miss Paulette, too."

"Yes, so have I," Charity told him. "She's a pretty little thing, smart too, and stubborn. She knows what she wants."

"And what she wants is to get Mr. Granville to return home to Louisiana," Elisha said. "I never blamed him for stayin' away before; figured he knew what he was doin' and had a right to do it. Now I'm beginnin' to wonder if Mr. Granville knows as much 'bout hisself as he thinks. He's changed since Miss Paulette came. Sometimes when he looks at her . . ."

Elisha shrugged his huge shoulders and went back to staring into the fire.

"He's a different class than I," Charity said. "I never understood him before. I do understand that girl's in for some heartaches. What she sees in her man just ain't there." Charity reached for the jug between her feet and lifted it to her lips. The liquor burned as it went down her throat, but it settled warm and soothing in her stomach. "We can only do what we can," she said, wiping her mouth with the back of her hand. "Maybe if she talks him away from here . . . well, maybe they'll have a chance."

"Not likely," Elisha disagreed. "Mr. Granville, he's got more than just the gold fever. There's somethin' eatin' at his insides. I've seen it before, back home, in my master."

"Never heard you talk 'bout your slave days," Charity observed. "The men say you're a runaway. That so?"

"Yeah, that's so, Miss Charity. I run to keep from gettin' killed for somethin' I didn't do. When I started runnin' I just couldn't stop—ran 'til the land disappeared and I was starin' at the Pacific Ocean."

"That's how you came to California? Just runnin'? You didn't come just for the gold?"

"No, the gold came after," Elisha told her. "Some men in San Francisco hired me to help bring their equipment to the camps. I came, and I stayed. Not much sense in doin' it, though. I've got me fifty dollars stashed away, and that for six months of workin' harder than when I was a slave."

"But you're free," Charity said. "You're in the land of the free."

"That's what Mr. Granville said to me," Elisha murmured.

"And he was right."

"You heard about the Chinamen's mine?" Elisha asked, and Charity said she hadn't. "They discovered them Chinese had found a rich vein and they took the mine away from them. Now they're tryin' to pass a law against anyone but the whites bein' allowed to stake a claim. If that law goes through, I'm no freer than I was in Georgia. The niggers and Chinamen, we'll just be misplaced creatures roamin' this great California."

"That law'll never go through," Charity said, but there was little conviction in her voice. "But considerin' that it's possible, maybe you'd best say yes to me, Elisha. Come work my claim with me and share what we dig out of the earth. If it's a rich strike—and I think it is—we will be gone from the camps before any law can be passed. You'll have enough money so you won't be just a-roamin' the country." She offered him a drink from her jug, but he refused. "You can also look after Miss Paulette," she added. "I know you're fond of her and that's what's worryin' you. You think Mr. Granville's goin' to do somethin' bad to her."

"She's a lady and I respect her," Elisha said. "Reminds me of my mistress, she does. And my mistress suffered somethin' terrible 'cause of the master. He was a mean one, always takin' his failures out on her. He had eyes like Mr. Granville, so pale and blue and cold they reminded you of the surface of a lake on a clear winter day."

"Is that why you ran away?" Charity pressed. " 'Cause you was tryin' to protect your mistress?"

Elisha stared into the fire and refused to answer. The set of his powerful jaw had gone rigid, the muscles in his neck protruded, and his eyes glazed with memories, unpleasant and best forgotten. After several moments of silence, he said, "I'll come in with you if you want me. I've got to get what I can while I can. There's somethin' I want to do more than anything, and I need money to do it."

Charity pulled her great long man's coat closer around her shoulders. The nights were turning colder, the winds blowing down off the Sierras biting to her bones. "And what might that be?" she asked, truly wondering what a black man would need with the kind of money he could make off her claim.

"My woman and child," Elisha said, "they're still with the master. If I had enough money and a friend to do the biddin', I'd buy their freedom and bring them out West. Even if they pass a law against non-whites stakin' gold claims, it's a better place to live." Elisha straightened his back and turned his head briskly to relieve the strain of tension in his neck. "You still want me in with you?"

"Need you and want you," Charity said. She reached over and took the big man's hand and shook it. "Then it's agreed," she told him. "You and I can put our backs to the hard labor and Miss Paulette can keep guard with the rifle against any bastard who might consider claim-jumpin' or worse." She saw his expression and added, "Yeah, I'm teachin' her how to use firearms. Even a lady's got to protect herself."

"She'll need more than firearms to protect herself," Elisha murmured.

He rose and strolled away toward his shack without explaining himself.

# Chapter Ten

FOR THE following few days Paulette rose with Dester, saw him off before sunup, and then joined Charity and Elisha to work the big woman's claim. The strike proved richer than even Charity had hoped, producing between two and three thousand dollars' worth of the precious material a day. Elisha worked with back-breaking speed, a man possessed. Together, they constructed a larger sluice box and rerouted a section of the creek so the water washed through the sluice box when it was lowered at one end.

Paulette proved an apt pupil at learning the use of the rifle and pistol; she might not hit the smaller targets Charity pointed out to her, but there was no doubt she could hit anything as large as a man, should the need arise. Only she doubted her ability to kill to protect them; Charity and Elisha trusted her completely and devoted their attention to their work.

News of Charity's strike spread and the camp was filling up with newcomers. A group from San Francisco told them Happy Valley, the eyesore of tents, had caught fire and burned to the ground. Paulette worried about Miriam and Chang, then convinced herself her house was far enough removed to be spared—besides, Jeremiah's mansion stood close to it, and in saving his own he would be forced to protect the smaller structure next door.

She thought of Jeremiah often—unwillingly. He had a way of creeping into her dreams and thoughts and she would fight to push him away. Often, sitting on the knoll with the rifle across her lap, she would think she saw someone hidden in the scrub and the first image she had was of Jeremiah, remembering how he had stood in the trees watching her house.

Dester had grown progressively stranger. With news of Charity's continuing success each day, he retreated more and more into himself. He was often short-tempered, even with her, and had taken to frequently drinking more whiskey than he had the capacity to handle. He made love to her nightly, but his savageness had returned, sometimes forcing her to plead with him. He never asked about her days, never questioned what she did while he was away—for that she was grateful, for should he ask her directly if she continued to go out with Charity and Elisha, she would not have been able to lie to him. At night, greeting him, she always pretended to be rested, although her body ached from the treks to and from Charity's claim and from spending too many hours standing sentinel.

Few miners approached Charity's claim. Those who did usually announced their visits by shouting long before they came into view. If Charity or Elisha knew them, they were invited closer, some even being permitted to use their pans in the creek beneath where the sluice box emptied, but Paulette had been warned to keep a close watch even on these invited miners. "There ain't no honest man where gold's concerned," Charity told her. "You might call a man friend and he'd still drive a dagger into your back or blow off your head if he thought he'd steal enough of the yellow stuff off you to make it worthwhile."

Paulette was not as distrustful, but she did as she was told—Charity knew more about the nature of men—and especially miners—than she. For guarding them, Charity and Elisha gave her a portion of each day's yield. Already the leather pouch she wore under her clothes bulged with gold; she had no knowledge of its value, only that its weight was beginning to pull at her waist and make her uncomfortable when she moved. She decided to find a place in the shack to hide the pouch and settled on a section of the floor beneath a loose board. That not only relieved her discomfort of carrying it around, but it also eliminated her fear of Dester noticing it when she undressed.

Dester had accepted her offer of money. With it he had bought better equipment and had hired the Malay boy to work with him. She ceased pressing him to return to Plantation Bend or even San Francisco. Her argument that there was more money for him to make in the port than the gold fields only angered him, made him feel she considered him a failure.

"I only need more time," he told her. "The big money's here! I know I'll strike a vein richer than . . . than Charity's." His eyes would glaze over, with expectation or dreams unfulfilled, and he would brood until the lamp was turned out and he drew her into his arms. After taking her, he said, "You'll go back with the next party. There will be one soon. No one's had Charity's luck. They'll get discouraged and go for an easier life. You'll wait for me in San Francisco. When I come for you, I'll have enough gold for us to live as we've been accustomed to."

He ignored the change in her: her rough and reddened hands, her sunburned complexion, her legs and arms, which had begun to harden with muscle. The soft, feminine woman she had been had begun to yield before the circumstances of this new life. Even she, when she gazed into the distorted shaving mirror, had difficulty imagining herself in a silk gown again. The woman she had been in Louisiana seemed but a vision of someone other than herself—and Dester seemed but a shell of the man she remembered.

Still, regardless of his moods and savage lovemaking, Paulette loved him as she always had, hoping one day he'd awaken having shed his obsession for gold. She began to think of it as an illness, as contagious as cholera—and as deadly. Men were constantly killing one another over claim disputes, or gambling—even over reasons that could not be determined later by those who had shot or stabbed a friend.

Elisha stopped shoveling gravel and dirt into the sluice box and stretched himself. He was shirtless, his trousers rolled up around his calves; the sun glistened off his smooth, black skin. He glanced up at Paulette on the knoll and nodded his head smiling. Charity also ceased working, and the two climbed up the embankment and settled on either side of Paulette.

"We're losin' light," Charity said, "but with the amount we're makin', we can afford the luxury." She leaned back, crossing her legs at the ankles, and turned her face up to the sun; she was already almost as dark as Elisha. "How much longer do you figure, Elisha?"

Wiping his brow with a coarse handkerchief, Elisha looked at Paulette and winked. "Figure 'bout what?" he asked teasingly.

"The vein, of course," the big woman said. "How much longer do you figure it'll hold?"

"Maybe a day, maybe a week, maybe forever," Elisha told her, smiling. "What difference does it make? We'll all be rich if it holds for another month. I can buy freedom for my woman and child, and you can go to San Francisco and play the great lady."

Charity sat up, laughing at the prospect. "Me, a great lady? Can you imagine that, Paulette?"

Paulette, not laughing, said, "You are a great lady, Charity." She slid the rifle off her knees and leaned it against a tree trunk. "You remind me of Dester's grandmother."

"That a fact?" Charity mused. Then she shook her massive head. "I don't want to be a great lady," she said. "I want to be rich, and that's the simple truth of it. I want a big home with stables and the best breed of horses this side of Kentucky. I want to hold my head up high when I go ridin' down the main street of any town and I want them to say, 'There goes Charity McGowan. She made it on her own in the gold fields. She didn't need no man to get what's hers.' That's what I want them to say." Her expression had turned serious; now she smiled again, embarrassed at revealing her innermost ambitions. "Of course, I want a man, too. But I want him to accept me on an equal basis. I don't want to be his slave—sorry, Elisha, but that's what women become to men—and I don't want him to be indebted to me. Equal, as I said." She laughed again, but with gallows humor. "Impossible dream, isn't it?"

"What would life be without impossible dreams?" Elisha murmured. "And you, Miss Paulette, what's your impossible dream?"

Paulette, busy taking food from their lunch basket, paused and looked at Elisha and Charity thoughtfully. "I . . . I can't really say," she told them. "My dream was always to convince Dester to leave here—to return home and take over the plantation; if not that, then to return to San Francisco and build our lives there, but . . . but something has changed inside me. I don't know why, or how, but . . ." She let the sentence trail off. "I guess I don't have a dream," she said, and she felt extremely empty and lost.

"Maybe your dream's just sleepin'," Charity said. "Even dreams must need a rest." She reached for the drumstick Paulette was taking from the basket and ate it hungrily.

Paulette offered Elisha food, but she declined eating. She hadn't been feeling well mornings, and the thought of eating made her nauseous.

Elisha ate silently, staring out across the creek, lost in his own thoughts. Then he said, "The creek seems to be goin' down some. Don't understand it." He pointed to the dark clouds capping the distant mountaintops. "It's rainin' in the Sierras. The creek should be risin' instead of gettin' shallower."

Charity, tossing her chicken bone aside, sat up and wiped her mouth on her shirtsleeve. She stared at the mountain and then the creek. "Seems the same to me," she remarked. "You're imaginin' it, Elisha."

"No, it's goin' down," he said with conviction. "See the rocks yonder? The water ain't yet dried where they was submerged yesterday. And the water should be higher 'cause of the rain above."

"Well, it's probably just beaver blockage," Charity determined. "The little devils. It'll break loose by mornin'."

"Could be," Elisha murmured. "We'd best drag the sluice box to higher ground tonight to keep it from bein' swept away."

Charity agreed to the precaution to please him, although she sensed no danger. The beavers were always blocking the creek with their dams; it never much changed the depth and didn't impair their digging. In fact, the change in water level might increase their yield, allowing them to wade farther into the creek bed and test the crevices the deep water had made impossible.

They finished the day with three-quarters of the amount of gold found the previous day, and Charity expressed fear that the vein was petering out. "I don't have enough yet," she complained as they trudged back toward the camp, "not for a grand house and a good breed of horses." Her massive shoulders were slumped, and for the first time Paulette saw exhaustion in the big woman, whom she had felt had an unlimited amount of energy.

"Ain't begun to work out that vein," Elisha said, encouraging her. "Just that all days can't be the same. Earth's not eager to give up her riches easily. They wouldn't be worth anything if she did. You'll get your horses and grand house, and I'll get enough to buy my woman and child free. Don't you worry none, Charity."

But Paulette could tell Elisha was worrying, too.

Outside the camp when Charity stopped to divide the day's yield, Paulette told them to keep her share.

"Lord, child! We can't do that!" Charity said, and Elisha shook his head in agreement. "You mustn't be so free with what's yours. You can't go givin' away what's yours and expect to survive. That's what it's all about—survival. We've hit on some luck, the three of us, but luck don't last forever. When that vein does go dry, we might not strike another for months. If the earth don't see fit to yield enough for us to realize our dreams, then we'll have to use what we've got to keep on goin' until she does."

"But I told you," Paulette protested, "I'm not sure I have a dream any longer."

"But you don't have no money, either," Elisha reminded her. "Your brother-in-law saw to that, and Mr. Granville, he took . . ." He pressed the gold into her pouch. "If your man goes broke again, he'll need it," he said and exchanged glances with Charity.

Paulette turned, hoisted her skirt, and tied the pouch around the waistband of her slip.

"You're too generous, child," Charity said as they entered the camp, "and generosity can be a curse. There are those who take it for a weakness and will take advantage of you. They'll take and take, and then hate you for givin' to them." She wanted to say more but decided against it. After all, she loved Paulette like a daughter, but she wasn't the girl's mother and she had no maternal right to express even the obvious.

It was dark when they entered camp. The fires were already glowing along the creek bank and the smell of cooking filled the air. Someone was playing a harmonica and someone else, in the distance, a guitar; the two tunes mingled in a sorrowful discord.

Paulette had a stew cooking on the pot-bellied stove when Dester returned to the shack.

His eyes were wild, excited. He dropped his equipment in a corner and came to warm himself beside the stove, watching her curiously, like a child pretending to hold back important news. Finally, when she did not question him, he removed the pouch from his belt, opened it, and shook gold out into his palm. "Look," he said and held it out to her. "I found it this afternoon—the most I've discovered in three months. I'm sure it's from an offshoot of a rich vein."

His happiness was infectious. She didn't tell him that the amount he had found was even less than Charity had given her for her portion of the day's yield. She threw her arms around his neck, laughing and kissing him. "I'm glad for you, Dester," she said and laughed. "I hope it's the richest vein in Hangtown's history—rich enough for us to leave here."

His excitement waned, but not so that she noticed. "We'll see," he said. "We'll see." But his expectation for riches was reflected in his voice.

They ate stew and corn pone. Paulette had a ravenous appetite and had begun to gain weight. After supper, she boiled water and Dester carried the large washtub into the shack. They bathed together, scrubbing one another; then she massaged the hard, stiff muscles of his legs and back. She herself ached, but she dared not admit it for fear he would question her. She did not want to spoil his mood. Still damp, she crawled into the pallet and watched him as he stoked the fire and turned down the damper so it would last most of the chilly night. The glow of the coals reflected on his naked body and she found herself wanting him more than she had for days.

"Hurry," she murmured. "Make love to me." Tonight he was happy—tonight he'd be less brutal.

He laughed, his teeth glistening white against his sunburned face. "Harlot," he teased.

"Yes, your exclusive harlot." She stretched out her arms to him, urging him to hurry to her.

Her clothes were on the floor where she had discarded them. When he stepped on them and she heard the crunch beneath his feet, she caught her breath in a gasp. The pouch containing her gold was still tied to the waistband of her skirt.

He stopped, staring from her to her clothes and back again. The smile had gone from his face; he instinctively knew what she had been hiding. He reached for the lamp and turned up the flame. Reaching into the bundle of her clothes, he drew out the pouch.

She would have risen from the pallet and gone to him, but the anger in his stare kept her where she lay. He emptied the pouch's contents into his hand, estimating the value she carried, comparing it to what he had found that day. She understood the anguish on his face—his discovery had been minimal in comparison. Again, he was a failure.

"I . . . I couldn't spend my days locked inside the shack," she murmured. "I help Charity and Elisha and they share with me."

"I told you I didn't want you going out with that bitch and nigger!" he shouted. "You're a lady! Can't you remember that? A lady doesn't grovel in the earth —even for gold. It's her man who grovels."

"I don't grovel, Dester. I stand guard while they work."

His face was crimson, distorted with rage.

"Charity taught me how to use a rifle," she went on. Talking kept her fear from consuming her, kept her from considering the change in him since he had left Plantation Bend. "It's easy, honest work, better than hiding away inside because of the miners."

"You'd belittle me in any way you could, wouldn't you?" he yelled.

"Belittle you? No, no! Why does it . . ."

"Bitch! You're no better than the others in the family we saved you from! Your half-sister Claudine —she thought she was better than any man. She laughed at men and tried to make them seem small." He shoved the gold back into the pouch and tossed it onto the pallet beside her.

She began to tremble, not so much from fear that he might strike her, but for him. Was he mad? Had his obsession for gold driven him beyond reason? They had an agreement since childhood that neither would ever mention the Favières. What she had learned of her family had mostly been from the slaves and from Katrina when she had been in her cruel moods. Dester had never thrown the evilness of her father or half-sister at her, even at his angriest. She stared at the pouch of gold, cursing herself for not having hidden it with the rest.

"The gold's for you," she told him. "I don't want it! It means nothing to me!"

"Nothing? Then you're a fool! You're as penniless as I am, thanks to Tom. Don't tell me you're bored with pretty silk gowns and hats and jewelry. Don't tell me you're happy living here in worse conditions than a slave. How you've done it, I don't know: cooking, boiling your own water to bathe, sleeping on a pallet instead of a soft feather mattress, no darkie to do your bidding, no ladies to dress up and serve tea to. Gold can buy all of that back for you—and it means nothing to you?"

"Nothing," she repeated. "You alone mean anything to me." She was weeping quietly, but her tears did not affect him, did not lessen his anger. "Take it! I don't want it! I can have all the things I'm accustomed to when you strike your rich vein!" She held the pouch out to him.

He snatched it from her hand and for a brief moment she thought he was going to beat her with it. She cowered against the pallet, eyes wide, waiting to be struck. But his face softened suddenly. He dropped the pouch to the floor and lowered himself to the edge of the pallet.

"You believe in me that much?" he asked in a whisper. "You'd go without things unless I provided for you?"

"Yes," she whimpered.

"You'd do as I tell you? You'll obey me as a wife even before we're married?" He was leaning over her, his eyes boring into hers. Although his anger was waning, there was still a fury inside him, a fury that frightened and puzzled her.

"Yes, I'll obey you," she said quietly. More frightening still was the fact that she was beginning to understand the innuendos Charity and Elisha managed to drop in their daily conversations—there was something not quite right with Dester. "I'll obey," she repeated. Although she had not wished to do so, she said, "I'll stop standing guard for Charity and Elisha."

He stared at her thoughtfully for several moments. Finally, he said, "No. I've no right to keep you locked up here. You're safer with them than alone."

I'd be safer with you, she wanted to tell him, but she dared not for fear of sparking his waning anger.

"As for your portion of gold, I'll keep it safe for you." He picked up her pouch and tossed it to where his lay on the chair. "There'll be a party leaving soon. You'll go with them."

"But . . ." She silenced her objection.

He rose, turned out the lamp, and crawled onto the pallet beside her. They lay separated for a moment, their bodies not touching; then he reached for her and drew her against him.

She suddenly felt empty and drained of emotion. The idea of his making love to her repelled her; she needed time to consider this new side of him, time to consider her uneasiness and fear. Her heart, thudding painfully, began to relax. She fought for words but could find nothing to say to him as he pressed his lips roughly against hers. Her body was taut with nerves and when he pressed against her she felt pain. His fingers dug into her bare shoulders and she winced.

"You're trembling," he mumbled. "Paulette, forgive me for my bad temper. It's . . . it's just that I can't bear you laboring like a . . . a strumpet."

"What I do is honest work," she managed to say. She tried to push away from him, but he held her tightly. "How dare you use that word in reference to me." Her anger was quietly voiced.

"I'm sorry, my love." He began to cover her with kisses, his wet mouth moving over her face and throat and down to the small crescents of her breasts. His left arm was crooked beneath her neck, his right hand caressing her legs and thighs. When his hand moved between her thighs, she shuddered at the roughness of his touch.

She fought her tensions and tried to give herself willingly, but the more submissive she became to his demands, the more savage the outlet of his lust. She whimpered and struggled beneath him, pleading with him for gentleness. It was with relief that she realized he had pushed deep into her, his body going rigid and then collapsing on her like a dead weight. She pushed at him then and he rolled onto his side, his arm still trapped beneath her neck. Within moments he was sleeping, the steady rhythm of his breathing loud and deep. She rose, and dunking a towel in the now tepid bath water, she washed herself gently, wincing at the pain. She dared not light the lamp for fear of waking him up, but she pushed back the covering of the window and in the moonlight inspected the marks on her breasts. She began to cry, not from the pain, but from the strangeness of the man she loved. She did not understand his savageness, his brutality, when before he had been a gentle, caring lover. She had often been grateful that they had discovered their sexuality together, for there could not have been a more thoughtful, tender teacher than Dester. Now, however, it was as if there was a great burning fury inside him that could be quenched only through savageness. Had she not known better, she would have sworn he hated her and used his sex to demean and inflict pain on her. Perhaps, she thought, there had always been this other side to his character, a side she had ignored because emotion had blinded her. She reflected back, trying to find evidence in memory, but only her happiness confronted her.

She dried her tears on the edge of the dusty window covering and, feeling suddenly embarrassed by her nakedness, fumbled through her trunk in the darkness until she found a nightdress. When she returned to the pallet she kept to her side, away from him, avoiding contact, and did not even draw near him for warmth after she slept and the fire had gone out and the shack was biting cold.

It was Elisha who first spotted the damage. He had been walking ahead of them, whistling, the shovels slung over his shoulder. When he stopped abruptly, Charity almost collided with his back.

"Damn, man!" But she then saw and was silent.

Elisha ran down the embankment.

The sluice box had been chopped into pieces, the splintered wood and gunny lining scattered in all directions. Elisha picked up the biggest pieces. Then, in his anger, he flung them out into the current of the creek.

Charity stood watching, her face dark and her heavily hooded eyes surveying the destruction. "No tellin' who did this," she said. "Some petty bastard who's jealous of our claim."

"It's not just the damage," Elisha said. He pointed to a section of the embankment. "They've been diggin', too."

Paulette, standing at Charity's elbow, asked, "How can you tell, Elisha?" The entire embankment looked the same to her, the earth dug away in great gaping holes.

" 'Cause I don't skip around like that," he answered. "They missed a good four feet." He stepped forward and kicked the ridge of untouched dirt, sending it flying into the air. "We've got ourselves claim jumpers," he said. "Someone waited 'til we went back to camp last night and then slipped in to mine by lamplight."

"Is that possible?" Paulette turned to Charity for verification.

"Sure it's possible," Charity said angrily. "Light is light, even if it's artificial. Not easy, though. Even with the best of sight, you'd miss nuggets, wash them right out into the creek." She moved to the embankment and lowered her bulk onto a boulder. "It's not the stealin' that sticks in my craw," she said, "though I'd kill the man who did it. It's the senseless destruction. That means we'll have to use pans today and build another sluice box tonight."

"Creek's down more, too," Elisha observed. "That's not right, either." He shielded his eyes against the morning sun and stared at the distant mountains. "Them clouds been there for days," he said. "It's been rainin' up there for almost a week. The creek should be high."

"Beavers," Charity repeated, as she did every time he mentioned the creek's level. She pushed herself off the boulder and rummaged through the sack she had carried for the gold pans. "No use cryin' over spilled milk," she grumbled. She tossed one of the pans to Elisha, who caught it in the air above his head. To Paulette, she said, "You watch careful today. If our thief took much gold last night, you can bet he'll get braver and come back for more. He might not even wait to hide his crime under the cover of darkness. Keep your eyes alert and your finger on that trigger. Tonight I'll stay hidden in the scrub. If the bastard comes back to steal more, he'll get more than he bargained for." She hoisted her narrow, coarse skirt and tied it around her hips.

"Water's cold as ice," Elisha called.

"Build a fire," the big woman told him. "We'll dry out after each pan. I brought whiskey that'll keep us from catchin' our deaths. Hell, we might even hit a glory hole today," she said with forced cheerfulness.

Paulette asked, "What's a glory hole?"

"A pocket where the nuggets get caught up in roots or under a large stone," Charity told her. "But no one's found a glory hole at Hangtown. Most likely we won't, either. That'd be askin' the Lord for more than our share. Still, it's a dream—to pick gold nuggets out of roots like pickin' strawberries from a vine." She turned and waded into the icy water. "You stay alert now," she called back. "Shout if you see anythin', even a deer movin' in the scrub. Elisha, keep your rifle where you can get to it fast."

Paulette climbed to the top of the knoll, where she had the best view of the surrounding area. Her hands were damp, the metal of the trigger cold against her finger. Today, she thought, she might have to prove how much she had learned from Charity in using the rifle. The thought of killing a man sickened her, but his crime also made her tremble with fury.

She scarcely glanced down at Charity and Elisha. She knew they were suffering from the cold—she heard Elisha complaining when he came to warm himself by the fire; he stamped his feet, resembling one of the Indians in camp who danced for the miners in return for whiskey. Charity did not complain; she took her time for warming herself, quietly surveying the surrounding area, as if her aged and hooded eyes were stronger than Paulette's and could pick out movement the younger woman might miss.

Paulette moved back and leaned against the trunk of a tree to rest herself. Charity was only a few feet away, throwing more logs onto the fire. "You think it was Crimmon?" Paulette asked, remembering the ugly, evil man Charity had driven away.

"Could be," Charity answered, "but I don't think so. He's not doin' bad on his own claim. Don't need to go stealin' from others. Still, he's mean enough to steal just for the hell of it." The big woman poured herself a cup of coffee and stood looking down at Elisha in the creek while she drank. "A good man, Elisha," she said. "Never known a white man to work as hard as him, even my Pa." She turned and looked at Paulette. "There are those in camp who don't think we deserve this claim," she said, "us being women and a nigger. If they hadn't mined on our claim, I'd have thought they'd axed up the sluice box out of pure meanness. But we'll show 'em we won't be driven away. It's our claim and no male bastard's goin' to take it 'cause he's white and has a pair of balls!"

Paulette felt her face flush at Charity's words.

"Excuse my language, child," Charity said. "It's just that I'm angry, and when I get angry . . ."

"It's all right," Paulette assured her. "I'm angry, too." And it surprised her that she was. Until seeing the senseless destruction, she had felt no personal attachment to the claim. Since she did not value the gold for herself, she had thought of herself as merely assisting Charity and Elisha. Being with them permitted her freedom, of not having to stay locked in the shack while Dester was away. The destruction of the sluice box and the evidence that someone had stolen from them had awakened her and made her feel involved.

"I'm glad you're angry," Charity told her. "Elisha and me, we were beginnin' to wonder if maybe love for your man had put your other emotions to sleep."

Dester showed little interest when Paulette told him about the destruction on Charity's claim. "It happens," he said. He was quiet, withdrawn, and they ate supper without conversation.

When Paulette had finished rinsing the dishes and was ready for bed, he was already asleep. She stoked the fire and turned down the damper, as she had seen him do. He had forgotten to refill the woodbox. She knew he would be furious if she went outside the shack alone after dark, but she did not want to awaken him. Besides, she reasoned, the miners had grown accustomed to seeing her come and go with Charity and Elisha. Although they continued to stare at her with lust on their faces, few had spoken to her and none had approached her. Unlike Dester, she did not suspect them of huddling in the dark outside the shack waiting for an opportunity to molest her.

She found her shawl and wrapped it around her shoulders. The night was cold, with a bright, full moon and high scattered clouds. She unlatched the door and stepped outside. The campfires were still burning, but there was no music, no forms moving around. Most had been driven into their shacks or bedrolls by the chill air. From the distant side of the camp she could hear hammering, and she knew it was Elisha preparing a sluice box for tomorrow's work. Charity was probably assisting him. She felt a twinge of guilt that she was not there with them doing what she could, although they did not expect it. She had given her share of today's yield to Dester for safe keeping. He had looked at the small amount and his expression had almost been smug.

She moved around the side of the shack to the woodpile. There was no wood chopped; Dester had forgotten. She looked around for the axe but couldn't find it. He had probably taken it to his claim and had forgotten to bring it back—as he had done in the past. Removing her shawl, she spread it out and gathered small chips and pieces of bark in it to carry inside.

When she put them in the pot-bellied stove, the chips flared and burned quickly, but the bark appeared as if it would last most of the night. She closed the lid and, rubbing her arms to rid herself of gooseflesh, turned out the lamp and crawled onto the pallet.

She was glad Dester did not awaken. Her breasts were still sore from the night before and she was too exhausted for his savage lovemaking. She snuggled beside him, drawing from his warmth, and closed her eyes.

Something was bothering her—something she could not quite grasp. She attempted to clear her mind so sleep would claim her. Dester groaned, turned, and she held her breath, her body going rigid. Let him sleep, she prayed.

His heavy breathing told her her prayer had been answered.

Elisha's hammering continued until long after she slept.

# Chapter Eleven

CHARITY WAS waiting for Paulette and Elisha when they came to the claim in the morning. After helping Elisha with the sluice box, she had come back and spent the night hidden in the scrub, her rifle across her knees, her head resting on a tree stump.

"Nothing stirred," she told them, "not even a deer or a raccoon." Her eyes were ringed with dark circles. "I guess our thief was a onetimer."

"Not likely," Elisha mumbled. " 'Cause of the way he axed up the sluice box, I don't think he was just a thief. He was a man with malice in his heart." He left the two women and moved to the creek bank to set up the new sluice box.

"You tell Dester about what happened?" Charity asked.

Paulette nodded, but she refrained from telling the big woman about his surprising disinterest.

"He'll want to look after his claim better, too," Charity said, "seein' how he brought out some gold the other night."

Paulette hadn't told either of them about Dester's yield. "How did you know?"

"When a man comes into camp with gold in his pouch, everyone knows," Charity said. "Some of the miners claim they can smell it. Wouldn't surprise me none, either. That's all they live and breathe for—

gold, gold, and more gold." She looked at Paulette curiously, seemed about to say more, but decided against it. She passed the younger woman her rifle and moved down the embankment to join Elisha. "We're wastin' light," Paulette heard her tell her partner.

Elisha protested her insistence on helping him. "You've not slept all night," he told her. "Rest for a while."

"You've been up, same as me," she argued. "I'll not rest. I'll pull my share."

Paulette moved back to the spot where she had spent most of the day before and let her gaze sweep out across the area. The leaves were now almost entirely off the trees, the ground a blanket of flaming colors. Gnarled branches reached into the clear blue sky. Birds were circling above. The dark clouds remained nestled over the summits of the Sierra Nevadas. Rain, Paulette remembered Elisha saying. It would soon begin raining below, not just misting as it had for the past two mornings. Work would become more difficult; the depth of the creek would rise and make shoveling mud from its bed impossible, and they'd be forced to move to another area of Charity's claim.

A buck shot out from the scrub behind Paulette. She spun around, rifle raised and ready for firing. She relaxed at the sight of the magnificent creature. It paused, as startled by her sudden appearance as she had been by its. Head raised, its crown of antlers thrown back, it sniffed the air, turned, and raced off into the underbrush.

When she turned back, Paulette saw that Charity and Elisha had been watching her. Both were smiling.

"If it'd been a man, you'd have shot him!" Charity yelled. "Good girl. We feel safe with you watchin' out for us."

Would she have shot a man? Paulette asked herself. Yes. She had been ready to fire without question had the buck been a man. Fear? For protection? The first

image that had entered her mind was of Crimmon—
the evil, foul-looking man springing on her from the
scrub. But what if it had been someone else, some innocent stranger tearing his way through the entangle-
ment for the creek bank? What if it had been Dester?
Would she have controlled her finger on the trigger in
time to stop herself from shooting him? She pushed the
thought away, but still she felt uneasy, the same as
she had felt last night when she had lain beside Dester
waiting for sleep—as if her mind was avoiding something important.

She was still deep in thought when Elisha climbed up
the embankment and went to the fire to see if the
coffee had boiled. "You should have shot the buck,"
he told her. "We'd have had venison for lunch and
supper."

"I . . . I wasn't thinking of food," she said.

He nodded. "I know," he said quietly. He poured
himself coffee; then he poured a cup for her. "Somethin' troublin' you, Miss Paulette? Somethin' you need
to talk 'bout?"

"No, Elisha."

"If there ever is, I want you to know you can come
to me," he said. "I ain't smart like Mr. Granville,
but I'm a mighty good listener. Sometimes that's all
that's needed, for someone to listen to what troubles
you." He nodded down at Charity, who was still
shoveling mud and gravel into the sluice box. "Miss
Charity, she's a good listener, too," he said. "She's
awful fond of you, thinks of you like a daughter. You
can come to either of us anytime you want."

"Thank you Elisha," she said. "I'm grateful; and
I'll remember that." She sipped the strong brew as
Elisha went back down to join Charity. They were
her friends, the black man and the big woman; she
wondered why Dester hated them so. Why did he
object to her being with them when he forbade her
to be with him? The strong coffee made her stomach
churn; she set the cup aside and wondered if it was the
coffee or the strange food that made her so easily ill

lately. If she ever got back to San Francisco, she would see a doctor. Surely that sprawling village, with its multitudes arriving daily, had decent medical men —if they hadn't given up their profession for the gold fields. It was impossible to look at the miners and know what sort of men hid behind their scruffy beards and fever-glazed eyes. She made a mental note to ask Charity if there was a medical man among the miners.

It was mid-afternoon when the gypsy wagon came into view.

Charity and Elisha had taken a break to share a roasted rabbit and were sitting with Paulette on the knoll. Paulette stood, alerted by the first sound.

"Gypsies," Charity said before the wagon was clearly visible through the underbrush.

Paulette glanced at her questioningly.

"You can hear the pots and pans and the chimes," the big woman explained. "The chimes keep the evil spirits away. Every wagon carries as many as there are occupants. It saves a lot of gypsies from bein' shot as they move between claims. The miners know the sound and don't pay much notice. The gypsies are safe. They'd steal the shirt off your back, but they'd never settle down long enough to work a claim. Lazy lot, they are." She bit into a rabbit leg, the juice squirting onto her wrinkled chin. "You seen any gypsies before, Paulette?"

"They weren't allowed on the plantation because of their stealing," Paulette answered. She'd seen them along the roadway to New Orleans, their wagons parked while the gypsy women gave fortune readings to the slaves and poor dirt farmers' wives. She herself had always wanted to stop to learn what future was reflected in her palms, but Vienna had always called it foolishness, saying, "Only the Lord knows your future, and I don't believe He wrote it on your palms for some wanderers to read."

"And you, Elisha?" Charity asked. "You ever had your fortune read by a gypsy?"

"No, Miss Charity. And I ain't 'bout to," Elisha

mumbled. "They're the devil's people. I don't want them touchin' my hands."

Paulette had a compulsion for a reading. Charity saw it in her eyes. Rising, the big woman flung her gnawed drumstick into the fire and waved her arms at the wagon.

The wagon came to a jerking halt; pots and pans and bits of glass on strings rattled and clanged, echoing in the chill breeze. A woman sat with the reins tight in her hands. She was old, with wrinkled arms and face and white hair that protruded from beneath her babushka. Her skirt and blouse and shawl were multicolored: cheap fabric that had been handpainted with various scenes and animals and symbols. Her shoes, one resting on the wagon's brake, were wrapped in gunny sacking to keep the cold from penetrating through the holes to her tiny feet. She wore countless bracelets on both wrists, dangling earrings, and necklaces with stones and more symbols pounded out of metal. Her eyes were dark ovals sunk deep into her skull. Her cheekbones had been heavily rouged, as were her lips. Blue dots had been painted at each corner of her deeply set eyes.

"Afternoon, gypsy," Charity said as she approached the wagon.

The old woman smiled, revealing uneven, darkened teeth. Her amusement, it appeared, was to discover that Charity was a woman, not the man she seemed at a distance. She nodded her skeletal head in a return greeting. Securing the reins of the horse that looked half-dead, its ribs showing and head too weak to lift, she climbed down from the wagon and stood before Charity, the big woman's size making her appear even tinier and more fragile.

"You read fortunes?" Charity asked.

The woman bobbed her head. "For gold," she said. Then, glancing toward the fire, she added, "Or for a share of your food—whichever you're willing to pay." She licked her dried, rouged lips, obviously salivating from hunger. "I've no man anymore," she murmured, "and I've had no luck with my traps. The animals have been spooked by all the miners and have grown wiser and harder to catch."

"Come, we'll share our food and give you some gold besides for readin' our young friend's fortune," Charity told her. "What's your name, gypsy?"

The old woman approached the fire. "Names aren't important," she said, then stared at the remainder of the roasted rabbit.

Paulette handed Elisha the rifle and fetched a plate from the gunny sack. She gave the woman the remainder of the rabbit—her share—and went to the creek and rinsed her cup and filled it.

The gypsy had seated herself beneath a tree and was devouring the rabbit. Grease oozed down her chin and dripped onto her blouse, but she was too hungry to notice, or care. Her fingernails were long and dirty, the ends chipped and jagged; her knuckles were swollen. She made an animal-like, grunting sound as she ate.

Elisha handed the rifle back to Paulette and moved down to the creek to escape the old woman. He wanted no part of gypsies and the evil of seeing into the future; she was a witch, and witches frightened him more than white masters with whips and thieves who came in the night. He was a superstitious man and believed the good that the Lord placed ahead of you could be altered by his anger at such actions of heathens. His Mama, although he had known her for only the first twelve years of his life before she had been sold off, had warned him to stay clear of those who claimed to have "the sight." He dug with fury, flinging shovels of gravel and dirt into the sluice box, but keeping a watchful eye on Miss Paulette and Miss Charity. Foolish women, he thought. Calling the gypsy over was the most foolish thing he'd known Miss Charity to do. As for Miss Paulette, he'd reserve his opinion—but as things stood now, her biggest foolishness was her devotion to Mr. Granville. She couldn't see that there was something wrong with the man—it didn't take a gypsy to forsee what lay ahead for her with him.

The gypsy finished the rabbit and looked around for scraps she'd missed in her first inspection. Satisfied there was nothing she'd missed, she drank the scalding coffee without consideration for her mouth. Licking her lips, she sighed and leaned her head back against the tree trunk. With her eyes closed, she appeared to be sleeping.

Charity, smiling, walked away to join Elisha, and Paulette was left alone with the old woman. She sat quietly, waiting. Then, deciding the old woman slept, she reached for the rifle and started to resume her duty of guarding Charity and Elisha.

"Don't you want to know your future?" the old woman asked.

Startled, Paulette turned and saw the old woman had spoken without opening her eyes. Her skin, beneath the heavy rogue, was pale and sickly.

"I must pay for my food," the gypsy said.

She pushed herself away from the tree and would have risen, except Paulette said, "You sleep. There's time enough to read my future."

"Nonsense," the gypsy answered. "Your future's moving rapidly. It's almost upon you. There is little time for delay." She stood with effort and went back to her wagon to return with a pack of cards. She handed them to Paulette. "Shuffle three times and give them back to me," she instructed. She squatted on the ground, pushing away twigs and small pebbles with her hands. When Paulette returned the shuffled cards, the gypsy lay them out carefully, her thin, dirty fingers following the pattern, her sunken eyes studying, calculating.

"You'll be married within two months," she said.

Although Paulette did not know if she believed in fortune telling, the statement sent a shiver of delight through her. How could the gypsy know that she was not already married? Her delight, however, fled with the old woman's next statement.

"It'll be a turbulent marriage." Her index finger stabbed at a card depicting a man and a woman standing with their backs toward one another, their heads bowed as if in sorrow—or heartbreak. In the distance between the couple stood another man, arms raised, dressed entirely in black. "Another man will come between you."

The image of Jeremiah Walker flashed through Paulette's mind.

"He is not good, this man," the gypsy told her, and her dark eyes expressed a warning from within their hollows. "You'll not know happiness until you've rid yourself of him. Ah, a child—a boy—very fair of hair. He'll bring you much happiness and much sadness." Her thin lips parted in a sly smile. "But all children are the same, are they not? Happiness when they are young, and sadness when they grow up and ignore their parents. The man was the same. He brought much unhappiness upon his parents."

"Which man?" Paulette found herself pressing.

The gypsy studied—or pretended to study—the cards. "I cannot tell you which man," she concluded. Her finger moved to the next card. "Your past shall catch you," she said. Then quickly she added, "You shall be very rich. Your wealth shall surpass your wildest dreams."

"I never dream of wealth," Paulette murmured.

"But you shall—for the child's sake." She stabbed at another card, but Paulette did not look. "Fire and water! Those are your most dangerous enemies!" she cried.

Paulette started to back away from the old woman. It was not the threat that alarmed her, but the sudden high-pitched terror in the gypsy's voice. She wished she had not consented to the reading and glanced in the direction of the creek for help from Charity or Elisha; both were busy and paid not the slightest attention to her.

The old woman grabbed Paulette's arm. Despite her frailty, her grasp was strong. Her dark eyes blazed.

"It's a fever with you! Like all fevers, this fever can be fatal unless your blood is purified! Remember that —cleanse your blood before the fever takes your soul."

"Fever?" Paulette queried. "Are you predicting I'll catch cholera?"

"No, no, not cholera," the old woman said with impatience. "It's worse than cholera, much worse, because you won't know you have it until it's almost too late."

Paulette, already worrying about her recent health, bit her lower lip with worry. "Enough," she managed to say.

"But I must finish," the old woman protested. "I was promised food and gold for your reading. I must earn what I get." She smiled. "What I do not steal, I earn. They tell you, of course, that all gypsies are thieves." She laughed, cackled. "It is not always true. I am too old to steal. I would be caught, so I earn what I get by telling fortunes. You'll know greater thieves in your long life than even I have known among the gypsies. Thieves and the fever will be your curse."

"Enough, please!" Paulette cried. "You'll get your gold! I don't want to hear more!"

Then Charity was at her side, her bulk blocking the warmth of the sun. "Enough, old woman," she said. "Take your gold and be on your way." She took gold from her pouch and passed it into the bony, shriveled hands.

The gypsy gathered up her cards and stashed them in a pocket of her skirt. On her way to her wagon, she stopped, turned, and met Paulette's eyes. "Remember," she said, "your blood must be purified before the fever conquers you." She stepped onto the wheel of the wagon and hoisted herself into the seat. "Beware of fire and water, thieves, and, above all, the fever." She undid the reins and slapped them against the aged horse's rump. "The golden fever," she grumbled. "Go on, Liebling. We've not far to go, you and I.

Get your old bones moving." She slapped the horse's
rump again and then let the reins relax in her hands.
The wagon began to move, and the pots and pans and
bits of glass on string again took up their chorus of
clatter and chimes.

"What'd she say that so upset you?" Charity asked
with concern.

"Noth . . . nothing important," Paulette answered.
"Something about my life being plagued by thieves
and . . . and a fever. I just found it unpleasant and a
bit annoying."

"Then don't give it no mind," Charity said and
patted her hand with affection. "I thought it'd amuse
you, that only. I never thought a lady such as yourself
would take a gypsy serious." She led Paulette back to
the crest of the knoll and stood with her until all
sound of the gypsy's wagon had vanished. "Gypsies
are like children," she said. "They're great for play,
but you can't put any stock in what they say. They
just don't know no better."

"I'm fine now," Paulette assured her. "Go on, you're
wasting light."

Charity laughed at hearing her favorite statement
thrown back at her, and Paulette's dark mood created
by the gypsy was soon forgotten.

It was late afternoon when Charity finally gave in
to her exhaustion. She allowed Elisha to coax her into
resting; then, out of stubbornness, she refused to climb
up the embankment and rest under the trees. Instead,
she stretched out on the creek bank with pebbles for a
bed, and she closed her hooded eyes. Within moments
her heavy snoring could be heard above the sound of
the rushing water.

Paulette removed her shawl, went below, and covered the big woman. When she straightened up, she
saw that Elisha had been watching her.

"She's a good woman," he said. "The others, they
don't like her 'cause she's rough as a man and can
out-drink them. No man has his way with Miss Char-

ity unless she's willin'.'" He jammed his shovel into the loose earth and leaned on the handle. "Me and Miss Charity, we were talkin' 'bout you. She said if things had been different for her and she'd married, you'd be what she'd want as a daughter."

Paulette glanced at the big hulk of a sleeping woman. "Thank you, Elisha. I'm flattered. Both you and Miss Charity are my friends and I cherish you." She climbed back to the top of the knoll and resumed her position. She knew Elisha wouldn't wake up Charity until it was almost dark and time to return to camp.

She had stood for sometime, her legs aching, when she heard a strange rumbling sound. She glanced down at Elisha and saw that he, too, had heard and stood with his head raised like an alerted deer sniffing out danger.

"Is it thunder?" she called.

He didn't answer, but he had turned to face up-creek. The sound was growing louder, almost deafening. Then Elisha spun around, eyes wide with terror, and flung his shovel away from him. "Miss Paulette!" he screamed. "Run for your life!" He dove toward the embankment and was shaking Charity. "Wake up, Miss Charity!" Before she could be awakened, he was dragging the big woman to her feet. "Run, Miss Charity! Run! Or we'll both be drowned!"

Paulette remained where she was in confusion and alarm, not knowing whether to run, as Elisha had instructed, or to dash below and assist him with the sleeping Charity. Run from what? What had Elisha noticed that she had not? Charity was on her feet now, shaking herself, disoriented and trying to determine what danger had caused Elisha to scream almost incoherently. Her gaze went up to Paulette and the terror of a sudden thought vanished when she saw the younger woman still standing with the rifle across her breasts.

"Run, Miss Charity!" Elisha repeated and gave her a shove up the embankment.

Charity began to climb. Still confused, her feet slipped in the loose dirt and she slid back to the bottom, dragging Elisha with her.

Then Paulette saw the reason for Elisha's terror and understood the thundering sound she could not previously identify. Coming around the bend in the creek was a wall of water. It was so high it rose above the embankment, using the creek bed only as a guiding track.

Both Charity and Elisha saw the wall of water at the same time as Paulette. They began scrambling up the embankment with as much speed as their terror— and Charity's bulk—would allow.

"Miss Paulette, hang onto a tree!" Elisha screamed.

And Charity shouted, "Save yourself, child!"

The terror in their voices drove Paulette's fear even deeper. She stared at the approaching water, and knew neither of her friends would reach the top of the embankment before it struck. A scream of anguish tore from her throat. She saw the gypsy's wagon riding the crest of the wave. *Fire and water! Those are your most dangerous enemies!* Flinging away the rifle, she ran to the nearest tree, wrapped her arms around the rough bark, and pressed her body against its trunk. Elisha and Charity continued to scream at her, but she could no longer hear them over the deafening sound of the approaching water. She screamed back, begging them to hurry, but they heard her no better than she heard them.

The water struck them first. She saw Charity, arms thrown wide, lifted as if she were weightless. She was thrown to the ground on the rim of the embankment and then swallowed up. Elisha struggled to keep his footing and fight off the power of the wave, but his efforts were futile. He gave a mighty lunge and grabbed for a clump of scrub, but the bush proved too weak and the roots pulled out of the earth. Elisha swept past as the wave struck Paulette.

Fortunately Paulette had clung to the tree with her back facing the onrush of water. The power of it drove her brutally against the tree trunk, the water swirling up and over and around her. She opened her mouth to scream and the water rushed in to extinguish the scream in her throat. If the tree held and she did not unlock her fingers from around its trunk, she would not be swept away, as Charity and Elisha had been. She could feel the tree's movement and for a brief instant thought that it would topple, the roots being torn from the ground by the water's force.

Then, as quickly as it had struck, the water began to subside. She felt its power slipping down her back and buttocks and then playing gently around her legs. She released her grasp of the tree and stood watching the water edge back toward the funnel of the creek bed. The sound was growing dimmer as the onrush moved on toward the mining camp. Stunned, shaking with terror, and cold, she staggered to the rim of the embankment. Her senses were reeling, and her body felt numb.

*Charity and Elisha!*

She began to run in the direction the water had carried them, screaming their names with the agony of thinking they had been killed. She was like a madwoman, screaming and beating her breasts in anguish and helplessness.

She found Charity first.

The big woman had been wedged in the V of two trees. Paulette did not have to touch her to know she was dead. Her head and back had been broken, her head twisted to one side, thrown back, with the heavily hooded eyes open and staring.

Paulette sank to her knees in the mud. Covering her face, she wailed through her hands.

She did not know how many times Elisha had called her name before his voice reached her through her grief.

"Miss Paulette, Miss Paul——"

Elisha lay only a few yards beyond Charity, his legs buried in mud and debris and only his torso showing. Paulette ran to him and started to throw herself on him in her relief at finding him alive, but then she saw that his arm was broken, the white stump of bone protruding through the flesh of his forearm.

He began to dig himself from the mud with his un-injured arm, using it as a tool to scrape away the debris. "Help me, Miss Paulette." His voice was weak and filled with pain.

She could find nothing to dig him out with, so she used her hands, driving them into the muck and scooping it away from his legs. She did not feel the pain of her fingernails breaking or the cuts being made across her hands and arms by jagged bits of stones and wood splinters.

"Thank the Lord, you've been saved," he groaned. He saw the tears in her eyes. "Miss Charity couldn't have known much pain," he told her, and his own voice broke in a sob. "I told her it wasn't beavers dammin' up the creek. Beavers don't . . ." He cried out when Paulette accidentally touched his broken arm.

"Pull your legs out now, Elisha!" she cried. But the mud was still sucking him down. She grabbed him under his good arm and struggled to pull him back onto more solid ground. When his legs were free, she fell back, panting and drained. "No time to rest," she said. "We have to find someone to set that arm."

"Won't be no one," Elisha groaned. "They'll be busy seein' to themselves, even if they would help a nigger. The water went right through the camp. Lord knows how many were killed or washed away." Elisha struggled to his feet. He stood swaying, fighting to keep from blacking out from the pain. Finally, he said, "Find me some saplin's for a splint, Miss Paulette. And tear me some strips of cloth from the bottom of your dress."

"You're . . . you're going to do it yourself? But, Elisha . . ."

"Please, help me, Miss Paulette. Please do as I say."

She found several small saplings sticking out of the mud. She stripped them of twigs and washed the mud away in the still-swollen creek. Her dress was also mud-soaked; she tore strips and washed them, avoiding glancing in the direction of Charity's staring, lifeless eyes. When she took everything back to Elisha, he had found a small tree with a fork the height of his shoulder. He had placed his hand in the V and was waiting for her.

"What are you going to do?" she asked in horror. But she knew; she'd seen Clabe set a slave's broken arm. He had placed it between a fork of a tree, just as Elisha had done. Jerking the slave's body backward, the bone had snapped back into place. "You'll pass out with the pain," she warned, remembering the slave's reaction.

"Might at that," Elisha said. "Put the stakes round my arm and tie 'em loosely. If I pass out, all you'll have to do is tighten 'em."

She did as he instructed.

When the splint was ready, Elisha looked at her through eyes half-clouded by pain. "Don't cry, Miss Paulette. I was luckier than Miss Charity."

She hadn't realized the tears were running down her cheeks. She wiped them away and stepped up next to Elisha. Her hands were trembling, but she secured the splint.

Perspiration was beading Elisha's forehead despite the cold. He closed his eyes, his muscles going tense. Then, gritting his teeth, he yanked his weight away from his arm. The bone snapped back with a grinding sound and Elisha's scream cut through the still afternoon air.

Paulette quickly secured the splint.

Elisha had not passed out. She helped him lift his arm out of the tree fork. He squatted, breathing heavily, waiting for the pain to subside. After several moments he rose. "We have to get Miss Charity down," he said quietly. "We can't leave her there like some pig hung up to be smoked. She deserves better, the way she treated us, sharin' her gold when she didn't have to. Did you understand that, Miss Paulette? She had no need for us. She could have hired men to stand guard for her and help her dig the earth. I'd have worked for her for a wage. She had no cause to give me a share."

"I'd have done the little I did for no wages," Paulette murmured, and she began to cry again until Elisha silenced her by telling her to stop and help him.

Together they managed to get Charity's body down from the tree. They balanced her bulk between them, Elisha carrying the heaviest burden on his good shoulder, and they started working their way slowly back to camp.

Along the way they passed the gypsy's wagon, splintered, pots and pans scattered along the creek bank, and the horse, its head buried in the mud, its legs sticking straight into the air.

It wasn't until they heard the shouting from the camp that Paulette thought about Dester.

She hoped he had been spared.

If he was dead, she would just as soon have had the water claim her, also.

# Chapter Twelve

PAULETTE AND Elisha took Charity's body to her shack and laid her out on her bunk. Paulette, unable to look into the dead woman's face, turned away as Elisha covered her with a quilt.

"We'll bury her later," he said. And they went out to check the damage to the camp.

Fifteen miners had been killed by the wall of water, five never to be found. The animals that grazed along the creek bank, two cows that supplied the camp's milk, a goat, and countless chickens had also been swept away to a watery death. Most of the shacks built close to the water were destroyed, the miners' entire possessions gone with them: sluice boxes, mining pans, shovels—all equipment was lost.

One miner, a burly man with a thick crop of black hair and a shaggy beard, was sitting on the stoop of a missing shack, his face in his hands, crying. Both his friend and his guitar had been swept away; it was difficult to determine for which he cried more.

Dester's and Paulette's shack remained standing, the water merely splashing along its lower sides and loosening the stump step. Paulette let Elisha go on without her and remained waiting for Dester. He came not long after, trudging through the mud with his rifle slung over his shoulder. He stopped when he saw her standing in the doorway and stared at her for a long while before wading through the creek and drawing her into his arms.

"I feared I'd lost you," he murmured into her ear. "My darling, thank God you're safe. I prayed all the way back to camp."

"Charity's dead," she blurted out, "and so far there are fifteen miners dead or unaccounted for." She buried her face against his chest and wept. Then suddenly she stepped back from him, breaking his embrace. Her face had been resting against his chest, and his shirt and coat were dry; her own clothes were still wet and sagging on her body. "The dam must have been below your claim," she murmured.

"No," he said. "I was lucky. I'd gone up to high ground to hunt food for dinner." He lowered his head. "The Malay boy wasn't as lucky. I'd left him to guard the claim. He must have been swept away with his wagon and team, probably trying to save them—he was so damned fond of those animals."

She remembered the boy and her tears started anew.

"All I could think of was you," Dester told her. "I came back by Charity's claim, and when I saw there was nothing left of it, not even a boundary marker, I feared the worst." He drew her back into his arms, cuddling her head beneath his chin. "I should have hired men to take you away from here the day you arrived," he said. "If you'd been killed, I'd never have forgiven myself—never!"

Paulette and Elisha buried Charity on the mountainside above the camp. Elisha could do little digging because of his broken arm, and it took Paulette a good part of the morning to complete the grave. One of the miners helped them carry up the big woman's body. They wrapped her in a quilt and buried what few personal belongings they could find with her. Elisha, silent and brooding, scooped the dirt in over the body, and Paulette, borrowing a Bible, read a prayer at the grave, although the words were blurred through her tears.

Dester had gone out that morning as usual, leaving before the sun was up. He had wanted to make love to Paulette during the night, but she had refused and he had honored her wishes. When he had risen and lighted the lamp, he had bent beside the pallet and kissed her. "I'm sorry about your friend Charity," he had said.

She had not understood the pang of anger that had struck her with his words, the lack of feeling behind them. For the first time in her life, she looked into his pale blue eyes and saw them as cold and calculating. When he had attempted to kiss her again, she had turned her face away.

Elisha lifted his head when Paulette closed the Bible. "She's at peace now," he mumbled. "I hope there's a personal heaven and Miss Charity's found her mansion and fine breed of horses." He turned and stared down at the remaining shacks of Hangtown. "Me, I'll know no peace 'til I find out who built that dam," he said.

Paulette had picked up the cross they had built with Charity's name and date of her death burned into it —they did not know the date of her birth—and was jamming it into the loose earth at the head of the grave. She looked up when Elisha spoke. "Do you really believe someone built the dam?" she asked doubtfully. "Maybe it was beavers, as Charity suspected, and the pressure of the water tore the blockage free."

Elisha shook his head slowly from side to side. "No, Miss Paulette. It wasn't one of the Lord's innocent creatures that built that dam. It was a man—or men—and I'll not rest 'til I know who's guilty." He glanced over his shoulder at Charity's grave. "Goodbye, Miss Charity," he said scarcely above a whisper. "We hardly knew you, but we loved you, Miss Paulette and me. We're goin' to miss you a powerful lot, but we hope you're at peace and happy with your maker." He pulled a cloth cap onto his head. "I'm goin' to make a trip up-creek now, Miss Paulette. I want to see where that dam was built that killed our Miss Charity and the other miners."

Paulette grabbed up her shawl. "I'll go with you, Elisha. I've a right to," she added when she thought he was going to refuse her company.

"Aye, you have," he conceded, and there was something dark in his eyes that she could not read.

They did not travel their usual route, but cut through the fields and woods, Elisha leading the way. It was a gray, sunless day, with showers likely to begin in the afternoon. The wind off the Sierras was biting cold, and Paulette clutched her shawl tightly around her shoulders. Off in the distance she could hear the cry of a mountain lion and hastened her steps to stay close behind Elisha.

When they emerged from the scrub on the creek bank, Elisha told her they were well above Charity's claim. "The creek's its narrowest 'round the next bend," he said. "If a man was goin' to dam it, that'd be the spot he'd choose."

His estimation proved correct. When they rounded the bend, Paulette saw the narrow gorge between two rocky knolls where the creek squeezed, as through a funnel. The water was white-capped and thundered into a large pool beneath the gorge. The ground was still wet here, great sections of loose dirt and gravel dug out by the sudden onrush of water. Great trees leaned ready to topple, evidence of the force of the water against them.

"You stay here, Miss Paulette," Elisha told her. He climbed up the side of the rocky knoll, moving slowly because of the use of only one hand. At the top, where the water spilled over into the pool, he stopped climbing and began looking around. When he returned to the lower ground, it was with a chunk of broken board. He held it out to Paulette. "Sidin' from a shippin' crate," he said, his face dark and angry. "A man built the dam, all right. There's plenty of evidence it wasn't no beavers."

Paulette took the piece of crate siding and examined the printing: ——ISON STEAMSHIP COMPANY. Below that: ——W ORLEANS, LOU——

"We have to show this to the other miners," Paulette said. It was still difficult for her to comprehend anyone unleashing the wall of water on all those downstream. Why? For what possible purpose? "They'll have to investigate. Whoever did this must be brought to justice."

"Aye," Elisha mumbled fiercely. "Justice at Hangtown is swift. But no one's likely to listen to a nigger, Miss Paulette."

"But you're a miner the same as they are," she protested. "This is California. You're not a slave. You stood to lose as much by this crime as any of them. You lost as much—more! We lost Charity."

"Still, I'm a nigger," Elisha repeated. "They ain't goin' to look at me as nothin' else. The miners never been fond of me—Miss Charity or you, either. They was jealous that two women and a nigger had the richest claim." He bent his head and stared helplessly at his feet. "Probably one or two of them that was envious who done this," he said. "I've got my suspicions, but I ain't goin' to say nothin' 'til the miners get together and show they're willin' to bring the criminal to justice."

"You speak as if you doubt they will," Paulette said.

Elisha shrugged his great shoulders. "If they don't, I'll see that justice is done," he mumbled. "It's a promise I made to Miss Charity when you was readin' the Bible over her."

Paulette shuddered thinking of Elisha taking justice into his own hands. It was not so different in California after all, she thought. If a black man touched a white man, he'd be hanged. She sensed that and understood Elisha's insistence that she herself produce the piece of shipping crate and make the accusation of the dam being man-made. "We'll do together what has to be done," she told him, "but promise me you won't become a one-man vigilante committee and kill someone unless we're both convinced of their guilt and the miners refuse to hear us."

Elisha looked at her for a long while, studying her face carefully. What he was looking for she did not know, but he finally said, "I promise, Miss Paulette, 'cause I know you'd want to kill the man who took our Miss Charity's life as much as me."

They traveled back along the creek bank.

They had gone only a short distance when Elisha stopped and said, "This here's Mr. Granville's claim."

Paulette stopped: Dester's claim. It could not have been far removed from where she had spent her days with Charity and Elisha—yet Dester had refused to have her here with him while he mined. She looked around, saw the gaping holes of water where trees had been torn from the earth, where the embankment had caved into the creek after the onrush had passed. "The water's fury was at its strongest here," she murmured. "Thank God Dester was hunting on high ground."

"Yes, Miss Paulette," Elisha said in a strange voice.

She turned and stared at him, but he had averted his gaze and was staring off into the distance. "I wonder where Dester is today?" she asked, more of herself than of Elisha.

"Probably huntin' again," Elisha answered, but she did not hear him.

Had she, she might have retracted the promise she had made to him only minutes before.

They heard the noise before rounding the bend in the creek and seeing the activity at Charity's claim.

There were at least a dozen miners crawling over the sight, digging, panning, tearing great chunks out of the embankment.

Paulette lay a restraining hand on Elisha's arm. "Why?" she asked. "What right have they?"

"They know there's gold there," Elisha said angrily. "It don't matter that we've just put Charity in the ground." He lowered his gaze in disgust.

Then Paulette saw Dester. He was working with a sluice box, working so hard that he had removed his coat and had rolled up his sleeves. His blond hair, damp with perspiration, was flattened against his head. There was something about the way he worked —the way all the miners were working, with a kind of possessed fury—that made the gooseflesh rise on her arms. She released Elisha's arm and hurried forward.

"No, Miss Paulette!" Elisha cried. "There's nothin' you can do now!"

Ignoring Elisha, Paulette rushed down the embankment and into the midst of the busy miners. "What are you doing here?" she shouted. "This isn't your claim! You're ghouls!" She was aware of Elisha standing behind her, urging her to come away.

Then Dester saw her. His face clouded over. Slinging his shovel into the sluice box, he pushed his way through the miners. "Go back to the shack," he commanded. "This place is no place for you."

"No place for me?" she cried incredulously. "You and these men—you're the ones with no right to be here! This was Charity's claim—Charity's and Elisha's and mine!"

The other miners had stopped and stood watching.

Dester's face was twisted with fury. He grabbed her arm and pulled her roughly toward the embankment. "Charity's dead," he snapped. "It's an open claim now. There's gold here and we intend to mine it." He gave her a push up the embankment. "Now, get back to the shack and quit messing in where it doesn't concern you." Quieter, so the others could not hear, he added, "You're embarrassing me in front of the men."

"Embarrassing you?" she shouted. "I don't even know you anymore! You're not the same man I fell in love with back home!" She fought to control her tears. "Has your greed taken you over completely? Can't you see what you're doing? Elisha and I just buried Charity, with no help from any of you! You're too busy stealing what was hers!"

Dester's face flushed scarlet. "Damn you, Paulette! Get back to the shack and wait for me!"

"No! You come with me! Come away from here! You don't need gold badly enough to steal it!"

"I'm not stealing it!" he yelled. "It's an open claim!"

Paulette's own anger matched his. "It's Elisha's claim!" she cried. "Charity made him her partner! All of you know that!"

Crimmon, standing behind Dester, laughed. "We're not lettin' the nigger have it," he said. "No nigger's gettin' the richest claim in Hangtown."

Elisha started to step forward but checked his movement. He understood Crimmon was trying to provoke him into attacking him. The other miners were waiting. If he made a move they'd beat him to death with their shovels. What did one black man's life mean when it stood between them and a fortune in gold?

Paulette waited for Dester to challenge Crimmon. When he did not, she could not believe it. "You always championed the freedom of the slaves!" she cried. "And you're not even going to attempt to defend Elisha's rights? You even parted with your own father over . . ."

"Shut up, Paulette!" Dester shouted. "I'm warning you, you little fool! Charity didn't register any partnership with Elisha. I told you, it's an open claim. We've sent a man to Sacramento to refile the claim in all our names. What gold there is here belongs to all of us."

Elisha stepped past Dester and climbed the embankment. "Come along, Miss Paulette," he said and stretched out his hand to assist her up the incline. "Leave the claim to 'em," he told her. "I'll see you back to camp."

Paulette pushed his hand away. "Never!" she cried. She stared unbelievingly from Dester to Elisha. "If neither of you will stand up for your rights," she told

Elisha, "then I shall! Charity would have wanted you to have her claim, not these . . . these animals." She raised the piece of crate siding above her head. "This came from where the creek was dammed!" she shouted. "You've all been so obsessed with your greed that you haven't even considered the dam. There's plenty of evidence it was man-made. That means someone—probably one of you—dammed the creek for the express purpose of killing Charity and Elisha and myself. How else would you get this claim? But you also killed fifteen other miners. What will the mining authorities in Sacramento say when they've been told? They'll not honor a refiling on this claim in any of your names because one of you is a murderer." She met Dester's eyes with a triumphant smirk.

The miners began to grumble and shout, some cursing her.

Crimmon stepped up beside Dester. "She's right, you know," he said. "Happened the same at Dry Gulch." His beady eyes turned on Paulette. "You goin' to let your woman stand up against you for the sake of a nigger?" he asked Dester.

Dester spun to face him, and Paulette, seeing his profile, noted that his face was hard and flushed and ugly in his anger. But he did not speak to Crimmon, did not challenge him; instead, he spun back to Paulette, glaring at her. "The dam was man-made, you say?" he said slowly. Raising his arm, he pointed an accusing finger at Elisha. "I accuse that nigger!" he shouted. "He built the dam. He wanted Charity's claim all to himself."

A shout of approval went up among the miners.

Elisha began to back away, glancing from side to side, seeking an avenue of escape.

Paulette was horror-stricken. "Elisha was with us!" she cried. "His arm was broken when the wave struck! You can't accuse him! He's innocent!"

"He'd have a hard time provin' it," Crimmon said and laughed, "especially with witnesses against him."

"But . . . but I'd testify on his behalf," Paulette sputtered. "Dester, you can't . . ."

"I told you to go back to the shack," he said through clenched teeth. "Now, go before . . ."

"Before what?" she challenged. But his expression filled her with fear. He's taken leave of his senses, she thought. It's the only explanation.

The miners began dropping their shovels and gold pans and advancing toward the embankment.

"Run, Elisha!" Paulette screamed.

"No, Miss Paulette. I'll run and they'll shoot me down," Elisha answered. "That's what they want, for me to run. Then they'll swear it proved my guilt." Elisha backed up a few short steps, wanting to put more distance between himself and Paulette for her protection. "Do as Mr. Granville told you," he said. "Go back to camp. What's goin' to happen here ain't for your eyes."

"I believe the nigger loves your woman," Crimmon told Dester. "I think maybe there's been some . . ." He was silenced by the fury in Dester's eyes.

Paulette rushed up the embankment and placed herself between Elisha and the miners. "What can we do, Elisha?" she asked helplessly.

"Nothin' we can do, Miss Paulette."

"You run and I'll stay behind you," she suggested. "I'll stay in the way of their rifle fire." Desperation was making it difficult for her to speak; her throat was constricted, her heart pounding loudly in her ears.

"No, Miss Paulette," Elisha said firmly. "Look at their faces. They'd shoot you down the same as me if they had to."

Paulette, staring at the miners, knew what Elisha said was true. "Dester, please!" she pleaded. "Don't let them do this!" She rushed to him and would have flung herself into his arms had he not pushed her aside.

Picking up a shovel, Dester advanced up the embankment with the other miners. Elisha was holding his ground; he knew his chances were nil, knew that if he tried to run he'd be dead before traveling a yard. His only hope was to stand and take the beating he understood they'd give him and to hope they'd show mercy and not kill him. He was a powerful man and knew he could kill several of the miners before they killed him—if he could have been certain which one had built the dam and killed Miss Charity, he would have given his life to take that one with him.

Paulette scrambled to her feet, from where she had fallen when Dester had shoved her. She hurried between the miners, pleading with them, but understood by their expression that her pleas fell on deaf ears. Hurrying forward, she threw herself on Dester, screaming and pounding on his chest. "Stop this! Stop this now or I'll never forgive you!"

Again he shoved her aside.

When she pulled herself up from the ground, she saw the first blow strike Elisha. The shovel handle thudded against his stomach and he doubled over from the pain. The second blow fell on his back and he stumbled and went down on his knees. Then the miners discarded their weapons and surrounded him, using their fists to pummel him to the ground. There were no words spoken, no cries of agony from Elisha. The entire scene seemed unreal, something from a nightmare from which Paulette could not awaken herself.

Dester had stepped back and stood watching. The expression on his face sent shivers of terror through her. When she had been told about her mother and her half-sister, the madness of one and the evil of the other, it was the same expression she now saw on Dester's face that always filled her imagination.

Elisha was no longer moving. The hands he had wrapped behind his head to ward off the blows were limp. Blood flowed from his scalp and was collecting against the side of his battered face.

"For God's sake, stop them!" Paulette wailed.

One of the miners had raised his rifle with the intention of bringing the butt down against Elisha's head.

Dester, hearing her scream in the otherwise silent attack, suddenly seemed to come to his senses. He stepped forward and grabbed the rifle from the miner just before the death blow was delivered.

Paulette cried out with gratitude. Struggling to her feet again, she pushed through the miners and bent beside Elisha. He was badly injured, but alive. She ripped away a section of her skirt and dabbed at the worst of the head wounds.

"Why'd you stop me?" she heard the miner with the rifle ask Dester. "If the bastard lives and your woman testifies in his behalf, they may just grant him the claim."

"She'll not testify," Dester answered. "And he'll not live. We'll hang him tonight, same as we hang all the criminals at Hangtown."

Paulette pulled herself tearfully off the pallet. She had lain there since Dester had carried her back to camp and locked her inside the shack, crying and trembling—and praying. It was late afternoon and the miners had returned to Charity's claim to steal from the earth what they could before darkness fell.

Elisha was also locked in one of the shacks. She had seen the miners carry him in, still unconscious, with blood dripping from the wound on his head. They had flung him inside as if he had been no more than baggage, and she had heard Crimmon tell one of the miners to stand guard until they returned. "It's a hangin' we'll have this night," he had said, laughing, and had dragged his hunched frame back along the creek toward the claim.

Paulette tore the gunny sacking away from the narrow window. The opening was too small to accommodate her body; otherwise she would have pulled herself through. There was no guard outside Dester's shack. The door had been bolted from the outside and a thin log had been braced against it should she prove capable of breaking the rusted bolt.

There were a couple of miners working the creek

near the middle of the camp. They were too far distant to hear her unless she screamed. The shack where Elisha had been locked up was only a few yards away. The man guarding him leaned against the door, his rifle propped against his leg. His arms were crossed over his chest and a smoking pipe dangled from his lips. Paulette did not remember seeing the miner before. He was young, perhaps in his midtwenties, with auburn hair and a ruddy complexion. His leanness and the gaunt expression on his face told her he had not been successful at the mines. His coat had been much mended with patches of varying colors of cloth and the leather heels of his boots were worn down almost even with the soles.

She glanced up at the sky, but because of the overcast she could not determine the time. The miners, she feared, would be returning soon to drag Elisha from the shack and hang him. Before leaving camp, someone had thrown a rope over a nearby tree. The noose had already been tied, so its purpose was unmistakable. She shuddered and pulled her head back inside. Pacing, she wrung her hands in frustration.

At that moment she hated Dester more than she thought possible, yet, at the same time, she blamed the change in him on some mysterious illness, a result of his obsession with gold. She hated him and still sought excuses for his vile behavior. Dark was the day he had left Plantation Bend; darker still was the day she had followed him.

Her pacing came to a halt before the door. Since her arrival, Dester had filled in the cracks between the saplings to prevent the miners from seeing inside. She pressed her weight against the door but it held firmly. She backed away and continued her pacing. She had to do something—and soon—if she was to save Elisha. She could count on no one to help her; even if they knew what was being done was unjust, they were more interested in the gold than they were in human life.

Then she remembered the gold hidden under the floorboards. She took a knife from the counter and pried the loose board free. The can she had stored the gold in was still there. She removed the precious metal and sat staring at it, thinking it incomprehensible that men would murder and die for it, that it could create a fever so intense that a man could take leave of his senses for want of it. She wrapped the gold in a scarf and set it aside while she dug through her trunks for the small pistol Clabe had given her before she began her journey. After having spent days handling Charity's rifle, the pistol appeared so much smaller and less lethal. She shoved it into the pocket of her dress.

When she returned to the window, the man guarding Elisha had stepped away from the door and was standing down at the creek. Putting his rifle aside, he squatted and began throwing pebbles into the water.

She swallowed, fighting the constriction in her throat, and called out, "Is he still alive?"

The man turned, surprise reflected in his blue eyes. He had apparently forgotten she had been locked in the shack. "Yes, ma'am," he said, rising. "I heard the nigger movin' about and groanin'. But he won't be alive long. They say they're hangin' him when it gets dark."

"Were you with the others at Charity's . . . when they took him?"

"No, ma'am," He moved toward the shack and stopped a few feet away from the window. "I've just come from Stockton, been here only two days. I heard stories about a rich vein at Hangtown. Me and my brothers, we came to try our luck." He was younger than he had appeared, not yet twenty, she judged. He was not only new to Hangtown, but also to the gold fields; he had not yet lost his manners and developed the crudeness of the other miners.

She felt an inkling of hope. "What they're doing is wrong. You know that, don't you?"

"Ma'am, it ain't for me to judge," he answered. "I'm only doin' what my brothers told me to do. I'm guardin' the nigger 'cause I have to." He scratched his head. "I don't think it's right, them locking you up.

You couldn't have done anything, your being a woman, frail, and dependent, but . . . well, I guess they have their reasons." He started to move away.

"Wait!" Paulette cried.

Bored with guarding Elisha's shack, he hesitated. He had left his rifle on the embankment, but, then, the woman was locked inside and was obviously not dangerous. It had been a long while since he had been in the company of a woman. "I ain't much of a talker, ma'am. I know you're probably lonely locked up in there, but . . . well, your man will be comin' back soon. I'm sure he'll let you out to watch the hangin'."

Paulette winced. She wanted to scream at the young man, scream about the injustice to Elisha and the cruelty of the miners, but she forced herself to remain calm. "How long have you been in the gold fields?" she asked.

"Three months, ma'am. We're from Maryland. Our Pa has a farm there, but things weren't goin' well for us. The crops failed last year, and then none of us were able to find other work." He pulled the collar of his coat around his neck because of the chill wind that whistled through the camp. "We heard all the tales about pickin' up gold nuggets in California and siftin' a fortune out of the sand. My brothers caught the fever and I came along 'cause there was nothin' else for me to do. As far as I've seen, the stories about gold were all fancy."

"Most of them are," Paulette agreed. "The richest strike in Hangtown belonged to my friend Charity."

The youth nodded. "The woman killed in the flood," he murmured. "I heard about her."

"It wasn't a real flood," Paulette told him. "Someone had dammed the creek deliberately. I'm not sure, but I think it was done to kill Charity and take over her claim."

He looked at her doubtfully. "Kill a woman over gold?"

"I can prove it," she assured him. "So can Elisha. That's why he's locked in there. The other miners are working my friend's claim. It really belongs to Elisha."

"The nigger?"

"She'd made him a partner," Paulette said.

"They told me he was a runaway nigger from Georgia—that it was him who was tryin' to steal the richest claim in Hangtown. That's why they're hangin' him tonight."

"It's not true!"

The youth stepped away, disbelief reflected in his expression. "Well, it ain't for me to say, ma'am. I told you I'm just guardin' him 'cause I was told to." He moved back to the embankment and picked up his rifle. "A nigger's a nigger, ma'am, no matter how you look at it. We owned two on the farm before Pa was forced to sell them, and neither one was worth the food they ate. You shouldn't upset yourself over what happens to him." He glanced toward the shack he was guarding, having heard movement inside. "You, nigger! Stay away from that window!" He lifted his rifle threateningly. "I can't talk no more, ma'am. I've got to watch this bastard 'til they come for him."

Paulette leaned out as far as possible, but she could not get a glimpse of Elisha. She turned back to the youth, desperation in her voice. "You came to California for gold," she said. "What if I gave you more gold than you'd possibly find in the ground?"

The youth looked at her suspiciously. "For what?" Then his eyes narrowed. "How'd you get so much gold?"

"I worked with my friend and Elisha," she told him. "I have a third of what we took from the claim."

"What happened to her gold, your dead friend's?"

"We don't know. She hid it and we weren't able to find it."

"And what do you want me to do for this gold?" he asked.

Paulette swallowed, took a deep breath, and said, "Let Elisha and me escape before the miners return."

The youth stared at her thoughtfully for a long while before saying, "Let me see this gold."

Paulette felt her hope rise. "It's inside," she said. When she saw his look of doubt, she said quickly, "Think what you and your brothers could do with the gold. Think of the things you could buy, the women you could have, how you could help your parents." She saw the familiar look begin to blaze in his blue eyes.

Suddenly, Elisha shouted, "No, Miss Paulette! He'd set us free and then shoot us as we ran!"

"Shut up, you black bastard!" the youth shouted. He stepped up to Paulette's window and she stood back for him to see in.

She opened the scarf on the table and the gold glistened under the light of the map.

"What would I tell my brothers?" the youth asked, more of himself than of her. "If I go against what they tell me to . . ."

"Tell them Elisha struck you through the window," Paulette suggested. "Tell them when you came to, we were gone."

She knew the youth was considering her suggestion; he was also considering what Elisha had said. If he let them free and then shot them, he'd have the gold and no trouble from the miners. She saw all this in his eyes —also his reluctance to shoot a woman. She suddenly knew she couldn't trust him. The gold again, she thought—it turned good men to evil.

"I'll take the gold," the youth announced. "Pass it out to me."

Smiling, Paulette wrapped the corners of the scarf over the gold. "You'll let me out first," she said quietly, "and then let out Elisha." She tied the corners of the scarf into a knot. "It's a small fortune I'm offering you, and for so very little. Still, if you don't want to take risks . . ." She made as if to return the scarf to the open can.

"All right," he said. He moved away from the window and she heard him scraping the wedge away from the door. The bolt was thrown, the door opened, and he stood in the doorway.

She tossed the scarf onto the table and it landed with a thud. "There," she said, "it's yours."

As he passed her, she drew the pistol from her pocket and aimed it at the back of his head.

He untied the scarf and whistled at the amount of gold. Then, scooping it into his pockets, he laughed softly. "Women ain't ever any good at business deals," he said. "My Ma, she couldn't even sell eggs and make a profit. You, ma'am, you're no better. I've got your gold and I don't have to do anything for it. They can hang the nigger for all I care, and your man can take care of you himself if you holler about my stealin' from you. No, ma'am, you're no good at business. My brothers would skin me alive if I'd let you and the nigger escape." He started to turn.

Paulette gently squeezed the trigger.

The youth stood for one long moment, surprise fixed on his face and in his eyes. Then his mouth fell open, all expression seemed to fade, and he crumpled to the floor.

Paulette covered her mouth to stifle her scream.

She heard Elisha calling her name, but it seemed as if from a great distance. To prevent herself from fainting, she forced her eyes away from the youth. "God forgive me," she mumbled, but she knew the youth's dead face would live with her for the remainder of her life.

"Miss Paulette! You all right? Miss Paulette!"

She came to the door and glanced out. The two miners who had been panning the creek had not heard the shot; they were stooped, sloshing the water around in their pans. She slipped through the door and rushed to Elisha's shack. There was no bolt, only a crossbar of wood. She threw it and stepped inside.

Elisha was standing near the window. He had wrapped a cloth around his head and the blood had already soaked through. "You kill him, Miss Paulette?"

She nodded.

"Lord, Miss Paulette, now they'll hang you, too," he moaned.

"No one's hanging anyone!" she cried. "We're leaving before the miners return." She grabbed a coat from its peg and tossed it to Elisha. "There are horses across the creek. We'll have to ride like hell, but . . ."

"Horse-stealin', too," Elisha mumbled. "Oh, well, Miss Paulette, they can only hang us once." He pulled his arms through the coat sleeves, something that required great effort because of his weakened condition.

Paulette, although the thought sickened her, dashed back to Dester's shack and took as much gold from the youth's pocket as would fill her own. When she came out again, there was a thin mist falling. Good, she thought, it'll make finding us more difficult.

When she said this to Elisha, he said, "Might also bring the miners back to camp sooner."

They rode hard until darkness fell; then they gave the horses free rein. The mist turned to rain and the rain soaked their clothing. Paulette longed to stop, to build a fire and dry herself, but fear of Dester and the miners finding them made her remain in the saddle. She closed her eyes, but opened them immediately when the face of the youth she had killed flashed against the insides of the lids. Near dawn they stopped and stretched themselves and let the horses graze. They drank water from puddles and Paulette felt cramps in her stomach and yearned for food.

Elisha, silent for so long, finally said, "Where you goin', Miss Paulette?" His voice was still weak; the loss of blood had drained his strength.

"We're going to San Francisco," she told him. "We'll be safe there. I have a small house and two friends who'll look after you until you're better."

"Then I'm comin' back," Elisha told her, "after you're safe and I'm better. I've still got my promise to Miss Charity. If they don't catch me and hang me for bein' a horse thief, I won't rest 'til her murderer's layin' beside her."

Paulette said nothing. She believed without doubt that Dester had been the one who built the dam. She had seen it in his face when he had stood watching the miners beat Elisha. It had been as if a great insight into his madness had been opened to her and she had glimpsed what she had hitherto been blinded to. It had not only been Charity he had wished to kill, but her, as well. The gold had meant more to him. Gold was his god and his lover. She had lost him.

When they reached Stockton, both looked more dead than alive. They bought food and slept on the docks until the launch arrived. Paulette bought their passage downriver. She huddled in the stern, shivering with fever, passing in and out of consciousness, and wondering, when she had control of her thoughts, if she would live through the journey.

# Part III

SAN
FRANCISCO

# Chapter Thirteen

THE FIRST pale light of dawn began creeping through
the cracks in the draperies. The coals in the fireplace
glowed red. Miriam, her head fallen forward onto her
chest, slept fitfully, awakening periodically from the
cramps in her neck. She awakened now, stretched
herself, and inhaled the aroma of coffee from the
kitchen. She rose and lighted the lamp, glancing at the
figure on the bed.

Paulette had been home for four days and had not
been out of her bed since Chang had carried her in
from the front porch. Senseless with fever, she would
awaken, cry out incoherently, and then fall back,
whimpering and drenched with perspiration, against
the pillows. The only nourishment she had taken was
the thin soup Miriam had forced between her lips.

Chang, who always rose before the first light,
pushed the coffee to the side of the flames. He removed his rifle and gun belt from the cabinet and set
them beside the door. Hunting, he had found, was always best done when the animals first began to stir.
Now that San Francisco had grown so rapidly, he had
to trek greater distances to the woods; if he was de-
layed, the other hunters would send the animals fleeing before them and he would come home without
food for supper.

Quietly, he peeled vegetables and added them to the soup he had prepared the day before. Miriam had been a good pupil, learning all he had taught her about cooking, but now that Miss Paulette was home he chose to resume his old chores. Thoughts of Miss Paulette caused his brow to furrow. There were so many unanswered questions: Why had she returned without her fiancé? Who was the giant of a black man who had carried her to the door and then vanished? What horrid experiences had she suffered at the mines? He shook his head slowly, wished he were the sort to question. But he was not—and Miss Paulette, when she wasn't sleeping, was not capable of answering questions, anyway. He heard the bedroom door opening and turned to see Miss Miriam slipping quietly into the kitchen.

"I think her fever's broken," Miriam said, answering the question she saw reflected on his face. "She's sleeping peacefully now." She took down a cup and poured herself coffee, thinking as she did so that Mr. Slater would have gone into a rage at this new addiction of hers to the strong brew. *Defiling the body the Lord had given her.* She moved to the table, groggy from lack of sleep, and held her hands around the cup to warm them.

Chang glanced at his rifle and decided another moment more would not lessen his chances of killing meat for supper. He sat at the table with Miriam and struggled to express a thought that had been plaguing him. "Miss Paulette, she's . . . she's not the same lady who left us," he said.

Miriam, who had come to know and read his expressions, said, "She will be, Chang. The fever's cracked her lips and the sun's baked her skin. I've been bathing her with oil and herbs. She'll be the same in time." But she understood Chang was not referring to Paulette's appearance. It was her nightmare cries that alarmed him, her ramblings during the height of the fever.

"Who is this man she claims to have killed?" Chang murmured. "And what does she mean by '*fire and water*'? She constantly screams, 'Fire! Water! Danger!' He laced his small fingers together and placed them in his lap. "It's most distressing," he said.

Miriam smiled at him, thinking how her English lessons had not been wasted. "Only a product of her delirium, I suspect," she said. "In a day or two she'll be up and about, and will most likely settle any mystery—if there is one."

Chang nodded, although not convinced. He pushed himself away from the table and began shouldering his rifle and gun belt.

"Now, don't let yourself be seen," she warned. "You know what may happen if they see you with a rifle." Several Chinese had been beaten when they had been caught with firearms, their single braids cut off to humiliate them. There were even rumors that the Chinese working the mines had been driven off or killed and in retaliation tongs were being formed. Chang was even in more danger because his own people resented his devotion to a white woman.

The little man nodded his understanding. "I'll try for a deer today," he said. "When she's better, Miss Paulette will need meat to gain her strength."

"A rabbit stew will suffice," Miriam told him. "Besides, there's that package of venison left so mysteriously on the doorstep."

"Wouldn't use it," Chang said excitedly. "Maybe poisoned." He had found the package and brought it in to Miriam. When they had seen the contents, he had urged her to throw it to the dogs, but she had refused.

Miriam was inclined to agree with him. There was too much going on that she did not understand—the black man who had carried Paulette to the house— and Jeremiah Walker was back again, although he had not been to his grand house since Paulette had gone away. Miriam had seen him for the past three days, riding his horse up to the clump of trees, dismounting, and standing staring at the house.

Chang opened the door and the wind whistled through. "Miss Paulette's letters," he said, "I put them beside her bed." He closed the door and Miriam saw him tramping across the yard toward the woods.

She finished her coffee, added more broth to Chang's soup, and slipped quietly back into the bedroom. Within moments of resuming her position in the rocker, she was asleep.

Paulette opened her eyes and watched the light within the room grow stronger. She had heard Chang and Miriam talking in the kitchen, but she had been too weak to call out to them. Her mind was a confusion of thoughts and memories. She remembered Elisha carrying her from the docks, Miriam's cries when she had opened the door, and Chang carrying her to her room. But it was unclear if she had been home for hours, days, or weeks, drifting as she had in and out of dreams—nightmares. She had been aware of Miriam smearing her skin with foul-smelling oils, of warm broth being forced down her throat. She had cried out for Charity, for Elisha—and Dester. Their faces haunted her along with the face of the youth she had killed.

She lifted her head from the pillow with great effort and gazed at the sleeping Miriam. "Miriam," she called, but her voice was scarcely a whisper and did not awaken the exhausted woman. She let her head collapse back against the goosedown pillow. Tears were stinging her eyes and her cracked lips trembled with sobs.

Then Miriam was hovering above her, soothing her brow with a cool cloth. "You're all right now," she said. "You're safe at home. Chang and I are taking care of you. You're weak. Don't try to talk now. Wait until you've your strength back."

She pulled the quilts up to Paulette's chin. When Paulette clutched at her hand and refused to relinquish her grasp even after she had drifted back to

sleep, Miriam sank to the edge of the bed and held
her until her fear had passed.

The following day Paulette sat up in bed and ate
all that was given her. She still did not feel strong
enough for conversation, but she managed to ask
about Elisha.

"The black man who brought you home?" Miriam
said. "He put you into Chang's arms, and when next
we thought of him he was gone."

"Poor Elisha," Paulette moaned. "He'll never manage to buy his wife and child free unless he sheds his
obsession for revenge."

The next day she insisted on being carried into the
kitchen and placed in a chair beside the window. Miriam, consenting against her will, wrapped two shawls
around Paulette's shoulders and tucked a quilt around
her legs. She forbade Chang to use the kitchen door
for fear of giving Paulette a chill, and he was forced
to carry the wood around the house and through the
front door.

Paulette stared through the panes with only half-
sight. The house next door—Jeremiah's mansion—
blocked most of her view and she could see but a
small corner of the bay. There were sparrows darting
about in the narrow yard and using the white pickets
as perches. Her flowers were in bloom in a profusion
of colors. As before she had gone to the gold fields,
she could still hear the sounds of hammering and sawing and men shouting. How long ago that seemed, she
thought. An entire lifetime. She would have liked to
have been taken to the front of the house for a view
below the hill, but she did not want to trouble Chang
or Miriam. They were busy, although she knew they
were watching her closely. "I heard Happy Valley
burned," she said.

"Yes, but it's built back again," Miriam answered,
"as much of a pigsty as before."

"The entire village is growing," Chang said.

"They're calling it a town now, but it will soon be a city."

Thinking back to the day she had sailed into the bay, Paulette could not imagine San Francisco as a city—it had looked like no more than a battleground. "And the hill?" she asked. "Have any other houses been built on the hill?"

"Just one, beyond Mr. Walker's," Miriam told her, and she glanced at her out of the corner of her eyes. "Mr. Walker's never moved into his house," she said quietly. "Men keep coming and bringing new furniture and carrying out the old, but he's never spent a night there to my knowledge. We've never seen a light, Chang nor I." Miriam waited, expecting Paulette to make some comment, but when none was forthcoming she turned her attention back to carving the rabbits Chang had killed.

"And letters?" Paulette asked. "Have there been none?"

Chang and Miriam exchanged glances.

Finally, Miriam said, "I put them away until you were stronger. There are two, both from Louisiana."

"I'll read them now," Paulette told her.

"Perhaps you should wait until you're stronger," Miriam suggested. "They've waited now over two months."

"No, now," Paulette said. She suspected the worst and there was no need delaying. She must write Vienna soon about Dester and she had no idea what to say, how much to relate.

The letters were both short. The first informed her that Clabe had died quietly in his sleep and had been buried beside his father and mother on the hill behind the plantation house. The second told her that Tom had been killed in prison and that Katrina, dramatically forcing herself back into society, had met a gentleman from Atlanta and was already talking of a wedding. There was no mention of Dester, no suggestion that she return—it was as if Vienna had given up hope and accepted the fact that their lives would from now on be separated.

Paulette let the letters flutter to the floor beside her chair. Her tears for Clabe fell silently. He had been like a father to her, the only father she had known.

"Bad news?" Miriam asked as she bent to retrieve the white sheets of paper. "Don't fret. You've yourself to think of. You must get your strength back." She wanted to say more, but not knowing about Dester, she dared not venture to make a remark about the future.

Paulette pushed the quilt from her legs and tried to rise; she was too weak to do so on her own, and Chang had to assist her back to her bed. She saw the worried look on the little man's face and patted his hand as he pulled the cover over her. "It's all right, Chang. Nothing to worry about. I'll be fine in a day or so." She closed her eyes, exhausted from her first venture from her bed. "There's so much to do," she murmured, "so much to consider. It's a new life ahead now—a different life from the one I anticipated."

Before Chang slipped out of the room, she was fast asleep.


On Sunday Chang carried a chair into the front yard and Paulette sat in the fresh air. Miriam, horrified by the coloring of Paulette's skin from the sun at the mines, insisted she not sit out without her parasol. "A lady's skin should be soft and as white as milk," she scolded.

Miriam and Chang, leaving Paulette, watched her quietly for a moment from the window. "I'm worried about her," Miriam confessed.

"She's much improved," Chang said.

"Physically," Miriam murmured. "But there's something on her mind, something she hasn't told us." She let the curtain fall from her hand and urged Chang into the kitchen, where there was meat to be cleaned. "Her fiancé, most likely," she concluded, "since she refuses to speak about him."

Paulette let her gaze sweep across the valley. How it has grown in so short a period, she thought. She had the vague thought that she had grown with the town, and for the first time since her arrival she felt a kindred spirit with San Francisco. The mud flats were being filled in and buildings were springing up, warehouses and storage sheds, too. The Union Hotel no longer occupied its entire block. There was a sprawling building beside it, constructed in the New Orleans style of architecture, a mingling of French and Spanish and colonial; the huge sign told her it was The Barbary Coast. The dirt streets, always nothing more than rivers of mud after a heavy rain, had been surfaced with gravel, and gas streetlamps had been erected on several corners. The hill opposite was now dotted with fine houses—although none so fine as Jeremiah's. Roads wound themselves upward where pathways had been only a few short months before. Trees had been thinned out and shrubbery had been planted. She sat twirling her parasol and considering the changes. Had it been similar with Dester's grandparents, she wondered, when they had come to New Orleans and watched the city sprawl beyond its original boundaries? Thoughts of home flooded over her and she shook herself to shed them. She did not want to think of home now, or of Dester—especially of Dester. There were too many facets that she did not feel quite well enough yet to consider. She closed her eyes and breathed deeply of the cool, crisp air.

She did not hear the horse's hooves or have the sensation of being watched. It was merely by chance that when she opened her eyes she was gazing in the direction of the nearby trees. She caught her breath with a little start and felt her back stiffen. How long had Jeremiah been standing there, his arm stretched across his horse's saddle, watching her? When he knew he had been seen, he waved. She nodded and averted her gaze, but she was aware that he was tying the horse's reins to a tree limb and knew he would approach her.

When she turned again he stood at the picket fence. He had removed his hat and was running a hand through his black hair. "Good afternoon, Miss Favière." Although it was a statement, she detected the question buried within by his tone of voice.

She met his dark eyes directly. "Good afternoon, Mr. Walker. And, yes, it is still Miss Favière," she said.

"I . . . I didn't mean to . . ." Her directness had confused him; still, she could see it pleased him, as well.

"There was no preacher at Hangtown," she said, although she felt no compulsion to explain.

A twinkle crept into his eyes. "Barbaric places, those mining camps." He became serious again. "I heard you were ill," he said. "I trust you're better."

"Much." She wondered if the sun-darkened coloring of her skin was unattractive to him—if, like Miriam, he thought a lady should be the color of white marble.

"I trust also you received the meat and wine and flowers I had left on your doorstep?"

So it had been Jeremiah. She had thought as much when Miriam had told her of the mysterious presents that appeared daily since her return. "Thank you." Then she could not refrain from adding, "A gentleman would have enclosed a card."

Jeremiah laughed. "You always told me I wasn't a gentleman," he said. "I thought it best to stick to form. I have not changed despite my success."

"Your gambling house must be doing well, indeed, for you to afford a house such as the one that blocks my afternoon sun and destroys my view." She glanced fleetingly over her shoulder at the great brown structure.

"The Barbary Coast is the rage of San Francisco," he told her, ignoring her complaint. "There isn't a miner who travels down from the gold fields who doesn't leave at least half his gold in my place." She detected the pride in his voice. "But, then, you consider it a non-gentlemanly profession, gambling."

"Gambling is a gentleman's prerogative. Being a professional gambler is quite a different story."

"But without professional gamblers, who would those gentlemen pit their skills against?" he asked, amused.

How devilishly handsome he is, she thought. He was wrong—he had changed in some unexplainable manner. She examined him as he talked about his profession. He still wore the stylish clothes that almost made him appear a dandy, black velvet-collared cutaway coat and frilled shirt with a ribbon tie. His black hair was shorter, just touching his collar. His face seemed thinner, the flesh stretched tautly over his high cheekbones and chiseled jaw. No, it was not physical this change; perhaps it was the aura of success. Then it occurred to her that the constant mockery in his eyes that so irritated her had vanished. The twinkle that sparked there now on occasion was not mockery, but amusement or enthusiasm—enthusiasm now as he talked about plans for expanding The Barbary Coast to even larger porportions.

". . . and then perhaps bring well-known entertainers from Europe and the East Coast," he was saying. He stopped talking suddenly and a tinge of color came into his face. "But I'm boring you," he said. He shifted his weight and, clutching the pickets, leaned over the fence. "Are you well enough?"

"Well enough?" she echoed. "To be bored?" She laughed, realizing as she did so that it was the first time she had laughed in a long while.

"No, well enough for a tour of . . . of my house?" The question was asked casually, but she could sense its importance to him.

"So long as I must stare at its outside walls, I may as well view its interior, too," she told him. "I must confess a certain curiosity. I'm told there is a constant shifting of furniture, each piece more grand than the last."

He held the gate for her and raised his arm so that

she might lay her hand on it. "The house must be perfect," he said quietly.

"Your house as perfect as your style of dress?" she mused. "I can't imagine it." She glanced up at him, but he kept his gaze forward. His profile, silhouetted against the pale sky, was unyielding to humor. "Is that the reason you have not moved in? Because the house falls short of perfection?"

They had reached the bottom of the steps. He went ahead of her, taking her hand and guiding her ascent almost ceremoniously. On the porch he hesitated, directing her attention to the many glass panels of the front door. "There are twenty diamond shapes set in a rosewood frame," he told her. Each was beveled and set so that when looked at as a whole they formed a single, larger diamond. Beneath the glass was a carved rosewood W, and under that was a smooth varnished block. "For when there are street numbers," he explained.

He inserted a key into the lock, threw the door open, and they stepped into a great entryway. Paulette had never seen one like it. Larger than her entire house, it had a great staircase that branched out above into a Y. Three stories above, a skylight cast reflections through stained glass that bathed the mahogany surfaces in a profusion of colors, colors that were also caught by the prisms of an enormous crystal chandelier. The gilt mirror and console were of the Louis XV period. The chairs on either side, also Louis XV, were covered in damask. The stand beside the the door with its silver tray for calling cards was carved from green marble, and a dragon twined around the column. The double sliding doors opening off the entryway were highly polished with brass pulls and carved insets of rosettes.

Paulette was speechless. She followed behind Jeremiah as he moved from door to door, throwing each open to reveal one room more grand than the last. In the ballroom she stopped and refused to go farther until she caught her breath. She stood, hands pressed to her breasts, quieting her heartbeat. "I never thought I'd see a house more grand than Plantation Bend," she told him. "Jeremiah, it is unbelievable. It truly is perfection. And to think I stared at those outside walls and hated it for hiding my afternoon sun!"

Jeremiah beamed with pleasure. She suddenly understood, as the tension drained from him, that it had somehow been extremely important to him that she approve of the house. "Come," he said, "you've still the upstairs to see." And he led her up the great staircase.

It was in the sitting room off the master bedroom that Paulette told him she must rest. She sank onto a down-filled French settee and fought the dizziness that had begun to blur her vision. She did not have to explain that she was still weak from her illness; Jeremiah understood. He left her and returned with a glass of water. Pulling a chair opposite the settee, he sat watching as she drank. His eyes had become hard, with concern, she thought, and his jaw was firmly set. He leaned forward, elbows on his knees, hands clasped tightly together.

"There are still inconveniences," he said. "The water must be carted up from below. We haven't been able to dig a well deep enough to supply the house. Then there are the furnishings for the servants' quarters. There's also the road to consider and the construction of a carriage house and stables. The fireplace in the drawing room doesn't pull properly and the stairs creak, not from settling, but from poor workmanship. I also plan a terrace above the front porch. It would command a magnificent view of the bay. I'm also considering buying the adjoining property. San Francisco is growing rapidly and I wouldn't want our . . . my view spoiled by new construction."

"As you spoiled mine," she said quietly with a smile. She finished the glass of water and set the glass aside. "A moment more and I shall leave," she told him. Her dizziness was passing and her heartbeat was almost back to normal.

Jeremiah rose from his chair and began pacing, his hands locked together behind his back. The natural arch of his eyebrows lifted even more, giving him a troubled expression. "You haven't told me about your experiences at the mines," he said.

Without hesitating, she said, "It's something I'm not ready to discuss." She would have risen and taken her leave had he not suddenly seated himself beside her.

He took her trembling hand in his and held it tightly. "I built the house for you," he said. "That's why everything had to be as perfect as possible. The twenty diamond shapes of the front door—I chose that number because we first met on the twentieth day of the month." He felt her try to pull her hand away and refused to relinquish his grasp. "I blocked out your afternoon sun because this spot commanded the better view of the bay, something I knew was important to you. I . . ."—he cast his eyes down in what appeared to be shyness—". . . I love you, Paulette. I was hoping you would return from the gold fields with a new awareness. Remember, I had met Dester Granville. I was only praying you'd see him for what he was and not what you imagined him . . ."

"Stop this, please!" Paulette cried. She tore her hand loose from his. Rising, she moved across the room to the window and stood staring out, her back to him. After a moment, she said, "I can't become mistress of this house, Jeremiah. If you built it for me, you built it in vain."

"I know if you married me, you'd be marrying below your station," he said, "but I love you, I'm a wealthy man, and I could care for you and make your life easier. What a man's social position was somewhere else is unimportant in San Francisco. This is a melting pot. Doctors and lawyers and laborers rub elbows at The Barbary Coast. Gentlemen sit down to dinner with dirt farmers and think nothing of it. The rapid growth has been an equalizing device. Roles played previously in society mean nothing now.

It is unique here. But, then, I'm not pleading the case for San Francisco, only my own. I want you as my wife. I want you to be mistress of this house. I will be good to you and give you all a woman could ask for."

Paulette turned from the window and stood outlined by the afternoon sun. "But I don't love you, Jeremiah," she said softly.

"But you will come to love me in time," he said.

Paulette doubted that statement; even after all Dester had done, her love for him had not died. During her recovery she had sought excuses for his terrible behavior—the gold fever, a temporary madness, anger at her disobeying him and questioning his authority as her future husband. She had not forgiven him, but she still loved him.

"Time," Jeremiah murmured. "If you would not deny me the time, I know I can earn your love."

Paulette did not move when he rose from the settee, came to the window, and put his arms around her. She stood limply in his embrace, unable to respond when he kissed her hair, her forehead, her eyes. Then, when he bent to press his lips to hers, she turned her head away. She felt him stiffen at the rejection. He pulled his hands from her shoulders and stepped back.

He sighed, and the sigh seemed to come from the very depth of his being. "Could I, I would purge myself of this obsession with you," he said. "A strange triangle we have gotten ourselves into, you and I: you are obsessed with Granville and I with you, and Granville is more obsessed by gold than either of us could come to understand." His heels clicked across the parquet floor as he paced back to the settee and sat down.

Paulette saw the unfamiliar slump of his body and understood his sense of defeat. Hadn't she felt the same with Dester? "There is another reason other than that why I don't love you," she said. "It has nothing to do with your social position or that you are a professional gambler. I have no right to cast stones, nor would I if I did. Marrying you would be doubly unfair of me." She crossed the room and sat beside him to say what she must. "You see, Jeremiah"—her voice was scarcely audible—"I am with child."

His head came up and he stared at her with an expression that made her feel he had not heard her.

"I did not know until after I fled the gold fields," she continued. "It was during the trek back to Stockton that I . . ."

"Fled the gold fields?" His brows came together. "Granville did not send you away for your own safety? I assumed he had hired the black man to bring you back to civilization."

Paulette, hands folded quietly in her lap, told him of the events at Hangtown, of Charity and Elisha and the strike, and of the strangeness in Dester. When she concluded with her story about killing the youth and freeing Elisha and their difficulties in reaching the river, she sank back against the settee, exhausted by reliving the experiences. She did not struggle when he took her hand and pressed its back to his lips.

She could sense his desire for her; something also stirred within her, as it had, she now admitted, on other occasions when they had been thrown together. She pulled her hand gently from his. "Your offer of marriage and protection is most generous," she said, "understanding that my heart belongs to another, but you now see that my acceptance is impossible."

"Lesser women would not have confessed," he said, "until after the marriage." Rising and going to the fireplace, he stood, his hands spread on the marble mantel, his head bent, staring into the unused pit. "If I could marry you knowing you did not love me, I could marry you knowing you carry another man's child," he said. "I could adjust. I could love the child because it would also be an extension of you. The child will need a father. Even if Dester were willing, better the father be me than Granville." He pushed himself away from the mantel. "And you, my love, need a husband. Regardless of the things I said about San Francisco's uniqueness, I fear unwed mothers are still regarded as they are in other sections of the country. You would be treated worse than those women you so despise who live on Maiden Lane."

"I have considered returning to Louisiana," Paulette confessed, "after the baby is born."

"And live a lie?"

"There have been worse scandals in the best of Southern families."

"In your own, for example," he said, not unkindly. "I've heard the stories of your father and half-sister."

"Yes, in my own—although I never think of the Favières as being of my blood. Their cruelties seem like nightmares from half-forgotten novels. But I suppose there is some of their cruelty in me," she said thoughtfully. "I was capable of killing that youth in Hangtown. I was also capable of considering your proposal of marriage and not confessing the truth about the child growing inside me."

"I still want to marry you," Jeremiah said with a voice that suppressed emotion. "But I also have a confession. I have never envied a man as I envy Granville. Someday I want to see the love in your eyes for me that sparks there when you mention his name. I would die for that, your love, and it does not make me a stronger man knowing this." He crossed his arms over his chest and stood, legs spread, chin tilted, as if he were about to face some enemy. "As I said, perhaps in time," he murmured. "For now I only require your answer to the question of marriage."

Paulette looked at him and again thought how handsome he was, especially when he was struggling to control his emotions. She also thought of the strange turn her life had taken in comparison to what she had planned and anticipated. She lowered her gaze and stared at her still-red and callused hands.

Quietly, she said, "I shall try to make you a good wife, Jeremiah."

Chang and Miriam took the news of her upcoming marriage with surprise and happiness. Joining hands, they danced around her like children until they collapsed in exhaustion at the kitchen table.

"You will be the wealthiest woman in San Francisco," Chang said. Then, remembering what she had told him about Tom's theft of her fortune, he said, "Again."

"But riches don't matter," Miriam scolded him. She turned to Paulette, her eyes bright with excitement. "I knew from the beginning that you were attracted to him," she said. "And, of course, his devotion was always so obvious, coming as he did to stand in the grove and stare at the house, hoping to catch a glimpse of you." She wiped the moisture from her eyes with an impatient swipe of her fingers. "I'm so happy for you." She sprang to her feet, bent down, and kissed Paulette's cheek.

"Not only will you be the wealthiest woman, but you'll have the biggest, grandest house," Chang said, watching them. "It will require a large staff." He cast his eyes down at the tablecloth. "With Mr. Walker rich enough to hire many servants, you will no longer be needing Chang."

Paulette smiled at him and winked at Miriam. "I'll need Chang for as long as he wants to stay," she said. "You shall be the one to run our house."

"No, no!" Chang was horror-stricken. "What would people say? A Chinese man for a head man? People would call you names and laugh at you. I will be kitchen boy and be happy."

"You will be head man," Paulette said firmly. "Let people say and do what they please." She already knew that people called her names for employing a "coolie" when there were now poor white settlers with young girls to be hired out. "And I'll see that Mr.

Walker pays you your back salary. You've been loyal and I should not have survived without you."

Chang, usually incapable of expressing emotion, was wild with excitement. "And a fancy uniform," he stammered. "Will I wear a fancy uniform like in the picture books?"

"If you like," Paulette answered.

"And me?" Miriam asked. "What position will I have?"

"Why, none," Paulette said. "You are my friend. You will remain a guest when we've changed houses."

"No," Miriam said with conviction. "I will be your personal maid. I shall care for your clothes and keep your things in order." Her eyes twinkled. "But I shall remain your friend always."

Paulette left them and retired to her room to rest. The day's events had drained her. She turned out the lamp and lay watching the patterns of afternoon light play across the ceiling. She could hear Chang and Miriam in the kitchen, still chattering and laughing. She felt their excitement, but only vaguely. She was still plagued by apprehensions.

# Chapter Fourteen

THE HOUSE on the hill was ablaze with lights.

The road from below, freshly made and covered with new gravel that crunched beneath the carriage wheels, was busier than the busiest streets. Men and women in their best finery alighted beneath the gas lamps, chattering and laughing, and in party moods.

Inside, Jeremiah gazed across the enormous drawing room at his wife, Paulette. The sight of her made him swell with pride. They had been married that morning, three weeks after he had proposed, in a small chapel north of the town. Only a small group had been present: Miriam and Chang; Mrs. Mason, who had returned from the gold fields the day before; and two of Jeremiah's employees at The Barbary Coast. Paulette had requested the wedding be such, although Jeremiah would have preferred the most crowded, elaborate ceremony possible to declare his happiness with the event.

The party had been his suggestion and she had acquiesced after considerable thought. "As Mrs. Jeremiah Walker, I guess I can't hide myself away," she had said, "so you may properly introduce me to San Francisco society."

How exquisite she looks, Jeremiah thought as he watched her move among the guests—the crowning jewel in the setting of this house I built for her.

Her gown was emerald-green silk. He had purchased the fabric from Dora, a fact that he'd never
tell her. Two Chinese women Chang had brought
from the Chinese settlement had made the gown in
record time, following the latest styles in a magazine
carried in on the newly arrived steamship *Bonadven-
ture* out of Paris. The neckline was plunging, daring,
and revealed deep cleavage; then, gathered beneath
the bosom, the silk hung free, flowing over the con-
tours of her body to within half an inch of the floor.
She had chosen the style for those experienced eyes
that might judge her pregnancy. When she moved,
the tips of her slippers showed a matching green with
small diamond clips fastened above the toes. The
necklace she wore around her tanned neck was of
emeralds and diamonds, his wedding gift. Her dark
hair was piled high in curls and swept to one side so
that her high cheekbones, the lovely hollows of her
face, were accentuated. A more gorgeous woman he
had never seen, Jeremiah concluded—and as gracious
a hostess as could be found.

Most of the men and women she spoke to were below her station, but she treated them with courtesy
and made them feel welcome. She let no one occupy
more of her time than was proper, although many of
the women attempted to corner her in long, gossipy
conversations. Yes, Jeremiah was pleased and his
pride was swollen and he told himself he had done
well by marrying her. In time she would come to love
him. How could she not when he loved her with every
fiber of his being? He listened to his friends compli-
ment him on wife and house, and he longed for the
moment they would all take their leave and he would
be alone with Paulette.

Paulette was uncomfortable and fought to keep the
discomfort from showing on her face. Not since
Dester had had difficulties with his father and fled
Plantation Bend had she attended a party; she had
never been the hostess at one. The strain was taxing.
More taxing was her fear that one of the women, who

all seemed to watch her with such consuming interest, would somehow discern the fact of her pregnancy. What, then, when she and Jeremiah were both disgraced by scandal? Trapped by three newly arrived ladies, she sought Chang's eye in the hope of being rescued.

Chang, having abandoned the fancy uniform he had so wanted and denounced it as silly, wore the silk robe of his countrymen. The garment was a brilliant red with black trim and multicolor needlework. Each time he answered the doorbell, the guests stared at him with shock and amazement. He met them smilingly, untouched by their reactions. He was now busy conferring with one of the maids and did not catch Paulette's look for rescue.

"Pardon me, ladies, but may I borrow my wife for a moment?"

Jeremiah took her arm and led her away to a corner of the drawing room. He handed her champagne and kissed her cheek before she could lift the glass.

"You are incorrigible, Mr. Walker," she teased. "But I thank you for rescuing me." She smiled and added, "Again." She let her gaze sweep the crowded drawing room. "Who are all these people, Jeremiah? Do you know them all?"

"Most," he answered. "The men frequent The Barbary Coast when they can escape their wives. You have the cream of the society of our town here, my love." He kissed her again. "And you have them at your feet."

Paulette, glancing around the drawing room, suddenly stiffened. "It would appear we have other than the cream, also," she said.

Jeremiah turned and followed her gaze.

Dora was entering from the foyer on the arm of a naval officer.

"Do be kind to her," Jeremiah said lightly. "She's now one of the star attractions at my club and brings in a tremendous amount of business."

"And takes a tremendous amount home, too, I'd

wager," Paulette said and laughed. "Now let's not be rude, darling. We have guests."

"Couldn't we send them away and be alone? Better still, let's abandon them and slip away to someplace quiet. I'd like nothing more at this moment than to make love to you."

She smiled and teasingly pushed him away from her though she felt uncomfortable at his remark. They had seen one another every day since his proposal and her acceptance, but she had always made certain either Miriam or Chang had been close by. Jeremiah had respected her refusal to be alone with him, saying he could wait until after the wedding. Paulette thought of his lovemaking, had questioned her capability to respond, but, even remembering their night together in Panama, she feared she would disappoint him. In Panama she had considered going to his bed a necessity. She watched as he moved away, mingling easily with the guests.

"Don't push him away too often. Men don't like it."

Dora had approached and was standing at Paulette's elbow. There was hatred reflected in her gray eyes.

Paulette smiled, but the smile was frozen, more for those watching than for Dora. She made as if to move away, but Dora put a restraining hand on her arm.

"No greeting for an old friend?" the redhead said. "Take my advice. You've caught him, but you'll never keep him by pushing him away."

"Perhaps if you pushed men away more often, we'd be invited to your wedding party," Paulette said softly. "Now, if you'll excuse me, I have the guests to see to."

A flicker of resentment flashed across Dora's face. She opened her mouth to speak, but she refrained from spitting out the angry words. She, too, was performing for the guests—perhaps, Paulette thought, at Jeremiah's insistence. Had he invited her to prove to those present that she meant little to him?

"Remember when I took you into my house?"

Dora asked in a whisper. "I referred to him as *our* Jeremiah, and you assured me he meant nothing to you. How horrified you sounded then at the suggestion that he held any appeal for you. I almost believed you." The woman laughed softly. "You not only steal my servants, but my man, as well." She shrugged her pale shoulders. "Oh, well, *c'est la vie.* We shouldn't be enemies, you and I. We should be friends since we have your husband in common." Gathering up her blue silk skirt, the redhead glided away into the crowd.

"The cheeky bitch!" Mrs. Mason mumbled as she stepped up from behind Paulette. "Don't let her kind worry you, my dear," she said and patted Paulette's arm. "Jeremiah's a man, and men have a penchant for such women before they marry—after, too, if you don't watch them. But I think you're safe with Jeremiah. He's one in a million. That woman's lost him and she's green with envy."

"I'm not worried," Paulette assured the older woman.

"A lovely party," Mrs. Mason said.

The older woman had changed since Paulette had seen her last. Her hair was now entirely white, her face and body were thinner, and her eyes lacked their old luster.

It seemed her Jamie had finally found a good woman and had married—and the new daughter-in-law had wanted her husband entirely to herself. Mrs. Mason had been sent packing by the son she worshipped. "Just like his father," she had told Paulette earlier that afternoon, forgetting how through the long days in Panama she had told her how unlike his father Jamie had been.

"But I'll be all right," the older woman had assured her friend. "I've a nest egg of my own. I plan on opening a small restaurant, something San Francisco needs to compete with all its slop houses. One thing I do well is cook. It's high time I stopped worrying about other people and started looking after myself. I'm not young anymore, and if a woman's own son can turn her out . . ."

Mrs. Mason stopped a passing waiter and took her fourth glass of champagne from his tray. "I always suspected you loved Jeremiah," she said. "You protested too much, my dear." She cut off her laughter with champagne.

"You're going to get tipsy," Paulette warned.

"Nonsense, my dear," Mrs. Mason retorted. "I'm going to get very drunk." She moved away in search of another waiter with a full tray of champagne.

Paulette, mustering her willpower, moved back into the mainstream of the party. She met and spoke with people whose names she would never remember, gazed into faces she would quickly forget, listening to conversation about San Francisco, the gold fields, the difficulties between the North and the South, the influx of Chinese and the sore spot now being called Chinatown. She spoke with women about styles of clothing, the need for the arts in San Francisco, the committees being formed to fight corruption and filth. Through the entire ordeal she was aware of Jeremiah watching her. He rescued her when he thought her to be trapped and he whispered words of encouragement when they would pass from one group to another.

At long last people began to take their leave. The circular driveway was crowded with carriages and the night was filled with laughing farewells and congratulations called over departing shoulders. The crowd inside was thinning out considerably and Paulette allowed herself the luxury of retreating to a settee. Her legs were aching—and her jaw, too, for having forced a smile for so long. She surveyed the waning group, saw Jeremiah politely edging a couple toward the door, and Mrs. Mason asleep in a chair beside the grand piano. Only Chang seemed to have any life left in him; he moved quickly about the room collecting glasses and inspecting the polished woods for damage. When he passed her settee, she asked him to bring her a glass of water.

She drank thirstily.

"Party a grand success," Chang whispered. "You are now the toast of San Francisco."

"Good God!" she murmured. "I want nothing less."

"Miss Dora? Did she bother you?"

"No, Chang. She's harmless."

"She's evil," the Chinese man said. Muttering, he hurried away to continue his duties.

When the last guest had departed, the long case clock in the entryway was striking midnight. Jeremiah threw the bolt on the door and sighed with relief. He lifted two glasses of champagne from a tray and carried them to where Paulette had collapsed on the settee. Handing her one, he saluted, "To us—and to being alone at last."

"Not quite," she said, and she nodded toward the snoring Mrs. Mason.

They laughed and sipped their champagne.

"You were a success," Jeremiah told her, "as I knew you would be. There wasn't a man present who didn't envy me or a woman not jealous of your beauty."

She sensed the uneasiness in him and understood that he was considering the awkwardness of their wedding night. To take one's true bride to the wedding bed was unlike taking a woman you married who confessed she did not love you and who carried another man's child inside her womb. He wanted her, yet he did not want to offend her or this strange agreement they had entered into.

It was Paulette who said, "Shall we go up?"

She instructed Chang to have the servants carry Mrs. Mason to a guest room and have Miriam undress her.

Then, hand in hand, she and Jeremiah climbed the great staircase.

When she came out of the dressing room, he was already in bed, propped against the pillows waiting for her. The gas in the lamp had been turned low, and the draperies had been opened. The night was

crystal clear, star-filled. Jeremiah turned back the
sheets and she crawled in beside him.

They lay for several moments, her head cradled
under his arm, staring out at the night sky.

"I'm a happy man," he whispered into her ear.

She said nothing. Turning, she kissed him, and en-
couraged, he lowered his mouth to her breasts.

During their last moments of passion, he did not
hear and she was unaware that she whispered Dester's
name.


In her seventh month of pregnancy, Paulette became ill. She confined herself to her room, and Jeremiah, beside himself, employed the finest doctor in
San Francisco. The doctor, a sour-faced Spaniard
with a yellowish pallor and hateful disposition, was
installed in a suite of rooms on the second floor. The
agreement was that he was to treat no other patients
and to remain within calling distance at all times. He
was not to leave the house unless leaving the address
where he could be reached, and even then his outings
were restricted to no longer than an hour at a time.

Paulette disliked Dr. Uribe. His lack of humor de-
pressed her and she was certain he was cruel and demanding of the servants. She would have dismissed
him immediately if she had not known how much Jeremiah relied on him. She herself felt like a caged animal. She spent hours in a chaise longue placed before
the window, watching the town beneath the hill growing; it had now spread to the base of the hill and
would have climbed halfway up its side if Jeremiah
had not purchased the land to ensure their privacy.
Her own modest house had been torn down and a
carriage house stood in its place; behind that were the
stables, with the breed of horses Jeremiah had had
brought from Kentucky. She never saw the horses or
heard them whinny without thinking of Charity. Then
thoughts of Charity would turn to Elisha and Dester,
and she would have to force her mind elsewhere.

She had few visitors. Mrs. Mason was busy with

her restaurant, and Miriam, two months after meeting
a young man from New York, had married him and
now lived contentedly in Santa Clara, south of San
Francisco. Paulette had approved of the young man.
He was handsome, attentive; although he had come
West for gold, he had chosen to "get back to
the land" and was raising cattle. Miriam, on her infrequent visits, bubbled with happiness and always
expressed her gratitude to Paulette for "saving me
from Mr. Slater."

A letter from Vienna had informed Paulette that
Katrina had remarried and that her husband had
taken charge of the operating of Plantation Bend. As
for herself, she was well. Bella had finally settled on
a single beau and was expected to marry in the
spring. Aaron and Mati had returned—"How grand
they looked in their eastern finery"—and had asked
to purchase freedom for Mati's mother. Vienna had
offered the old woman her freedom, but she had refused, saying she understood her life at Plantation
Bend and was terrified of leaving.

Jeremiah sat with Paulette in the evenings before
returning to The Barbary Coast. He talked about
things happening in the town. Wells Fargo had expanded its offices. A dry-goods center had sprung up
on Clay Street, and Kearny Street bustled with a great
number of retail shops. As always when he talked
about San Francisco's growth, Jeremiah's eyes lighted
with excitement. "Everything is in a state of transi-
tion. Hills are being leveled and there's a plan afoot
for reclamation of the bay and mud flats. Portsmouth
Plaza has changed overnight. The shanties and tents
are gone and it's taken on the appearance of a ba-
zaar. Several gambling resorts have arisen, but none
more soigné—as one of the women said—than The
Barbary Coast. I tell you, Paulette, there's no place
on earth I'd rather be than here."

She listened and she smiled and she understood his
excitement, but as for herself, she often longed for
Plantation Bend and the people she had known there.

She was confined while everything around her grew and flourished.

Jeremiah never spoke more of The Barbary Coast than to mention of its name. He knew she objected to his profession and he kept that profession to himself. Once when she was in a mood to annoy him, she suggested visiting The Barbary Coast after the baby came. He had stomped from the room and had not come in to kiss her good night when he returned that evening.

She did not understand why that night she had lain unable to sleep, listening to the new house settling, the horses whinnying, an owl hooting. Tears had collected on her cheeks and she had not understood them.

The day had dawned gray and stormy. Darkness came early and with it came the raindrops that spattered and streaked the windowpanes. A deep, rumbling sound approached from across the Pacific, grew louder, and eventually rattled the house with its fury. Lightning crackled and filled the night with its blinding glare.

Paulette forced her head deep into the goosedown pillows and bit her lower lip against her pain. The pain had awakened her despite the sleeping draft Dr. Uribe had given her before retiring. When the pain passed she trembled, knowing her time had come when it struck again before memory of the last had faded. She cried out, but her cries were deadened by the thunder. A bolt of lightning flashed across the sky and her room was illuminated as though it were day. She screamed, not knowing if from fear or pain. It had sounded as if the house had been struck.

She reached for the silver bell on the nightstand and jangled it loudly. When there was still no response, she flung the bell at the door; it struck and settled on the thick carpet.

Dear God, she thought, all these servants and a private doctor, and I'm left alone when I need them most. Then it came to her that she might die, and the horror brought her head from the pillows. *My baby!*

*Dester's baby!* She waited until there was a lull between the thunder and wind, then called out again: "Jeremiah!"

But the night clock on the mantel told her that Jeremiah would not be home for another hour.

"Chang! Help me, Chang!"

Then she heard footsteps in the hallway. Her door burst open and Jeremiah, in a sudden flash of lightning, was illuminated in its blinding light. When he saw her, his face twisted with rage.

"The baby!" she cried. "Jeremiah, the baby's coming!"

He stepped back into the hallway, bellowing for the doctor. Even the thunder could not drown out his voice. He vanished, and as the household was awakened, he returned to her room with the frightened doctor by the scruff of the neck. He literally flung the man into the room and would have, had not Paulette's screams stopped him, struck the man in his fury.

Chang hurried in, wiping the sleep from his eyes, and lighted the lamps and drew the heavy draperies.

The doctor, still trembling, set up his black valise and prepared his instruments. "Leave now," he said to Jeremiah, but Jeremiah had already crouched beside Paulette's bed and was clinging to her hands, as if trying to draw her pain into himself. "I need a woman to assist me," the doctor mumbled.

Chang left and returned with a pale and trembling serving girl who had been employed only the day before. The others had conveniently made themselves scarce. "You help," Chang told the girl, reverting back to his thick accent in his nervousness, and he quickly dashed away to see to the preparations he had been informed to expect.

"Breathe deeply," Jeremiah said. Perspiration beaded his forehead, as it did Paulette's.

"Yes, breathe deeply," the doctor echoed. "Don't fight your pain. Now, Mr. Walker, if you'll leave us? This is no place for a husband."

Paulette clung tighter to Jeremiah's hands.

"I won't leave her," Jeremiah said strongly. "My place is with her."

And it's not even your child, Paulette thought. Thank God for you, Jeremiah. A sudden pain so sharp passed through her body that she thought she would faint. She screamed and arched her body against it; then as it subsided she felt the doctor forcing her back against the mattress.

"Let the baby come," he said without emotion.

She felt the sheets being thrown from her and a cold mat being forced beneath her. Unable to get her to lift her shoulders, her sheer gown was ripped away. Perspiration had streaked into her hair and taken the natural curl away; she felt it sticking to the sides of her face. Even her eyes ached and felt as if they would suddenly sink into her skull. "The pain . . . the pain!" she wept when she felt the wave begin again.

The doctor, since he could not convince Jeremiah to leave, forced him to the head of the bed out of his way. He bent where the husband had been, and Paulette could feel his cold, rough hands pressing, exploring her body. She clung even tighter to Jeremiah, whimpering between cries.

"Is . . . is it always . . . like this?" Jeremiah asked through clenched teeth.

"Sometimes," the doctor answered coolly. His fear of his employer had passed and there was resentment in his voice. His hands, trained to be gentle, went against their training as he felt and probed.

Paulette squirmed beneath his touch, hating and fearing him.

It was the young serving girl who cried, "You're hurting her, Doctor! Good gracious, she's not a cow!" Then, stricken by her own outburst, she backed away from the bed and put her hand to her mouth, as if to silence the statement that had already escaped.

The doctor glared at her. Jeremiah, too stricken by Paulette's pain to take his eyes from her face, did not notice—but Paulette did. In a sudden surge of strength, she pulled herself up and flung the doctor's hands from her body.

"Send him away!" she shouted. "Jeremiah, send him away!"

Jeremiah was at a loss. "But we have no one else. Who will . . ."

"I hate him!" Paulette cried. "He hates me and my baby! I won't have anyone with that much hate in him delivering my child! Send him away!"

The doctor rose to his feet, his face flushed crimson. "I assure you, Mrs. Walker, that I do not hate you or your baby. I'm a doctor and I'm dedicated to relieving the pain of others."

Jeremiah looked from Paulette to the doctor. Perhaps, he thought, the pain had driven her senseless. If he sent the doctor away as she demanded, who would deliver the baby?

Paulette, sensing his indecision, turned pleading eyes on the serving girl.

The girl understood the plea. In her one day at the house she had come to understand the doctor. He was a man who hated everyone better off than himself; he especially hated his employer and his employer's wife because they lived so grandly while he himself had to grovel for enough to support the women he visited an hour at a time on Maiden Lane.

"Send him away," Paulette repeated, but her voice had grown weak and was losing its conviction. —

The doctor, seeing Jeremiah's confusion, again bent over the bed.

The serving girl drew a great breath of air into her lungs before saying, "Do as she says, sir. Send him away. I've helped with babies. Leave the mistress to me and . . ."

"How dare you!" The doctor straightened. He drew back his arm and would have struck the girl if Jeremiah had not clutched his wrist and forced his hand down. Sputtering, the doctor stormed from the room.

Paulette, between seizures, thanked the girl with

her eyes. She squeezed Jeremiah's hands. "Leave me now. Send Chang to help . . ."

"Annie, madam," the girl said.

"Send Chang to help Annie," Paulette said.

Jeremiah hung back, wanting to leave and yet believing he should be with her.

"Go," she repeated.

He bent and kissed her damp forehead, turned pleading eyes on the girl, and left them.

Chang appeared almost instantly. The little man came to the bedside and took Paulette's hands. "An old Chinese proverb says," he said, "the harder the birth, the stronger the child."

She smiled because she knew he feared for her. "You've been loyal and good to me, Chang. Should I . . . should I die . . ."

"Hush!" he said. "Miss Paulette, you're not going to die. Don't think about dying. What we're doing here is concerned with life, not death." Yet his lips were trembling.

Paulette drove her head deep into the goosedown pillows as a new surge of pain spread through her body. Tears rolled unchecked from the corners of her eyes, and her lips whitened from being pressed so tightly together.

"It's coming!" she heard Annie cry. "Breathe deeply, madam! Stop fighting! Let it come! There . . . there, it's . . ." A clap of thunder cut off her words.

Paulette felt too weak for the next surge of pain. She lay still, feeling as if her body would split into halves. Eyes wide, her ears filled with the howling of the wind and the rumble of thunder, she thought how auspicious it was that her baby had chosen the time of the storm to make its entrance into the world.

Then the pain was more intense than before.

She heard Annie cry, "There!"

And Chang clapped his hands together and laughed.

The baby, a boy, was born at the height of the storm. Chang claimed the honor of the first gentle slap, and the baby unleashed a torrent of cries. He had not come gently into this world, and he would not face life meekly. His cries brought Jeremiah bounding through the doorway from the hallway, where he had paced the polish from the parquetry. He did not glance toward Chang and Annie, who between them were preparing to bathe the baby, but went directly to the bed and knelt beside Paulette.

"Good God!" he said. "The agony of not being able to help you!" He buried his face against her shoulder and wept.

Paulette ran her hand gently through his dark hair. "You helped," she whispered. "You were here, you cared." And she refrained from adding: "And it isn't even your son."

Annie brought the baby to Paulette and she examined his tiny head and hands and body as if searching for some defect. Finding nothing wrong, she kissed the baby's head and broke into tears of gratitude and relief. She had never told anyone how she had feared for the baby's life when she had learned of her pregnancy. The horror of those last days at Hangtown, her fever and illness, they had not—thank God—touched her baby.

Jeremiah touched the baby's face as if it were made of fine porcelain. "He's handsome," he said softly.

"As handsome as his father," Annie beamed. "You must be very proud, Mr. Walker, sir," she said as she took the baby from his mother.

"Very proud," Jeremiah echoed.

When Annie and Chang had left them, Paulette stared deep into Jeremiah's eyes. "You will love him, won't you? You will always treat him as if he's your own?"

"Yes, of course," he answered.

"Even if he's blond-haired and blue-eyed?"

"Even then," he assured her.

She slept peacefully while outside the storm continued to rage.

# Chapter Fifteen

DAYS AND nights turned into weeks, and time passed quickly and contentedly for Paulette. She continued to avoid thoughts of Dester, although that became more difficult as the child grew. She had named him Clayborn, after his grandfather, and the resemblance was uncanny. He began walking at eleven months, talking at twelve. His hair was blond, his eyes a pale but vibrant blue.

Jeremiah was true to his promise. He was devoted to the child, and if embarrassed when his friends commented on the lack of resemblance to either parent, he did not show it. He took to taking Clay on Sunday carriage rides, although where they went during these excursions Paulette did not know. The child was as devoted to Jeremiah, preferring his company to that of his mother. Paulette felt no jealousy, only pride in their relationship.

Jeremiah lavished her with gifts—jewels and silks and items for the house. Although she had never come to love him, she never turned him away from her bed. Five months after Clay's birth she became pregnant again.

"Life is going to pass you by," Mrs. Mason warned, sometime later. "You can't keep yourself pregnant and locked away in this house, no matter how grand it is." The older woman had grown even thinner, working herself to exhaustion every day in her restaurant. Sunday, the only day each week that she allowed herself freedom, she visited Paulette, always drank too much, and had to be sent home in a carriage. She leaned to the window and pulled back the sheer curtain as Jeremiah and Clay departed for their Sunday outing. "A jewel of a man," she murmured. "Have you ever considered how fortunate you are to have married him?"

Paulette, busy with her needlepoint, glanced up and smiled. "I remind myself at least once a day," she confessed.

Mrs. Mason's gray brows pointed to the middle of her forehead. "And yet you don't love him, do you, my dear? Oh, you can tell me I'm prying if you like. I know I am. But I love you like a daughter and I can't understand this quirk in you. You have a jewel of a man for a husband, yet you pine away for some . . ." She let the sentence trail off and lifted her sherry glass to her cracked lips.

"I assure you I'm not pining away," Paulette told her. "I am contented with Jeremiah. He's a good husband . . . and I've tried to be a good wife."

"He's more than a good husband," Mrs. Mason told her. "It's not many a man who'd take in someone else's child and treat him as his own."

Paulette caught her breath. "You know, then?"

"Of course, my dear, although you didn't see fit to tell me. Little Clay doesn't have one feature of Jeremiah's—or of yours, for that matter. Then, not that I'm one who ordinarily counts such things, but he was born a mite soon to have been conceived after your marriage to Jeremiah. Clay's father is that Granville man, I presume." She drained her glass and rose to refill it. "Well, I don't want to pry. I can't force you to confide in me, but if you ask me"—she ran her index finger around the rim of the overfilled glass and then brought it to her lips—"you did the right thing—that is if you were honest with Jeremiah."

"I was honest," Paulette assured her.

"Good." She resumed her seat and sat staring out the window. "Amazing, isn't it, how rapidly this town is growing? My restaurant cannot accommodate all who seek to dine there."

"It's the food," Paulette said, glad for the change of subject. "Jeremiah tells me it's excellent. He told me he offered you a tremendous sum to close the restaurant and cook for us."

"Aye, that he did," the older woman murmured. "But it wasn't the thing for me to do. I told you the night of your wedding party that it was time I started looking after myself. If I became your cook, I would spend all my time worrying over you and Jeremiah. My life wouldn't be my own again. Ever since Jamie threw me out . . ."

"But you're working yourself too hard," Paulette said with genuine concern.

"I'll slack off when my employees learn to cook properly," Mrs. Mason said quietly, her tone indicating she did not truly anticipate that day dawning.

Paulette laid her needlepoint aside and folded her hands on the mound of her stomach. "I worry about you, Maude. My concern is partially selfish. With Miriam living so far away, you're the only woman friend I have in San Francisco. What would I do without you and your Sunday visits? I talk to no one else outside of Jeremiah, Annie, and Chang. The other servants seem frightened of me and avoid me when they can."

"You should get out and make new friends," Mrs. Mason said bluntly, "instead of locking yourself away here. Do you know people are beginning to talk about you? They use your name in the same sentences with that man they call The Emperor of San Francisco—and him a character, an eccentric." Despite her efforts, anger had crept into her voice.

"Do you think I'm eccentric?"

"No, but I know you, my dear," she said more gently. "Other people don't. They look at this great house perched on the hill and naturally want to know who lives here. They see your husband coming and going, see him at The Barbary Coast, but no outsider has set eyes on you since your wedding party. You refuse invitations and never entertain. Why, they ask themselves, does the wife of one of San Francisco's wealthiest men hide herself away? What secret is she hiding?"

Paulette began to hunt for excuses. Jeremiah had said much the same to her.

"And," Mrs. Mason went on, "is it fair to Jeremiah?"

Paulette stared at her friend and said nothing.

"He's thinking of running for office. Did you know that?"

Paulette sat forward on the settee. "He didn't tell me."

"Well, he is," Mrs. Mason blurted out. "And he should, too. He's the sort of man we need to organize us. Do you know the citizens have formed a vigilante committee? That's how high the crime rate is becoming and how ineffectual the law is. Jeremiah is a man who can grow with the city. He can make the people keep up with its growth. He's a natural leader and we need him. But"—she left her chair and came to sit beside Paulette on the settee—"there are those who are fighting him. They don't want a man like your husband to hold a position of power. It would curtail their greed and graft and prevent them from exploiting the poor."

"But why didn't he tell me?" Paulette stammered. "I understand how much he loves San Francisco, how much a part of it he feels. Why has he hidden this from me?"

"Perhaps because he hasn't wanted to call on you for support," Mrs. Mason suggested. "He'll be running against some very influential men—men who are married and have families that are socially active. None is as qualified as Jeremiah. But Jeremiah has several strikes against him. Mainly, he operates The Barbary Coast and many of the people think the gambling houses are linked with the rising amount of crime. Secondly, he . . ."

"Secondly, he has a family that lives very privately," Paulette finished for her. "He has a wife people are calling eccentric, maybe crazy."

Mrs. Mason sighed and patted her friend's hand. "That's about it, my dear. Jeremiah wouldn't stand a chance in hell if you didn't support him. A man, especially a man who is going political, needs a woman behind him to entertain and charm the voters." She slumped back against the cushions. "But here I'm lecturing you," she said. "I didn't mean to. It's just that yesterday I had a woman in my restaurant asking about you. Something about her made me furious."

"Who was this woman?" Paulette asked.

Mrs. Mason bobbed her head from side to side. "I don't know. But one of my customers told her she was seeking The Empress of San Francisco. The customer was being a smarty, comparing you to that character who rides around the streets on his two-wheeler, but the point is that he isn't the only one, and it's your own fault for locking yourself away in this beautifully lined coffin."

"I've never felt the need to go out," Paulette confessed weakly. "Everything I want is here, or brought in to me." She rose with difficulty, her body now large in the last months of pregnancy, and began pacing the Aubusson carpet. "I didn't realize," she mumbled more to herself than to her friend. "Jeremiah should have told me what people were saying, what he was planning. And this woman—I can't imagine who she would be. I know no women here, and no woman has called on me."

"Perhaps she's from New Orleans and has brought a message for you from home," Mrs. Mason suggested, "although I can't imagine trusting one like her with even a message. She was a sour-looking creature if I ever saw one. And she had a young man at her elbow young enough to be her son, him bowing and scraping."

Paulette continued to pace long after Mrs. Mason had finished the bottle of sherry and taken her leave. She pondered the mystery of the unknown woman and of Jeremiah's reluctance to inform her of his intentions of running for office.

When she heard the carriage wheels crunching on the gravel of the driveway, she returned to the settee, picked up her needlepoint, and attempted to wipe the distress from her expression.

Clay was clinging to Jeremiah's hand. Each time Paulette saw him, she was amazed at his size and his resemblance to his grandfather and father. Clay ran to her, kissed her cheek, and settled beside her.

"Nap time," Paulette said. Her voice must have been more stern than she intended, because she was aware of Jeremiah's sudden glance. She patted Clay's hand, bent over, and kissed his cheek. "Mama wants to talk to your father," she told him. "We'll have Annie take you to the kitchen and give you one of her delicious apple turnovers."

Jeremiah rang the bell, and Annie appeared promptly. Jeremiah lifted Clay from the settee, hugged him, and sent him away with Annie. "Now," he said, "suppose you tell me what's upsetting you."

She decided to be direct. "Is it true you're considering running for office?"

Jeremiah's brow furrowed. "Mrs. Mason's visited, eh? Yes, it's true, I considered it, but then I rejected the idea."

"Because of me?"

"Did she tell you that?"

"She told me you'd need me if you decided to run," Paulette answered. "I understand living as a recluse couldn't help you. I want to know if I had anything to do with your deciding against running."

"You have something to do with everything I do," he said. "You are an important part of me. How could it be otherwise? But there were other things I took into consideration, so, you see, you were not the only reason I decided against becoming a public figure."

He came and sat beside her, taking her hand. "I am the owner of a gambling house—and as you so often reminded me before our marriage, I'm a professional gambler. The profession is not highly respected among San Francisco's finest. They have a penchant for linking crime and gambling."

"But it's not so."

"Not always—not in my case. I'm quite respectable, my dear. The Barbary Coast is the most honest gambling establishment in San Francisco."

"Then you could overcome the stigma."

"I could," he said with conviction, "if I had not decided against running for office."

Paulette pushed his hand away and rose. "Then it is essential that you change your mind," she said. She was forced to smile at the surprise mirrored on his face. "You love this city more than any of its citizens. How better to serve them than by holding a responsible office?"

Jeremiah looked questioningly at her.

"I'll try to be a gracious hostess," Paulette told him. "I know this is important to you." She glanced down at her swollen body. "At least I'll have time to have the baby and get my figure back, won't I?"

Jeremiah laughed. "Campaigning won't begin for another two months."

"And what office will you be running for?"

"Mayor."

"Oh, I see. I don't know if I'm prepared to be the First Lady of San Francisco."

"Why not?" he said. "You're already the finest."

Paulette gave birth to a daughter and named her Anna. The child was Clay's opposite, small, with dark hair and dark eyes; she had Jeremiah's high forehead and Paulette's high cheekbones. She was a quiet baby, seldom disturbing the household, and became the darling of the servants. Clay, suffering from sibling rivalry, became moody and moped about at Paulette's heels when Jeremiah was away from the house. As much time as his parents spent with him, he refused to be consoled, thought of himself as betrayed, and refused to remain in a room when his baby sister was carried in by a nurse.

Jeremiah said his difficult period would pass, that he would become accustomed to sharing the spotlight, but Paulette worried. She wished even more that she had Vienna to talk to; instead, she made do with long letters.

She had carried her lap desk into the drawing room and set it up near the window the morning she heard the carriage coming up the hill. Thinking Jeremiah, who had departed only minutes before, had forgotten something and was returning, she went to the front door and opened it.

It was not Jeremiah's carriage that had stopped in front of the house, but a smaller, foreign model pulled by an aged horse. The driver was vaguely familiar, but it was to the occupant that Paulette turned her attention.

The woman, ignoring the offer of assistance from her driver, alighted from the carriage and stood impatiently smoothing the wrinkles from her black gown. "You drive like a madman," she complained to the driver. Her face was pale, the lines severe, the severity accentuated by her choice of hair style—black-and-gray-streaked hair pulled straight back away from her face and fastened at the nape of her neck with a tortoiseshell comb. She wore a hint of color on her lips and cheeks, but that only served to make her complexion look paler. Her eyes were deepset, dark, and not unlike those Paulette stared at every morning when she faced her vanity mirror. The woman's clothes were stylish but worn; she was either poor or had been in mourning far longer than her wardrobe warranted. She apparently found a tear in her skirt and turned her anger on the driver. "I warned you!" she cried. "I'll deduct the cost of mending from your wages!"

Then, glancing up, she saw Paulette standing in the doorway. Dismissing the driver with an impatient wave of her gloved hand, she climbed the steps. "Mrs. Walker?" The exertion of climbing the steps in addition to her taxing anger at the driver had left her somewhat winded; she pressed a trembling hand against her bosom. "You are Mrs. Walker, are you not?" Her pronunciation was somewhat clipped and accented.

Paulette forced her eyes away from the woman's face and nodded, "Yes, I am Mrs. Walker." Jeremiah had told her he would send a woman to teach her the fundamentals of public speaking for a rally to be given the following week. Her contribution was to be small, a few short words spoken from her husband's side, but she had felt incapable and had asked for tutoring. But surely Jeremiah would not have selected such a woman as the one facing her across the porch. Something about her stirred forgotten memories that made shivers plait along Paulette's spine. Her dislike was instantaneous. Still, Jeremiah must know best. She read the woman's accent, and so she said, "And your name, *madame?*"

The woman stared at her for several moments, her dark eyes appraising openly. Finally, she said, "I am using the name Colette Fouche." Aptly chosen, her tone seemed to add, since even you backward Americans must remember that gentleman's fame.

Paulette waited for the woman to say more, but when she did not, merely continued to stare out of the dark hollows of her eyes, Paulette said, "Did my husband send you, Madame Fouche?"

The question seemed to amuse the woman. "Your husband? Oh, no, my dear." She laughed softly into her gloved hand. "I've never met your husband, although I've seen him at his place of business. How handsome he is—and, I understand, quite wealthy besides." She stepped closer and Paulette backed away from the door and into the entryway. "I've trav-

eled halfway around the world for this meeting. You
have not been easy to locate. New Orleans, San Francisco, the gold fields. What adventurers Maurice
Favière bred."

Paulette stifled a scream at the mention of her father's name. She continued to back away until the
heels of her shoes touched the first step of the great
staircase. She did not understand the fear building inside her. Scenes, words, and dreams stamped on her
memory and forgotten since childhood began to con-
jure up images she wished to push aside. She grabbed
for the banister and clung to it with such force that
her knuckles whitened.

The woman advanced until she stood in the middle
of the entryway carpet, the fragments of light from
the stained-glass skylight feeding color into her pale
face and dark clothing.

Paulette's senses seemed to become acutely alert.
She heard Clay in some distant upper part of the
house yelling for Annie. Someone in the kitchen
dropped a pan; it clattered and settled noisily. Outside, the driver had turned the carriage and was walking across the gravel, whistling.

"Come now, my dear," the woman said, "aren't you
going to welcome me?"

"Who . . . who are you?" Paulette managed.

The woman laughed again, the thin red lines of her
lips pulling back over yellowing teeth. "I told you I'm
using the name of Colette Fouche," she said when the
laughter had passed. "Only you and I need know my
true identity."

"Wh——who?"

All hints of amusement faded. The pale face became stern and unyielding. "Do you truly have to
ask?" she demanded. "Can't you identify me by my
eyes? Look at them. Aren't they the same as yours.
And the Favière cheekbones. Come, come, my dear,
blood should recognize blood." Spreading her black-
cloaked arms, she moved forward, as if for an em-

brace. "I'm Claudine Favière, of course! Your beloved half-sister!"

Paulette fainted before the arms could embrace her.

When Paulette opened her eyes she was in her own bed, Chang and Annie hovering over her.

"I send Mr. Walker," Chang said, reverting to his thick accent as he always did when disturbed or excited.

Clutching at the sleeve of his robe, Paulette sat bolt upright in bed, eyes wide as they scanned the room behind the loyal servants. "Where is she?" she cried.

"Where who is?" Chang asked, confused.

"The woman!" Paulette cried. "Claudine Favière! Where is she?"

Annie, her lower lip trembling, took Paulette's shoulders and coaxed her back against the pillows. "We saw no woman, madam." Her eyes began to fill with tears. "We heard you scream, and when we came running . . ." Her voice broke and she fought for control. "When we saw you at the bottom of the great staircase, we . . . we thought you had fallen."

Paulette understood their distress and waited to assure them she had not been injured, but she could not erase the image of Claudine Favière confronting her in the entryway. "The woman? Neither of you saw her?"

"No see woman," Chang mumbled, "only carriage going downhill—fast, very fast." He reached into his robe and drew out an envelope. "And this, Miss Paulette—this was on floor beside you." He put the envelope into her hand and turned to soak a cloth in the basin. Placing it across her forehead, he said, "I send for Mr. Walker now?"

Paulette raised the envelope. *Paulette Favière Walker* was scrawled across its face and underlined with two bold strokes. "No, Chang. It won't be necessary to summon Mr. Walker. Leave me now. You, too, Annie. I'll be fine—really I shall."

Chang and Annie reluctantly moved away from the

bed, hesitating in the double doorway as if questioning the wisdom of leaving her.

She waved them away and tore open the envelope as soon as the door had closed behind them.

> *My dearest sister,*
>   *I write this note in the event you refuse to see me. Coming as I am from the dead, so to speak, I know I shall be a considerable shock to you . . . you who thought yourself without family all these years.*

Again Paulette felt faint.

She let the sheet of paper flutter to the bed and closed her eyes. *Considerable shock!* An understatement. Dear God, how was it possible? Hadn't Clabe verified Claudine's death in order for her to claim the Favière estate? She remembered the report: *found in the Seine with her throat cut.* How that had haunted her—and yet, hearing the stories of Claudine's cruelties since her childhood, she had considered it poetic justice.

Her hands trembled as she lifted the sheet of paper and continued to read, the words blurring. The note ended with a request for a meeting. The address was on Maiden Lane.

Paulette stiffened with recognition. Dora! It was Dora's address.

Paulette lay for several minutes, her gaze fixed unblinkingly on the ceiling. When realization hit her of the effect Claudine Favière's sudden appearance could have on Jeremiah and his campaign for office, she rose and began pacing her room. Claudine was infamous, still whispered about by enemies of the South as an example of the cruelties whites inflicted upon their slaves. Southerners still remembered her with anger and disgust and spat when her name was mentioned. Jeremiah already had enough strikes against him—owning a gambling establishment, a wife who was called an eccentric. Claudine's appearance and

the opening up of the past would surely bring about
his defeat. She collapsed in a chair beside the window.
There was so much churning about in her mind that
she was incapable of thinking coherently. All she
knew was that she must prevent Jeremiah from being
injured because of her.

Rising, she went quickly to the bell pull and summoned Chang and Annie, instructing them that Mr.
Walker was not to be informed of what had happened. Then, because she thought best while soaking
in a bath, she had the porcelain tub filled with scented
water and submerged herself for nearly an hour.

When Jeremiah arrived home for supper she was in
control of herself. She sat opposite him at the long
dining table, discussing the upcoming election as if
nothing troubled her. Still, she was aware of his watching her closely. He's so attuned to me, she thought,
that the slightest inflection in my voice alerts him.
She toyed with her food, pushing it around on the
plate to make it appear she had an appetite. Chang,
who was serving them, remained aloof, never attempting to catch her eye. He took her plate away at the
earliest opportunity and saw that her helping of des-
sert scarcely covered the bottom of the plate. She
declined coffee and sat quietly while Jeremiah indulged
in his usual liqueur.

She heaved a sigh of relief when he pushed his
chair away from the table and offered her his arm.
Now, she thought, there's only the hour with the children to get through.

When Jeremiah put on his greatcoat and stopped at
the door to kiss her cheek, she felt a surge of guilt for
not confessing to him. She clung to him, suddenly
wanting to hold him back, but then, knowing she
must not, she let him go, then watched him hurry
down the steps and climb onto his horse. When he had
ridden away, she turned to summon Chang and found
him standing in the shadow of the great staircase.

As he stepped into the light, he said, "I thought you
would need me, Miss Paulette."

"Yes, Chang, I need you. Bring the carriage around. We'll be going out."

The Chinese man nodded without question and scurried away to do her bidding. When he brought the carriage around in front, she was waiting concealed against the darkness of the shrubbery in her long black cape. "Where to, Miss Paulette?"

"Maiden Lane," she told him. "Miss Dora's. And hurry."

The redhead opened the door when the carriage pulled up. Silhouetted by the light behind her, she appeared smug and amused. "Welcome once again to my house," she said with sarcasm. She stepped back to make way for Paulette to enter. Only for Paulette's ears, she whispered, "What would Jeremiah think to see his wife again in Maiden Lane?"

"No doubt you're enjoying this," Paulette said as she swept into the small entryway.

"An underestimation," Dora said and smiled.

"How much have you been told?"

"Enough to appreciate your circumstances," Dora answered. "You'll find your sister in the drawing room." She pushed the outer door closed, blocking off Paulette's view of Chang as he sat atop the carriage in his red silk robe. "There's a great similarity between your sister and yourself, not only, I think, physical."

Paulette gritted her teeth and refused to dignify Dora's remark with an answer. She threw open the drawing room doors and stepped inside.

Claudine Favière sat in a straight-backed chair before the blazing fire, her hands extended toward the warmth. She did not pull her gaze away from the flames, but said, without looking up, "Come in, sister. I have looked forward to this reunion."

Paulette remained standing just inside the tawdry room. She could see Claudine in profile, the thin, sharp features and sunken hollow of the eyes, the black-and-gray-streaked hair pulled severely back and knotted at her neck. Her back was slightly bent, her shoulders stooped, and the hands extended toward the fire were bony and gnarled.

"Why do you stare at me so?" the woman demanded.

Because I've feared you and hated you all my life, Paulette wanted to cry—feared and hated you because I dreaded that some of you would be reflected in me! But she held her tongue. The doors behind her remained open, with Dora lounging in the entryway listening. She turned and brought the doors together with a slam. Then she crossed to the settee and perched on its edge. "What do you want of me?" she asked directly. "Why have you sought me out?"

Claudine turned slowly until their eyes met. There was hate there and mockery mirrored in those cold, dark irises. "Why, sister dear, one would think you unhappy to greet your only living relative." The thin slash of a mouth spread in a humorless smile. "You are so . . . so *de mauvaise,* little sister. Does it depress you that I am alive and not buried in Paris with my throat cut, as that bastard Granville was informed?"

"What do you want of me?" Paulette repeated.

*"Mon dieu!"* the woman cried and raised her bony hands in a gesture of helplessness. "Can you think of nothing else? Can we not converse as two sisters would after so long a separation?" She crossed one leg over the other and leaned back in her chair. "There must be many questions floating about in that pretty head of yours."

"I've asked the most important one," Paulette said coolly, "and you seem indisposed to answer it. I repeat: What do you want of me?"

Claudine's face went even paler. "Very little of you, my sister," she said, "since your foolishness deprived both of us of our rightful share of our father's plantation."

"Oh, then it's money?"

"Is there anything more important?"

"To me there is," Paulette murmured.

Claudine stared at her quietly, her slash of a mouth

twisted in a mocking smile. Finally, she said, "Since you will not bring yourself to question me, I shall offer my own explanation. You were told, of course, of my narrow escape from New Orleans."

"And of the reason for it," Paulette told her.

"A wretched misunderstanding." Claudine laughed. Then her laughter faded abruptly. "If that madwoman of a mother of yours had not set the house on fire . . . ah, but then I do not want to call attention to the weaker genes of your heredity. Father was a fine figure of a man, but your mother . . . she was a bond woman, you know. Father found her scrubbing floors in a New Orleans brothel. He bought her, married her, and carried her home. She must have had some endearing qualities that evaded me, because Father was a very discriminating man. She went mad, I think, when she became pregnant with you."

"You mean the two of you drove her mad," Paulette blurted out. "You needn't go over all this. I've heard it before. The Granvilles hid nothing from me."

"Oh, yes, those meddlesome Granvilles," Claudine mused. "Nothing but trouble from the moment they swindled that surrounding land from the government. They did, you know. Zelma Granville's father was a senator. He saw that our father didn't get a deed to the land surrounding Favière plantation, but that his daughter's husband did."

"I'm not here to defend the Granvilles," Paulette said sternly. "Even if I believed what you're telling me, those that Maurice Favière fought with are dead."

"But they're still stealing from us, aren't they, little sister? Wasn't it a Granville son-in-law who stole the fortune you entrusted to his care? And do not refer to our father as Maurice Favière—so unfeeling of you, my dear."

There was a rap on the door and Dora entered. She set a tray with crystal bottles and three glasses on the table between Paulette and Claudine. "I thought this reunion called for something stronger than tea," she said.

Claudine Favière glanced at the tray, saw the third glass, and rose from her chair. Taking the glass from the tray, she handed it to Dora. "You're being paid for the use of your house," she said bitterly. "That doesn't include your prying inclusion. Now, if you'll leave us."

Dora appeared about to object, but the expression on Claudine's face made her hold her tongue and back away quickly through the doorway.

Claudine poured a stiff drink into a glass and downed it in one quick gulp. "Do you indulge, little sister?"

Paulette said she did not.

"A pity. Liquor can be such a comfort when there are no other comforts for body or spirit." She poured a second glass and carried it back to her chair before the fire. "Such a whore's house, this one," she mumbled. "But then I've lived in far worse places since fleeing America."

"Forgive me for being unsympathetic. I can't help considering the reason you had to flee. If you hadn't, you would have been hanged. They still whisper stories about you to frighten children and enrage adults. I understand Harriet Beecher Stowe was so enraged when she heard of you that she wrote that damnable book that is creating such a controversy." Paulette, rising, moved to the hearth and stood staring down at Claudine. She had to make an effort to control her agitation. It would not do to have the woman see her hands trembling. She did not know why, but she understood she was being challenged. Again, she asked, "What do you want of me? Money? You already know I have nothing left of the estate."

"Because you let the Granvilles cheat you out of it," Claudine snapped. "Is there no end to what they will take from us?" She pushed at the bun of hair on her neck as if it were coming loose, and she tried to compose herself. The anger did not fade easily from her gaunt face. "Well, little sister, I do not intend to suffer because of your stupidity. I want my share of Father's estate, and I mean to have it!"

"I have no money," Paulette told her. "How can I share with you what was stolen?"

Claudine rose; she was surprisingly tall as she faced Paulette. Her eyes burned in their deep hollows. "I am no fool," she said through frozen lips. "I did not arrive in San Francisco today—or yesterday. I have been here for sometime, watching and waiting for the proper time to approach you. So, you see, little sister, I have been with you for a long while. My man, Jean-Paul, even became your traveling companion when you ran to that Granville in the gold fields."

"Jean-Paul!" Paulette cried. Memories of the young Frenchman and her mistrust of him flooded over her. She remembered that on their parting he had said, "We'll meet again. It is destined." When she remembered the driver who had brought Claudine to her house that morning, the sense of familiarity she had felt when she had glanced at him. "Your driver," she mumbled.

"Yes, my driver," Claudine said. "My handyman, my servant and my lover, too. Jean-Paul was quite taken by you. I believe you even temporarily made him forget his share of the reward when he helped me claim half the estate."

"But there is no estate!" Paulette protested. "You have wasted your time and efforts! I cannot give you what I do not have!"

Claudine stepped closer, so close that the warmth of her breath touched Paulette's cheek.

Paulette stepped back and stood pressed against Dora's flocked wallpaper, as if the wine-red rose stems had her caught in their grasp.

"You married well, little sister," Claudine said with a sneer. "Unlike our father when he bought and married your mother, your husband is wealthy. It is his duty to pay your debts."

"Jeremiah? Never!" Paulette cried. "He doesn't even know you're here . . . alive."

"I didn't think you'd tell him. But no matter. He must be told"—she held her index finger toward Paulette, shaking it threateningly—"unless you can come up with the money on your own."

"I have no money of my own," Paulette told her.

"You have jewels!" Claudine cried. "He'll give you money if you ask for it!"

"I . . . I never have," the younger woman said. She moved away from the wall and collapsed on the settee, her face buried in her hands. "I cannot. He is good to me. I can't deceive him."

"Then he must be told," Claudine said firmly. "If you don't tell him, then I shall. How would he like it if his sweet little wife's past was brought out from the closet, especially now that he has his eye on an office of responsibility? Yes, I know that also. I told you I've been watching you, waiting. I've seen the money drawn in over those gambling tables. I've seen that lavish house built for a queen, and I've heard of the emerald-and-diamond necklace he draped around your slender young neck the day of your marriage. He would pay to protect you, if not himself." Returning to the chair before the hearth, she leaned toward the heat but kept her eyes riveted on Paulette. "Call me evil and greedy," she said, her voice coldly ominous. "Think of me as you wish, little sister. But do not think anything but money will silence me. I will drag you and your devoted husband into ruin if I must."

"Even if you ruin yourself in the bargain?" Paulette managed to say. "You escaped a lynch mob once. Would you risk it again? You are hated no less now than before."

There was a strange flicker in the older woman's eyes, but it lasted only momentarily. Paulette knew it to be fear, but fear was short-lived. It vanished and the thin lips parted in a cynical half-smile. "Are you threatening me, little sister?" Claudine asked with amusement.

Paulette pulled herself erect on the settee. "No

more than you're threatening me," she answered. "If it becomes necessary to incite a mob against you, so help me, God, that's exactly what I'll do."

Claudine threw her head back in laughter. "You? The eccentric Mrs. Walker who lives on the hill? The mock empress of San Francisco? My dear sister, who will listen to you? You could not incite gold-starved miners to a claim with promises of riches beyond their expectations. You poor, pathetic creature! You are but a pawn in a game beyond your understanding. It is only because of our shared blood that I came to you first. I felt you should have the opportunity of settling your debt before I approached your husband. A mistake on my part, I can see now." Her thin chin tilted upward and the muscles in her scrawny neck protruded as if they would pierce the tightly drawn flesh. "Go," she said drily.

Paulette, wavering between sheer terror of what the woman could do and the impulse to strike back, continued to sit in utter silence, her shoulders slumped warily forward, her fingers laced tightly together in her lap. Anguish rose up in her throat like bile, and tears threatened to streak down her cheeks. She was aware of the eyes in that skeletal head fixed on her, reading her every thought, understanding she had been beaten. With sullen resignation, she asked, "How much money do you want?"

Claudine sighed and cleared her throat. "So you are sensible, after all," she said victoriously. "I knew there had to be some Favière blood coursing through your veins despite those years of Granville intervention."

Paulette, caught in the black, sullen mood of the defeated, did not bring herself to defend the Granvilles. She merely repeated, "How much will it cost for you to go away and be dead once again?"

"Fifty thousand dollars," Claudine answered without hesitation.

Paulette gasped at such a sum. "The entire estate was only eighty thousand," she ventured.

Claudine smiled. "More proof of your Favière blood," she said. "The estate was three times that amount. I'm merely being generous with you—because of our relationship, of course."

"Of course," Paulette murmured. "You did your research well."

"I am my father's daughter," Claudine said expressively, "as are you."

Paulette shot her a disgusted look.

"And now," Claudine persisted, "how shall we make arrangements for payment? Jewels, or money, or both? I am not difficult to satisfy, so long as the entire fifty thousand is paid."

Paulette rose, trembling with fury and an inexplicable sadness. My blood, she thought. My God, it's even worse than I imagined.

"Do not be so crushed, little sister," Claudine said, rising to see her to the door. "Think of it as paying a debt and not buying my silence. Or think of it as saving your handsome and ambitious husband. When will you bring the money?"

"I'll need time," Paulette answered.

"Ah, yes—time," Claudine said. "I am an expert on time—a time to sow and a time to reap, a time to . . ."

"Please spare me your limited knowledge of the Bible," Paulette said with disgust. "I will contact you as soon as I've raised the money."

"Not more than a week," Claudine said with emphasis. "I will wait no longer. If the money isn't in my hands within one week, I shall begin working toward your husband's downfall."

Paulette disengaged herself from the claw-like hand that clutched at her arm. She threw the doors open and saw Dora standing beside the banister, her face an obvious mask of interest. How she must be gloating, Paulette thought. Damn her! Damn both of them! But then, she thought, it was she who was damned—damned by the blood that flowed through her veins.

Turning, she closed the door and blotted out Claudine's smiling face.

"You look like a woman facing doom," Dora told her with gay mischievousness.

Ignoring her, Paulette crossed the entryway and let herself out into the night.

Outside, her bravado abandoned her. She leaned a hand against the door frame to support her weight. Her head was swimming and her vision was blurred. Her legs threatened to cease supporting her, and she would have slumped to the step had not Chang suddenly taken her arm and guided her toward the carriage.

He handed her inside and arranged the fur lap robe around her legs. "We go to Mr. Walker now?" he asked, and she understood that it was more of a plea than a question. "You tell him everything and he fix it. Miss Dora evil, I told you long time ago. Evil woman does evil things. Mr. Walker stop her from hurting you."

Paulette stared at his troubled face in the illumination of the gas streetlight. "There are women far more evil than Miss Dora," she said. "I do not think even Mr. Walker could comprehend them, least of all save me or himself from the destruction they are capable of inflicting." She pulled the lap robe tighter to ward off a sudden chill and leaned her head against the soft leather. "Drive me home, Chang. Drive me home." She wept.

# Chapter Sixteen

USUALLY WHEN Jeremiah returned from The Barbary Coast at night, he did not awaken Paulette until he crawled into bed beside her.

This night was different.

He flung open the bedroom door so that it slammed against the wall, reverberating throughout the house. The gaslight in the hallway silhouetted him in the open frame.

Paulette, dozing after fitful hours, sat bolt upright in bed, clutching the covers around her. Before she recognized Jeremiah's silhouette, she was reaching for the bell pull.

"Damn you!" he cried.

Her hand froze in mid-air. She whimpered. Then, reaching for the lamp, she turned up the wick. If thinking him a stranger frightened her, seeing the expression on his face terrified her. She had seen that expression before when he had saved her on *The Falcon* from her would-be rapists. Then he had killed two men. Her blood chilled with the realization that his anger was now directed at her. She looked around like a trapped animal seeking an avenue of escape. There was none unless she chose to fling herself through the upstairs window—and she seriously considered doing that for a brief moment. Leaping to her feet, she placed the bed between them. "Jeremiah," she called, but her voice cracked and his name came out as more of a wail. Never since she had known him had she been the object of his wrath. She repeated his name in a scream as he started to advance toward the bed.

He faltered, as one coming from a fit.

"Jeremiah, for God's sake, what has happened?" she cried.

Doors were being thrown open throughout the house; there was the sound of running footsteps, confused shouting, and the children's crying.

Spinning around on his heels, Jeremiah slammed the door just as Chang appeared in the hallway. The door groaned and threatened to splinter in its frame. A painting tore loose from its hook and settled on the floor in a broken frame. Jeremiah remained with his back to the room, his body heaving as he drew great breaths of air into his lungs.

Trembling, Paulette reached for her dressing gown and pulled it over her shoulders. She wanted to run to him, to put her arms around him, but she hesitated leaving the bed that separated them.

Jeremiah turned the key in the lock and shouted for the servants to return to their beds. Then, instead of turning to face his wife, he let his forehead fall against the polished surface of the carved door. He drew back and struck his forehead a second time.

"Jeremiah, please!" Paulette pleaded. "You're going to injure yourself!" She moved to the foot of the bed and clutched at the post. "You terrify me! Why? Please talk to me! Please explain!"

He turned then, slowly, his face pale except for the red mark already forming on his forehead. His dark eyes were ablaze with anger, and his black brows were raised to meet the tousled black hair. "Need you ask?" he shouted. "You were visiting Maiden Lane tonight!"

She thought at first to deny it.

But he read that thought on her face as readily as if she had verbalized it. "Don't deny it! How many carriages are driven by men wearing red silk robes?"

"Jeremiah, please let me . . ."

He waved away her explanation with an impatient gesture. Crossing to the chaise longue, he dropped into it.

She saw then that he had been drinking, something she had never known him to do to excess. She still refrained from going to him; instead, she sank to the goosedown mattress and continued to clutch at the bedpost.

"Why did I ever think you'd get over your obsession?" he asked, more of himself than of her. "Especially since I know I will never conquer mine for you."

"I don't understand!" she cried. "You're not making sense, Jeremiah! Obsession? What obsession?"

"This fever of yours!" he cried. "Weren't you with him?"

"With whom?"

"Granville!" he yelled.

"Dester?" She released the bedpost and clutched at her throat, instead. In all the days of their marriage, Jeremiah had not once mentioned Dester's name; it had always hovered there between them, a name not to be acknowledged or brought from the shadows into the light. It had been a silent agreement between them, as much a part of their marriage vows as to honor and obey until death do they part.

"Don't tell me he didn't contact you," Jeremiah told her. "Don't pretend you weren't aware that he's been in San Francisco for the past five days."

"I didn't! I swear I didn't know!" she cried. It felt as though her chest would collapse with the pressure from within. So much in one day—Claudine and Dester both reappearing in her life, her past becoming the present, frightful dreams becoming a reality.

"He's living on Maiden Lane," Jeremiah said, "in fact, at the very address in front of which your carriage was seen. The right place for him, too. A male whore on the street of whores." He drawled the words out hatefully so they might sting her more.

Tears of anguish and frustration filled Paulette's eyes.

"Shall I tell you about your precious Dester Granville?" Jeremiah shouted. "Tell you why he's a whore for gold, more than I, whom you detest for being in the honorable profession of gambling? Would your delicate ears comprehend such truths?"

"Stop it!" Paulette shouted. She clamped her hands over her ears in an attempt to drown out his angry words. *Dester here! Dester here!* kept echoing through her head. God forgive her! The news that he was in San Francisco excited her as much as Jeremiah's anger frightened her. That realization brought more tears than her frustration and anguish. She let herself slip from the mattress to the carpet, her head lolling against the bed frame. Her anguish found expression, and the sound was deafening.

She felt Jeremiah's hard, muscular arm go around her waist and lift her back onto the bed. He was speaking, but his words did not reach her. Chang was pounding on the door, shouting her name; she could hear that, but not Jeremiah's softly spoken words. It was as if she were deaf or he a mute, whose lips moved without sound.

The anger had vanished from his face. There was fright there now, concern, apology. She knew by his eyes that he was pleading with her, begging her forgiveness. And then, when she continued to wail, he struck her.

The pain exploded inside her head. Her screaming stopped and her hearing returned.

Jeremiah drew her against his chest and held her tightly. She could feel the coarse fabric against her cheek, smell the odor of alcohol on his breath. "My beloved, my beloved," he moaned. And then, like one discovering he was being duped, the words caught in his throat, and his embrace became less comforting, lax. Releasing her, he rose and stepped away from the bed.

Paulette collapsed back against the pillows, but try

as she might, she could not pull her gaze from his; it
was as if some unseen force kept their eyes locked together.

"Forgive me if I wronged you," Jeremiah said, his
voice softening. "Forgive me if I must wrong you
again. But I must ask you to swear you did not have
Chang drive you to Maiden Lane tonight."

Paulette pulled her back against the headboard.
Her tears had ceased; so, too, had her trembling. "I
swear," she said slowly, "that I did not see Dester
Granville, and that until you told me, I did not know
he had returned to San Francisco."

"But you were on Maiden Lane?"

"I was," she confessed.

"But why would you . . ."

"I was at your friend Dora's house," she interrupted. "It was not a visit I relished. I would have
avoided it if I could."

He did not ask for further explanations. A great
shudder went through his body. As if his legs suddenly became too weak to support him, he dropped
to his knees beside the bed and crouched with his head
across her breasts.

Dear God, she thought, he's weeping! Jeremiah
Walker is weeping! She had at that moment of realization the strongest sense of closeness she had had for
him since marrying him. She ran her fingers through
his hair and, pulling him tighter against her breast,
lay her cheek against his head. "My devoted husband," she whispered, "how I must have made you
suffer. It is you who should forgive me." She pulled
his head back and wiped the tears from his eyes with
her finger.

Embarrassed, he tried to hide his face from her.

"No," she told him. "Don't hide them from me.
Those tears make me realize how much you love me."
She brushed the hair from his bruised forehead and
kissed each of his eyes. Then she rose, went to the
door, where Chang was still pounding, and told him
to retire. When she turned back into the room, Jere-

miah was standing before the fireplace, his legs spread, his hands resting on the mantel to support the slump of his body. She went to him, ran her arms around his waist, and rested her face against his back. "I was not going to tell you about my visit to Maiden Lane," she said, "nor of the visitor I had this morning. I wanted to protect you—from me, from my past."

He straightened up then and turned to stare down into her eyes. "I have no right to question you," he said quietly. "I married you knowing you belonged to another man. I thought that in time you would forget him and transfer your love to me. Still, it's plagued me these past months. I am used to getting whatever I want, except where you are concerned. I married you, but marriage did not blot out the reality of Granville. Even after you bore our child, I feared he would return and take you away from me. When I learned that he had returned to San Francisco, I was beside myself. Then tonight when our carriage was spotted . . ." He let the sentence remain incompleted.

Paulette, taking his hand, led him to the chaise longue and sat beside him. "We have a far greater problem than Dester," she told him. Then, before he could question her, she told him of Claudine Favière's visit and of her threat unless the money was raised within one week.

Jeremiah listened attentively until she had finished. Then, rising, he walked to the window and stood staring out at the darkened city below. "She's obviously a fraud," he said. "In New Orleans I was told that your adopted father verified her death before you could claim your inheritance. Such matters are not easily falsified by the French authorities. They are an officious people. Details are as important to them as are their wine and *amour*."

"But she is my half-sister," Paulette protested. "It's there—in her eyes, in her cheekbones, in her knowledge of our family. I never doubted her authenticity, not for a moment. As I looked at her and talked to her, I only regretted that the same blood flows through both our veins."

"What proof did she give you other than her appearance and stories that could have been taken from any meddlesome neighbor?" Jeremiah demanded. "Did she produce documents? Affidavits?"

"No," Paulette admitted. "I did not feel it necessary to ask for further proof. God, I wish that it were not so, Jeremiah, but she is my half-sister."

Jeremiah, turning from the window, offered her his hand. Then, lifting her into his arms, he carried her to the bed. "You should have sent for me when she first presented herself," he said, "instead of trying to protect me from scandal. If I, instead of you, had made the trip to Maiden Lane, I dare say the outcome would have been much different. Our Mademoiselle Claudine Favière, dead for these past fifteen years, would be unmasked as a fraud and returned to her grave, where she would no longer haunt you."

"You are mistaken in this, Jeremiah," Paulette insisted. "I would know my own sister even if I could not remember her. She was no fraud. And even if she were, can you imagine the harm that could be done if she speaks to the press, whether it be the truth or a lie about her identity? You would be defeated in this campaign before you had ever begun."

Speaking with such earnestness, she had been unaware that he had been removing her dressing gown and undergarment as she spoke. Now naked, she stared up at him in surprise.

"I hope to God I never fight with you again," he said as he undid his tie and shed his coat, "but it has made me want you all the more."

Paulette opened her arms to him and welcomed the weight of his body on hers. She clutched at his neck, her passion equaling his. In the final moments, however, with her eyes clamped closed, it was Dester's face that flashed across her eyelids—it was Dester to whom she surrendered herself.

From somewhere in the recesses of her mind, an

old gypsy's voice murmured: *"It's a fever with you
. . . fatal unless your blood is purified."*

Paulette did not agree with Jeremiah's belief that
Claudine Favière was a fraud. The resemblance
aside, the woman was too confident and knew too
many intimate details. True, some of her information
could have been picked up from gossip, rumor, or
conversation with someone from the New Orleans
area. The fact that her mother had gone mad near
the end and had set fire to the Favière plantation was
well known, and so were Claudine's inhuman treatment of the slaves and her narrow escape to France.
But that her mother had been a bond woman, purchased and taken in wedlock by her father, was
something that had been known by few. Even
Paulette had learned of this through confidences with
Vienna, the dear woman telling her it was best if she
spoke of it to no one and not fan the flames of her
family's unfortunate legend. And the exact amount of
the estate—Claudine had known that, also. Claudine
had taken Paulette's figure of the estate's value as a
lie, but, even being convinced the woman had been
whom she said, she had been making a feeble attempt
to trick her and prove her an imposter.

Last night when Jeremiah had suggested that Claudine was a fraud, Paulette had wanted desperately to
believe him. For a moment, perhaps she had. Even
this morning when he had kissed her good-bye and
promised he would see to the matter, she had clung to
that belief. But after he had left her alone, her cer-
tainty had vanished and she had once again accepted
Claudine as her half-sister. It was Jeremiah who was
deluding himself, not her.

And exactly what had he meant by "taking care of
the matter"? When he left the house, had it been his
intention to drive to Maiden Lane and confront Claudine? She wished he had been more specific. He had
been gone for several hours and had not returned or
sent any message. The waiting was pure torment. Had

he gone directly to The Barbary Coast from Maiden Lane with the intention of not informing her until he returned for his evening meal? Had he thought he had convinced her so completely that Claudine was not whom she claimed to be? It was so like Jeremiah, she thought, to cloak his activities in an aura of mystery.

Unable to remain in her rooms any longer, she went to the nursery, thinking the children would divert her attention. Anna, having just been fed by the wet nurse, was sleeping, and Clay, although excited by her sudden appearance during his lessons, soon lost interest in her and devoted himself to the young tutor Jeremiah had employed in the belief that "it is never too soon to begin an education."

The young tutor was named Ralph and was the son of a local businessman. He was a genius for one so young, Jeremiah had told her. His genius did not appear evident. He stammered and repeated himself several times as he coached his charge. His pale face reddened when he caught her eye and he looked as if he were about to close the book and end the lesson.

Realizing her presence made him uneasy, Paulette smiled encouragement and left them.

Even the servants seemed to have made themselves scarce this day. Usually the house bustled with their activities and chatter. Today, when she was seeking diversion, there was no one within sight or hearing. She descended the great staircase to the drawing room and absently picked up the needlepoint she had left on the settee. On the first stitch she pricked her finger. She tossed it aside impatiently.

Of course, the servants were moving about in a hushed silence because of last night's argument between their employers. Never had such a thing happened; not even a cross word had ever been exchanged between the Mr. and Mrs. Well, they would adjust, she thought. She had—or almost. There were moments during the morning hours when she had been swept back to last night, to the fear she had felt from witnessing Jeremiah's anger.

If only someone would visit.

She thought of sending Chang for Mrs. Mason, but she decided the older woman would be furious at being dragged away from her restaurant at its busy noon peak.

Sighing, she rose and returned to her rooms.

It was Annie who rapped gently and entered. The young woman stood with her eyes downcast. Paulette glanced at her twice before noting the tears streaming down her cheeks. Annie, since helping to deliver Clay, had become Paulette's favorite; she considered her to be a friend and often gave her small gifts and sent her on buying sprees to Kearny Street.

Leaving her windowseat, where she had been staring down at the city with half-sight, she moved quickly to the young woman's side, lifting her chin and brushing away the tears with her fingers. "There, there, Annie," she said. "It can't be that bad." Her own anxiety was forgotten as she tried to comfort Annie. "Come in. We'll order tea and spend the afternoon chatting."

"No, madam," Annie whimpered. "I've my duties and . . . and I came with a message."

A message? Tears? Paulette's heart fluttered. She had an instant vision of Jeremiah lying dead in the gutter of Maiden Lane, shot perhaps by Claudine Favière or Jean-Paul when he had confronted them. She grabbed Annie's shoulders and shook her to stop the flow of tears. "Tell me," she demanded.

"A . . . a gentleman, madam," Annie stammered, "he frightened the life out of me, jumping out as he did from behind the woodshed." She reached into her pocket and extended her hand to Paulette. "He told me to give you this and that he would be waiting in the stables." She cast her eyes down again to hide their expression. Then, as soon as her mistress held the article the man had given her, Annie turned and fled.

When Dester's ring with the family crest dropped from Annie's hand into her own, Paulette drew back as if a deadly spider had bitten her flesh. The ring fell to the carpet and rolled against the bedpost. She stood staring at it, wide-eyed, trembling, memories flooding over her. A queasiness attacked her stomach and her blood pounded at her temples. She moved to the foot of the bed and sank to the floor, her eyes fixed on the ring, but her fingers refused to obey the command of her brain to pick it up.

A distant door opened in the hallway and she heard Clay's excited laughter. Lessons had ended and he was free to spend the balance of the day at play. His tutor's footsteps echoed down the great staircase, the front door opened and closed, and presently she heard his horse's hooves on the gravel.

Like one coming out of a daze, she suddenly snatched the ring from the carpet and struggled to her feet. *Waiting in the stables! Dester!* Although Jeremiah had told her he was in San Francisco, she truly had not expected him to call on her.

Despite the chill in the air, she left her room without her cape and hurried down the back stairs, avoiding the kitchen and pantry, since the servants would consider it odd that she was leaving the house by the rear door. The wind was blowing in off the bay; it touched her arms and face, causing her to realize she was hot flushed. Bending into the wind, she grasped the folds of her skirt and ran for the stables.

The doors stood open and she ran through, almost colliding with the carriage Chang had moved near the entrance to polish. The horses were in their stalls, feeding, watching her with vague interest. The place smelled of fresh hay and dung and animal sweat. She stood, hands pressed to her breasts to quiet her heartbeat, and let her eyes roam from corner to corner; Dester was nowhere in sight.

Softly, she called his name.

"Here," he said, and he stepped from behind bales of newly delivered hay. He was as she remembered him, tall and handsome, with his hair bleached almost white by the sun, his pale eyes appearing an even paler shade of blue because of his tanned complexion, his head slightly tilted upward so that his chin jutted out defiantly. He was not dressed as he had been at the mines, but wore a dove-gray cutaway coat with a high collar. There were ruffles at his neck and at the bottoms of his sleeves. A gold watch chain swagged from one pocket of his vest to the other. He carried a silver-tipped cane.

More as he looked at Plantation Bend, she thought. But still he looked out of place in the fancy clothes. His hair was unkempt and hung too low on his collar; his hands were too rough and red to be protruding beneath such elaborate cuffs. And a cane—she had never known him to carry a cane, even for effect.

All this she discerned in an instant. Then, dashing forward, she flung herself into his arms. Jeremiah, her children, the servants—everything was forgotten except that Dester was holding her. His savageness and and the madness of gold fever were no longer evident in his face. The pale blue eyes that stared into hers were kind and filled with loving. He whispered her name over and over as his lips moved around her face and eyes and ears. The sound of his cane dropping to the stable floor was muffled by the covering of hay. He tossed the high hat he had been holding after the cane, and, pulling her back behind the bales, he lowered her gently to the floor.

In a quiet, thoughtful voice, he said, "I love you, Paulette. It's always been you and me. It always will be." He buried his face against the curve of her throat while his fingers fought with the buttons of her gown.

She did not resist; her only thoughts were of the moment.

Naked, bits of straw clung to her feverish body and entangled themselves in her dark hair. She clung to him, her fingernails digging into his shoulders, her passion matching his. Only when she felt his mouth painfully on her breast did she emerge momentarily into reality, remembering his savageness at the mining camp and the brutality with which he had taken her. Her passion waned, she became less responsive—but she seemed not to notice or care.

When he rolled off her to lay panting on his back, she lay staring at the planks of the ceiling, listening to the horses whinny, the wind rattle the windowpanes, and suddenly she was consumed with guilt and self-reproach. She sat up and reached for her clothing, her nakedness a sudden embarrassment. Her breasts were bruised, the imprint of his teeth still visible about the crescents of her nipples. While she dressed, Dester, raised to one elbow, watched her closely.

There was an unfathomable expression in his blue eyes, as if he were attempting to read her thoughts through her skull. "It's true, isn't it, Paulette?" he asked quietly. "It's been just the two of us since childhood? It will always be just the two of us?"

She refrained from speaking for several moments. Then she said scarcely above a whisper, "I have children of my own now, Dester. I have a husband. When I was forced to flee the gold fields . . ."

He rose and when she turned away from him he slipped his arms around her tiny waist and kissed the back of her neck. "Forgive me," he pleaded. "I was not myself. The gold fever had driven me near madness."

"I understand about fevers," she murmured. "A gypsy once warned me . . ." She stepped away from him and stood combing her fingers through her hair to remove the bits of straw. Her eyes were fixed on a corner of the great house Jeremiah had built for her—it was all she could see through the open stable doors. "I have a husband," she repeated.

"I heard," he said casually. "The gambler. But you married him for convenience. You would leave him for me, wouldn't you?" he asked broodingly.

He took her silence as an affirmative answer.

She heard him moving behind her, gathering up his

clothing and dressing. So many thoughts were crowd-
ing into her mind that she felt befuddled: Jeremiah,
the children, Claudine Favière—and, most of all,
Dester. When she had seen him standing beside the
bales of hay, she had lost all control. The love for
him she had buried had easily resurfaced. She suffered now because she had not been faithful to her
emotions. When she had fled from him, she had
thought his gold madness would never pass, that he
had been lost to her—and she had carefully constructed a new life as Jeremiah's wife. The fact that
she had been truthful with Jeremiah about her love
no longer seemed to matter. She felt trapped by her
marriage and by her children—and something else
festering inside her that would not yet let itself be
known. Could it be possible . . . ?

When she turned, Dester had finished dressing and
had seated himself on one of the bales. How handsome he looked—and how confident—as he smiled
and beckoned her closer. She went to him obediently,
sat beside him, and leaned her head against his shoulder. Perhaps, she thought, if she could talk it out with
him, she would find understanding. "When I fled
Hangtown . . ."

"Everything collapsed at once," he interrupted.
"The claim petered out and I was . . ." He stopped
speaking and lifted her chin to stare into her eyes.
"You don't still believe I was the one who built that
dam, do you?"

The dam. Charity's broken body caught in the fork
of a tree. Elisha. How long ago all that seemed: a de-
cade, two, memories that crept into her dreams and
haunted her. The youth she had killed. Dester's being
here beside her dredged it all up. Things she had
struggled to forget bombarded her. And Dester himself—how she had fought to think of him as little as
possible.

"Well, it wasn't me," Dester told her. "Crimmon,
perhaps. He always coveted Charity's claim. Another
miner killed him in a fight. The bastard deserved it."

He drew her close. "But we must forget all that," he said. "It's behind us and best forgotten."

"Your fine clothes," she said. "Then you finally struck your rich claim?" She remembered his promise to come for her only after he had had success at the gold fields.

"That I did." He laughed. "Not at Hangtown. That nigger . . . Elisha drove me out of there. He was a madman, stalking about in the scrub watching me, threatening me. Elusive, he was. None of the miners could catch the bastard. I finally was forced to hire a man to stand guard over me while I worked my claim. When that petered out, I moved on to Dry Gulch." He sighed, stretched, and rose. Moving to one of the narrow windows, he stood staring out at the cliffs and the bay beyond. "My strike wasn't as rich as I'd dreamed, but it produced enough gold to keep us comfortable for a long while."

"And the children?" she asked.

"And the children," he echoed.

"Dester, I . . ."

He glanced at her over his shoulder, his blue eyes suddenly cold. "You're not having second thoughts, are you? You still love me? You'll leave this place with me?"

"I . . . I still love you," she murmured.

"Then why the sad face?" he demanded. "Things are finally going to be as we wanted them. You should be elated, as I am."

"Gold wasn't required for the way I wanted things," she said quietly. "I would have consented to live like a dirt farmer's wife merely to be with you, to have your children."

"But now you won't have to live like a dirt farmer's wife," he told her. "We'll return to Louisiana and live as we lived before everything happened here."

Suddenly remembering that he had not been informed, she said, "Your father is dead, Dester. Katrina's new husband is running the plantation." Your responsibility, she wanted to add, but she refrained from doing so.

A flicker of emotion that she took for grief passed quickly over his face and then vanished. "What did you write my mother about me?"

"Only that I left you well in the gold fields," she told him truthfully. She had never been able to bring herself to write Vienna of Dester's obsession with gold and how it had changed him. Vienna, in her letters, had ceased mentioning her son at all. Paulette looked at him more closely now, trying to determine if he had indeed shed the madness she had witnessed at Hangtown, and she saw only the old Dester, the Dester of her youth, her love.

The back door of the main house slammed and Paulette stiffened in alarm. Dester drew her back behind the hay bales and crouched with her.

Chang entered with a pail and rags to clean and polish the carriage. Fortunately, before he began the task he realized he had forgotten something and turned and left.

"Why did you wait days before coming to me?" Paulette suddenly asked.

He was taken aback by her question, by her knowledge that he had been in San Francisco for almost a full week. "I had to see how things stood with you," he answered. "You didn't expect me to come barging into another man's home and announce that I was taking his wife from him, did you?" He kissed her before she could answer and then rose from behind the bales. "I'll go now," he said, "before your servants find me here and send for your husband." He spat out the word "husband" with distaste. "I'll come for you in a few days. Be ready, my love. Take only what you cannot bear to part with. I'll buy you more fancy clothes when we reach New Orleans."

Paulette clutched at his arm to delay him. "One thing, Dester—when your father tried to secure my inheritance for me, he was forced to produce proof that my half-sister was dead."

"Yes, I remember. She was found with her throat cut—or at least that's what the report stated. Why the sudden interest in something that's over and done with?"

"Why did you say, 'at least that's what the report stated'?" she demanded. "Why did you say it in that tone of voice?"

Dester stared down at her, questioning her reasoning in broaching such a subject when he was about to be discovered by her Chinese servant. "The report was falsified," he told her. He smiled at the shocked expression on her face. "You never really knew my father," he said. "He was not above doing such things if they achieved his purpose."

"But . . ."

"Not now, my love. We'll have the rest of our lives to review our pasts." He took her hand from his arm, and after kissing her quickly, he hurried through the opened stable doors and vanished around the side of the building.

# Chapter Seventeen

THE SUN had gone behind dark clouds and the sky gave a promise of rain before nightfall. The wind was creating whitecaps across the surface of the bay, and the willow Jeremiah had planted beside the house was bending over almost double in the sudden gusts. The stable doors, left unlatched, were banging against their frame.

Paulette sat beside the window, her forehead touching the cool pane. After she had returned to her rooms, she had been struck by the full guilt for what she had done. The guilt had brought a sense of clarity with it; both made her suffer.

She realized that even if she loved Dester, she could not leave Jeremiah. Her abandoning him like a common wanton would destroy him, perhaps her and the children, also. She had the happiness of more than herself to consider. She respected Jeremiah—and she owed him a debt, many debts. She owed Dester nothing.

That *something* that had plagued her when she had been with Dester in the stable once again rumbled inside her as if demanding recognition. She closed her eyes and tried to free her thoughts, but she was too guilt-stricken and confused to understand the elusive feeling; she was like a woman talking to herself and not hearing.

She rang for Chang and told him to bring her a bottle of sherry. "No, cognac," she decided.

When he returned with the decanter and one glass and set them on the table before her, Chang remained, waiting for her to glance at him. When she did, he said, "May I do something to help you, Miss Paulette?"

She knew by his expression that he had been talking to Annie. They had been inseparable since the night they had delivered Clay. They knew they were her favorites, and that had created a close bond between them; together they ran the household and made life easy for her. Now she had disappointed them, she thought. She had even toyed with their happiness. Resting her elbows on the chair arm, she buried her face in her hands.

"Miss Miriam," Chang said hesitantly, "always told me that no sin was so great it couldn't be forgiven if one asked for forgiveness." The Chinese man waited for her to speak. When she did not, he shook his head sadly and left her.

Chang's words continued to echo inside her skull, mingling with other memories, half-forgotten phrases, and a collage of familiar faces that appeared and vanished with rapidity. She had heard that a drowning man saw his entire life pass before him; it was the way she felt now, drowning and reliving her life. If she had been a religious woman, she would have summoned a priest or minister. If she had not been what the people were calling "eccentric" and had made friends, she would have sought out their companionship and advice. As it was, she had no one— except Jeremiah—and she suddenly realized how much she had come to depend on him since their marriage. He had become her husband, her lover, her friend. She had become more devoted to him than she had realized. She pulled her hands away from her face with the shock of sudden understanding that she also loved him. It was not the same sort of love she felt for Dester. She did not love him with wild aban-

don and insatiable passion. Her love for Jeremiah
had grown slowly, nurtured by him, kindled by his
kindness, their love of the children, and mutual respect. Unknowingly, she had helped him build a solid
foundation for their relationship.

She poured herself a cognac and felt the warmth as
it settled in her stomach. She put the top on the decanter. Another drink would make her dizzy, and she
needed her full senses to think clearly.

That, then, was the *something* that had plagued her
in the stable. She had given herself to Dester, but in
so doing her love for Jeremiah had surfaced. She
knew now that she could not, would not, abandon
Jeremiah for Dester. Although she still loved him, her
hope of building a future with him had died in the
gold fields. She had stopped considering him as a
husband as Vienna had stopped mentioning him in
her letters. Only her desire for him had not died,
probably would never die completely. The ghost of
him would always stand between her and Jeremiah,
but she knew now it would only be the ghost of memories. She did not want to see Dester again.

Then it occurred to her that she might also have
lost Jeremiah. Their relationship had been founded
and based on honesty. She could not lie to him about
Dester's visit. He was a proud man, a jealous man.
Would he turn away from her in fury and disgust
when she confessed her infidelity?

No matter, she thought, she must tell him. If she
did not, it would be like a great lie standing between
them. Jeremiah would forgive her Dester more easily
than a great lie.

She decided she would tell him when he returned
home for his evening meal.

Determined, she permitted herself another cognac.
Then she summoned Chang once again and asked
him to have her tub filled with scented water. She
bathed and dressed in Jeremiah's favorite gown,
emerald-green silk, a copy of the gown she had
worn on their wedding night. The emerald-and-

diamond necklace was in the drawing room safe; she went downstairs, opened it, and had Annie fasten the necklace around her neck after the young woman had coiffed her hair.

Then there was nothing to do but wait.

The long case clock in the entryway struck off the hours.

One hour past the time when Jeremiah usually came home, Paulette began to panic. He was a man of habit who adhered to a rigid schedule. If he was to be late, it was his custom to send a message with one of the casino employees. Tonight he would have been especially thoughtful since he knew she was concerned about his seeing Claudine Favière. Again, she imagined him dead in the gutter of Maiden Lane, shot by Jean-Paul or Claudine herself.

Trembling, she rang for Chang and told him to bring the carriage around. The little man looked at her oddly, perhaps thinking she was returning to Maiden Lane or going to some clandestine meeting with Dester. "We're going to The Barbary Coast," she told him. "Hurry!"

Chang, who had often been sent on errands to the gambling club, drove the horses into a back alley and stopped in front of a door with a dim light. He jumped down to help Paulette from the carriage, fighting the wind for her cape. "The employees' entrance," he told her. "I'll take you to Mr. Walker's office."

She followed him through the door into a dimly lighted passageway. The din of noise immediately assaulted her ears: laughter, conversation, music, a woman's voice singing—they all blended together in what sounded to her like pandemonium. There were employees moving through the passageway with trays full of dishes and bottles, but Chang was a familiar figure and no one questioned their right to be there, although she was aware of their questioning stares.

Chang led her to a narrow staircase. "Mr. Walker's office is at the top of the stairs," he told her. "I'll wait in the carriage, Miss Paulette." Before she could object, he was gone.

Paulette rapped on the only door above, but there was no answer. She rapped again, then pushed the door open and stepped inside.

Jeremiah's office was not as she had expected it to be. He had taken such care with the decoration of the house, but the office was extremely casual, almost sloppy, with a massive mahogany desk covered in clutter. His desk chair was high-backed, tufted brown leather with a tear at one corner. The wall behind his desk was book-filled shelves. Two chairs and a sofa, both upholstered in a wine-colored velvet, faced the desk. The wall opposite was draped from floor to ceiling in matching fabric. The only evidence of expense was the Oriental carpet—perhaps, she thought, one he had bought and rejected for their home.

She pushed the door closed and moved thoughtfully around the room. The din of noise from downstairs was muffled. She moved to the draperies and parted them and was startled to find herself staring through glass panes at the main floor of the casino below. A game she had played as a child came to mind: King of the Mountain. Here in his office Jeremiah was king. She wondered vaguely if that thought had ever occurred to him. Fascinated by the scene below, she continued to hold the draperies apart to watch the activities.

There were many gambling tables; some she recognized as roulette, blackjack, and baccarat. All tables were crowded with men eagerly wagering their money, with waiters and women in brightly colored dresses moving among them. There was a long bar to one side of the room that also was crowded, and at the far end was a stage. A woman in a flowing crimson gown with matching feather boa was singing, although few of the customers were listening. A thick blanket of smoke hung over the room like a cloud. So this, she thought, is the men's world of gambling and relaxation. Vienna had told her that Clabe, during his bad time, had frequented such places in New Orleans.

Paulette scanned the various tables searching for Jeremiah. He was not among the dealers. Then she remembered his telling her he no longer indulged in actual gambling unless a special customer requested it.

She was about to let the draperies fall back into place when she caught sight of Jeremiah. She caught her breath in a gasp. Jeremiah was not alone. He had just entered from the street. Behind him, blond hair catching reflections of the light, strode Dester. Behind Dester, cloaked in black, came her half-sister, Claudine. They were proceeding through the crowd and she knew instinctively they were headed for the second-floor office.

She rushed to the door, opened it, and stepped into the hallway, her heart pounding. The staircase was narrow and long. The hallway below, where the waiters were passing, was also long and open. Even if she reached downstairs, Jeremiah and Dester would see her as she hurried toward the exit. She hesitated, trembling. If she was forced to face both Jeremiah and Dester—and Claudine—at one time, she knew she was lost.

Panicking, she stepped back inside Jeremiah's office, but there, too, she was trapped.

She had scarcely concealed herself behind a corner of the draperies when the door opened and she heard them enter. Holding her skirts back, she pressed herself against the wall, grateful that there was a solid space on either side of the window so she could not be seen from below.

"Sit down," she heard Jeremiah say. She heard him cross the room. From the opposite side of the wall from where she hid, he pulled a cord and the draperies opened the width of the window.

Paulette thought she would surely be discovered now, but the angle of the desk and the sofa where Dester and Claudine had sat kept her from being seen. She watched Jeremiah as he moved behind his desk, pulled out his chair, and sat down. His face was dark, his brows furrowed, and she knew that he was angry.

"All right, Granville," he said sharply, "let's get this over with. If it could have been settled on Maiden Lane, I would have preferred it. I don't like your type in my establishment even as customers." His gaze moved from Dester to Claudine. "And you, you're even more despicable. How could you have agreed to this monstrous scheme?"

"Monstrous, but profitable," Claudine answered with sarcasm. "Besides, who are you to call it a scheme, to dispute me as the woman I claim to be?"

"My dear Madame Fouche," Jeremiah said with matched sarcasm, "or shall I refer to you as Mrs. Nunally? Do you still persist in continuing this charade?"

"It is no charade," Claudine said hotly. "If it is, prove it."

"How foolish you are," Jeremiah told her. "I can produce a dozen witnesses who will swear you have been in San Francisco for the past four years and that your dead husband, Martin Nunally, is buried in the cemetery at Sacramento. The only authenticity to your absurd claim is your French heritage. I am told you came from France during that country's most recent upheaval and settled in Maryland until your husband insisted on moving out West." Rustling through the papers on his desk, Jeremiah drew out a crumpled sheet and read from it. "You worked as a maid in the hotel, a laundress, and, when you could find a man who'd have you, as a prostitute." He dropped the sheet back onto the desktop. "The only reason I am seeing you at all and not turning you over to the authorities is because of my wife. And even then I'm considering it the proper thing to do. There are two areas in which my wife refuses to see clearly. One of them concerns her family's past."

Paulette, her breath caught in her throat, could not believe what she was hearing. Jeremiah was not only convinced Claudine was a fraud, but he had proof. Is

that why he had not returned home or sent a message
—he had been investigating the woman's claim?

Paulette could see the woman's profile. Her hawk-
like features were frozen in anger, but there was also
fear there, revealed by the quivering muscles above
her thin lips.

But Dester? Paulette thought. Why was he here?

Madame Fouche suddenly turned her sunken eyes
on Dester. Paulette's question was answered when the
woman cried, "It was your scheme! You said it was
foolproof!"

Paulette felt a stab of pain in her chest so severe
she thought she would double over. She had to fight to
maintain her position against the wall. Dester's
scheme! Dear God, how could he? And only hours
ago she had given herself to him in the stable. She
had been tormented about choosing between Jeremiah
and Dester, even though she had determined to give
Dester up. "I love you," he had sworn. "It will always
be just the two of us." His words echoed in her head
and made the betrayal even more shattering.

"It was not difficult to guess who was behind the
scheme," Jeremiah said, "after I had proved you to be
an impostor. Who else but Granville would know
enough details of Paulette's life to make your per-
formance credible?" Jeremiah's gaze went from Madame Fouche to Dester, and the hate in his eyes
intensified. "You are that second area in which my
wife refuses to see the obvious," he said. "I have attempted to expose you exactly for what you are to
her, but she refuses to have the film of youth from
which she sees you torn away from her eyes. For
what's it worth to you, I consider you the lowest bastard ever to have crossed my path. I would have
killed you long ago if doing so had not meant losing
Paulette."

"And I could kill you now!" Madame Fouche cried.
"You are a lowly bastard! I trusted you. You were so
cocksure. You swore the scheme was foolproof. Now
look at the fine mess you've gotten us into."

"Shut up!" Dester shouted. Sitting forward in his chair, he looked as if he were about to strike her. As she cowered against the upholstery, he got to his feet and, leaning his knuckles on Jeremiah's cluttered desktop, met the man's stare. "Exactly what do you plan to do, Walker? You may frighten this bitch with your threats of calling the authorities, but I'm still not quivering. If you call in the authorities, the entire story of Paulette's infamous family would come out into the open. What chance would you stand then in running for election? I can tell you. None! So now what? Will you slap our wrists and send us away?"

"I'd send you into hell if I could," Jeremiah answered.

"Kill me?" Dester laughed softly. "You'd break Paulette's heart and lose her, besides."

"It's still tempting."

"But not practical," Dester countered. He slipped back into his chair and assumed a relaxed position. Taking a cigar from his breast pocket, he bit off the end, rolled it, and lit it. The smoke curled above his blond hair. "So if I had not been more clever than you anticipated, we would now be at a stalemate," he said. "But since I am a clever man . . ."

"You are nothing but a greedy man," Jeremiah interrupted. "I knew that the first time I met you in the gold fields. I paid you off then to insist Paulette remain in San Francisco and not join you."

"But you lost. She came, anyway—of her own accord," Dester reminded him. "What did you call it? Her obsession with me?"

A flicker of pain flashed across Jeremiah's face.

Paulette also felt another stab of pain. Tears formed in her eyes and ran unchecked down her cheeks.

"And look what you did to her!" Jeremiah shouted. "How could any man be so unfeeling about someone who loves him? You treated her like a slut, a slave! You, who profess to support the sentiments of the North!"

"And I almost killed her," Dester said drily, "when

I built the dam on the creek and collected enough water to drive that cow of a woman she befriended from her claim."

Paulette felt the hair on the back of her neck prickle. She stood rigidly, scarcely daring to breathe for fear of unleashing a scream of protest. So Elisha had been right. Elisha had understood and she had been blind.

Madame Fouche's eyes were darting from one man's face to the other's. She did not entirely understand what was happening, but she understood enough for her fear to leave her. They—she and Dester—now had the upper hand again. It was obvious by the expression on Jeremiah's face.

"Your Achilles' heel, Walker, is your wife," Dester blurted out. "I am hers."

"And yours, Granville?"

Dester puffed his cigar thoughtfully before saying, "Gold, until I discovered I'd no knack for finding it. Now it's money."

"Any way you can get it?"

"The easier, the better."

"How much easier than duping an innocent woman," Jeremiah murmured, "a woman who loved you and whom you claimed to love?" He shook his head in disgust. "If you were not so despicable, you'd be pitiable. Tell me, with your standing to inherit from your father, why did you argue and leave home?"

"We argued over many things," Dester answered calmly. "He thought our main disagreement was over the slavery question. It wasn't. I'd read his will. He'd left everything equally divided among my mother, my two sisters, and Paulette. Paulette already had a fortune, and my mother and sisters would be sharing the wealth while I toiled to operate a plantation for my portion. He even stipulated that I was to be disinherited if I refused my manly responsibilities."

"Then your father knew you well," Jeremiah murmured. "Both of you get out of my sight before I summon the authorities, the consequences be damned!"

Madame Fouche looked to Dester for instructions. Since he remained seated, she did, also.

"I told you I am a more clever man than you give me credit for," Dester said. "I am not leaving without fifty thousand dollars. And you, Walker, are going to want to give it to me when you hear my terms."

"I wouldn't want to give you the sweat from my brow if you were dying of thirst!" Jeremiah raged. "You're worse than a parasite, Granville."

"But Paulette does not agree with you," Dester said flatly. "She would never believe any foul stories you told her about me, and you know it." He paused dramatically to give his words emphasis. "What I am offering to do, Walker, is sell you your wife."

Jeremiah's face flushed and his dark eyes blazed. The muscles around his jaw tightened and the veins in his neck protruded.

Madame Fouche, seeing this transformation, sprang from her chair and backed trembling toward the door. Dester continued to sit casually; if he felt threatened, he did not show it.

Paulette thought she would faint with indignation and rage. She would have revealed herself then, but she clung to her hiding place, forcing herself to hear more.

Jeremiah was obviously struggling with himself to keep from leaping across the desk and seizing Dester by the throat. Paulette knew the power in him, had seen his rage, and knew that he could kill Dester with little effort. With forced quiet and clipped words, Jeremiah said, "Explain yourself, Granville."

Paulette knew and dreaded what was coming. She did not pity herself, but she pitied Jeremiah for what he must suffer because of her.

Dester inclined his head mockingly. "I learned this morning that you were investigating her," he said, indicating the hovering Madame Fouche. "I had not anticipated Paulette coming to you with her pathetic story of a half-sister risen from the dead. I thought she would sell her jewelery, beg, borrow, or steal to rid herself of the legendary Claudine Favière. When I realized she must have come to you, I knew I must cover myself or be arrested for fraud."

"How stupid you are, Granville," Jeremiah told him, "not clever at all. Had you gone to my wife directly and asked her for money, you would have stood a far greater chance of getting it. Even I understand that. Knowing you were in need, she may then have sold her jewelry, or, as you put it, begged, borrowed, or stolen for you. But the evil in you is so ingrained you cannot see the good in others." Jeremiah rose; hands folded behind his back, he walked to the window and stared down at the busy casino below.

Paulette held her breath. All he had to do was glance out of the corner of his eye to discover her hidden there. The stricken look on his face filled her with anguish. She fought the impulse to reach out to him, to hold him and beg his forgiveness.

Jeremiah sighed almost soundlessly, and without glancing in her direction, he returned to his desk.

Dester crushed his cigar out in an ashtray. "I went to Paulette," he continued, taking great pleasure in what he was relating. "It was not difficult to convince her of my love and devotion. What woman does not like to feel everything a man has done is for her, to make their life together easier? The obstacles in between, the little disappointments and betrayals—they can be forgiven and forgotten. Should you confront your wife tonight, Walker, I am certain she would confess to you that her bags are packed and she is going away with me. That is what I mean by selling your wife back to you. For fifty thousand dollars I will vanish and never be heard from again."

Jeremiah looked defeated. Quietly, he said, "For fifty thousand dollars, you would leave the woman who loves you to the mercy of a husband you have informed of her indiscretions?"

"I would," Dester said flatly. "What happens between the two of you is no concern of mine. She is, after all, your wife."

Jeremiah straightened himself up in his chair. "What would Paulette think of you now?" he asked, his voice gaining power.

"She would be angry for a time," Dester said with a laugh, "but she would eventually forgive me, as you will forgive her. When there is a fever such as you and she have in your blood, it never completely abandons the system."

"Perhaps we should ask Paulette if she agrees with you," Jeremiah said.

Even before he called her name, Paulette understood that he had seen her behind the draperies and had not revealed it even to her.

She flung the draperies aside and stepped out into the office.

Madame Fouche screamed and dashed hurriedly out the door. "Fool!" she shouted over her shoulder. "You bloody fool!"

Dester's face became a twisted mask of surprise. Leaping to his feet, his leg struck the ashtray stand and it clattered to the floor. His mouth hung open, all color draining from his face.

Paulette's eyes never left Dester's, but it was to Jeremiah that she spoke. "For what it means to you, Jeremiah, my bags are not packed. I came here to tell you what happened and to plead with you for forgiveness."

"That," Jeremiah said, "means considerably more to me than you realize."

Paulette took steps toward Dester, and he, remembering her fury as a child, backed away an equal number of steps. He was still close enough for her hand to find his cheek. Even before the sting of the blow had ceased echoing around the room, the imprint of her hand rose on his face. "Even after making my decision, I thought the ghost of you would stand between us," she said. "I was too blind to see you as

the man you really are. Tonight I have seen you
clearly for the first time. Your ghost will not haunt me,
only the pain my stupidity has caused others because
of you."

Turning her back on him, she stepped to the win-
dow and stared down at the main room of the casino.
She heard Jeremiah rising from behind his desk, heard
Dester's footsteps as he ran through the doorway after
Madame Fouche.

Things happened then in quick sequence.

Jeremiah, coming up behind her, slipped his arms
around her waist. He spoke, but she did not hear his
words. Below on the casino floor she saw Elisha. She
saw Dester hurrying forward unsuspectingly toward
him. Then the outer doors were flung open and a man
screamed, "Fire! San Francisco is burning!"

The casino crowd panicked. Already smoke was
drifting in through the opened doors. Chips and
money were abandoned in a mad dash for the exits.

Jeremiah grabbed Paulette's shoulders and tried to
pull her away from the window, but she fought him,
her gaze transfixed on Dester and Elisha. She saw
Dester's terror as the black man suddenly loomed before him, saw him turn and try to flee through the
stampeding crowd. Instead of escaping, they pushed
him forward almost into Elisha's arms. There was a
flash of steel and Dester crumpled beneath the trampling feet of terrified customers.

Paulette turned to Jeremiah. He had seen, also. Silently, he turned her away from the window and hurried her from the office and down the stairs. The
smoke was getting heavier, making breathing difficult.

"The back way," Jeremiah said. He half-carried,
half-dragged her through the milling waiters and sa-
loon girls.

Outside, she collapsed against him, struggling for
breath.

"Hurry," he told her. Then he was screaming
Chang's name.

The Chinese man, leaping from the driver's seat, opened the carriage door. Before allowing Jeremiah to hand her in, Paulette turned and stared up into his face.

"You knew Chang was here?" she said.

He nodded.

"Then you knew all along I was inside!"

"I did. Now, get in the carriage," he demanded and almost threw her through the door. "Get her home, Chang!" he shouted, then disappeared into the crowd.

When the carriage pulled up outside the hilltop house, all the servants were standing in the front yard.

Clay, tearing away from Annie, dashed to Paulette and threw his arms around her legs. She lifted him into her arms and held him protectively.

Below, San Francisco was burning. Great walls of fire spread rapidly from building to building with the force of the wind. The Barbary Coast was already a great ball of flames, as was the hotel and the bank. The air on the hill was thick with smoke. Paulette glanced at the servants and saw no hope in their eyes. She passed Clay back to Annie and told her to take him inside.

She remained on the porch with Chang long after the servants had silently retired.

The first light of dawn was streaking the sky when she heard horse's hooves on the gravel. She left the sleeping Chang on the porch and came out onto the road to meet Jeremiah.

His face was smeared with soot. His hair was singed and one hand was bandaged.

Forgetting about her emerald-green silk gown, she threw herself into his arms and thanked God that he was alive. They stood silently holding one another for several moments. Then Jeremiah, pulling her into the protective curve of his body, turned and they stared down at the smoldering ruins of the city. The sun was breaking out in a golden light through the overhanging smoke.

"Your beautiful city," Paulette whispered in distress. "I'm so sorry, so very sorry."

"We'll rebuild it," he told her. "We learned from our mistakes and we'll rebuild it even better than it was before."

Clinging to one another, they entered the house and closed the door.